Check out these other books by C. A.A.:

Love Can Always Be Found
Love Can Always Be Found Part 2

Coming Together Series:
    C & B Diner
    Discovering Friends
    Eric's Reunion
    Father's Day
    Friend Love
    Hating to Be Right
    Love is Deep
    Moving On
    Niki Finds Silence
    Saving My Own Corner of the World
    The Making of a Family
    Who Will Save Geri

Copyright © 2017 written and illustrated by C.A.A. All rights reserved. Except for the use in any review, the reproduction or utilization of this work in whole or in part in any form by any electronic, mechanical or other means, now known or hereinafter invented, including xerography, photocopying and recording, or in any information storage or retrieval system, is forbidden without the written permission of the author or illustrator directly.

This is a work of fiction. Names, characters, places and incidents are either the product of the author's imagination or are used fictitiously, and any resemblance to actual persons, living or dead, business establishments, events or locales is entirely coincidental.

For questions and comments about the quality or content of this book, please contact us at dailyreader.caa@gmail.com

If you enjoyed these stories, you can find more on: https://www.thedailyreader.online   free library and subscription

The Daily Reader, A Commuter's Library

Index:

Maybell's List - novelette - realistic fiction

Mismatched - novelette - realistic fiction

Odd Friends - novelette - magical realism

Photo Shoot - novelette - dramatic romance

The Cottage - novelette - romance

The Night of the Full Moon - short story - magical realism

Timmy and Kim's Longest Year - novella - drama

Maybell's List

Maybell is a real planner, from the time she was a teen she had her whole life planned out. Life, on the other hand, had a different list for her to follow. When Maybell looks at her life now she is not sure if she has been successful or a complete failure.

Maybell had it all worked out when she was a teenager, she had every step of life worked out down to the age it was going to happen. She was so confident that her life was going to happen the way she wanted, that she never gave much thought to the fact that maybe something wouldn't work out the way she wanted. She had showed her list to her father and he praised her for even remembering that there is life after high school. Her mom didn't have much to say, but then again, she rarely does when Maybell had anything to say or do, and even less since she turned sixteen.

Her parents both came to this country and had to immediately work in their respective family businesses to help their families pay simple bills and to make sure there was always a roof over their head and food on the table. Maybell's father did not have a chance to finish school past ninth grade, her mom didn't even have schooling that far, but both of them read as many books as they could get their hands on in their spare time. Her mom's family owned a simple bakery and they specialized in breads. Two of her cousins took over the bakery about ten years ago and have made it a community staple. Maybell is proud of her cousins, they had asked her for some financial advice until her mom got wind of them talking to Maybell and told them to keep financial information in the family. Not the first time she pushed Maybell out, Maybell is certain this won't be the last.

Her father, on the other hand, had vowed that all of his children would have a better education than he did as a child. He worked hard at making his father's business big so that he could put his children through college. First generation of high school and college graduates. Maybell is the last one. She has two brothers who already finished college and are well on their way to making their own successful career. Her younger sister Angie finished with a business degree last year and now works side by side with their father, she plans on keeping the business open for generations. Maybell's father is getting ready to retire so it's good someone will take over for him. Although Maybell is not confident that Angie truly understands how to run a business but that's neither here nor there.

Maybell wants to make him proud, she has in some ways, she supposes, but not as much as her brothers and definitely not as much as her baby sister. Her so called plans have been jumbled almost since the day she made them. But she is happy with her life; she loves her children tremendously, that has to account for something, doesn't it?

Now, as she sits and looks at her closet trying to put an outfit together for tonight, she finds herself lost in contemplation of that list she made so many years ago. So much of it went awry from the very first part of the list to the last. Maybell could use her father's advice right about now.

"Hmmmm, where did I put that list now?" Maybell gets up from her bed and walks to her dresser to find the list she had laminated when she was twenty, so it would never be ruined. "Ah, here it is, let's go over this one more time for good luck." Every time she reads this list, she hopes the next item will come in a natural order, but as of right now, she has not had one item come to her as she had planned. She has done many of them backwards. Her best friend, Adam, is the only one who knows about this list, besides her father and mother, and he teases her about keeping such a thing all this time. The only reason she takes the teasing from him is because his own list is as messed up as hers.

Maybell and Adam met during high school at an interstate retreat for teens who plan on going into finance. They hit it off immediately and kept in touch ever since then. Staying in finance is the only part of her plan that came true. Adam left for college swearing to her that he was going to graduate in three years instead of four, move on to his career, find the love of his life and by the time he was thirty, have lots and lots of children. His reality, however, took him on a different route. Took him five years to graduate because he ended up doing a masters and undergraduate combination. He married a girl he dated throughout college but they divorced after their son was born a year and a half later. Adam has custody of Mick because Cindy never wanted to have children in the first place. She now lives far away, and the last they heard, she is still trying to keep up appearances of being young and innocent so she can get into the upper echelon in her field.

"Ok, Maybell, let's review this one last time." She reads the list out loud.

18-22 go to college get degree in finance – you love working with numbers

22-26 secure career and get married – but only to a hairless guy – icky, no chest hair

27-30 take time to have children and start to enjoy life

30s make the most of yourself and start putting away for retirement – plan, plan, plan

"Oh, Maybell, you've done it all wrong haven't you? Adam would be laughing right now if he saw this paper out again. For someone who was smart enough to plan at the age of sixteen, you've blown all of this. ALL!!!! God, you're such an idiot Maybell, you should call off tonight." Maybell sits down and lets a few tears slide down her face, she drops her hands by her sides and then she falls back onto her bed, for the first time in a long time, she lets herself cry out of loneliness.

"Momma!" Neeli calls to her, Maybell jumps up, wipes her tears and runs towards her daughter's room.

~ ~ ~

"Adam, you're acting as if this is the first date you've ever been on. For goodness sakes you dated all through college and were married for almost two years." Adam's mom says.

Adam looks to his mother who came over to babysit tonight. "I know, it's so weird, isn't it? I mean Maybell is doing the same thing tonight and she isn't losing herself because if she was, she'd have called me already like she always does. And she doesn't even have a reason to be calm, she isn't lucky tonight like me Mom, she called me earlier today to tell me she may have to show up with Neeli and the baby because her babysitter canceled on her. That's definitely ensuring her evening will be short. And she hasn't called me, so, either she found a different one or she is resolved to taking the kids, but me? Even with my parents to support me, I'm a nervous wreck." He paces away from her again.

"Well, she didn't lie on her profile about the kids, did she? I mean, it won't be a total shock to him if she comes and admits the babysitter backed out at the last minute." Adam's mom asks, thinking about the kids.

"No, of course not, we both filled them out at the same time remember? You were here, you gave her some pointers on what to say. I can't believe the site set us both up on the same day or I'd take Mick over there and babysit for her myself." He says worried for his best friend.

"Oh, Adam, that's terrible, why did I even suggest such a thing, and why didn't you tell us? Joshua!!! You have to go to Maybell's right now!" Adam's father comes running into the living room holding Mick on his hip. "What?! Why? What's the emergency?" he asks.

Adam explains the situation to his father. "Ok, don't tell her I'm on the way or she'll call and convince me not to come, not that I will stop driving though." He kisses Mick and hands him over to his wife then grabs his keys and runs out the door.

"Ok, now that this problem is solved, what else is bothering you Adam?" his mother asks calmly, seeing that her son's nerves are really on edge.

"I don't know, Mom, I wish I could tell you. I guess, it's the whole blind date idea. Who knows what kind of woman they set me up with? They don't even give you names! I know it's supposed to have been done in a scientific sort, because you answer so many questions that they match you up based on the percentage of questions you answer the same but is that really how I want to meet someone? I mean who are these people to say that those questions I answered are really me? For all I know I could be meeting up with some Amazonian woman with big teeth and wild hair. Or what if she is beautiful and she takes one look at me and says oh crap I got stuck with you for the night. So many things could go wrong, what if she is expecting some bedtime antics? Mom? Mom?! Why are you laughing at me?" Adam questions his mother, his voice frustrated and nervous at the same time.

Julienne calms down and faces her son, "Oh, Adam, you're really fretting over this way too much. You should take the same attitude that Maybell is and think of it as a night out and nothing more. You're not going to marry this person tomorrow but you may learn to like yourself again and maybe you both will find out that dating is not as horrible as you've made it out to be. Now, go put on those nice blue pants I brought you last week with that multi colored vest to match. It's not too dressy and not too casual. Go, go." She pats her son's knee and takes Mick back out of the room to play with him.

~ ~ ~

"Oh Neeli honey, you're ok. You only bumped your head on your chair, not the floor or something harder, you see? Look in this mirror, I will show you, you're not even bleeding." Maybell is much calmer now that she sees the scream was more out of fear than pain. "We should go check on your sister to make sure you didn't wake her up with your screaming." Maybell takes Neeli back to the bedroom and checks to see the baby is still calm. She places her hand on the baby's back to make sure he is breathing comfortably. "Shhh, let's go back to your bedroom and find a good book to read ok?" Neeli shakes her head yes to her mother.

The doorbell rings and startles Maybell, Neeli begins to cry again at being jolted by her mother. "Oh, sorry honey, I'm ok, the doorbell startled me is all. You want to come with me to who is there? Of course, you do." Maybell walks to the front door of her townhouse. She purchased this place all by herself when Neeli was born because she didn't want to live in a cramped apartment like so many of her friends and co-workers do. She ended up not even using all of her savings for a down-payment. This purchase is one thing her father really praised her for, he complimented her on knowing how to make such a purchase work and to do the transaction with sound financial planning. He was so proud he helped her out by making the first few payments so she could spend her own money for furnishings without making sacrifices.

Maybell looks through the peephole, then swings the door open. "Joshua? What are you doing here? Is Adam ok? Is it Mick?" she asks smiling but nervous.

"Hello Neeli, Uncle Joshua came over to play with you tonight so Mommy can go out by herself, is that ok?" he grabs Neeli out of Maybell's hands and walks back upstairs to her bedroom, he knows she should be in bed soon and taking her out only means tomorrow will be horrible for Maybell.

Maybell slowly closes the door because she is in a bit of a stupor, pulling herself together she runs upstairs after Joshua. She finds him in Neeli's bedroom already. "Really?" she asks softly. She knows Adam must have said something about her canceling babysitter.

"Maybell, even if the guy knows you have kids, he doesn't want meet them on a first date. Besides you know I love these guys to pieces anyway. Come Neeli Uncle

Joshua thinks you need a bath, how about that? Maybe with bubbles too." He smiles at Maybell and shoos her away with his hand so she can finish getting dressed.

Neeli squeals and jumps out of his arms to grab her bathrobe from her chair. Nothing makes this two and half year old happier than a long bath and Joshua knows this because he has seen her many times before.

Maybell heads back to her bedroom and sighs. If she lived in the same state as her parents, she is sure they would have come by tonight but having Adam's dad here is as good. She will have nothing to worry about except this mystery guy.

"Ok Maybell, you're not getting married tonight, only a date. How about you go for something casual. Oh, and this whole talking to yourself is really helping with the nerves." Maybell smacks herself on her forehead and walks to her closet.

She was told to wear a blue flower to be unique so he can find her easily. They told her everyone uses red or white flowers and blue is a safe one. So she looked through her clothes and found she had a headband that has blue flowers all around, now that she thinks on this, she has a great shirt that has a similar pattern and she pulls them both out of the closet and then finds a nice grey pencil skirt to pull on and simple flats for shoes. Heels would tell him she is looking for something more, and right now, this is to "get her feet wet in dating" as Adam's mom says.

Satisfied with how she looks she walks back out of her room and over to the bathroom where she hears Neeli giggling and splashing about. "How do I look?" she asks Joshua. He turns around and smiles, "You look lovely, honey. Where are you going to meet this young man anyway?"

"Oh, the guy picked the place, he said he wanted to meet at the new deli, you know the one on the corner of fifth and Grand? Seems like a good idea to me, casual yet not fast food." Maybell watches as Joshua smiles. "What?" she asks.

Joshua realizes he is smirking at Maybell and he quickly composes himself, "Nothing honey, I think you're right, the place is not fast food and yet it's not too fancy either. He picked well. I give him two points for that at least. What time does she really need to be in bed?" he asks quickly changing the subject.

"A half an hour ago." She says.

"Wait, how were you going to go out if the kids were asleep?" He asks.

"Well, I was hoping they were both going to stay asleep and I could transfer them into the double stroller, another reason to like the deli – the place has a lot of space between tables, but this is a much better solution, thank you Joshua. I owe you guys so much. Without having my family close, you've always been there. You've taken such good care of me without any judgements. It's more than I deserve." Maybell says softly.

Joshua stands up, "Two minutes Neeli," he says first then turns to her mom, "Maybell, we care for you a lot. I can't tell you how happy I am to help out. Next time call us, no hesitation. Julienne and I are thankfully retired young enough and we have the time to help out, we enjoy being here, I promise you, you area never a burden to us. Now go before you're late." He smiles again.

Maybell gets up on her toes and gives Joshua a kiss on the cheek, "Be good Neeli Uncle Joshua will only read you one book tonight because your bedtime is already late, ok?" she says to her daughter.

"Bye bye Mommy. Nights" Neeli says.

"Nights." Maybell says and walks out and down the stairs. She grabs her purse and heads out the door.
~ ~ ~

When Joshua hears the door close and the car start, he quickly sends his wife a text "*it's her!!!!*"

"*What? What's her?*" Julienne asks back

"*His date!!! Maybell is wearing blue flowers and is meeting him at the deli!! Keep your fingers crossed that they wake up ☺ Love you!*"

Julienne laughs out loud while looking at her phone.

"Someone send you a joke Mom?" Adam asks.

Julienne looks up surprised, she forgot Adam hadn't left yet, but it makes sense he lives much closer to the deli than Maybell does. "Your father sent me another little love note." She says sweetly.

"Oh man, I hope I find the love you have with Dad. I want to be sending my love sweet notes after being married for thirty years. Bless me Mom so that I can get what you have." He pleads with her.

"Consider yourself blessed." Julienne says and kisses her son. "Now go, you look great, enjoy."

Seeing his mom look happy at the small note his father sent, puts Adam in a really good mood. He met some of his friend's parents over the years but he has never seen the same love between two people as he sees daily between his parents. He met Maybell's parents once, when she had the baby, they are wonderful people but their love for each other is more of a mutual respect than a deep never ending love that you find once in a lifetime. He thought he had real love with his girlfriend in college, they had so much fun together every day.

They would go on impromptu picnics between classes, have all night study nights together helping each other out. Adam even remembers those times when she would sneak into his classes simply to hand him a note. If it wasn't for her encouragement, he would never have even considered a master's degree. Although, now that he really thinks about her encouragement, she only wanted him to go for the extra degree because she thought a secondary degree would put them in a higher financial bracket and get him noticed more.

"No, that's not true Adam, she wanted her own career to be the biggest and the best, you know that. It wasn't about money, she was all about advancing to the best in the best place possible. Cindy wanted, probably still wants, to earn accolades as much as she wants the money. The problem was, I didn't care enough. I never cared about being the best of the best. Being at the top is not something I ever wanted. Sure, I want to do well, but my aspirations were not, and still aren't, the same as hers. Turns out we were never on the same page, not even a little.

I want to be happy, I want to be a role model for Mick and to make sure he grows up in a home that is full of love like mine was. Cindy was beautiful, is beautiful, but she wants more, she wants everything I could never give her. However, she left me with the best gift ever.

Cindy never wanted to have a baby; she was waiting for the baby to be born before she left, only because she didn't want to take anything with her. She told the judge during the divorce proceedings that she wants to sign over her parental rights right now, so no custody decision needs to be made. Remember that Adam? Do you? Remember how cold she was in court?" Adam takes a deep breath, he has to stop talking to himself in the car about the past. The past is done, over, and yet those words haunt him still. He can't take these memories into a blind date or the woman will think he's stuck on Cindy still.

The only person who understands his demons is Maybell. Without her support he is not sure how he would have gotten through the divorce and adjusted to single fatherhood. His big brother supports him so much that he helped Adam establish a daycare center at the office for all their employees. The employees all pitched in to make this added bonus work out for everyone. This addition raised morale tenfold and has been a big hit these past couple of years. They even have a van that picks up the kids who go to half day kindergarten nearby and brings them back to the daycare. But these kinds of accomplishments were not what Cindy was looking for.

This is an accomplishment that Adam is very proud of. His brother is too, in a few months, his brother's new baby will be joining the daycare with his cousin Mick. Adam and Guy are best friends and best brothers. Their younger sister Wendy lives across the country with her three children and husband. But unbeknown to his parents, they are moving back to this area soon because Wendy's husband has accepted a transfer closer to his parent's home. They will be here for the Fall holidays, Adam has already found them a place to rent, should be ready for them in a month, they will arrive in six weeks. Adam can't wait to surprise everyone. He is the only one who knows so far.

Somehow this fifteen minute drive is taking much longer because his head is all over the place. Now, stuck at a red light, Adam has to make a decision. "Deep breath Adam, it's only a date." He exhales and proceeds through the green light. "Three more blocks and I meet a so called scientifically picked mate. Let's try and enjoy tonight." He says out loud.

~ ~ ~

Maybell is almost halfway to the deli and realizes she is way too early. She doesn't want to wait there by herself in a booth, so she pulls over into the next available parking lot and parks under a light. "Ok Maybell, what are we doing now? You've got five or so minutes to figure this night out now. Speak it out loud, how do we describe your life to a perfect stranger?

Let's start with, ok, I am almost twenty-six and I'm still finishing my education. No, that doesn't sound good. How about we go with the beginning? Ok, here, at the age of eighteen, I graduated high school and thought I was going to college in the Fall only I didn't.

My brother called me and told me to come stay with him the summer before I go to school because his office was offering job training for three months and I qualified. I went, only I haven't been home since. But my brother moved away shortly after that summer and I have no family near me now."

Maybell puts her head down on the steering wheel, shaking her head, "god that sounds awful Maybell, you sound like a jerk. Maybe you should turn around and go home, send a quick e-mail saying you suddenly got sick."

Maybell pulls down the sun-visor and looks in the mirror and takes a moment to really look at herself, "You look like a waste. Who would want you Maybell? Really, you have had a weird life, no one is going to accept that." She takes another deep breath with her eyes closed but before she turns the car into reverse, she hears some noises around her. The next thing she knows there is a group of teenaged boys around her car all yelling at her and shaking her car up and down, up and down.

Maybell is terrified, she grabs her phone and dials the emergency number of the town, "Please come fast, there is a group of guys all pushing my car up and down. Oh my god, I'm so afraid, please don't let them break in. Please, I have children, I need to get home to them. You have to come soon." Maybell's voice is crying already

"Maám, can you tell us where you are?" the dispatcher asks.

"Ummm, I was going west on Route 52 when I pulled into a parking lot, it's um." Maybell tries to look around, one of the guys is standing on the hood of her car now, and he is holding a baseball bat. "Oh god he has a bat!!!! He is going to smash my windshield!!!!!!" she looks around some more and sees someone on the side trying to bang on her passenger side door handle. She gathers up all her strength and looks around and beyond the boys attacking her car, "I'm at the Quickmart parked under the light."

"Ok, maám, I know you're nervous but we have cars close by and they should be there before anyone can get to you. They said they are almost there." The dispatcher tries to keep a calm voice to help make sure this woman in trouble keeps a level head.

Maybell hears the sirens but her nerves aren't calm at all, the boy on the hood of her car is looking rather angry that she called the police, he begins to smash her car's hood with the bat, he even swings at one of his friends who is trying to tell him to stop, the boy falls down as the bat comes down on his head.

Maybell jumps and screams loudly. "Oh, no, that poor boy!!!! Stop!!!!! Stop!!!!!" The sirens are right behind her but the boy on the hood has not left, he must be high on something, she thinks to herself.

The boys around her car have all darted away but the boy on the hood and the boy on the ground are all that is left. From the left side of her car the police grab the boy on her hood by the feet and pull him down before he has a chance to fight them, he falls on his face on her hood. They quickly confiscate the bat.

Maybell rolls her window down and yells out, "There is a boy on the other side. Check him, he was hit in the head with the bat, please check on him." Maybell finds her hands shaking now, the reality of what she has sat through is beginning to hit her. She was only supposed to stop for a couple of minutes to gather her thoughts.

"Maám, are you ok?" one of the officers asks.

"Physically? Yes. I was only here to kill a few minutes. I've been at this Quickmart a million times. The store is even open now, how can this happen? Is the boy ok? The boy, check on him please." She pleads.

Another siren is coming near her car and Maybell turns around to see an ambulance. "Please don't be dead, oh please, he has a mother somewhere who will be crushed." She says softly in a prayer.

"Maám, do you know these boys?" the officer asks. "You seem very concerned for their safety." He says.

"Know them? I was sitting here deep in thought when they decided to surround me. Three of them ran into the parking lot to the left here." She says pointing out her window. A couple of the other police officers walk over there to check out the situation.

"You're sure you don't know any of them?" he asks again.

"No, I don't know any teenagers, If I did, I wouldn't have had to get my friend's father to watch my children tonight." She looks out her window now to see the EMTs attending the boy on the floor, he looks alive, but badly beaten.

"Maám. I don't think you should drive home by yourself, do you have someone you can call to come get you?" he asks.

"Yes, yes, that's a good idea." She says.

"Ok, you go and call, we're going to be here a while. The young man that was on your car is going to have one heck of a hangover in the morning. The boy he beat is probably his friend and he doesn't even know what he did. We will need you to come down to the precinct to press charges, but you can come down in the morning. This young man will still be there." He points to the boy from her hood and then he hands her one of his cards so she knows where to go and whom to ask for.

Maybell shakes her head, she dials the only number she can think of right now. "Joshua? Are the kids ok? Please tell me my kids are ok." She pleads with him.

"Maybell? Where are you honey?" He knows she can't be on her date because Adam already sent him a text saying how down he is because the girl didn't even bother to show up. "Maybell?"

Maybell hands the phone to the officer near her car, she can't find her voice. "Hello, this is Officer Gentry, who is this?" he asks. The officer begins to explain all he knows about what has happened to this young woman in a very professional manner to the man on the phone.

Joshua's voice quivers a bit as he says, "We'll have someone from the family get to her in less than ten minutes."

"Very well, we'll still be here." The officer says and hands the phone to Maybell, "Someone will be here within ten minutes." He smiles.

Maybell can only shake her head.

~ ~ ~

Adam wonders how long is a polite amount of time to wait until you know for sure you are stood up. His phone rings. "Hey Dad, what's up?" he says.

Joshua tells him what has happened to Maybell, he also tells him that his brother and sister in law are on their way to him. "One of them will drive you over there so you can drive Maybell home. They will take your car back home to Mom. You can stay with Maybell tonight or I'll take you home in my car, let's play that decision by ear. She needs a friend tonight Adam, no teasing about date night." Joshua says to drive home the point.

"I hear you Dad. Oh, god, if she is hurt, I'm going to choke that boy myself." Adam finds himself breathing heavy. He stands up to walk out of the restaurant and passes the waitress. Feeling bad for not ordering this whole time he stops next to her, "An emergency has come up, not your fault. Here, thank you for waiting patiently with me." He hands her a generous tip.

"Wow, thank you sir I hope all is well." She calls after him.

Adam is outside as his brother and wife are pulling in. He opens the back door and throws his keys in the front before they are fully in park, "Move" is all he says. His sister in law jumps out to take Adam's car and his brother moves over to take Adam over to Maybell.

His sister in law pulls out right away in Adam's car and heads home. Guy takes Adam with him. Adam notices that they have taken the baby out with them and he holds the baby's hand to help keep himself calm. The infant wraps his little finger around Adam's finger. Right now, the baby is the only thing that is real to Adam, the idea of Maybell going through this trauma is more than he can handle right now. Sure, she is ok, so why is this hitting him so hard?

"Guy, Dad didn't say if Maybell is hurt. Do you think she is ok?" Adam asks his brother, his voice quivering.

"Adam, he said she never left the car, she is ok, shaken up is all and the cop told Dad she should not drive home but listening to your voice I'm not sure you should either." Guy says.

"I'm ok, I need to see her. This whole night was a disaster from the moment it started. I should have watched the signs, they were all there. How can this happen? Dad says the Quickmart is open. Why did she stop in the first place? Why didn't anyone from the store call the police? Are they all blind!? I'm sure those boys were making a lot of noise, someone should have seen or heard them." Adam rambles off in one breath.

"Adam, take a deep breath my dear brother. Really, inhale slowly and exhale slowly because if you're not calm, we may have to juggle the cars and drivers even more. Because you can't drive in this state of mind." Guy answers him

"I'm ok, really I am." He holds onto his stomach trying to make sure he doesn't lose his lunch. "Your son is beautiful Guy, I hope he and Mick are good friends, they are only two years apart." Adam tries to change the subject to get himself thinking clearly but his stomach isn't listening, his nerves are so on edge he feels he is about to explode.

Guy doesn't answer, he knows what his brother is doing, he also knows that he is secretly dying inside. Guy, his wife and his parents all know that Adam and Maybell belong together, but they have to realize something like that themselves. By the way Adam is reacting tonight Guy feels the realization may come to his mind, but then again, they both may be so caught up in the moment they won't realize what is going on and they will rationalize their feelings tonight out to being nothing but the comforting of good friends.

"Be there in five minutes, be ready with a smile." Guy says.

"Yeah." Adam says quietly.

~ ~ ~

A car pulls up next to Maybell's car, she looks over to see Guy driving, and bends her head down. "Great, big brother to the rescue." She whispers to herself. "I miss my brothers right now. I should call my own mom, I should call on my own family not Adam's." She says to herself with a big sigh

The police officer walks over to Guy's car and speaks to him to verify their relationship with the woman in the car. He then walks back to the victim's car. He taps on the window. She opens her window to hear him.

"Can you identify the men in the car next to you?" he asks.

Maybell looks over at Guy's car, she sees Guy and then she sees Adam get out of the back of the car, her heart skips a beat. Why? She does not know. "Yes sir, that's my best friend getting out of the back seat and the man driving is his brother." She says, her voice still shaking.

"Ok, then I will let them take you home then." He says to her and walks over to the men to let them know she has positively identified them and that they can take her home.

Adam walks slowly over to Maybell's car after being given permission to take her home. With the window open he steps up to the car, "Hey Bell, you ok?" he asks as strongly as he can.

Maybell looks up at Adam she shakes her head, she can't speak right now. He opens the door and puts his hand out to her so she can stand up with his help. Maybell takes his hand but as soon as she stands, she falls into his arms and he holds on for dear life and allows herself to whimper into his shoulder. Adam pulls her in close. Holding her right now is doing things to him that shouldn't happen between friends. Behave yourself Adam, now is not the time, this is not the place and she is certainly not the person, he thinks to himself.

He walks her around to the passenger's side of her car and opens the door for her. "Come, let's go home." He whispers into her ear as he helps her to sit back down. Maybell finds herself shaking but she is very confused as to why, is it the trauma or is it being in Adam's arms at the time of the trauma that has her trembling inside? Maybell decides to be quiet during the ride home, assuming that Adam will figure her silence is because of what happened when in reality it's because she is afraid to open her mouth right now. She wants to say thank you to him but she also wants to hold him and nothing else, hold him tight, he felt so good, to be in his arms felt so comforting. Maybell's emotions are all over the place, she has decided to sit back and concentrate on the fact that she is physically ok. Oh but that boy. Her voice catches.

"What boy?" Adam asks.

Maybell looks to Adam, she does not realize she spoke out loud. "The boy at the car, he was beaten by his friend with the bat, straight in the head." She points to the top of her head to demonstrate where the bat came down. "His mother is going to be so worried, we should find out what hospital they brought him to Adam. We should visit." She says in what Adam defines as her mommy voice. When Maybell talks about her kids or anyone else's for that matter, her voice softens and her eyes glisten. Adam loves that about her, she is so genuine. How could these boys attack her car? Something is not right with this scenario. He will ask the police tomorrow.

"Bell, you can't adopt every wayward child you see, you do know that, right? Just because you see things happen in movies and television does not make them practical for real life. I'm sure his own family is at the hospital and the last thing they need is for you and I to be hanging around them showing how much they don't have or trying to prove that we know better how to parent their child. I'm sorry Bell, but I can't encourage you to visit. You understand?" he asks softly.

"I know, but you had to see his face when his friend went wild on my car. He was so scared Adam, really, really scared. It might as well have been a gun to his head, I think he knew his life was over. That shouldn't be. We don't live in a bad neighborhood, these boys happen to be on something and they probably had too much or mixed it with something they shouldn't have. I would love for my car to be fixed but then again, I'd like to drive the car around for all to see so that everyone will take a better look at what is important. It's a car and god has given me a job that will allow me to replace this one if I want to. I believe, for these boys, that is not the case, especially with the boy who was hit or the one who was on my car. Please Adam, as a father you should understand." She pleads.

"Let's get you home, we'll talk tomorrow. You've been through a lot and you may or may not be thinking clearly. No offense. Do you want to call your mom and dad?" Adam asks changing the subject.

Maybell sits back in her seat. Her hand goes to her heart as it always does when she thinks of family. If her family was near, they would have come for her, wouldn't they? They've met Neeli, decided that Maybell was entitled to one mistake but when she became pregnant again, they have not been so forthcoming with any love or support really. Her brothers sent her presents, one came to visit and her sister has refused to speak to her since she became pregnant the first time.

Maybell misses her family, don't they know that? Don't they understand how much she loves them? How much she wants them to be proud of her? But she keeps ruining that option for herself. She wanted to be a mother, the procedure was done in an office like any other office procedure. The funny thing is, she has had two children but she has never been with a man in bed. That part doesn't matter to her who the father is, the doctor assured her that everything was tested for any kind of problem that could arise. She made sure all medical testing was done on the sperm before she had agreed to going through with this. She didn't wake up one day and say, hey Maybell lets go have a child. She had given careful consideration to all of her options. There were no men in her life at all, her schedule for having children was now, so she decided that one part of her list was going to come true.

She did not expect the backlash from her family. Adam's family doesn't seem to care. Julienne supported her when she told them she was pregnant again. His mom was with her while Joshua watched Neeli when she went into labor with Jerimiah. She held her hand and told her everything was going to be ok. Julienne has taken Maybell into her life with no judgement at all.

Maybell stays deep in contemplation as they pull into her parking lot. She did not really notice they were home until Adam put his hand on her shoulder and said, "Bell, we're home. You ok?" he asks softly.

Maybell shakes her head and proceeds to get out of the car. She reaches down and grabs her bag, at this moment Adam notices what she is wearing. She has on blue flowers in her hair and she was headed in the direction of the diner. His date never showed up. Holy....Adam slaps his hand on his mouth before he says something stupid. The last thing Maybell needs right now is to know some silly computer program set them up on their date tonight to be with each other. Maybell sits back up and sees a look on Adam's face that startles her. She quickly looks behind her thinking someone is coming to her car again, then back at Adam who is now looking at her and smiling. "What? Tell me Adam what's wrong?" her voice cracks as she asks.

"Bell, I'm sorry, I guess the events of tonight have me jarred as well. I saw a cat jump on the car next to us and I startled is all. Let's go check on the kids and show my dad you're ok." He turns his back to her to get out of the car, Maybell gets out of her side as well.

Adam runs around to her side and guides her up the few steps to her front door. They walk in together and Joshua jumps up from the couch and runs over to Maybell to hold her. "Oh, you poor dear. Come, let me make you some tea, or would you prefer orange juice and seltzer?" he asks leading her into the kitchen.

"Plain o.j. would be fine, thank you." She says as she sits down. Her head spinning now, she puts her head down on the table. I can't call you Dad, can I? You won't come, you won't want to, neither will Mom. Especially Mom. I've let you all down. But I sure could use you now. Her tears begin to fall, and she lets them.

Adam heard every word she was whispering, he looks to his dad to see if he heard them too. Joshua looks to his son and picks up his phone. Then he heads out of the room to call Maybell's parents. They need to know what happened and they need to get here tomorrow.

Adam sits down next to Maybell and begins to rub her back softly to help her calm down. She looks up at him and without knowing why she gets up from her chair and sits on his lap and continues to cry into his shoulder. Adam holds on to her tightly, she needs some strength, he continues to rub her back.

~ ~ ~

"Hello?" Mike answers the phone abruptly because he does not recognize the call and assumes this is a telemarketer.

"Hello, is this Mr. Winkler?" Joshua asks.

"Who wants to know?" he answers in a not so friendly tone.

"My name is Joshua Hardgrove, I'm Adam's father. I believe you've met him a time or two, a friend of Maybell's." he answers.

In a softer voice Mike answers, "Ah, yes, fine boy you have there, Joshua is it?" he asks.

"Yes. Um Do you have a minute to talk father to father?" Joshua asks.

"All ears." Mike says.

Joshua begins to tell him about how wonderful Maybell is doing with her two children, how much he has seen her grow in both parenthood and in her career. She is sought after for her abilities in the finance world and is doing quite well for someone her age.

"All nice to hear, thank you, but I don't believe that is why you're calling out of the blue and at 9:00 at night." Mike says.

"Correct, there is more." Joshua says. He then regales Mike with the tale of what happened this evening and how she is currently crying, not because she is hurt but because she can't call her own family. To add a little more information to the situation, he then shares with Mike that Maybell chose to get pregnant out of the love of children. That she took her choice to a respectable doctor's office in town and not some shady place, that she has, at least not to his knowledge, ever shared a bed with a man. Her reputation is impeccable.

"You say she wasn't hurt though, right?" Mike asks with concern in his voice.

"Shaken, yes. She is actually more concerned with the boy who was hurt than herself." He answers.

"Hang on a moment. Don't hang up." Mike says.

"Ok" Joshua waits, and paces the living room waiting a full five minutes before Mike comes back on the phone.

"Ok. We can leave in half an hour. We'll be by her in the middle of the night though and that will scare her even more. We will get to a hotel this evening and arrive in the morning. How bad is the car? Do I need to bring her a new one?" Mike asks.

"The car is banged up but perfectly fit to run. Your presence is all that is needed sir and I'm sure it will be very much appreciated. I may have my son sleep here tonight to make sure she is not alone, if that's alright with you." Joshua says.

"Um, yeah, she probably should not be alone. You sure she is ok? Physically." He asks again.

"I didn't see any sign of any physical trauma. Thank you, sir, I look forward to meeting you tomorrow morning." With that Joshua hangs up hoping he did the right thing explaining all that he did to Mike.

He walks back into the kitchen and sees Maybell curled up onto Adam's lap. He questions his son with his eyes and his son shrugs leaving him to believe she did this on her own, to find some comfort. Before anyone could do anything else for Maybell, the baby begins to cry and she perks up immediately and runs upstairs to him.

She quickly picks him up and sits down with him in the rocking chair Julienne gave her for nursing. Once he latches on, Maybell finally stops crying. "If you ever do anything so stupid as to take drugs, I'll kill you, you hear me?" she asks the suckling baby. As if to say yes, he looks up for a moment into her eyes then continues to nurse. She melts into the natural state of nursing and allows herself to relax so the baby will have what he needs, comfort and food.

Food? Hmmm, she never did eat dinner, and as she thinks the thought her stomach growls at her quite loudly. She hears rustling downstairs and begins to get nervous but then she remembers she is not alone, Joshua and Adam are downstairs. "Those are two of the finest men I've ever known Jerimiah, you know that? It will be perfectly ok with me if you grow up like them. Either one, take your pick. Uncle Joshua loves you and so does Adam. You can't go wrong trying to be like them." She kisses the baby's head and holds him up to burp him.

Jerimiah was having none of that, he wanted to continue to eat. Unlike Neeli, he likes to eat until he is full then he will allow himself to be burped. She puts him on the other side to finish and he latches on as if he hasn't eaten in hours. Maybell smiles down at him and her heart melts a little more.

"Oh that poor boy, some mother is at the hospital right now with great heartache. Her boy has been beaten. Oh, the horror of this all. Please, stay safe Jerimiah. Stay safe." She whispers.

There is a knock at the door, "Yes, I'm decent." She says covering herself for a moment.

"Hey, I realized that neither one of us ate dinner. Nothing fancy, but I made us some noodles and cheese. Should be ready soon. Is he done?" Adam asks.

"Never" she smiles and so does he. Adam has given him a bottle before and knows that he won't come up for air until the bottle is empty.

However, at the mention of his eating habits, Jerimiah finishes and pulls away from his mother. She covers herself and puts herself back together while handing the baby over to Adam. "See if he'll burp for you, I'll meet you downstairs, I must use the bathroom."

Adam walks around with the baby for a minute or two trying to coax a burp out of him, instead he gets a shoulder full of warm milk followed by a burp and a smiling baby. "Thank you." Adam says and brings him over to the changing table to clean them both up. After changing the baby, he gently puts him back into his crib and walks downstairs.

"You going home tonight Dad?" Adam asks.

"You?" Joshua asks.

"Mom is there, Mick will love seeing her in the morning. I'm sure he will get her to make biscuits, he always does. Save me some though." Adam says.

"Ok, sleep on the couch please." Joshua says softly.

"Every intention, but thanks for the gentle reminder." Adam smiles at his dad.

Maybell walks in as the two men laugh, "Again, I miss the joke?" she asks.

"I'm headed home Maybell. Adam is staying. I insist you not be alone tonight." He uses his best don't argue with your father voice.

"Ok Joshua. Thank you. I'll say it again, I don't deserve you people." She gives him a big hug. Joshua kisses the top of her head and heads out the door.

"Let's go eat." Adam says looking at his friend. She looks at him with her eyes big, "No, I still don't think it's a good idea." He says

"Adam, he needs to know I don't care. He needs to know I don't think less of him, his choice maybe, but not of him. We'll ask the police officer tomorrow his opinion, ok?" she stares at him

"Ok, ok we'll ask, but he is going to tell you no, and you're going to go anyway so why bother?" Adam asks.

"I will listen." Maybell says.

"No, you won't." Adam says as he pushes her a plate of noodles and cheese. They eat in silence.

~ ~ ~

Joshua calls Adam at 7:00 in the morning. "Yes Dad, what's up? Mick ok?" he asks sleepily.

"Yes, I heard from Mike, they're headed over to you, will be there soon. Is anyone up? I don't want to scare her. Aw, she is going to kill me, isn't she?" Joshua asks. "We'll be there before them. Don't answer that question." Joshua hangs up before his son can answer.

"Honey, let's go, we have to buffer, well, in case." Joshua says to Julienne.

"I agree. Mick, shall we bring Maybell and Neeli some biscuits too?" she asks her grandson.

"I like Neeli," he says with a big smile.

"Ok, first we have to get dressed." Joshua grabs the boy to go find clothes. Julienne finishes up the biscuit dough, they will bake them at Maybell's she has a better oven than Adam anyway. The three of them leave, hoping to beat Mike and his wife to Maybell's.

"ADAM!!!" Neeli squeals as she sees him in the kitchen.

"Hey little one, how are you this morning? Is Mom up too?" Adam asks.

"She has baby." She answers.

"Well, how about we set the table up for people to eat breakfast. I think Uncle Joshua and Julienne are going to come with Mick this morning, how about that?"

he asks her as he scoops her into his arms.   She gives him a big hug, "like Mick" he smiles.

Adam and Neeli continue to put out plates, cups and silverware as the knock on the door comes, they go to answer together. Thankfully it's his parents and Mick.

"Are we first?" Adam nods. "Good, come Neeli, I have biscuit dough and you and Mick are going to help me bake them." Julienne says.

"How was the night?" Joshua asks looking up the stairs.

"She woke up once, but that once kept us up for two hours. She wants to go see the boy who was injured, we aren't going to get out of going, she is pretty insistent." Adam says.

"Ok, maybe her parents will distract her. We'll see." Joshua says and looks up as he hears her come down. "Good morning my dear, Julienne insisted on baking the biscuits here" he says.

"Of course, my oven is much better than Adam's" she says as she walks by. "Your turn" she hands the baby over to Joshua, who takes him willingly.

The doorbell rings before they walk into the kitchen. Maybell turns around, she sees Adam and he smiles, she looks to Joshua and he shrugs which tells her he knows exactly who is at the door. Maybell walks over to Joshua and hugs him, "Thank you." She whispers and heads to the door.

She opens the door to see her parents and her oldest brother, he must have been recruited to drive them. "Good morning, you're just in time for biscuits, Julienne is famous for them." She smiles

Her father is frozen, he looks to her and then to his left where he sees her car all banged up. Maybell, for the first time looks to her car too. In the light of day, the car looks a lot worse than it did last night. "I'm ok Dad, come in. Please." She says pleading.

Maybell's mom walks in first and hugs her daughter, then her brother comes in and does the same, finally, after much head shaking at the car her father walks in. "Belly, why didn't you call us? Why" his voice broke before he could continue talking and he pulls his daughter in for a long overdue hug. She feels good in his arms, his little girl. Not his baby but still Daddy's little girl.

Julienne walks in because no one has come back to the kitchen, "I hope you're hungry everyone, sit down, the biscuits will be done soon." She says startling everyone into moving towards the dining room table.

After introductions, Neeli squeals again "Poppop!!" this is a name she knows well. They video chat all the time but in person, she knows she will have fun. She runs to Mike, who willingly picks her up and squeezes her tightly. He did not realize how much he wanted this until he holds this little girl. He has been an old fool, he has wasted too much time listening to the people around him.

Someone is pulling at his pants, he looks down at the little boy not much bigger than his granddaughter, "Mick" says the little boy. Mike leans down and says, "Hello Mick."

Mick gives the man a hug because Neeli is so he must be good. Mike grabs both of them and sits down with them both on his lap. Maybell's mother is still somewhat taken aback by all of these people and the children. Jerimiah starts crying in Joshua's arms and for some reason Maybell's mother instinctively takes him out of his arms and holds him in a very specific position to get him to calm down, he is quiet in seconds.

"Mom?" Maybell asks.

"It's the same cry your brother had, the only thing that helped is this. I'm sorry. Do you want him back?" Maybell's mom looks to Joshua.

"No maám, he who quiets a baby that fast is deserving of my gratitude. That is one piercing sound when your ear is so close." Joshua laughs and so does everyone else.

Julienne brings in the biscuits and conversation begins to open up to other items. The drive in, crazy traffic this morning from the hotel, Maybell's penchant for numbers and organization which is why she is so quickly successful in her chosen field. Adam watches as Maybell's heart swells as her father speaks of how proud he is of her. He is non-stop talking about all her accolades and Maybell is overwhelmed, she never thought he was proud of her, this is a defining moment for her and Adam sees relief all over her face. His heart skips a beat watching her, he shakes his head. That can't be happening, he thinks to himself.

~ ~ ~

Most of the morning goes fairly well. Both mothers get along swimmingly, the kids love everyone. Adam is busy taking pictures of everyone with everyone and smiling. Then Maybell drops the bombshell on everyone, "Who is going with me to the hospital to see the boy who got hurt?" She looks around the room at a group of shocked faces, except her father.

Mike looks at Maybell, "Did you ask the police officer yet? He may say this is the wrong thing to do Belly." He looks at her wondering how she is so caring when he can't be bothered to see her more than once a month and only through a computer monitor.

Maybell looks around the room, everyone seems to agree with Mike. "Don't you all understand? That boy is only destined to do bad if everyone believes he will. If one person stands up and says, I don't think you are your actions, he may never change. Please, one of you has to be brave enough." She pleads.

Adam's heart is breaking and he is not sure why. "Ok Bell, I'll go, there are enough people here to watch all the kids, let's go now before I change my mind. There are two pumped bottles in the fridge." He says.

Maybell walks over to Neeli, "I'm going to go out with Adam, all these people are going to stay here with you and Mick and Jerimiah, then when I get back, we'll make a bubble party. Ok?" Neeli jumps to her mom and hugs her, then she runs over to Joshua and pulls him over to her toys. Her mom is still holding Jerimiah, "He shouldn't be hungry for at least two more hours. His bottles are in the fridge. Oh, yeah, Adam said that already. See you all soon."

~ ~ ~

They swing by the police station first to check on where the boy is and how the other boy is doing. "Ah good morning you two. How does the car look this morning? The officer asks.

"Bumps and bruises. Nothing that can't be fixed." Maybell says. "We'd like to know which hospital the boy is in that was taken last night."

"Which one?" ask the officer

"Which one? The one who was hit with the bat? Is there more?" she asks.

"The one we arrested, ended up having a bad reaction to whatever he was on, ended up, we had to take him over to join his friend at about 2:00 this morning." He says.

"Oh my, this is going from bad to worse. Does he know what he did yet? Is the other boy alive?" she grabs Adam's hand for support.

"He has not been of right mind yet to tell him what he did last night. He is under the care of good people over at Good Hearts Hospital, they take in wayward children no questions asked. The other boy was taken over to Valley Hospital for head trauma. Both have an officer by their doors, pending charges. We also found two of the other boys last night hiding in the bushes. They gave the name of the last boy. How would you like to handle this? Charge each one separately?" he asks.

"Charge them? Oh, no, Adam?" she gasps. Holding her hand to her heart and the other on her mouth.

"Maybell doesn't think they should be charged for being stupid. She is hoping that once they learn what they are capable of under the influence of illegal drugs that they will have regrets." Adam quickly explains to the officer.

"Well, my dear, that may be a nice thought but I will tell you, the ones who ran, ran because they have a record already and this is not going to help them. I don't really have to get you to press charges, it's more involved than you think." He says.

"Officer, may I go see them?" she asks. "Their names please" she says as she takes out a paper and pen. He shrugs and gives her their names. First stop is to the see the one who was beaten. His name is William. They find him easily in the pediatric ward, the officer sitting in front of the room.

He stands as they approach. "Funny, you don't look like parents." He says.

"Actually, I am..." Maybell starts to say.

"I know who you are, captain already called. Good luck." He says. Maybell and Adam walk in together and they see a young man staring at them as they approach his bed.

"Who are you?" he asks.

"Do you know why you are here?" she asks.

"Bad accident, I suppose." He says.

"Have you seen your parents? Family?" she asks.

The boy stares at her even harsher than before. "Lady, I am my family. I don't go asking for handouts from the likes of you and I certainly don't want my family contacted because no one has the money to pay for all of this." His face angry now.

"No need to get in a snit," Adam says. "this is the woman's whose car you and your friends chose to pounce on last night. Ring any bells? How about the fact that your own friend is the one who pounded a bat on your head, which is why you are here. Does any of that bring back some memories for you?" Adam was not in the mood to be nice, so he spit out the information as is.

The young man's face goes whiter than the sheets of his bed. Realization comes flooding to his brain, you could tell. Images that he thought he was imagining all night, have been confirmed. His best buddy, high on who knows what and how much, had done this to him. What had he done to this lady? She doesn't look harmed, thankfully.

Maybell puts her hand on his foot, through his sheets, "We all make mistakes, some stupider than others, you have a lot of stitches and they are watching you for a concussion or other damages. He almost came down on you a second time but I screamed and distracted him, then the police arrived and they got him before he could get to you or me." Maybell rummages through her purse. "Here is my business card. When you are discharged from here, you call me. I want to give you a job." She says.

"Why?" he asks.

"Because, you owe this to yourself to prove to yourself and the world that your stupid actions last night are simply that, momentary lapse in judgement caused by a lack of care for yourself. Well, I want you to learn to care for yourself and about yourself. No preaching, no obligation to stay." Maybell pulls on Adam so they can leave.

Adam turns to the boy and says, "By the way, she is not pressing charges, but if you have other things behind you, they may find a way to charge you without her. Good luck man." He says and walks over to Maybell who is already at the door.

"Wait." The boy calls to them

They turn around. "Does he know? I mean does he know what he did to me?" the boy asks.

"I don't think so. He will be told today," Maybell answers, and with that, they walk out.

"A job Bell?" Adam asks

"Adam, if I press charges he will forever be there, maybe, one can hope, that if he has a real job, some real responsibility, he will become a part of society that people like. I don't think he comes from a bad family or a poor one, did you see the watch he is wearing? They want him to be a model citizen as much as we do. But no one he knows will open any doors for him, he caused that, so maybe I can be that last door. I may even be his only open door." Maybell says.

"Bell, you amaze me every day. I'm ready to go see the other boy." Adam says and takes her hand in his to walk out.

Her hand in his feels right. Everything about the past twenty-four hours has been an emotional overload for Adam. By the time they get to his car, his heart is pounding, he opens the door so she can sit down. When she releases his hand, his body misses her. This is not good, he says to himself. This is Bell, his best friend not a girlfriend but he can't let go, holding her feels so good.

~ ~ ~

"Joshua, does it appear to you that our children should be together?" Mike asks shortly after they leave.

"That notion appears to both of us, only they don't see this yet. I'm sure they will soon." Joshua says.

"Maybell is so smart, but all the planning in the world can't make love come. I told her that, but she insisted that her list is exactly how her life is going to work. She said a list worked for her brothers, so it should work for her." her mother says.

Julienne chimes in, "Adam had his own list as well, which was thrown out the door after the divorce. He is looking for his forever now, his words." She says.

"My Belly has a mind of her own, always has. As a child she would only do things in order as well. Even the way she ate, she only ate one item on her plate at a time, when one was finished, she went to the other item. Her life list made sense to me. Not what she wrote was but that she made one." Mike says.

Joshua begins to laugh, he has eaten with Maybell many times and she still does that, he always found it a part of her that made her who she is, a little qwerky, yet loveable. He looks from Mike to his wife, she is so unassuming, her demeanor is so quiet she can get lost even in a room by herself. Her son hasn't said two words either, Joshua makes the assumption that Maybell takes after her father, qwerks and all.

"Joshua! Joshua honey, didn't you hear what he asked you?" Julienne says strongly.

"Oh, sorry, I was lost in my own thoughts, I do that sometimes. Do you mind repeating yourself?" Joshua says.

Mike smiles at Joshua, "I asked you how long do you think we need to stay? My son is itching to get back already to his wife and job, highly unusual for him to take a day off and my wife is more comfortable at home, always has been." His voice is quiet so his wife and son can't hear him, which is probably why Joshua didn't really hear him in the first place.

"Stay as long as you want Mike, I'll make sure you get home either by train or plane, if they want to leave, send them home now." Joshua says a bit annoyed. How can they leave these kids? Why do they want to walk away so quickly? They've only seen them a couple of hours.

"I wouldn't mind staying with my Belly for a couple of days but I didn't really pack, we kind of left in a hurry because I needed to make sure she was ok. She is my little girl you know." Mike says a bit choked up in the voice.

"You and I aren't that much different, I'm sure I can lend you some clothes for a couple of days. Will Maybell be upset to see her mother gone when she gets back?" Joshua asks because he doesn't need her to have more drama now, she needs stability.

"She will expect them to be gone." Mike's head bows a moment. He picks up his head again and looks Joshua in the eye as if to tell him something very personal, "Joshua, she is *my* baby girl." The emphases is put on the word my and Joshua quickly understood that Maybell has a different mother. Joshua puts his hand on Mike's shoulder and shakes his head. He repeats, "Stay as long as you want."

Mike took this acceptance and went over to his wife and son to tell them to leave without him. They seemed all too happy as far as Joshua is concerned. All these years and she still can't love Maybell? What is the son's excuse? Does he know the true story? He should hold that angst against his father not Maybell. We all make mistakes, some are bigger than others but we all make them.

~ ~ ~

"Adam, did you or your father call my father last night?" Maybell asks.

"Dad did, you mad?" he asks.

"No, surprised more that they came than the fact that he called." She states simply

"Really Bell? Your dad loves you, it's so obvious." He says.

"Right, my dad. Maybe my oldest brother likes me, at least a little, he is the one who got me my summer job that turned into forever. But then, after I stayed, and he left for another job closer to my folk's home, I realized he did this to get me out of their house. I think he knew I wouldn't be going back home. Don't look at me like that Adam, I know the truth, I've always known." Maybell says.

"What truth is that?" Adam asks.

"I have a different mother than the rest Adam. When I found out, everything else made sense in my life. All the missed school activities, all the birthday dinners 'accidently' forgotten. The hand me downs given to my sister and not me. My mom showing up today is a farce, my brother drove them because my dad was probably too nervous. Bet you a night at Benny's Diner that they are gone when we get back." She says matter-of-factly.

"Bell? Are you kidding me? Do you think that's why they don't approve of the babies? Thinking that you are sleeping around? I can assure you my father put them straight on that. I know he did, Bell." His hand reaches over to hold hers again.

Adam's hand holding hers makes the world right again. Being on his lap last night was exactly what she needed. But Maybell doesn't want to lose her best friend. They've been through too much together, what if this doesn't work? She can't lose him, ever! Unconsciously, she squeezes his hand, he squeezes back, and there they stay in silence all the way to the other hospital.

The officer at the door looks a lot more intimidating than the first one did. Adam approaches slowly, "Excuse me, we are here to see the young man inside. Is he ok?" Adam asks.

"You the woman whose car he jumped?" he asks sternly.

"yes." Maybell answers.

"He has been mumbling all morning about something about a car and a woman. At least some of his memories are coming back. He probably won't remember all of the events of last night. Go on in, but tread lightly please." He says.

They shake heads and open the door slowly. Again, they see no family, Maybell looks to Adam and he already knows what she is thinking, he nods his head to let her know its ok. They walk together to his bed.

"Hello." She says softly.

The boy sits up and looks at them, he looks at Maybell smiling at him, a moment of recognition hits him. "Why are you here?" he asks.

"I want to let you know, I'm not pressing charges." She says.

"Why not?" he asks

"Because being incarcerated will not help the problem. But maybe being supportive will." She smiles again at him. She continues, "Stupid actions don't make stupid people. Give yourself a chance. We saw your friend this morning, he is going to be ok, they are holding him one more day because of his head trauma." She says softly to try and get him to remember what he did.

The boy looks at her and at Adam questioningly. He closes his eyes to try and remember what the hell happened last night. He remembers being on her car, he remembers the guys daring him to drink something, he remembers.........

He looks up at Maybell and she shakes her head, out of nowhere and for the first time since he was a young child, tears begin to fall. Maybell approaches a little closer and puts a hand on his foot through the sheets like she did his friend, a simple touch means a lot. "He will be ok. You two took some powerful stuff, I'm happy to see that the memory of this has come back. Maybe it will help you not repeat something so foolish. Here is my card. When they discharge you, come to me for a job. Prove yourself above this incident. I'll bet there is a lot of untapped potential in you and I'd like to make sure you see that."

Before the boy talks, Adam interjects, "No we aren't missionaries, we don't want you to repent and say a thousand prayers, but we do want you to know that it is possible to get out of the predicament you're in. We stopped by to tell you, there are people in this world that don't think you're trash, we want to help you prove to them your real worth." Adam stands behind Maybell and pulls her away, they've said their piece and now it's time to go. Maybell taps the boy on the foot again, smiles and turns to leave with Adam.

Her card dangles in his hands. He has really screwed up this time. If his parents know about this incident, and he is sure they do by now, he is sure to lose everything from them. If this woman looked into who he was she could have sued big time, his father would have paid it to shut her up and make sure the incident doesn't make the papers. But she didn't, she isn't even pressing charges and oh god, he put his friend in the hospital. This has to end, he squeezes the card, now.

~ ~ ~

Adam and Maybell are quiet walking back to the car this time, no words. Holding hands and walking out together, no words are necessary. Maybell leans her head into his should and he releases her hand to put his arm around her. This feels, well, it feels right to him, how can he tell Bell that without sounding crazy? Adam thinks to himself.

As she sits down in the car, Maybell begins to cry. Adam walks around to get in the car and sees her. "Bell?" he asks.

"I've done this all wrong Adam, all of my life. Don't you see? I was born wrong and it's all been downhill since then." Her tears pour out of her and Adam watches because he knows Bell needs to get this out once and for all.

He reaches over to hold her hand, she lets him and continues, "After high school I was supposed to go to a local school, I was going to help my dad in the store and take classes in the afternoons. But then my younger sister decided she was going to get a business degree when she finished school and she was going to take over Dad's business. Mom was thrilled to see the business would be going to her daughter and not me."

"What are you saying Bell? Do you really think your mother, the one who raised you would not want you to help out your father?" Adam is confused.

"Adam, on my sixteenth birthday my mother told me the truth, I knew anyway but it was harsh to hear the words from her. I woke up thinking it was my birthday and then got the teeth knocked out of me. She came to my room and said, and I quote, 'No party today, I'm tired of making them for you. You know you're not mine anyway and your only here on borrowed time until you leave for college. We were separated for a year but shortly after your father came back there was a knock on the door and there you were. For sixteen years I've had to live with a constant reminder of that time in our lives when we both went astray. You're old enough to deal with the truth now.' So happy sweet sixteenth to me, huh?" Maybell says.

"Ouch, Bell, I met you only a year later, you never told me." Adam says.

"I know, you know everything else there is to know but this you needed to know to explain why she won't be there when we get back. She picked up Jerimiah today on instinct when she noticed she was holding him she offered him back immediately. Only because Joshua didn't take him that she continued to hold him. My oldest brother, who knew the whole time because he was nine when they were separated, he is the one who called me out here, he had a job and it was good, so he asked me to come out because they were offering these tremendous internships with pay.

So, I came, they loved me. So much so that they begged me to stay, paid for my education at night and well, you know the rest." She bows her head in shame.

"Bell, your children are beautiful, don't ever feel bad that you had them." He says.

"Why didn't I wait Adam, what was my big damn rush?" she cries some more.

"Your list, you felt you needed to make good on one of them, your age was right you simply didn't have the rest yet." Adam says quietly.

"I have nothing Adam. I'm twenty-six years old and I'm still working on my degree because my job demands so much of my time that I can only take a couple courses at a time. Year round. I still have eight more classes to take before I actually graduate. Then I owe them back the time because they are paying for my education." She says.

"I think they've made the investment in you because they believe in you. And you've proven them to be right. No one at work is complaining how long it's taking you to get your degree, you know why? Because you landed the biggest account in their history, that alone makes up for the money they've invested in you. You make more money on commissions with them than some people make after being there for ten years. Bell, you have a gift and they recognize that. Please don't doubt your self-worth, you are everything." Adam says and then realizes what he admitted to her. She is everything, everything he would ever want in a woman of his dreams. Even the computer said so. His heart begins to beat faster at the thought, right now he wants to hold her again, in his lap and make this all go away, this pain she has been carrying for so long.

"Adam," her words are failing her. She picks up his hand to kiss him, she doesn't know what else to do right now, his words have hit her hard. She is everything? No one has ever said anything remotely like that to her before. Everything?

Her kiss on his fingers tingles all the way up his arm and through his body, all through his body. Whoa boy, settle down. He thinks to himself. But then again, why?

Maybell is his best friend, she knows all the good and the bad about him and now he knows even more about her as well.

Maybell takes his hand and puts it up to her face, she is leaning her cheek into his hand, he opens his fingers slowly to touch her. Maybell turns to face Adam, her heart is pounding and her body is responding to his touch in ways she didn't know she ever could and all she could think to say is, "We should head home, no?"

"No." Adam says and stares at her, "Bell, not yet." He says and he slides his fingers towards the back of her head and entwines his fingers into her hair, so much softer than he imagined, he pulls her closer to him and as their faces are close, he leans in and their foreheads touch. "I like this." He whispers and lifts his other hand to the other side of her head, he lifts her head to look into her eyes, she is not afraid, as he thought she might be. No, she is inviting him in, he kisses her softly on the lips and pulls away. "Now we can go home." He whispers. Maybell nods.

Adam starts up the car and the two of them drive in silence, both lost in thought as they ride along. Maybell does not know what to do with this new found affection for Adam, maybe it was always there, she hopes she doesn't blow this, she can't lose him, she simply can't.

Adam's mind is going to all kinds of places, he is almost hoping that her mother is still there so he can tell her off and kick her out. But then again, he is hoping that her father is still there because he wants to make sure Maybell doesn't feel like she was a mistake. She is too perfect to be a mistake. He looks over at her, yes, she is too perfect. How will he be able to hold on to her? He really needs his mom's advice right about now.

~ ~ ~

They pull up next to Maybell's car. Maybell walks around Adam's car to her own, she runs her hand along each of the dents in the hood of her car, it could have been so much worse, she will leave them on as a reminder to be appreciative for all she has. Adam comes up behind her and slides his hand around her waist, "I say leave them." He says over her shoulder.

"My thoughts exactly." She says They stand there a moment when they suddenly hear a child scream. "Oooo, that's Mick!" she says. The two of them run into the house and see Mick holding his head. Adam runs to him but Joshua has already picked him up.

"What happened buddy?" Adam asks.

"Dat!" he yells at him. Adam looks down and sees a toy on the floor.

"Did you try and pick it up fast?" Adam asks. Mick shakes his head.

"Neeli, go get Mick the ice man." Maybelle knows she can reach this, she has a side by side refrigerator/freezer and she keeps this on the bottom shelf on the door. Everyone looks at Maybell, Mike smiles, he knows exactly what an ice man is, he made one for her years ago, a tear comes to his eyes when he sees Neeli carrying a bag that resembles a man with a big belly filled with ice. She hands the man to Mick and kisses his head where his hand is.

"I wonder who taught her that?" Mike asks smiling.

Joshua isn't watching the little kids, he is watching the sparks from the bigger ones in the room. While it took a bit of trauma to pull them together, at least together finally happened. He knows this is a forever girl that Adam is looking for. He smiles at his son, giving him a knowing smile and Adam walks closer to hug his father. "She is forever." He whispers to Adam. Adam shakes his head

"How are the boys doing?" Juliene asks.

"Ok, I handed them my business card, now the ball is in their court, we will see what happens." Maybell answers.

"Good idea Belly, no one should be defined by one stupid act." Mike pipes in. Adam looks over to him with a bit of disdain. Mike feels Adam's feelings and knows why too. Maybell must have told him why his wife is gone. If he can even say wife anymore, more like roommate.

Mike walks over to Maybell and takes her hand, he grabs Adam's as well and leads them to the kitchen. Joshua and Julienne look to each other, "Truth has to come out some time." Julienne nods.

"Sit please." Mike says.

They do and he paces the room for a moment, takes a deep breath and begins to talk, not facing them, "A long time ago, your mom and I split up. Her eyes were wandering all the time and some rumors came out that it wasn't only her eyes. I needed to leave, needed to clear my head. That clearing took a long time. I made some investments while away, did things she would never allow me to do with my money. My wife has plenty of her own, she didn't need all of mine as well. We've always had separate bank accounts because she had said she didn't want me controlling her spending. So, while away, I met with my own financial guru, Mr. Markus, remember him?" He turns to Maybell, she shakes her head.

"Anyway, in the time I was away I almost forgot about my life in that house. I called the boys each day to see how their day went, met them at any and all games they played, but I was detached somewhat. I met a woman, who knocked my socks off, we talked all the time, we had fun. Belly, I was having fun again, in my life. We went on roller skates, saw movies, laughed out loud at the park. I had forgotten all the things I used to do before I married. Her name was Tory, she was from down south and had the cutest dimples on her left cheek, you only got one of them, she had two. Her eyes were the color of sapphires, really they were.

At one point I told her I was married and she didn't care. We talked for hours about heavy things and about nothing. I was falling in love all over again. I felt good. I felt really good, whole even. We were two consenting adults with a lot of love for each other, that much I can promise you. We made plans, I spoke with an attorney, I was going to get a divorce, no doubt about leaving my wife. It was going to happen within the next couple of months.

Then, my wife fell ill, really ill and I needed to set an example for my sons about what to do. How one is supposed to be there for people in their lives. She was an old friend, and that is exactly how I thought of her, an old friend. Tory understood. But when I went back, her phone was disconnected, I couldn't find her again. I looked for weeks. My heart was broken, I didn't know what to do.

Turns out, my wife was not as grave as she made herself sound, she only was looking to get me back. Did you hear me? Get me back, not win me back. My marriage has been a farce ever since. I never left because I never found Tory, she would be the only reason for me to leave. I even hired a private detective, he worked for months on my case and could not find her." Mike comes to sit down in between Maybell and Adam.

He holds both of their hands and continues, "I loved her from deep down, really I did Belly, you have to know that and I believe she did too. One day there was a knock at the door, I saw the private investigator, he was standing there holding a tiny little baby. When I say tiny, I mean tiny. You were only six pounds, had been released from the hospital finally because you were a preemie. He found her, my Tory, but he was too late.

She spoke with him for a day or two, he held her hand, she was not alone, her family was with her in the end. But they never wanted to take you because they said having you would be too hard, they knew I had a wife and other children so everyone thought you would be better off to be with your real dad.

Tory had gone home after going to the doctor finding out she was pregnant, but she also learned that she had some form of cancer. They were not sure she would be able to have the baby at all. She decided not to do any chemo because she wanted you to be as whole as possible. The doctors checked you upside down and backwards. You were given a clean bill of health. Your mother was not. They were going to start the chemo shortly after you were born but her body did not hold out." Mike reaches in his pocket for his wallet. He pulls out a picture he has carried all these years and shows Maybell a picture of her mother.

She looks down at this picture of her father and mother, so happy, smiling as if the world revolved around them. She could see the love that she never saw at home. He truly loved her, she was born from love not a mistake. "See Belly, everyone's list gets jumbled up. Seeing your kids has changed me in only a few hours. I think I'm done lying. I want out, I want to live my life and not hers. Before we came, I called the lawyer back and asked him what to do. He is going to have everything done within a week. My happily ever after never came but I watch you every day, I miss you every day, I want to be back in your life all the time." He says.

This is a lot to load up on Maybell but she knows where he is coming from and she doesn't mind. Adam speaks first, "Well, that's a hell of a story to tell Mike, got any more?" he asks with more sarcasm than necessary.

Mike understands why, he loves Belly and won't stand for more pain, good for him. "Only one." He turns to Adam and says, "I want her to have a happily ever after, are you prepared for that?" he asks. "I want Belly to never know pain again, not from me, not from you, or anyone." He looks to Maybell.

"What about the store, Pop, you worked all your life for that." She says.

"Right, to stay out of the house, I worked there to stay out of that house, not a home. She can have the whole thing. Like I said, I made some investments of my own. She doesn't really know what I'm worth and since we've always kept separate accounts and filed taxes separately, the lawyer says she won't be eligible to get anything, she has been living on her own money this whole time. He can prove she doesn't need mine. And as far as your brothers are concerned? Half-brothers, they take her side all the time. Everything has always been my fault. But the truth is, I've never asked for DNA proof of their parentage, I'm not sure they are all mine and if I ask during a divorce hearing, she will have to admit to her own faults. I'm really not sure how your sister came about, I don't think she is even your half-sister. But I don't want drama, I want out. I'm still young enough to enjoy life and retiring as a grandfather sounds good to me. If my sons don't want to be a part of my life, then that is their choice. I'm open to anything. Adam, any open apartments you can steer me to?" he asks

Maybell looks at her father, "You're not disappointed in me? My lopsided life? Job first, then college and children in the middle, with no marriage? I mean, I couldn't have screwed up any more than that, could I?" she asks.

"Maybell, you have your mother's mind. She could do numbers in her sleep. I swear sometimes she even did. It was the most wonderful year of my life. I carry those memories all the time, those happy memories. Adam will help you make happy memories too." He looks to Adam, who has finally come out of his sulk.

Adam looks at Mike, he thinks to himself what a rarity his parents are, he wants his children to have that too. One thing is for sure, there is already three children involved and he hopes to make even more. Life with Bell, will never be dull.

Joshua and Julienne come in the room, each carrying a sleeping toddler in their arms. "Small apartment, sorry, we heard everything, not going to lie." Joshua says.

Mike looks to them, "It's ok, don't know about anyone else but right now I feel like celebrating." He says.

Julienne looks to Adam, she can see he has finally admitted to himself that Maybell is his forever girl. "We're going to go put the kids down for their naps, then we can talk about how to move forward." She says quietly.

~ ~ ~

Mike moves in with Maybell for the time being. All of his belongings were sent to him by his lawyer. He packed them himself and anything else Mike asked for, then before he left, he handed over the divorce papers to the Mrs. He said signing them now would help eliminate any court dates but that she could have her lawyer look them over.

He told her she had twenty-four hours then he was going to go straight to court with a lot of information that she would not want made public. She practically pushed him out of the door.

Mike's wife called him the day after the lawyer came. "What the hell? Twenty-four hours? Really?"

"I gave you more than twenty-four years, seems fair. What do you want really? Why are you calling, mad I beat you to the punch?"

"This is crazy, you won't really leave me, you came back before."

"That was a mistake, I shouldn't have made, I've regretted that day ever since." He says "We're over, you haven't loved me since the day after our first son was born. Stop pretending. I am."

"My lawyer says I have all the time I want. You can't make me sign sooner than I want to."

"Ok, but know the longer you take the more paternity tests will be taken."

"You wouldn't!"

"Afraid of something? Sounds like an admission to me, I'm not stupid, I did the math, a few times and I always came out to the same answer. I only had one child with you. The longer you give my lawyer the longer he has to investigate our life together."

"But the children?"

"Are yours to deal with. Explain to them however you want. You've turned them on me for years, this won't be new. Goodbye, and good luck." Mike hangs up and walks back into the living room with Maybell and the kids.

"Adam's parents are right, you can hear everything in this room." She says.

"I don't mind. It makes me feel like it's private. Belly, I can't stay here, you're a grown woman with children and possibly more when Adam and Mick move in. Oh, don't look at me like that, you know that will happen."

Maybell's smile grows, she and Adam have done nothing but talk about the future and then about nothing at all. Like her father said, it's the nothing conversations that mean more. She always knew he loved her, but never knew why they were so close. Knowing matters, it really does. Maybell has made another list, this time she made one with Adam, first they are looking to get married, then they will find a place to live together, one that is big enough for all of them, then they plan on making this all work, each day, each year, together. A simple list but it's one they know they can follow through with.

"Ok, you have me on that, we were possibly thinking of buying the neighbor's place, he said he might be willing to sell, then we will combine the two town houses and instead of having three bedrooms, we will instantly have six, double the living space and even have two separate basements. Adam is hoping to use one of them as his office so he can work at home without anyone interrupting. His online presence is much greater than his in person one and he thinks he can really make that business grow. In the meantime, stay here, the kids love having you around. And afterwards, maybe we can convert the second basement into an apartment for you?" she asks.

"Belly, you don't want this old man living with you always."

"I don't see an old man. I see a live-in babysitter who will love to take the kids out, watch them like a hawk, and be a chick magnet for all the other eligible widows around here and divorcees."

"Hey, why do I always miss the good jokes." Adam says as he puts Mick down. He kisses Maybell and greets Mike with a nod.

"We've decided that I'm going to buy the place next door as your wedding present."

"What!!? That's not why I mentioned the idea and I also said this is only a possibility."

"I know why you spoke, but I only have *you* in my life to spoil and it's about time I started. Come Adam, let's go make the man next door an offer he can't refuse, then we'll come back and make a date. Enough wasting time."

Maybell makes a mental note, "add to list – thank your father for his undying love every day for the rest of your life." She watches as her two favorite men in her life walk out towards their future. This is going to work, it's most definitely going to work now.

~ ~ ~

Mike has been living with Maybell and the kids for three weeks now, the process of buying the next-door neighbor's townhouse is in the works, his divorce is final and

Maybell and Adam will be married in two months. There didn't seem a reason for them to wait longer, their lives are already so entwined.

Mike had looked at the basement next door, he could probably make a nice bachelor pad there, he will only have to be there at night to sleep because he is officially going to be babysitting all the kids, with the help of Joshua and Julienne, his two new best friends, he has begun to love life again.

Mike proceeds to get dinner ready for the kids when there is a knock at the door. "Door!" the kids shout. "Yes Neeli, I hear, come here." He picks her up and Mick follows holding on to Mike's pants.

Opening the door, Mike gets a very big surprise. His son, his only son is standing before him with his wife and child. "Room for a few more?" he asks.

Mike steps aside and lets them in. "I'm not going to beat around the bush here Dad. I forced Mom to do a DNA test on all of us. I knew the truth, but I wanted them to know too. The ungrateful bastards were badmouthing you all over town and instead of playing their game, I put them in their place. Knowing you took them in regardless of who their father was shut them up pretty damn quick. But leaving her the business is a bad mistake. She may think she knows what she is doing but it's going to fail in a year, maybe two." Brian is done with his tirade.

"Nice to see you, won't you come in?" Mike says. "This is your niece Neeli, and behind me is Mick, the one crying behind you is Jermiah, Belly's newest baby. How are you dear?" he asks his daughter in law and kisses her cheek.

"I'm good Mike, she is so beautiful. Wow. I can't get over her, I mean really she is. Say hello to your cousin Neeli, Victor." She smiles at the child. She knows her husband has been bursting to say what he had to say for days now. So, like Mike, she is letting the information go.

"What time does Belly get home?" Brian asks.

"In about an hour, I was making the kids dinner. Come Neeli, help Grandpa set the table we have new people to eat with." He smiles.

~ ~ ~

Adam and Maybell walk in the door together, they take one car now because they work near each other. "What the hell?!" Maybell shouts as she sees Brian and Carol standing in her living room playing with the kids.

Brian runs over to his sister, "You're all we have." He grabs her and hugs her tightly.

A horn honks outside and within a couple minutes Joshua and Julienne walk in with the rest of dinner. Every Tuesday, they all eat together. "Sorry we're late today. Damn traffic." Joshua says but before he can say more, he looks around and sees more people.

"Bloody hell, even two townhouses won't hold all of you. Come, you guys will stay at our house tonight yes?" he laughs.

Note to self, add to list, 'staying with family is important, forgiving even more so.' Maybell thinks to herself She squeezes Adam's hand. He leans down and whispers to her, "add to the list, family first." She smiles and laughs because she knows he knows what she was doing, adding to her list.

With everyone around the table, Brian proposes a toast, "Here is to tragedy." He says. "Because it makes us remember what is really important. Adam, treat her well, because we will be moving back shortly. The office is bringing me back to this location, says I can do more here than half way across the country. Carol is going to be working from home and hopes to create, what did you call it?"

"I want to create a home business where I make my own products to sell but also sell the supplies for others to make. I think I'll make more money on the supply sales than the finished pieces so I'm only going to do a few at a time. I work with so many things. A hobbyist turned pro I guess you can say."

"Bravo my dear" Julienne shouts. "Oh my, my heart has expanded even more. This family is growing by leaps and bounds. Adam's brother is going to have another baby soon, and his sister is about to be promoted as well. Oh, we are so blessed." Julienne's eyes begin to tear, Joshua pulls her in for a hug and Adam sits a little straighter with pride, he finally has what they have. He leans over and kisses Maybell on the lips, right in front of everyone.

The whole crowd laughs. "Hey Belly, maybe you should add to your list, never fix your car, it will always remind us of how we almost lost each other. No more." Brian says.

"Speaking of which, what happened with the boys?" Mike asks.

Adams speaks for Maybell because it always brings her to tears. "The boy who was hit in the head is doing an internship at my office. They are teaching him everything there is to know, he will be earning more money soon and may even be offered an actually full-time position. His father stops by unannounced every so often to check that he is actually at work and not fooling around anymore. It's a process, but it's going to work. Maybell took a chance on them and the boys have pulled up to the challenge. The other boy, the one who did the damage is working with Bell learning how to type and do coding from one of her tech guys. He says the kid has a lot of potential and doesn't mind working with him. His parents check on him too. But the boys don't seem to mind. It's what they both needed. A wake-up call and more importantly, someone to believe in them.

Oh, and we almost forgot to tell you, with all the goings on tonight, we forgot." Adam takes a breath but Maybell blurts out. "We close in two days!!!"

Happy tears, things are working out for everyone. Maybell knows that even though it took her here in a roundabout way, life knew what it was doing. She needed to experience all of what she has experienced to get here to this day. Now that happiness has set in, she can internalize and accept her life wholly for what she has.

Family, loving, dedicated, family.

Mismatched

Society makes a check list of the perfect features a person should have. People have erroneously decided what is socially accepted and what is not. However, sometimes fate and genetics, let's not forget them, play a part in who receives what features. But it is these people whose features don't match societal norms, they have a big choice to make, either suffer their whole lives, or make the best of life with what they have. Gilly has tried to get past the snickers behind her back, but even as an adult, they follow her. Herbert, on the other hand, has embraced his out of the norm features as part of what makes him unique. Can these two societal misfits find their way to happiness?

The car radio rings out with, "...here you go again, looking better than a body has a right to" at least this is what the words sounds like to Gilly, these words really resonate a little too well with her. This is a song sung by a female country singer, it has that quality that will make the melody stick in someone's mind for the rest of the day. Gilly is certain the song is not talking about her personally because she has never met this singer but that line keeps repeating in her head.

Gilly considers herself to be a simple person; living modestly and working hard. She doesn't own all the latest gadgets; has no need to have five hundred or more contacts on social networking sites, and her phone still flips up. For now, anyway. This week it's still working. This song clicks with her because of how close the words are to what people have been saying to her since puberty and that was a long time ago. People stare and then mumble, "Why does *she* get to have those legs?" or "Is she seriously only buying a size small?" The worst part is when perfect strangers assume she has had work done to her body and ask her why she didn't do anything to her face. To Gilly, and apparently many others, she looks better from the neck down. She has heard the same thing said over and over again that she doesn't deserve to have the body genetics gave her because it doesn't match her face.

Her eyes are green but not the nice emerald green society loves, her nose protrudes out a bit more than is fashionably acceptable these days and her lips are so thin they are almost nonexistent. At least, that is what she has been told by the make-up lady in the department store, more than once. One time, she had a man say to her that if he drank enough to not mind the face he sure as hell would love to go after the body. Gilly has worked hard to get to where she is at work and people give her some respect because the rumor is that no one would sleep with her so she must have come by her promotions with honest hard work and achievement. Actually, if she is honest with herself, they pretty much ignore her in the office because no one wants her job. Ok, so it's not the most glamorous of jobs, but she does her job well and enjoys what she does immensely.

Gilly started at this company as a phone receptionist, then kept taking on work from different departments because she was bored and her supervisors asked her to do more. She does some work for the accounts receivable and accounts payable departments and found herself working on a statistical report for the VP. She maintains all this while still answering and screening all the calls that come into the company. Her work keeps her busy now all day.

She willingly takes on more responsibility while others in similar positions haven't moved up or even tried. Some of the women say that Gilly is always trying to prove something because she has to. The guys in the sales force (mostly men) love to make comments at her backside, it's when she turns around that the smiles leave their faces.

One day she turned to tell one of the salesmen off and instead she merely said, "Blame it on genetics, I'm may be mismatched, but I could sell you under the bus." That's a title her own brother gave her one year during high school. There was a costume party to go to and they went together as Jekyll and Hyde, only the other party goers kept asking who her brother was because it looks as if Gilly could be both with her body as Hyde and face as Jekyll. That got her brother into a lot of trouble, he "accidently" found his fist falling into a couple of guys' faces". That's what he told their mom anyway. In fact, on the way home from that very party he said to Gilly, "Don't worry about being mismatched, I love you and think you're perfect." It was the first time the term was used, and since then, the name stuck, she began to believe herself to be mismatched. Although there is nothing she can do about her physical attributes, short of surgery, which she has no intention of doing, still, her mismatched features are always spoken of.

The women in the office and other places are no better. Starting back in high school, when they had to change into gym uniforms, the girls used to watch her because they thought they would see the "real" body, in other words - she must have had padding in her bra and panties in order to have that body. When they didn't see what they wanted to see they would make comments regarding her body. There was that one time when the captain of the cheerleaders said, "Well, natural boobs is it? Why is it that the girls with the less than perfect faces get all the curves? Not sure how you expect to get a boyfriend though. Maybe he will text you a lot so he is not obligated with full frontal conversation." There was one girl who thought she was helping Gilly that time by saying, "Leave her alone, it's not her fault she has the body of a woman and the face of a man." Those weren't even the worst ones. Of course, there are also the rumors about her not wanting to be with a guy in the first place.

Gilly tries to ignore them all, then and now. Her family has been very supportive throughout adolescent and college years but now that she is on her own, the same words are much harder to walk away from without being told you're being cold or unsocial. She had assumed, that as an adult these annoyances would go away, but evidently that is wrong. She thought about getting one of those jobs where the employee can work remotely and no one has to see them. But then she'd be bored with no one to talk to face to face except for the ladies at the lunch counter at the nearby deli.

Currently, Gilly considers herself the chameleon at work. Wherever they place her, she is ready and able to adjust to the job or take on any new roles. Her boss loves that he can give her anything and she is willing to learn and do the new responsibilities the right way.

Gilly works for a company that sells to both wholesale and retail customers, a large variety of people come through the doors each day. The sales force works mostly on commission so they are always trying to sniff out the wholesale buyers and sometimes they ignore the retail sales. Retail sales are going directly to the end user and therefore are usually smaller sales hence smaller commissions. A couple of times Gilly has been out on the floor doing some inventory work when she stopped to talk to a customer and made a sale on her own. Of course, this always causes problems with the sales people, but the manager put a stop to their complaining, asking them why an office personnel was the only one on the floor to help that person in the first place. While she appreciates the support and the commission, this only gives them one more reason to not like Gilly.

    This doesn't always result in a sale though because she has had experiences where a customer will approach from behind and then when she turns to face them, they say, "Oh, I am looking for a salesman." Last week this happened, and when she told the person she could help him he stammered his response with, "No that's ok. I'll wait for a real salesperson." Not wanting to be a bad sport, she called over to one of the sales personnel to help him. The boss says she is too valuable behind the scenes. Gilly hasn't decided if she wants to take that as a compliment or an insult. She prefers compliment but it's not always easy to keep thinking that way.

    Sometimes she feels like that piece of the puzzle you don't know where to fit in. Her brother once told Gilly that she'd be great at voice overs for cartoons. He said they could make a great picture of her in cartoon form, everyone will love you, he used to say. Sounds insensitive to say to a sister but he has Gilly's best interest at heart. He has the bumps and bruises to prove his loyalty too. But what he doesn't understand is that Gilly doesn't feel the need for everyone to love her, that she'd be happy with one or two. Her brother always made sure she never felt unloved. Gilly wants some real friends. Someone to understand her and not care about her outsides. Her brother is both traditionally handsome and physically put together. He loves her as any brother would, unconditionally.

~ ~ ~

Today Gilly is going down to the community center for a change of pace to see what this place is all about. People at the office as well as customers talk about the fun times they have there. She actually took a personal day off today. She is all caught up on paperwork so she won't be too far behind herself when she goes back tomorrow. The community center is always advertising that they have something for everyone at any age.

The doors to the center are outlined in orange trim and bright as an autumn sunset. The doors themselves are a blue sapphire with handles of a complimenting burnt orange inviting patrons in. Once inside the smell of the cooking classes to the right entices Gilly and the mini market is to the left with all the fanfare of an outdoor street market is equally as inviting. Gilly gravitates to the market first. There are at least thirty different booths she can see immediately with people who either made or grew their own wares. Some of the pies look amazing, and the cookies, breads and casseroles are quite tempting as well. However, what has completely drawn Gilly in is the man who is weaving his own carpets. The patterns are nothing like she's ever seen in a conventional store. Stripes with polka dots, greens with fuchsia, plaids and swirls, but woven with such precision that the designs all makes sense. 'They are mismatched, like me.' Gilly thinks to herself. She can't believe her eyes, the textures, the colors, the designs every bit of it mismatched to itself and to the one nearby. She feels lost in the kaleidoscope of colors and patterns, there is no way she can leave the center today without buying one. The hardest part will be deciding which one.

"Can I help you, maám?" says a man with the most radiant eyes she has ever known. He is sporting a cute little goatee of auburn hair on his chin, and he wears a red striped shirt and simple black jeans. Upon a second look, his hair does not match his goatee at all, in fact they are two completely different colors and his eyebrows are a third. Gilly is so mesmerized that she almost forgets to acknowledge his question. He clears his throat and is still looking at her straight in the eye.

Gilly finally takes her eyes off of him and says, "Oh, hello, sorry, I'm looking around right now." She says trying to recover. "I know I want one, however, I need to figure out which one best suits my place. They remind me of myself, completely mismatched." She looks to him but his eyes look confused.

"Is that a compliment? Because I'm not sure I've ever seen or heard a woman describe herself as mismatched before." He continues; "Everyone has their own beauty, we have to find what that is, accept, and be proud of what has been given to us. In art it's the same way. There are no real rules for what you can put together and what you can't. Look at any classic Picasso. Depends on what you like. An artist takes what they like, and what they see and marries them together to make something new. I'd rather think of them as similar to a compound word than a mismatch." His voice doesn't match him either. Seeing him from afar Gilly would have thought his voice would be rough and scruffy and yet he sounds as smooth as silk, like a professional baritone singer. He's not defensive, quite the contrary, he is stating how he feels and is sincere.

"You are quite the artist" she replies, "I don't think I would ever have thought to 'marry' what you have put together. The old phrase of stripes and spots not working together doesn't seem to work here. You've taken things that go against conventional thought and put them together in a way that makes them sing in harmony. Yeah, that's what I see, you've taken all the instruments of the orchestra and made a beautiful symphony of color and texture." Gilly says while still staring at the carpets hanging around this man's booth.

"Many people describe my apartment as eclectic so I guess I could put any of these in one of my rooms. I don't have a color scheme either, I buy what I like. May take a while for me to decide. Do you see any of them for me?" Not sure why she is asking him, it's not as if he knows her at all.

When he smiles, Gilly melts a little inside. 'This is wild, why would a stranger's smile affect her like this?' she thinks to herself.

"I would have to see your apartment before I could tell you that," he answers. "My girls would be proud to be part of an eclectic apartment but I wouldn't want to throw off your energy with the wrong one. Can I come by later and see for myself? I will be packing things up here at around 5:30, takes me about half an hour to load the truck so depending on where you live, I can be there sometime after 6:00. Does that work for you?" He says to her all the while looking in her eyes. At this point, however, Gilly feels he is all salesman, not one part of him is looking for anything else, again, not sure if she should be flattered or insulted. This happens a lot with her, she is never sure if the person is looking at her or looking her over.

"Sure, why not. I'm going to look around the rest of the center anyway and I have some errands to do today. Here is my business card. I'll write my home address on the back. Here is my cell phone number, call me if you're running late. I have a doorman, he'll check your identification before letting you in though, I hope you don't mind." Gilly is not really sure the doorman does that but she already said yes so, she wants him to understand that the doorman will have a record of him being in her apartment.

He takes the card and smiling says, "If you want to enjoy the day here, I'd suggest you check out the classes on the first floor, some allow walk-ins because they do different activities each week. You'll find the list on the blue board back in the lobby." He holds up my card like you would a glass of campaign to toast and says, "See you later." 'And there's that smile again. Oh, my I'm going to fall over if he keeps that up.' Gilly ponders as she turns to walk away.

"Thanks, see you later," she says. As she glances back over her shoulder she notices he is rubbing his thumb on her card and smiling. Gilly is hoping this means he is looking forward to seeing her again and not that she is going to be buying a lot of his carpets.

~ ~ ~

Gilly spends the rest of the morning going from class to class on the lower level of the center. She makes a ceramic mug that she has to pick up next week, takes a class that teaches how to turn around your life in five easy steps, creates beads from clay which will also be fired and finished next week, and she took her first ever salsa dance class. If nothing else, she certainly had a good workout before lunch. Before she leaves, she remembers to stop by the rug man because she never got his name. She walks in to see that he is busy with another customer. He looks up and smiles again as she comes closer. 'There go my legs. What is it about him?' she thinks.

"Excuse me, sorry to bother you while you're with someone, but I need a name to give the doorman." Gilly thinks this is a good way to ask.

"Herbert Lawson II, now you know. I'll see you later."

'Well, that's weird. I couldn't tell if he was annoyed at the question or at me for asking. Smile or no smile I suppose there will be nothing coming from this encounter. No worries, nothing and especially nobody ever comes to me, I usually have to be the one who comes forward. I've had a great day and all I can do is find the one thing that can bring me down. Ok Gilly, don't ruin your day. Let's move on to errands and by all means find a friend to talk to, not always yourself.' By the time she is finished with her rant she is out by her bus stop.

On the bus, she notices that she is sitting near a mismatched couple. They are a couple for sure by the way they have no concept of waiting until they get to a private place to express their feelings for one another. The woman is long and lanky with beautiful dark brown tresses while the man is a full head shorter than her and definitely not as physically trim. His hair length is more in his beard than on his head. All day today Gilly sees mismatches everywhere. 'Why is that? I should call my brother and tell him about my day, he'd get a good laugh. Especially at the idea of me salsa dancing.'

Instead of calling she sends a text message to her brother. He quickly writes back, '*you took a salsa class? Any pictures?*'

Gilly laughs a little and responds with, '*sadly, no but I had a lot of fun dancing with a man as old as Uncle Bernie, he could sure move though. We were a great mismatched pair.*'

After a moment or two her brother answers, '*Aw man, I really wish I was there to see that. Laughing my head off right now trying to picture Uncle Bernie moving to the salsa beat. Headed into a meeting, glad you had a good time. Send me a pic of the carpet you pick out. I love your eclectic style* ☺'

Gilly tries to picture her uncle in that way and she laughs out loud on the bus, everyone looks at her in a funny way but she can't help but laugh at the image in her mind. Her laughter even interrupts the couple next to her to come up for air. This makes her laugh harder.

Gilly ponders her day, 'Maybe there is something wrong with me, maybe all I see is what shouldn't be instead of seeing what is. I'd complain about my job but at least I have one and I'm definitely never bored. I like my eclectic things too and I should be proud of my mismatched body, but when it keeps being pointed out to me; it's hard to ignore that part of my life. But not today.' She sits up a little straighter at this thought. Not one comment, not one exclusionary comment. Gilly sits tall in her seat until she gets to her stop.

The bus ride is quick, not much traffic today. She stops at the fruit stand before entering her building and almost forgets to talk to the doorman because her head is full of her day. She tells him the name of the rug man and his response is, "Herbert? How on earth do you know him?" his voice emphasizing the word you.

"What? You know him?" she asks in shock.

"Sure, everyone knows him. He's the most eligible bachelor in the whole county. How did you get a meeting with him?" He almost appears annoyed with Gilly, as if she doesn't deserve to be meeting him.

"I met him at the community center this morning if you must know. He offered to come over I didn't have to beg him or anything, not that it's any of your business anyway. Just let him in, will you. He said he will come sometime after 6:00 tonight." Her good day now ruined; she walks away steaming with anger. 'How dare he talk to me that way? I don't care if he is the king of his country, I did not deserve to be talked down to like that.' However, as soon as she walks into her apartment, she turns on her computer to look up Mr. Lawson to make sure it is the same person that the doorman is talking about.

The first thing that comes up is a picture of him and his adopted daughter. They couldn't look more different if they tried, (mismatch again). But their happiness is contagious through this picture and through their smiles.

Somehow, she has the same smile as he does. It is him alright, hair colors and all. She reads further and figures out that she must be the only person this side of the bridge that doesn't know who Mr. Lawson is. She definitely would not have forgotten his face had she seen it on TV or the papers before today.

 Gilly decides she knows enough and goes about doing whatever has to be done in the apartment, cleaning, laundry, e-mails, and other personal projects. Before long she realizes she is hungry so she starts to make dinner. On occasion she really enjoys cooking up a storm when the mood hits. She is so lost in what she is preparing that she doesn't notice the time and without realizing, time flies by, there is a loud knock at the door.

 Gilly drops her spoon and runs to the door while wiping her hands on a towel, but unbeknown to Gilly she also is wiping flour on her face. She opens the door and sees the same man she saw before, only this time he isn't smiling. "I'm sorry sir to make you come so much out of your way" I say. "You must think I'm a crazy person. Oh, where are my manners? Won't you come in?"

 He follows her in and then asks "What are you making with so much flour flying around?"

 Gilly turns around quickly and see her reflection in the front hall mirror. "Oh my, I'm a wreck. And here you've come all this way to be greeted by an ugly mess." She quickly runs to the kitchen to make sure nothing is boiling over or burning all the while wiping her face with the back of her hand. As she turns to go back, he is right behind her stirring the sauce while she begins washing the dishes. Her radar raises and she watches him with caution out of the corner of her eye.

 It is as if he knows exactly where to go for the spoon and knows exactly what to do. "Smells good, mind if I join you for dinner? I didn't leave my booth all day and I'm starved." He asks in a most gentle way. The sounds of his soft, low voice does things to her that have not happened before. Here in my apartment stands 'the most eligible bachelor' and he has invited himself to dinner. Something about this makes no sense yet it also feels good at the same time.

"Sure, I was in the mood to cook this afternoon, not sure why I made so much," She says "There's probably enough for five people to eat. I won't have to cook the rest of the week. I hope you don't have any allergies. The plates are right above you in that cabinet, if you'd like to set the table." After the words are out of my mouth Gilly realizes she asked a man that probably has servants do these things for him all the time to set the table for her. Immediately she turns around, "I'm sorry sir, I didn't mean to ask you do to that, I'll get it, it's my house, you're a guest." She crosses the kitchen and jumps in front of him to get to the dishes before he does.

Of course, she also loses her balance, why would things work out easy? She falls into his arms and to her surprise he laughs, a real belly laugh. It is quite a funny picture and as they laugh harder, they both end up sitting on the floor in each other's arms laughing until eyes are watery.

"Please don't tell me, let me guess, you looked me up when you came home." He says. "I'm afraid I wasn't totally honest with you this morning. I didn't lie about my name or anything like that but I did misguide you about the inspiration for my carpets. You see I have a young child that I adopted. She loves to take out her colors and go after a piece of paper with unclouded fervor. As I watch her, I take to my designs the same way. Oh, and one more thing, I never make house calls, I thought for sure you knew who I was by the way you smiled back at me. But when you asked my name that I realized your smile was genuine and not planted on to attract me. I was attracted from the moment I saw you walk in. I'm sorry for being so forward, but hearing you call yourself mismatched sealed the deal for me. If ever there is a mismatched person it would be me. Take look at my hair." With this he laughs again and so does Gilly.

Gilly starts to stand up and he comes with. They set the table together and discuss everything from the spices in the food to his daughter and politics. Conversation seems to flow with ease. "When you first came to my door you had such a sour face, I'm so glad to see you happier now."

"I apologize for that, I was still mulling over the words of your doorman," he says. "A rather uncouth fellow, I gave him a few words of advice about how to treat people that will enable him to keep a job. But it left a sour taste in my mouth. I was rather looking forward to seeing you tonight. My daughter is with her grandmother, my mother, and I always get lonely when there is no one to go home to."

For the next two hours they continue to talk about everything under the sun. Gilly thinks to herself that she has never experienced this before with any one. She is even surprised at herself that she was able to hold the conversation considering he probably knows so much more about the world than she does.

"This may sound like a ridiculous question, but do you think that you and I could try and make a go at a genuine friendship?" He asks this question in a hesitant voice.

"Herbert, I've had a wonderful time with you tonight and I couldn't imagine a better friend to have. But why are you hesitant? You probably have hundreds of friends whereas someone like me, well I have less than a handful. My only real friend is my brother." She tells him.

He reaches over and lets his finger run down from her hairline to her chin. Quick as the wind, his lips are on Gilly's in a kiss as soft as new silk. When he pulls away, he smiles that smile, "maybe more than a friend?" and he sits back down but doesn't let go of her hand.

"I am flattered, but I have to admit I'm also confused. I know we have been speaking for a long time but maybe I should share a little bit more about myself. I'm not exactly of the same caliber social circle as you are, nor do I run in the same circles business wise. I am but a simple worker. I go to work every day, pay my bills, eat dinner and read the paper each night. I have few friends and even less family to speak of. The bigger question isn't would I like to be with you but why would you want to be with the likes of me?" now her voice is quivering a bit. We are having this conversation while holding hands across the table. What started out as a simple day off work has certainly turned out to be so much more, Gilly's mind is swirling with possibilities, however, sadly, all of them end.

Herbert sits straight back in his chair and crosses his arms on his chest, and taking a deep breath he says, "I care not for status, I hate being in the limelight, I'm only there because people know I have money, that's public record I suppose. My daughter, Madeline, and I live a simple life. She goes to school, I work on my art and sell only at the community center. I refuse to use a gallery. Madeline comes home from school and we usually eat dinner together unless my mom has her, she likes to spoil her once a month or sometimes more. We play some games, have tea parties and dress up together. I cook my own meals (yours is delicious by the way), she showers and we read books until bed. Does that sound like too much for you? Please let me know and I'll see if I can tone my life down a little." He is in a huff right now and Gilly knows she put him there.

"I have a brother who is the social butterfly of any gathering," I explain. "But I'm always the one who walks along the wall trying not to get noticed. I don't have refined social graces to speak of and usually speak my mind, which often gets me into trouble, like now. I'm forever saying "I'm sorry" for the words I blurt out. I suppose I'm no different from your young daughter, I have no filter. It's not an excuse but an explanation. Please don't be angry and yes, in response to your question before, I did look you up but only after the doorman was so rude to me as well. I wanted to find out if he was telling the truth. I wanted to see how much of a bubble I live in to never have heard your name before. I'm sorry but I really never did. You don't look any happier, how about I get your coat and walk you to the door. I'll clean up later." Gilly stands up and walks towards his chair because that is the only way to the couch where his coat is.

He jumps up in front of Gilly. "I don't want to go yet." He takes both of her hands and holds them in his. "The papers will have a field day with the two of us. You should know that in advance. Some of their comments may not be very kind - like your stupid doorman. But if you're willing to take a chance, so am I. I'm sorry I get in a huff easily. I hate when people make presumptions about me. Do you know your doorman said that if I drink enough tonight, I might have a good time? I wasn't even sure what that meant at first, and as I was about to walk away, I realized and I about punched his lights out. Instead I gave him in a tongue lashing he will not soon forget, neither will anyone else who was in the lobby I'm afraid. Sorry for that. The papers follow me around and their words may be better or worse than his. Please, I haven't wanted to be with anyone in so long. People are spreading rumors that I'm not interested in women anymore only because they haven't seen me in public recently. Don't get me wrong, I really don't care what the papers say and I'm not out to prove them wrong." He looks over at me through eyes that are telling me he will protect me.

"I don't know what to say" I answer him. "We are so different, I'm a contradiction all by myself. I...." His finger is on Gilly's mouth to shut her up, his other hand on her lower back as he pulls her in. "Don't talk about my girl like that. I like eccentric ideas and I see nothing wrong with who you are. Do you hear me? Nothinnnnnnng." That last word is whispered in my ear and he starts to kiss my neck. His head fits so exactly on my shoulder as if it'd been there before.

His kisses keep coming, gentle, soft, and sincere. All around my neck to the front and up to my lips, he pauses, smiles and then we kiss, a long careful yet tender kiss.

This forward man, this introverted woman, he is from society, she is girl with a regular job, he is exotically handsome, she is plain or less than plain, a mismatch if she ever saw one. And yet.

~ ~ ~

Three months have passed since that first "date" and Gilly learned how to see things differently. Life is not all about seeing the mismatch but about seeing how everything works together. Today is her last day at work. Herbert does not like the way he hears Gilly is being treated and when he came into the showroom, he heard some of the comments for himself before they realized who he was or even that he was there. No apology is going to get the salesmen a reprieve. He immediately spoke to her boss and told him Gilly is unable to work under such a hostile environment and practically dared him to deny the comments made behind her back. Gilly stood there and watched as did everyone else in the showroom. These last four days have been the best since she started here. No comments, no sneers, well really, there has been no conversation at all that didn't involve her new "status".

The women hate her because she hasn't introduced them yet to her boyfriend. They keep telling her that all girls introduce their boyfriends to friends. It sounds like a nice sentiment except these are the first three months anyone has talked to her since she started working here over four years ago. If she had friends here, she is sure she would have shared him with them.

Gilly discusses her job options, and Herbert explains how he wants her to join him in his work. Gilly tries to tell him that is where they are mismatched again – first of all she knows nothing about his day job and second she can't even draw a straight line and she might be colorblind. He chuckles and tells her she can do anything she wants to but he would prefer it being done with him. She tells him that maybe she could help him with sales because in the past four years she certainly learned a lot about that.

Gilly feels they are the strangest couple there is in local society, and with his daughter in tow they make an even weirder family picture. She knows this because she sees a new picture of herself in the local society pages of the paper every week. Her brother calls her to tell her about each one. Then he asks her again, if she is happy. He even threatened that if Herbert hurts her in any way, he will personally wring his neck. Gilly laughs but she knows her brother loves her.

"Have you asked your Marcy to marry you yet?" she asks her brother one day.

"Gilly, I can't lie to you. I'm frightened to death to ask. She is like us, no real family around. Hard enough to be on your own but don't you think it will be harder to be on our own as a couple?" her brother asks.

"If you want to wake up in the middle of the night and see her smiling right back at you, then you aren't on your own anymore, are you? Herbert told me that one." She says.

"Yeah, he is a good one, I hate to admit it but he is. He said he would help Marcy make contacts to grow her business. He says family should help family, I guess he sees us together as well." Her brother says softly.

"Hey, since when are you so chummy with Herbert?" Gilly asks.

Gilly's brother completely forgot that Gilly does not know they met up more than once already. Herbert made him swear to secrecy. "He has my phone number, took it off your phone one day. Is it true you still have me down on your phone as Jekyll?" he asks laughing.

Gilly laughs, "Yes, why yes I do." She laughs with her brother for a long time.

She loves her brother and he loves her; she has Herbert and Marcy in her life as well. Maybe she isn't as alone as she thought she was.

~ ~ ~

On their fourth-month anniversary (if there is such a thing) Herbert and Madeline announce they are planning a special dinner for Gilly and that she should show up wearing violet or indigo. Knowing them, this could have meant they want her to match them or even match the food. Although Gilly can't think of any violet colored food so it has to be clothes.

She still hasn't gotten used to having a car show up for her when she needs to be somewhere but it always does, and every time the driver will not let the doorman open the door for her. In fact, he usually stares him down so he can continuously put him in his place. As she rolls up to Herbert's house, nothing appears out of the ordinary. She walks in and sees at least a dozen vases full of big white fluffy flowers, cloud-like actually. Madeline comes running over wearing a beautiful green dress. Well, it isn't clothes she is matching. They walk into the dining room and she sees that it is decorated in the most exquisite red silks she has ever seen.

"Wow, what is this for?" Gilly asks.

Madeline giggles and runs to get her dad. He comes into the room wearing, of all things, an orange silk smoking jacket. While the color may seem odd, the style suits him well. The lapel is black and so is the trim, but the body of the jacket is a muted orange that fits him like a glove. He looks like a million bucks. He is also wearing the biggest smile she has seen so far.

"I feel so under-dressed. You said violet, not silk and beautiful. I hope I'm not a disappointment." Gilly says trying to smile.

"Haha Daddy, you owe me a trip to the sundae store, I told you she would say the word disappointment." Madeline is dancing over to her dad who gives her a big hug.

"Yes, you most certainly did. You must learn a new word, my dear, you are obviously becoming predictable." He smiles at her.

"Old habits die hard," Gilly says with a smile. "But I sure hope I get to go to the sundae store as well." Madeline jumps for joy.

There is definitely something going on that Gilly is still not privy to. Herbert picks up Madeline and whispers something in her ear, and then she darts from the room giggling all the way. "Come have a seat darling." He pulls out the chair for her as he has done so many times before. As she is about to sit down a lovely woman walks in and he pulls the chair opposite Gilly out for her as well. She is wearing a chiffon dress in the softest shade of yellow. Gilly doesn't know too many people who could wear yellow, but she is sure pulling off the color splendidly. Then she jumps up from her chair. "Oh my, you must be Herbert's mother." Gilly runs around the table to greet her. "I'm so happy to meet you finally. You look beautiful in this dress. The color suites you well." Gilly is holding her hand and Herbert's mother puts her other one on top.

"Not as much as I am to finally meet the one who has stolen my son's heart. Took him long enough to find you. Come, sit, sit, sit let's eat." Oh my, she has his smile too, or he has hers but it is remarkable. Gilly thinks to herself.

Gilly walks back around the table to sit down and it is then that she notices the tablecloth and dishes. They are using their finest blue china. A simple set, blue on blue but very elegant at the same time. Dinner starts and everyone is really at ease with conversation and each other. Gilly thinks that with his mother around she will surely stumble on her words and be a disappointment to them. Oh my, I thought of the word again. Thankfully, she didn't say it out loud this time. The meal lasts for quite some time because his mother and Gilly keep talking and talking and Herbert and Madeline keep giggling at each other throughout the meal. It's as if they have a million personal jokes that they aren't sharing. Part of Gilly is jealous, she would love to be able to giggle like that with Madeline.

On special occasions, Herbert uses a service to serve a meal and tonight is one of those nights. He says he didn't want his mom getting up and down so much. Made sense to Gilly but she is still weary. The butler brings out the desserts on silver platters with cloches over them. Each one has a different style dome and Gilly supposes that means a different dessert. Knowing Herbert, he was playing in the kitchen today and made everyone their favorite dessert. His mom loves sorbet, he adores chocolate chip cookies, Madeline likes anything with coconut, and Gilly is partial to a fruit cup sprinkled with a little chocolate liqueur.

Herbert starts to tap his glass with his spoon to get everyone's attention. He stands up like he is about to make a toast. "I want to thank everyone for coming and being a part of tonight." More giggles, from both his "girls" this time. There is no doubt in her mind that there is a private joke going around tonight and Gilly is the only one in the dark.

He raises his wine glass towards Gilly and says, "My dear, we are here to celebrate a special occasion. Tonight, is the night of our anniversary. We have known, and dare I say, loved, each other for four months now. You have brought so much light and color into my life." Madeline is about to fall off her chair with giggles and his mom has her hand on her mouth to hold hers in. Gilly can see why the two of them get along so well. When she looks back around, Gilly sees Herbert is laughing too.

"Ok, do I have spinach in my teeth? What is the big joke? Out with it one of you." Gilly is glaring at all of them now.

Madeline speaks first, "You know how much we all love you right?" Gilly shakes her head yes. "Well tonight we want to do something special. And, well, you see…" she is hesitant but not giggling anymore.

"Special about what my dear," Gilly, now sounding annoyed.

"Sometimes you don't see things that are right in front of you – look at all this color. What does it remind you of?" the child asks

"Like your father's art studio, why?" Great outbursts of laughter follow that. People are holding their sides, and Gilly realizes she must have said the worst thing possible. She starts to look around again, mulling over all the colors that she sees and is still only seeing a kaleidoscope of color, nothing more, nothing less.

As she positions herself to get up from the table, no longer wanting to play the game and not in the best of moods, knowing all of them are laughing at her and not with her. Herbert races over to her side and turns her around to face him. He has one arm on each of her shoulders. He gently pulls her chin up to face him. "I'm sorry love, but the fact that you can't tell we set the room up like a rainbow is simply too funny. As you walked in, you saw the clouds. That represents the state of mind I was in before I saw you tonight. Here on this table now you see that meeting you is my silver lining. I found you by accident as the rain lifts, the sun comes out, and then there is a rainbow." She looks into his eyes and his eyes are as watery as hers feel. He pulls her over to the table and turns her to face the cloche on her plate. As he uncovers hers, he says in a voice that is choked with emotion, "Under every rainbow there is a pot of gold." He puts the dome to the side and she realizes that on her plate is an open ring box with a gold ring that has three interlocking circles on the top. It is so simple and so beautiful at the same time.

Both Madeline and Herbert are at her side now, and in unison they say, "Will you marry us?" Oh, genius that's the three circles and of course it's a rainbow, how stupid of me, Gilly thinks to herself. We are so mismatched Gilly's head is swirling yet again.

She doesn't know which of them to hug first. She chooses Madeline and whisper in her ear "yes." She grabs Gilly so tight she isn't breathing well. "Grandma!! She said yes!! We're going to be married!" She jumps down from Gilly and runs to her grandmother. Then Gilly turn to Herbert and smiles. "Mismatched to the max."

"Just the way I like everything." He pulls her in and gives her a big kiss right there in front of his mother. It goes without saying that the rest of the night was a lot of fun too. Gilly doesn't want to leave but she doesn't live here, so she is getting up to start saying goodbye when his mom speaks up.

"You know, now that you're engaged, there is no need for you to keep that apartment. Why don't you sleep here tonight? Besides, I sent the driver home already." Herbert looks at his mom and she smiles that Lawson smile.

"Woo HOO!!! A sleepover! That means Daddy makes chocolate chip pancakes in the morning doesn't it, Daddy?" Herbert laughs and so does his mom. Then she winks at him and excuses herself for the night. "Come on Madeline you have to help me out, we have a wedding to plan."

Funny, but Gilly doesn't think pancakes are the first thing on Herbert's mind right now. He speaks first, "In case you're wondering, I asked Jekyll for his permission before I did all of this. He is coming for breakfast, he assumed you would say yes. I told him to bring Marcy and we can make a double wedding. Think he will follow through?" Herbert asks.

"Stranger things have happened you know." Gilly looks down at her ring again, three rings looped together, each with a small stone sitting in the middle, "Birthstones?" she asks as she shows him the ring.

"Yes" he says quietly. The idea that Gilly will be his forever has hit him in the gut and in the heart, he doesn't know how to handle all of the emotion right now.

Gilly watches him and then says, "What happens when there is more of us?" she asks softly.

Herbert smiles at her, he is looking forward to making children with her, "Ahh, for that my dear I plan on filling both of your wrists with small loops." He grins.

"One at a time, my love, one at a time." Gilly laughs.

They spend the next few hours discussing the simple wedding they both want and how their future will be together.

~ ~ ~

"I'm so nervous Mom." Gilly tells her mother.

"You're nervous?! Imagine how I feel? All of my friends are watching to see if the wedding and their own picture will make the society pages. Can you believe people asked me if they can take pictures with you guys so they can show them off to people they know? Oh Gilly, I couldn't be happier for you but this society crap is way out of hand don't you think?" her mom asks.

"Yes, it annoys us all." A voice from behind them says. Gilly and her mom turn to see Herbert's mother.

"I'm sorry, I didn't mean to insult you." Gilly's mom says quickly

"No need to apologize, I mean what I say. It's annoying. Once my husband made some good money, people who never spoke to us before were inviting us to gatherings as they called them. Networking bullcrap. My husband always said he was coming then politely declined at the last hour. He made his money through a lot of hard work, a bit of ball busting and good old fashion ingenuity. We didn't ask to be in the limelight, we were thrown into this nonsense. So, we do our best to ignore as much of them as we can.

When they printed something bad about my parents once, heads rolled off and into the unemployment line faster than you could purchase the paper. Retractions were printed and asses kissed but my husband knew who gave them the information and he destroyed the man the only way he knew how. Through business. He was ruthless, my parents and I never saw him so enraged. He made it clear, that no one messes with our family no matter how far reaching they are. The press didn't seem to get the idea very quickly because every time they tried, another head rolled.

So, I extend my apologies to you my dear and your lovely family. I hope they aren't pulled into this mess too much, but don't you worry, before my husband died, he taught me everything he knows about getting back legally and without press. Herbert knows how too and his baby sister does as well. She married out of the country, we see her a few times a year, but nearly weekly on the computer." Mrs. Lawson was about to say more when the door burst open.

"He proposed!!!!!!" Marcy yells shaking her hand in front of everyone. "Right outside there by the fountain" she runs to the window and everyone follows her, Gilly's brother waves to everyone and Gilly's mom says, "About damn time." She hugs Marcy.

"A little cheesy, I know but he said he would feel a lot more comfortable walking down with me than for me to watch from the sidelines. He said we can consider it practice for the future then he presented me with this ring of sapphires. We share a birthstone you know." Marcy's eyes are so big everyone can see the love.

"You will make one hell of a bride." Gilly says. She has always loved Marcy.

"Oh, Gilly, I'm sorry for taking a moment away from you. But I couldn't hold my excitement in. Herbert was there as a witness, he said, no one will believe your brother if there wasn't a witness. Guess he knows him well enough already huh?" the girls laugh.

"Ever the sworn bachelor that son of mine. Only because he hadn't met you yet Marcy." She smiles at her soon to be daughter in law.

"Oh, well we need to change things up a bit now don't we. All the bride maids are wearing silver dresses, come darling, I'm sure I have something that you can wear." Her phone rings. "Hello? Ok we will leave in ten, sudden need for a wardrobe change thanks to your best man." Herbert's mom says.

"Ok, the men are leaving now for the hall to get ready for the ceremony. Come, I know just the dress." She grabs Marcy's arm and the two of them whisk away to find a different dress.

"This place is so big Mom, I can't believe my future husband has been here all day and we didn't run into him. How will I keep this place up, upkeep alone will be a full time job." Gilly's mind is racing now, and so is her heart.

Her mom walks over to her and pulls her in for a long overdue hug. "He has people for that, you will either get used to them doing the work, or you will work with them, you have plenty of time to figure that out. After tonight, you my baby will be a married woman. However mismatched you believe you two are, you work and work well. Come let's go find everyone and leave for the wedding hall." She smiles.

~ ~ ~

The ceremony is simple, Madeline walks first, siblings walk down and then the parents walk the new couple down. Cheers and a large bouquet of balloons go up with the first kiss of the new couple. The press was allocated to the back of the room, only the paid photographer was allowed any closer to take pictures. Mrs. Lawson made this very clear.

The after party lasted until Mrs. Lawson said it was over, at which time all the guests filed out happily. She walks over to Gilly's parents. "Welcome to the family. I look forward to getting to know you better." With that she and a very tired Madeline walk to her car and wave back at everyone.

    Marcy and Gilly's brother did not let go of each other the whole night. To send off the new couple, a blue limousine drives up to the front of the wedding hall. The new couple gets in the back.

    "Well, Mrs. Lawson where to?" Herbert asks.

    "To the end of the rainbow." She smiles.

Odd Friends

Friendships come in all shapes and sizes. Katie begins to realize that her newest and closest friend she has ever had in her life, is old enough to be her father. He accepts her for who she is regardless of her past. Nat, too, has found the woman he thought he had been looking for, only she's not for him. How can these two friends help each other find what they are really looking for?

Nat and Katie are good friends. Normal circumstances would not have led to their friendship, but both are thankful for the other in their lives. Nat is turning sixty next week and Katie is twenty-five. Their friendship started by accident late one afternoon at a nearby park. It had become one of Nat's routines since he moved in with his son, after his wife's death. He used to go out with his wife every Wednesday night, since her death, he still feels the need to leave the house on Wednesdays. Even if it means he takes a walk to the park and sits and watches the people go by, all alone.

Nat and his wife were very close partners. They started off as best friends, became lovers, became a married couple and had three beautiful and healthy children together. None of life's stages came as easily as listing them though. Nat's brother didn't think she was pretty enough for him, his mom didn't understand how a woman can grow up not knowing how to cook. However, in the end, none of this mattered to Nat, he knew how to cook since he was young, and to him, her beauty was beyond anything he thought he was entitled to. Their love won out. When his parents saw them together, they realized no one could break such a bond. His father told him on his wedding day that their love would carry them through everything it was so strong. Nat was inclined to agree.

Her parents were not so forthcoming with praise for Nat though. Her father thought Nat could be more than a simple salesman, thought he didn't have enough drive to succeed to be much of anything. He told his daughter often that a woman of her stature and abilities should attract someone who had higher aspirations. In fact, she later informed Nat that on the morning of their wedding, her father told her she could call off the wedding still and he would not mind. She laughed at her father's face and told him he didn't have to walk her down if he felt that way. Her words shut him up pretty quickly. Nat and his wife laughed about this for many years.

    They showed everyone that with a strong love connection, the two of them can achieve anything they put their minds to, and they did. Nat was not a simple salesman for long, he became the head salesman for the region and not only that, he surpassed all the other regional sales teams, single handedly. On her deathbed, his wife told him that her father was never good at sharing and probably didn't want to share his baby girl. At her funeral, Nat and her father shared a long and tight hug. No words needed to be spoken then, thirty plus years of emotions were understood. They both loved her with all their heart.

    Now, Nat sits on his lonely park bench waiting for Katie to show up. His beautiful young friend. They met when he had only been living with his son Samson a few weeks. Katie goes running on Wednesday nights and that is the same night he leaves the house and sits in the park. On the night they met, Katie had been running and twisted her ankle, she hobbled over to the bench where Nat was sitting. A conversation started easily and they have been fast friends ever since.

    She could be his daughter by age but she has an old soul, as the saying goes. She seems to understand his need for a friend that his children do not. She speaks with him about older music, even older television shows. He meets her sometimes for lunch near her work, for something to do. Nat retired when his wife became sick and he gave her his full, undivided attention until the day she died, as he promised her he would, so many years ago. Nat has always been good with his money and they made sure there was enough to retire on and also to take care of her parents in their old age. His father-in-law knows nothing about how his care is being paid for, Nat and his wife decided this is better.

    Retiring at such a young age, has worked out well for him. Since his wife's death his children decided that he should not be living alone, and since Samson has his own house and is not married, it became the best plan. He could have stayed in his own house forever, the house was theirs and he had a lifetime of memories there with his wife but his children insisted that he move out so he would not wallow in those memories and become recluse.

Never one to argue, he saw the logic and some fear in their eyes and gave in. The house sold well, and the adjustment to living in Samson's house has not been hard at all. Nat and his wife always considered themselves very lucky because all of their children live as adults within twenty-five miles of each other. So, in the end, moving in with Samson still allows him to see everyone easily and yet still have time when he doesn't.

Belinda and Nat speak on the phone all the time as well as see each other twice a week. The idea of seeing another woman is amazing to Nat. Nat is amazed he found time to meet Belinda at all. Belinda is a tall, slender widow who is in much need of attention. Nat, having the time and energy, gives her that attention.

Which brings us to today, the wedding day. Belinda and Nat decided that being together is better than being alone, they care enough about each other to make themselves a duo. Not nearly the same kind of love he had with his one and only, but enough to keep him from being lonely, and her as well.

The nuptials are being held at the gazebo in the park. Samson arranged everything for the permit they needed, the band, the flowers and even the dinner back at his house. Nat's daughter Cora, along with her husband and two children, have made sure that all the finer details were attended to. His youngest son, Kirk and his wife are in charge of set up and take down of everything. Katie is Nat's best man. Sure, he has an official best man, the kids call him Uncle Bart, but he is not Nat's brother, he is his best friend since life began.

Nat's brother decided to show up at the last minute at the insistence of his own children. They told him if he is expecting to be treated with respect as a father, he had better show respect to his brother. Nat's nieces and nephews can be very persuasive. They responded with resounding applause when he told them he was getting married again. Nat's brother, simply told him, "ok".

Katie has been hovering over Nat all day. She won't let him have a minute's peace and he knows why. If he is given the chance, he will leave the situation, she knows him well. His love for his wife filled his heart and is too great to let another woman in, there simply really isn't enough room. He told her numerous times he feels as if he is cheating on her. Katie talked sense into him and he realized how foolish his heart can make him. She told him he will never love Belinda the same, and she knows that but he can't have the ghost of his wife interrupt his chance of being happy for the rest of the life he has yet to live.

Belinda and Nat will be living with Samson. His house is big enough for a small army and Nat already lives on only one side of the house, and he rarely sees his son during the week. Belinda did not bat an eye when the arrangement was proposed to her. She currently lives in a small one room apartment.

~ ~ ~ ~

"Hey, what are you doing outside?" Katie asks Nat as she approaches the bench on the far side of the backyard.

"Thinking. I've been talking to my wife a lot lately. She says she likes you a lot and that you should be married." He smiles at her.

"Very nice, does she happen to know whom I should marry as well?" she asks with a smirk.

"Actually, she does, but I'm not allowed to tell you yet. Come sit with me a moment, we only have half an hour until we leave for the park anyway." Nat scoots to the side and pats the spot next to him.

Katie watches Nat's eyes. Something is off, she can feel something in the air is wrong. Something is scarily off and she doesn't know what or how to react right now. Her stomach starts churning a million miles per second as she walks over to him and sits down. She sits down and leans her head onto his shoulder for comfort. She picks up his hand and places it into hers.

"What else did she say to you Nat? Something is bothering you I can sense your pain." She says to him in a quiet voice.

"I'm not sure this is fair to Belinda. I loved her too much. We shared so many ups and downs in our lives, you can't simply throw that away. I know Belinda needs someone to take care of her, but I'm not sure that someone should be me. I have Samson to watch over, my grandkids, Cora and Kirk." He pauses and taps her hand with his free hand. He turns to look at her and Katie sits up and looks him in the eye, "and you. Who is going to watch over you?" he asks slowly.

"You say that as if I'm going somewhere. I fully expect to see you every Wednesday night at our bench in the park and at least once for lunch during the week. Nothing will change Nat. Your friendship means too much to me. No, you're stuck with me whether you like it or not and Belinda will have to get over the attention you give me." Her voice a little tighter than she wanted it to be. Could he be saying goodbye to her? That can't be. Something is really wrong.

"Let's get you inside. You need a drink so you won't get too hot at the park and dehydrate. You're already looking sluggish." Katie pulls Nat up to stand, he walks with her slowly, slower than usual. She looks at him and he looks and feels as if he is walking through thick mud. Katie wraps her elbow around his and interlaces her fingers into his, together they walk but she is pulling more than walking together.

Three steps later and Nat falls to the ground, pulling Katie with him as he goes. His grip tightens on her and stays that way as they hit the ground. Katie quickly makes sure he has not hit his head and leans him on his side, not his back because she doesn't want him to puke and choke on his tongue. She quickly calls Samson on her phone with her other hand because she is too far out in the yard for anyone to hear her.

"Samson!! Call 911, Nat has fallen, he is unresponsive, he has a pulse but it's weak. The weird thing is, he feels at peace. I can't explain that part." She calls into the phone.

"On it." Samson hangs up,

Petrified, he dials 911 and says the exact words that Katie did to describe his father, gives them the address and calls Cora and Kirk to handle Belinda and the guests. Samson looks outside from his bedroom window to see Katie and his father on the ground. She is so beautiful, he can't believe his luck in having to have met her in his life. She has been great with his father, she speaks with him too but not the same way. She speaks with Samson like most people do, as if he is fragile. Sure, he walks differently than most, but his mind is there, how else could he have achieved so much professionally? He owns his own house, car and he recently even put money down on a vacation home in another country. He told Cora and Kirk they could take their families there anytime so they don't have to pay for a hotel.

Along with his walk, his voice and his speech are not what would be described as normal, however, it's not that far off that women should see him as so different, but they do. Women at work smile at him, men at work shake his hand often and ask for his opinions, however, no one invites him to their nights out after hours; no one includes him in their gatherings for anything. Samson is a lonely man too. Often questioning why no one can see that. He looks out again at Katie and his father. What is taking the ambulance so long?

He should go outside but someone has to let them in, so he stays and walks downstairs waiting for them. He paces the foyer about a dozen times and calls 911 again to make sure they heard him and how urgent the situation is. He remembers to speak slowly like his mother taught him to on the phone. The dispatcher said someone is on their way and should be there soon. She reminded him he is fifteen minutes from the nearest hospital where the ambulance is coming from. She reassured him, at least a little.

Samson tells her he is going to leave the front and back doors open so they can go straight through the house to find him. She told him she will let them know and that he should feel free to call back if he needs to. Reassured, he decides to walk outside to Katie.

He sees Katie holding his father's hand and her eyes are closed, her lips moving. He is not sure if she is praying or talking. He sits down next to his father, puts his hand on his chest to feel the heartbeat, it seems to be there but not as strong as he remembers it being as a child. Nat has been his strength through everything in his life. He has shown him, Cora and Kirk exactly what it means to love someone unconditionally, he taught them how to stand on their own two feet and plant them firmly on the ground when necessary and when it's time to walk away. If it were not for his father, Samson knows for sure he would not have made it this far in life. Love can take you a long way.

Samson lies down next to his father and says, "Hello, are you listening to me? I need you to come back, you know. I can't do this on my own. Not yet anyway. I know I'm thirty but I still need you Dad." He leans over and kisses his father's cheek. He feels cold and warm at the same time. He sits up and sees that his father's lips are moving too. Samson can't decide if the two of them are in a trance together or if it's a coincidence that they are doing the same thing.

He watches Katie and a part of his heart swells, he wishes she would hold his hand like she is his father's. If only she could open her eyes and see him for the man he is and not her friend's son. Maybe then, she will understand that when he looks at her it's from deep inside himself, not only a surface glance.

~ ~ ~ ~

After hanging up with Samson, Katie begins to cry. "Don't you dare die on me Nat. I'll kill you. I swear I will." She thought she felt something in her hand and then she realized she had. Nat's hand became tighter around hers. So tight that she actually closed her eyes for a second in pain.

Once her eyes were closed though, she became pulled into a conversation, or a dream, she is not sure which. Nat starts to talk to her, "Katie my dear, I'm not leaving yet, but I'm not sure I will have much voice left though soon, so you need to hear me out, ok?"

"Ok Nat." she answers

"Belinda is not for me, you will see after today that she will not want to hang around, but I'm ok with that. I have you, I have Samson. We will all be ok." He says.

"What do you mean by me and Samson. Where will you be?" she asks.

"The mind is a wonderful thing Katie, but I'm afraid mine is being fried right now. Literally, as I speak to you, synapses are being broken." He tells her.

Katie does not know how to respond. She wants to scream, only she finds she has no voice. She wants to run away but she can't seem to move her body. Her phone, she will call Samson again, but she can't bring her hand up to grasp the phone again. Is she sick as well? Have they both fallen and hit their heads?

As if hearing her thoughts Nat replies, "Nothing like that has happened Katie, you're fine. Listen to me though. I have a lot to tell you and you need to hear the whole thing. Can you listen without questions?" he asks.

"I'll try." Is all she can muster.

"A long time ago I met a wonderful woman. As you know we married under some duress but at the same time, we married in what I've known as eternal bliss. I never thought it was possible, but I had achieved that. You're right, my wife would want me happy but the thing that makes me happiest is her, and my children. Adding Belinda into the mix will actually only add the heartache I feel about cheating on my wife." He pauses

"Nat, I don't agree, but I will not argue any more. I believe you feel that much for your wife and I am turning green with envy that any one person could love so strongly." She interjects.

Nat smiles at her, he knew she would understand. "You need," he takes a breath, "you need to know a little history about my family. I'll be quick, they're coming for me soon." Another pause.

"After we married, we tried to have children right away. We wanted a million of the little beggars, but that was not in the cards for us. Many doctors told us it was of no use. Medicine is not like today where they know how to manipulate the women's cycle to help out or do some minimally invasive procedures to help in getting someone pregnant. My wife had three miscarriages." He bows his head down.

Katie is not sure how he is doing that when part of her clearly sees him lying on the ground and yet he is sitting right next to her at the same time. She sees that Samson has come out and is lying next to his father, a gentle giant is really the best way to describe the scene. She wants to talk to him, but her mouth won't open. She merely watches him lay there with a tear rolling down his cheek for his father's wellbeing.

"Fast forward" Nat's voice brings her back to looking at him, "we find ourselves pregnant with Samson. We also find a doctor who is willing to help her out and keep this baby. By then, I was making enough money to pay for our expenses, small as they were, but she quit her job and sat down or laid down for the next seven months. Seven months!!!! Can you believe that? She and I wanted this baby so much that even before he was born, we made sacrifices. Her family came to see her often, to keep her company. Her mom would cook and leave me food for dinner for the next few days.

Her sister came a few times as well. Our neighbors got word of what is going on and they pitched in as well. The old phrase it takes a village to raise a child surely came true for us. They were all there during this time and the child hadn't even been born yet.

This is where Bart came into our lives. He is a neurologist who came to talk with us in the hospital when Samson was born, he said, his exam was good and that he is as harry as his namesake is said to be. We were good with him and him with us, but were yet to be friends." Nat puts his head down again, this time his face has a grimaced look on it.

Katie puts her hand out to touch his face. "You ok?" she asks

"I'm ok, they will be here soon, let me finish." He pauses again, but before Katie can answer he says, "Don't worry my boy, I'm coming back." She looks over to Samson and sees him kiss his father, another tear rolling down his square jaw. He must get that from his mother because Nat's features are much softer, however, there is a certain appeal to how Samson looks as well.

Katie looks back at Nat who is smiling at her now, "There is a lot more to a book than its outside isn't there?"

he asks. "Katie listen to me, I need to speak quickly while I still can." Katie looks at Nat with tears in her eyes, "OK" she responds.

"Fast forward, we had Cora three years later and Kirk three years after that. Not for lack of trying mind you." He winks at her and Katie stifles a laugh, now is not the time. "We loved our children almost as much as we loved each other. We never wanted our children to know anything but love. A deep love will carry you through so much, you're never prepared for a test, but it's not always up to us.

Fast forward again, we are at a ball game, professional baseball, Samson is almost thirteen, he has been studying for his bar mitzvah reading already for months and my brother, his teacher, decided to treat us all to a game for all his hard work. The game was a bit slow in pace but then the action picked up in the fifth inning, one hit after another, our team had a four hit lead all of a sudden and it didn't look like anything was going to stop any time soon.

The fans were all on their feet cheering wildly, one of the best players was up at bat, we heard the crack of the bat and then a second crack only moments later. I felt the hit before I saw it, Samson was on the floor in front of me. He had turned his head to me to ask a question and the ball had gone straight from the bat to hitting the back of his head, down he went. The crowd stopped cheering, the silence in the stadium was deafening. My brother's cool head prevailed, he reminded everyone not to move the boy because movement could make the injury worse. The game went on around us to distract the fans. The paramedics were there in seconds or hours, I don't know which, it became one long blurry moment of hell in our lives."

Nat takes what looks like a deep breath, Katie sees Samson pick up his father's head and lay it on his lap, he begins stroking his head like a father would to a child. Must be a familiar thing with him, considering the story she is being told.

Nat continues, "The kids went with my brother, my wife and I rode in the ambulance to the hospital. I had the wherewithal to remember Bart and requested him in the ambulance, they called ahead to see if he was there, he was. Thankfully." Another pause.

"But something had changed in him. He came to us and did the exam as thorough as we would have wanted him to. He spoke to everyone around him with urgency, as the situation was serious. Samson was out for a full twenty minutes.

He called for a head scan, x-rays, blood work, you name the test; it was done. But we both noticed his actions were not done out of love for the patient but out of rote for doing a job he knew too well. He was following procedure, not his gut. Finally, he came to tell us we have to wait this out, and see what damage there might be. He said he did all he can.

My wife went into a fit I had never seen before, yelling at him about how he lost his passion for his job and that if he had any passion he would be fighting for this boy he saw nearly thirteen years ago as an infant, she yelled at him about how as a young doctor he would have done everything in his power to help their son, not simply speak mechanically to them after running procedures like a robot. She told him to grow up and not come back until he did.

Bart left the room with his tail between his legs. Took me a couple of hours to calm her down, but I had been as agitated as she was so maybe it took us both that long, only she was able to verbalize her anger, I was not. I held my son the best way I know how, with love.

We both did, we took turns in holding his hands, rubbing his feet, even his belly for fun. She tried to tickle him but he told us tickling hurt so she stopped right away. But at least we knew his nerves were still there in his feet. That made us happy." Nat looks up at his son, and smiles.

"Now he will be the caretaker and he can too Katie, you will see how strong he is. But he is going to need you." He says.

"Nat, what happen, did Bart come back? Is there permanent damage to Samson? He seems fine to me, I've never seen anything different about him." She tells him

Nat smiles at her again, "You don't see anything different? Katie that is what makes you so amazing. One of the many things I should say. I'm sorry your parents never saw that in you but you, my young friend, are amazing. I promise you that." He puts his hand on her shoulder, or at least it feels that way to her, because when she looks in front of her, she sees him on the ground holding her hand steadfast.

"Bart went home that night and had a bar b que with his family. His two-year-old son decided to play with the big boys and ran into their game. A whiffle ball hit him smack on the forehead and Bart jumped out of his skin, as he explained to us. He knew full well the whiffle ball can't do damage but it was the idea of the ball and his child that snapped him into place.

He told us that had the ball hit Samson in the front with the same force, he would not have survived the night at all. Then he spent the whole night making phone calls, he called doctors from all over the country and even some out of the country to find out everything that can be done for Samson. Had it been his child he would have done everything in his power, he apologized for losing his heart to the bureaucracy of the hospital and the health care system.

He found many new ideas, some of which were against traditional medicine and he was clear as to which ones have worked and which ones are still being tried, but we wanted our son to be as perfect as he was before. He understood that now.

We all worked together. My brother decided that he would still study his bar mitzvah reading with Samson, even if all Samson did was follow with his finger, when his voice came back, he was confident his nephew would know the whole thing."

Nat puts his hand on Katie's again. "He learned it all Katie, every word he learned, the week before, he began singing out of the blue. He knew every word by heart when most others never do. It was a song in his heart, it was his love that saved him; our love that helped him as well. We never gave up on him. We pushed him through school, pushed him through college and the rest is history. He is the man he is because of love. Remember that Katie. Love is key."

With that last word Nat began to move, Katie's eyes finally open and she hears the paramedics calling to them. Nat's fingers are still interlocked with hers but they no longer hurt. As the paramedics begin to check him, Samson steps aside and puts a hand on her shoulder that she should stand and do the same, finally, Nat's fingers slide out of hers. She stands with Samson's help and she leans onto him for support. She is not sure what happened there on the ground. She is not sure how much time passed. For her, time felt as if she and Nat were speaking on their bench for quite a while, like their regular meetings, but if the paramedics just got here they couldn't have been down there more than five or ten minutes. Maybe fifteen at most.

Her head is feeling a bit dizzy, so she leans herself back onto Samson's chest. His hands go to her shoulders to comfort her and give her strength. He leans down to her ear, "What did you two talk about?" he whispers.

She looks up at him questionably. "Your lips and his lips moved but not at the same time. I know you two were talking. I don't know how though."

Katie reaches up and touches his hand with hers, she pats him and says, "Let's discuss this when he is settled." But instead of taking her hand down she slides her fingers under his hand to hold him. His strength is great and his support is already emanating from him to her. Katie questions the feelings she is having right now. This day is something she has to let sink in before she can internalize all that has happened. The paramedics call to her, "Are you the one who took his pulse initially?"

"Yes sir, I found his pulse to be faint but it was there fighting its way to be heard." She says.

"That's a funny way of putting it but I feel the same way. Don't worry the pulse is still there, thankfully. You did all the right things here. Laying him down, comforting him and waiting. Not much else you could have done. We think he had a massive stroke. But we are only guessing. Will you two be following in a car or do you want to ride along?" he asks.

Katie and Samson exchange glances, "She will ride, and I'll grab the car and meet you there. I have to go get Bart. She has full permission to make any decisions necessary. My brother and sister will be there shortly." Samson says with strength and conviction in his voice.

When he takes his hands off of Katie, she feels a sense of loss. Without him as part of her, touching her, she is not as sure of herself as she was minutes ago. "We have to go now." The paramedic says, so mechanically, Katie follows them, she glances back at Samson, who is rubbing the hand she held. He must feel the same loss, she thinks.

~ ~ ~

The hospital room finally calms down, Bart and his team of experts have been in and out all day, Belinda sent regards but that is all she could send. Nat was right, she won't stay around now, he needs care and she can't give, she needs to be the receiver.

Katie has been sitting in the same chair all day, holding Nat's hand, he holding hers. The doctors are all baffled, except for Bart. He knows that Nat's love is what is holding onto Katie. Over the years, he has felt the power of that love and is happy to see this part of his friend is still there. He is not sure how much else is there, but this is the strongest part of Nat and maybe that strength will work for him once again. Only, this time, even his powerful inner strength may not pull him to full recovery, but may allow him to heal and accept his new lot in life.

Bart likes Katie, he knows that Nat and she are close. An odd pair, but a good one. Now that there are no more intrusions, and Samson is out in the waiting room with his siblings, he has a chance to talk with her alone.

"So how much did he tell you with his hand?" Bart asks her.

Katie looks at him in surprise. Bart continues, "He sat next to me when I lost my mother, we were close and I wasn't handling her death well. He took my hand and we sat there quietly, only there wasn't quiet, he told me everything I needed to hear, good and bad but needed to hear. I can only imagine what he had to say on the morning of his wedding. The wedding that won't happen." He says quietly.

"He spoke as he knew he would not be able to speak to me again. He told me his brain is losing synapsis as we speak. We talked of love and Samson. How does he do that Uncle Bart? Makes no sense." She says

"I agree, but ever since I met him and his wife, I've learned not to question. Something very special about him. His wife was the same. The two of them were literally made for each other. I suppose he told you about Samson's accident. Feels like I've known him my whole life, he makes everyone feel that way." He says.

"Yes, as a matter of fact he did tell me about the accident and also about how hard it was for them to have children in the first place. I told him I never noticed the speech problem. He smiled." Katie responds.

"You are the only one in his life to do so then my dear. Even Cora still can't understand him sometimes and she was a big part of his recovery." Bart starts to pace.

When he continues his voice shows big concern for his friend, "Katie, I'm not sure this time. I'm really not. I don't know how much of his love will get him through this one. This is a tough one. I don't know if he will be able to feed himself, dress himself, I really don't know what he has lost and not knowing is killing me right now. He is my best friend Katie, I've never had someone like him in my life." Bart walks over and takes Nat's hand out of Katie's hold him. "Can I have a few minutes alone with him?" he asks in a choked voice.

Katie nods and walks out to the waiting room. The first face she sees is Samson's, he is looking through to her soul, not at her outsides. She can feel his eyes on her and she is not sure if this feeling is comforting or scary. She walks on and before she knows why, she is enveloped into his arms and her tears are flowing down her cheeks and hence down his shirt. Cora and Kirk join in a group hug for a moment.

The four of them scoot over to a set of chairs near each other in the waiting room. Samson sits down and pulls Katie onto his lap in one swoop. She does not argue because sitting here is giving her the comfort she needs right now.

After being thrown out of her parent's house at the age of sixteen, she has longed to belong to some kind of family, this is the first one to embrace her for who she is. A little weird, a bit off the normal when it comes to dress and job. However, she has been supporting herself since she left. Her parents did not believe she could. They assumed she would come crawling back to them in what they feel is their perfect picturesque setting. But Katie does not fit into nice and neat, she needs disorder in her life and in this she functions better. Chaos brings her into a better creative state and she can sit down and write in her blog or create another sculptured piece within hours of the chaos hitting. She can only imagine what will come from today. But she is not feeling energy to create, she is feeling real emotions, hurt and pain. Something she is not used to.

Cora speaks first, "Katie, Dad has an amazing gift, he speaks to people in ways no one else understands. Samson said the two of you were speaking while Dad was out. Did he tell you anything we should know?"

Everyone knows this unique gift of Nat's, now she does not feel as confused. Katie sits up a bit more but does not leave Samson's lap. "He said love is key." She doesn't want to explain that he told her their life stories. She is not sure Samson would want her to know. She tries really hard to listen to his words, but she does not hear the slur or the lisp everyone keeps mentioning. Either she is crazy or it's not as bad as they make him out to be.

Samson sits up a little more in his chair, careful not to jostle Katie too much. He knows that he is ridiculous to have a grown woman sit on his lap but he needs to hold her a little longer and she does not appear to be in any hurry to get off. That is comforting to him in a big way.

Kirk breaks the silence, "He has been saying that our whole lives. Cora and I feel we are lucky to have at least half of what our parent's love was for each other. We hope it's the same, but theirs is hard to match, their love was, no is perfection. Either way, as you've seen, we are very happy, so, I guess that means we learned that lesson well. But let's talk logistics here, Dad has to move back home with you Samson, we know that. You'll have to bring him down to the first floor though, maybe you can get that guest room off the kitchen fixed up real nice in the next couple weeks and add that shower room you were always talking about so guests don't have to walk through the house in a robe for a shower. Katie can move into Dad's room upstairs and keep to eye on him. This will be the best scenario as I see." He sits back in his chair.

Katie feels the energy emanating from Samson, heat comes through his hand that is on her back right now, she is feeling a flight or fight response is necessary. No one is going to tie her down to mundane activities like caring for a man who can't feed himself. She has a job she has a career in fact and she is not tied down to anything. As her blood boils over, Samson puts a little bit more pressure on her back to calm her down. "Kirk, how very nice of you to offer up Katie as Dad's caretaker but what is to stop you from stopping by once a week and Cora can take another day and you each have spouses, that is four days right there, Katie and I can probably be ok with the other three days, but he gave birth to the three of us, not to the one of me. Plus, Katie here is a friend, no relation at all. Remember that." His voice sounding stern and very oldest brother-like.

Cora's eyes open a little more, then a large tear rolls down her cheek. She has never heard her brother sound so clear in what he has to say. "Samson, I.." She can hardly speak. Kirk too seems bewildered. Samson and Katie look at each other, neither one of them knowing what is going on, seems to Katie that the plan is a good one. Before she can respond Cora continues.

"I'm sorry. Samson, I've never heard you speak so clearly before. Ever. I suppose that is what Dad always spoke about. Love will come through in strength. Dad needs your strength, and here you have plenty to give. Yes, we are in Samson. I'll talk to Craig and figure out which days work for us. I may not be able to give a whole day but certainly before and after work, possible lunch if our schedule's work out. Katie, I'm sorry you are dragged into this family this way, but you are so much a part of Dad's life since mom died, we can't think of you as anything less than family. Your parents are foolish for pushing you out of their lives. And maybe, just maybe your daughter is still out there in foster care and you can adopt her now. You have so much love to give." Cora realizes she may have opened her mouth too much by the look in Katie's eyes but she needed to let Katie know her self-worth. She has a lot.

Samson takes his hands and runs them up and down on Katie's arms to let her know he is behind her no matter what she decides. She looks back at him. "I can get Nat's room ready in two days, no need to pay a contractor for a job an artist can do. Although I can't do the plumbing."

With his hand rubbing her back he simply shakes his head. Bart's voice startles all of them. "Ok gang, let's talk reality. I've been sitting with Nat for the past hour. He knows I'm there. He can sit up, thankfully, he even went to the bathroom by himself. Although I'm not sure how long that will last. Sorry, being honest. He can't pick up the fork or cup but he pointed to a steak on my laptop and we both laughed. Going to be a long, long recovery do you have plans?"

The four of them laugh, then they explain what they have decided to Bart.

~ ~ ~

The schedule works out nicely, there is not a single person who does two days in a row. Nat is being a good patient because he knows, deep down, he knows how hard this is for his children to do.

Samson is the only one who bathes him though. Cora and Craig both cook amazing dinners when they come, enough for all of them to eat together. Kirk and his wife popped the news that they were expecting their first child, coming in six months. This news made Nat smile, albeit a crooked one right now, but a smile nonetheless and everyone is thrilled to see him do so. Bart did not think he needed to be in a rehabilitation facility but reserves the right to change his mind if he doesn't see good progress at home.

Katie has managed to finish Nat's new room in his favorite colors, she also put in a built-in bench on one wall and made sure the bench was surrounded by the same flowers that grow in the park. Upon seeing the bench Nat reached for Katie's hand and he pulled it up to kiss. He held her hand for a moment and in his eyes, she knew there was acceptance to his new fate. The two of them would now sit on this bench for a while. Katie keeps telling him this situation is only temporary because she plans on dragging him out to the real bench soon enough. Nat tries to do something that resembles a laugh.

Bart's official diagnosis is a stroke, so far, he has some of his daily functions down pat. Everyone is thankful he can walk, he drags one foot but at least he is moving on his own. He needs to be fed but he can chew small pieces. All of this could have been worse, is all they keep telling themselves.

The new rhythm of the house keeps everyone on schedule. Katie moved in under duress, but in the end, she realizes this is where she wants to be. She mentions to Samson all the time that she is still paying rent on her apartment and can leave at any time, he usually smiles at her and nods.

Cora and Kirk say they have never seen Samson happier. Cora thinks it's because he gets to pay back their father for all the years their dad took care of him, Kirk thinks he likes to be in charge and so he is in his element. Bart, on the other hand, sees what Nat sees. Katie keeps Samson going. Bart can tell by Nat's eye movement that he wants Bart to encourage this. To make something happen even.

~ ~ ~

Eight weeks of this new life and Nat is already getting antsy. He pushes himself to take walks outside in the backyard. Katie is usually the one who finds him outside. She sits with him on the bench out back, she talks, he listens and he sends her as much information as his mind will let him. Never very long, he can't seem to hold his thoughts.

Katie pats his hand in hers, "I know you love me Nat admit it. You're my best friend, I could not have asked for a better one. But this constant lack of conversation is killing me. You have to go to the speech therapist. They will help you. We, your family, aren't trained for this you know that. Your wife did this for Samson didn't she?" she asks suddenly.

Nat shakes his head the best he can, he squeezes her hand, this she understands better. "She pulled everyone together and each person was given a task to help Samson recover and look at him now. He is strong, kind and everything you'd want him to be. Let him do the job you trained him for. Let him take care of you, you stubborn old fool. Don't you want to be able to read books to your grandchildren? I'm making the appointment, and short of dying, you are going. Do you hear me?" Katie is trying her hardest not to lose her temper at Nat but his refusal is downright selfish at this point and she can't stand his silence either.

Nat squeezes her hand again. She looks into his eyes, there is a tear running down his cheek. Katie wipes it off and leans into him, he tries to hold her the best he can. She pulls his hand around her and they sit there for a while.

Samson sees Katie and his dad from his window again, he longs to hold her again. He hasn't been able to since the day of the wedding. His arms long to have her in them again, for her to accept him as a man in her life and to stop thinking of him as Nat's son. He is older than her anyway.

Samson sits down and hangs his head into his hands, elbows on his knees. "Tough day?" Samson jerks his head up and sees Katie standing in his doorway. His heart begins to pound and he sits up a little straighter.

Seeing him sit up, his full height really hits Katie in the face. This man is so big, so strong, so kind, so...... 'Stop it Katie, you are a house guest' she chides herself.

"Kirk came to relieve me outside. He had a craving run for his wife and as long as he is out already, he brought some ice cream to Nat as well. She doesn't mind as long as he brings hers home first." She smiles. Katie looks at Samson, he does not look right. She walks closer, never having been in his room before she didn't know what to expect, it's beautifully decorated. Eclectically so. She brings her head back to see Samson watching her walk in.

She is not sure she should be here now but he looks like a lost puppy so she sits down next to him and puts her hands on his, "Seriously, are you ok? Been a long time since we brought Nat back and you've had to shoulder a lot of this burden. Want to talk?" Katie's voice is soft now.

Samson turns his hands over so that their palms are touching, Katie does not move. He is afraid to speak, and when he gets afraid, his voice is worse. But he has to answer her. "I'm ok" his voice squeaks out. "You?" he asks.

"Funny you should ask, I just got done yelling at Nat about going to speech. I told him he has to get over his fears and deal with reality; that I'm going to make the appointment and put him on the back of my bike and drag him over if I have to. I think he tried to smile, he made that weird face again at me but his eyes were bright." She takes a breath, knowing she is rambling.

Samson simply stares at her. This beautiful woman is in his bedroom and he can't think of an intelligent thing to say right now. Not one. "Hello? Are you listening?" she asks him.

This makes Samson smile. She learned the family question. This same phrase is the one they ask each other all the time when they aren't sure the other party is even paying attention. It is how they used to get Samson to focus on his studies so he could catch back up in school.

"I'm here but why are you? You could have waited until I came downstairs to tell me this." Samson stands up because he can't trust himself to be this close, in his room and not pull her in for a kiss. His whole body wants her, his head and heart do too.

"I'm sorry, you're right. I should not have invaded your space. I wanted to let you know that your father will go to speech and I'm going to make the appointment for tomorrow. I wanted to know what time you're available or if you need me to the appointment a different day." Her voice is now quiet, like a chastised child. Katie begins to walk out of the room.

Samson rushes over to her before she gets to the door. He spins her around and pulls her in for a kiss he has been waiting for two years to give her. He is slow and yet deliberate at the same time. 'I'm not a stupid little boy anymore, I'm a man' he says in his head.

Katie's hands slowly slide behind his head and before she can talk herself out of her own actions, she brings herself further in. If she is not mistaken, he is speaking to her in her head like Nat. The way she feels right now, she certainly knows he is a man.

Katie starts to pull away and lets her hands slide back down, all the while looking Samson in the eye, as best she can for someone who is more than a head taller than her. "I heard what you said." She told him.

"I didn't say anything, I thought something though." he responds

"No, you said, and I quote 'I'm not a stupid little boy anymore, I'm a man' right in my head. I heard you loud and clear. But Samson, I never thought of you as stupid, and certainly not as a boy. Never. Please don't say that about yourself again, things like that me uncomfortable that you feel that way about yourself. I was once with a boy, and that ended very badly." She says and steps away.

She has never told anyone about what happened to her so many years ago. She turns to walk out of the room again, things are getting too open here, too close. Samson grabs her shoulders and pulls her into him, still having her facing the doorway. He is holding her arms, at the top near the shoulders. "My dad told me about your daughter. I guess he told Cora too. She didn't mean to upset you in the hospital. Cora loves her children so much she wants you to be happy and have yours is all."

Katie wants to cry, she hasn't talked about her daughter to anyone but Nat. and even then she didn't give him the full story. "I'm a broken person Samson, you don't want to be involved with me. I will stay until Nat is better but then I'll have to leave this area. I hope you understand." Her tears flowing now, she can't control them.

Samson spins her around and lifts her chin. "If I'm not allowed to be stupid, you're certainly not allowed to be broken. You can tell me as much or as little as you want the decision is all up to you. I'm here to listen when the time is right." His voice is soft with understanding.

"Why does everyone say you can't speak Samson? I hear you loud and clear." Katie asks.

"My momma said that too. She said people hear what they want to hear. My dad can hear me too. People I work with sometimes ask me things in email so I don't have to talk to them. I've been told my lisp is irregular and can't be fixed. If I speak really slowly like I did in the hospital, my words come out close to perfect, but no one speaks like that, I think speaking slowly makes me sound even more stupid. Sorry." His eyes apologizing for using the word stupid.

The two of them stand there a few moments until they hear a voice. "Yo!!!! Samson!! Katie!! I have to leave. Dad is in the den, someone!" Kirk calls.

"I've got this one." Samson says but before he leaves, he leans down and kisses her again gently on her lips. "Whenever you're ready." He says again. And walks down to greet his brother and find his father.

~ ~ ~

Another month has gone by and Nat is making very slow progress with his speech but his ability to eat is improving. He can now drink from a straw. Craig's parents sent over a blender to be able to make all kinds of smoothies so that Nat can get proper nutrition in him. They all balked at first, but now it has become the family toy. Cora and Craig make the best ones, especially when they bring the kids over.

Kirk and his wife came over to fix dinner one night. Kirk walks over to Samson and hands him an envelope. On the outside of the envelope it reads, "Get the hell out of here for a night. Take Katie, our treat." Samson opens the envelope and sees a gift certificate to a nice restaurant downtown. Kirk shakes his head and Samson pulls him in for a hug. He walks over to hug Kirk's wife too but she shoos him away because she is in the middle of cooking and once she is in the beat, you can't bother her.

Samson walks over to where Nat is sitting with Katie and shows her the envelope. Nat sits up a little straighter in his chair and says, with all his might "Go". Katie leans over and kisses Nat. "That was clear as a bell. Stubborn old man." She teases. Nat smiles.

"Do I have to dress better?" she looks down at her paint stained outfit then looks up at Samson in his suit pants, blue shirt and tie. "Hmmm, guess that's a yes. Ok give me five. Promise." She rushes past Samson.

Samson sits next to his father and says, "Hello, are you listening?" Nat shakes his head.

"It hurts Dad, what do I do?" Samson is referring to his heart and Nat knows he is. Katie can be aloof sometimes and other times pay full and close attention to someone. She pulls back the instant she begins to feel. With Nat it was a safe friendship. Samson is not so safe. He told his father about the kiss, and Katie did as well. He heard both sides of the coin. Both of them need each other, both too scared to let the other one in. Nat works hard to open his arms to hug his son. His eyes speak to his son. Samson nods.

The ride to the restaurant is quiet. Both people trying to figure out what to do on this outing. Is it a date? Is it a thank you? Can it be both? Right before they get to the restaurant Katie begins to fidget in her seat, she seems agitated and nervous. Not normal nervous either, but big time nervous. 'What could she be thinking I'm going to do to her?' Samson thinks to himself.

Katie recognizes the restaurant. She was here once before, on the night that changed the course of her life forever. Now she wishes she would have asked where they were going. She trusted the place to be nice if Kirk said it was. Samson jumps out of the car to run over and open the door for Katie, she sits their frozen in her seat, the door is open. Samson leans down and speaks softly, "We don't have to go in, I prefer a simple hamburger anyway. No one has to know we didn't go. We'll give the certificate to the next couple who we see going in." Katie shakes her head no, she can overcome this. Ten years now, she needs to overcome, she can do this.

She stands up out of the car and Samson takes her arm to lead her into the restaurant. Katie rushes passed him and starts running out of the parking lot. Doesn't take much effort on his part, and with his long legs, to catch up to her. He literally picks her up and holds her. He looks around and sees a bench and carries her over to the bench where they sit down, she on his lap, again. Only this time she buries her head into his neck and cries like he has never seen her cry before or anyone for that matter.

"I'm sorry. I had no idea this is a bad place for you. No way Kirk knew anything either I promise you." He says eager to calm her.

Katie shakes her head into his neck. She knows he could not have known, no one does. Samson is rubbing her back and calming her down. With each stroke of his hand she breathes a little easier. What is it about the men in this family that can reach into her so well? Finally, she lifts her head and sits up a bit. She wipes her face with her sleeve to clear the tears, "I'm sorry Samson. I owe you an explanation." She says weakly.

"No, you don't. Obviously, a bad memory for you. Let's go to the car and we will go get that burger I was talking about earlier." He says continuing to rub her back and arms.

"I have to face this. I have to grow up sometime." She says

"Katie, this is not about growing up, it's about owning up. We all have to own up to our past. No one is free from one. But you don't have to do everything in one tonight. Not even tomorrow or the next day. When you're ready, ten years from now, we can come back and you'll tell me all about this place, ok?" Samson is trying to comfort her and get her to talk at the same time. He wants to hurt whomever it was that hurt her so long ago.

Katie shakes her head yes. "Ok, can we get fries with that burger?" she asks trying to make a joke.

Samson smiles at her, and lets her slide down off of his lap so she can walk back to the car. There are two men standing at his car. Katie freezes and stands even closer to Samson. He is at full attention now. "Is there something I can help you with gentlemen?" he asks authoritatively.

"Why are you here Katie? We told you never to come back. Someone saw you get out of the car. Guess who that someone was Katie?" One gentleman asks her in a very accusatory voice.

Samson pushes Katie behind him, clears his throat and very slowly speaks to them, "I suggest you move away from my car this instant. If you have something to say to this woman, it had better be I'm sorry. Clearly your presence is enough to make her sick and I'm beginning to feel the same way." He looks at each man daring them not to listen. They begin to walk back to the entrance of the restaurant.

Samson sees another couple walking across the parking lot, he looks at the young woman and calls over to them, "Excuse me young man. I'd be careful about bringing that pretty young thing into this restaurant. Apparently, woman aren't really invited to be there. You'd best be finding another place." His voice was loud enough that two other cars heard him as well and began to back up.

The man and his date quickly turn around and head back to their car. Samson takes out his pocket lighter and lights the gift certificate on fire and drops it on the asphalt to burn. Then he looks at the man about to protest what he has done and he simply stares them down. Samson's full presence can be quit intimidating. His full voice can be heard like thunder. Katie slips behind him and into the car in one quick movement. Samson gets into his car and pulls away quickly.

The silence in the car is a comfortable one. Samson will wait for Katie to say anything or nothing, the decision is all up to her. "You're very good at playing protector Samson. Thank you." She sinks into her chair a bit.

"Easy to protect you Katie." He wants to say it's easy to protect those you love but he could not. Not today, not now. Maybe soon.

Samson drives for about a half an hour, Katie does not notice the time go by, her body is shaking for most of the time and she has to get herself under control. This should not have happened. She heard they had left, this should not have happened. This is so messed up.

Samson pulls into his favorite restaurant from when he was a child. Owned by an old family friend. Someone who lets him come in any time when he was a teen and work there when no one else would let him. The son now runs the place and Samson knows two important things, one is that they will allow them to stay as long as they need and two, they serve amazing food.

When the car comes to a stop, Katie doesn't move, she makes no move at all in fact, almost like she is in shock. Samson walks around and opens her door for the second time of the night. "Katie, it's safe to come out now. I promise. Katie, come with me, please." He pleads.

At this Katie looks to her right and sees the welcoming arms of a man she has grown very fond of. Carefully she steps out. Samson slides his arm around her waist and brings her closer to him as they walk into the restaurant. The smells of good food wake Katie out of her stupor. She takes a moment to look around and she sees a beautiful room, lit with simple chandeliers, the wooden tables all have lace looking paper place mats on them. She looks up at Samson as her stomach actually growls loud enough for both of them to hear. "Hmmmmm, glad I brought you here, you won't leave hungry. For anything." He grins at her.

A man about the same size and age of Samson comes out from the back room. "Sammmmmmsonnnnnnn!!!" he calls out. Samson turns to see the owner coming towards him. He drops his arm from around Katie hugs his old friend. "You look fantastic my old friend. Who is this beautiful lady you have and why is she with someone like you?" the man teases.

Samson smiles at Katie, "This is Katie, the woman who befriended my father after mom's death and who I am proud to say is my friend as well."

Katie looks up at Samson, her heart pounding ever so slightly more than it should. "I'm happy to meet you. This place is really nice. I've never been here before." She answers quietly.

"Never? Is that even possible?" he looks at Samson. "In that case, dinner is on me. Come sit down in your favorite spot, it's open now and I'll bring you the works. Starting with my famous onion rings, you will be spoiled and never eat them anywhere else my dear. And don't get me started on our burgers. Any allergies?" he asks.

Katie smiles, the thought of food sounds great no matter what kind he is serving. "I can't eat peppers, they don't really agree with me, not an allergy more like an aversion." She answers still being very quiet. Her insides are still shaking from the events that took place not too long ago. She looks up at Samson and he can see in her eyes, she needs to leave this conversation. He hugs his friend one more time and pulls her to the corner booth where no one can hear them or see them.

"This is the place my father took me to after my accident many years ago. The only place that didn't judge me for my differences. The only restaurant I know of that has no steps to get into so that all handicapped people can come. These booths were made like cubbies with walls around them that are sound proof. If a child sits here and yells, the rest of the room is not disturbed. I hope you aren't claustrophobic." He smiles

Katie looks up and notices that they are in a mini room with bench chairs to sit on. "I'm ok, this is really nice. Your friend is kind of boisterous, isn't he?" she asks.

"No, he always makes a big deal out of me coming in. We grew up together here. My father made sure we went to the same schools so he knew I would have one person in my corner. We happen to have the same birthday. He calls me his twin even though we look nothing alike, but in school sometimes it was fun because people believed us for many years. Wait until you eat the food. You really will be spoiled. I'm sorry about the other place, we had no idea it was a bad place for you. Kirk never would have given me the certificate to the place if..."

Katie puts her hand on his across the table. "I'm ok. There is no way for you to know. I haven't been there since I was sixteen, you'd think I've moved passed that memory but obviously they haven't either." Katie takes a deep breath. "I should explain, I owe you that much." She looks down at her hand holding onto Samson across the table. His arm is so strong, even only holding one hand is enough to give her the strength she needs to finally open up. Nat knows some of the story, that's the part he obviously told Cora.

Samson looks across the table at Katie, she looks so fragile right now that if he holds her hand too tight she will break. "Katie, you owe me nothing." He says simply.

Katie gives Samson a smirk, he is so gentlemen-like, his caring for her is showing more and more and lately she has been enjoying him more and more That first kiss still sits on her lips when she is feeling lonely.

Before Katie begins to speak, the onion rings show up. The plate is piled high and the smell goes right to her stomach and all other pleasure senses. She has to grab one before she starts talking. "Hmmmmmmm, this is out of this world. Almost hits you in places food shouldn't." Her eyes pop open realizing what she actually said out loud. Samson is smiling at her and he slides his legs out to reach hers and he surrounds her legs with his, he gives a small squeeze and holds them. Katie looks across the table at Samson and his eyes are being very expressive. He wants all of her to be his, she feels him and hears his thoughts. She is not sure what to do with this, so she begins to tell her story, he will either hate her afterwards or simply think she is nuts. Either way, she is sure his legs and his affections will dissipate quickly.

"When I was sixteen, I was dating a young man who was in college. He is one of the owner's sons from the place we went to. I met him at a fair near where I used to live. He was nineteen at the time, not so crazy for us to be dating except people thought he was older because he was in college and had a beard. That was because he was too lazy to shave.

Anyway, we really did get along well. We liked many of the same things, he appreciated my artsy side, or so he told me then, later he told me he thought it was a phase I would outgrow when I finished high school.

His family didn't seem to care that I was only sixteen. I fit right in with them, got along with everyone, even the boys we saw tonight. They are his older brothers. One of them is married, the other one, well, I personally don't know why he hasn't ended up in jail yet." Katie pauses, she knows why he is not in jail. They have an uncle that is a prosecuting attorney and he keeps getting him off on technicalities. One day, he won't be so lucky. She could have pressed charges for rape, but she saw the idea was futile and therefore put her daughter up for adoption. No child should know they are a result of rape and not love.

Katie eats a few more onion rings and remains silent in her own world for a few minutes. She feels Samson squeeze her legs a bit again and she realizes she has actually been mumbling not silent, he heard every word she just said, she can tell by the look in his eyes.

"I, well, the thing is, I…" Katie is at a loss for words.

"Dinner is served!" came a loud voice next to them.

"As usual, you've outdone yourself my friend. I see one mushroom burger and one with onions and avocado. What no side salad?" Samson tries to joke for Katie's sake.

"Still such a pig, are you Samson? I'll bring one out fit for a king. And you my lady will receive the royal treatment as well. Anyone who can keep him smiling this long must be made of something special." He turns on his heals to retrieve the rest of their dinner.

Katie stares at the burgers, they look amazing. Almost too good to eat. She grabs for half of the mushroom burger and digs in before she begins talking again and inserts her foot even further down her own throat.

They eat in peace for a few minutes. She can tell that Samson is being patient, he is not asking questions, he is letting her do what she feels she can. This man in front of her clearly learned from the best. Nat always had a way of letting her talk when she needs to and stopping her when she needs to as well.

"For almost a year we were boyfriend and girlfriend. Coming upon our one year anniversary and we were talking about how much we cared for each other and that maybe it was ok for us to express this physically. He made all the right arrangements. They have a condo that they use when they go down to the shore and he figured the place was far enough away that I would be comfortable, no one would know us there really. A whole weekend for us to get to know each other intimately.

Everything was going well. My parents even let me go. I said I was going away to his family's condo at the shore and they assumed the family was going with. I made no corrections, but in the end, I never directly lied, did I?" she looks at Samson for some kind of confirmation, his smile reassures her that she was right.

"The first day we spent at the beach, laying around playing as if it was the most natural thing in the world to be together, to be hanging out like this. We joined a group playing volleyball and we went to the local bar and had a couple of drinks with them. He ordered virgin drinks for me without anyone there knowing except the waitress. I was not insulted because I felt he was taking care of me.

He told me later he did that because he wanted to make sure I was going to go ahead with everything with a clear head and that I could not blame him for anything unwanted. Which sounds twisted doesn't he? I guess he really only wanted to be with a virgin, and not really with me. But why would he wait a year?

The whole ordeal was baffling afterwards. As that first evening went on, he became more and more amorous and I really began to feel that this was the right person, the right time. When we got back to the condo, the place was quiet. Just us, he turned on some music and went to prepare the bedroom. He put out candles and even had a pretty piece of lingerie for me to wear. I went in the bathroom and changed, and so did he.

We came together on the bed, things moved very slowly. When we suddenly heard a loud boom sound from the living room. His brother had come in, drunk as a sailor on his first leave, or so I have heard.

He was calling our names, he knew we would be there. He called out things like, "are you done yet? Was the cherry red?" Katie drops her eyes down, this is the most degrading thing for her to tell this story. But she has come this far, she might as well finish.

She takes a deep breath, "Anyway, my boyfriend jumped up to prevent his brother from coming into the room. I heard a scuffle then I heard him yell, Stop!! You Can't!!! Untie me!!!!. At that point I knew I was in trouble. Before I could get into a closet and hide his brother was on me, way too powerful for me to handle, a mean drunk who is over six feet tall and as wide as a barn is no match for a sixteen year old girl with minimal muscle. You can guess the rest of the story." Katie looks down at her plate and realizes she has scarfed down an entire burger while talking. She hopes her words actually came out clear.

She looks over at Samson and sees by the looks in his eye, the whole story registered, loud and clear. She clears her throat and sits back to finish, the rest she has to look at him to say because she has to regain some amount of dignity. "When he finished with me, he laughed and told me the night was never going to happen with his brother anyway. He stomped into the living room and untied his brother yelling at him, 'Fags don't get to be with beautiful girls, even for a test run.' Then he laughed so loud the walls shook. Two seconds later the door was slammed closed. I sat there not knowing what to do. Then my worst fear happened. The door closed again. He left me there. Alone, scared and hurt. I went to shower, not knowing what else to do.

I came out and cleaned up the bedroom by stripping the bed, I even found new sheets to put on. I rolled up the soiled sheets and put them in a garbage bag to bring down with me. I found my purse and realized I had enough money to catch the next train home.

I walked the two miles to the station because I needed to clear my head. I came home with bruises on my face and legs and the first thing my parents said to me was, 'Get out!! How dare you go away with a boy! How dare you bring shame to this family!!!' I stared at them in disbelief. How did they know? I asked them.

  My father said one of his friends saw me on the beach with a boy and he knew who the boy was. They apparently went to the restaurant to see if the family had gone too and saw they did not. Cover blown. Worse yet, they didn't even notice the shape I was in.

  I went upstairs and packed a bag, I've never been back. Never called them to tell them I was pregnant, never called to tell them I gave her up. Nothing. They know nothing to this day. When I was halfway through the pregnancy, I showed up at the restaurant to see if there would be a reaction. There was, they kicked me out too. My so-called boyfriend and his brother both physically picked me up and dragged me out of the place through the back door.

  The 'boyfriend' told me, with a smile. 'Well we know it's not mine. You're not my type, are you?' he laughed. He actually laughed. His brother looked down at me and said, 'Can't be mine, I don't lay with scum. So why are you here? To try and put this on us? Our parents would never believe you. You can't prove a thing.' As they walked away my then boyfriend turned back and smiled. 'Looks like you may need a real job after all.'

  Before he could leave though I shouted to him, 'We were seen there, don't think your parents don't know. My parents came looking for your parents that weekend. They know you were with me down there.' He froze, he turned around and stared at me. 'What do you want? I can't take care of a baby and you and I both know the kid's not mine.' I told him I could get the baby tested and then his parents would know the truth both about him and about his brother and how they play games with girls.

He walked right up to me and slapped me as hard as he could. Can you believe him? He slapped a pregnant woman! I grabbed his hand on the way down and I told him he was going to be sorry he did that. I turned to walk away. His father came out and yelled 'Stop' as I turned around, I saw him with a heavy box over his head, he was going to kill me. 'Young lady you've caused enough damage to this house. Enough you made a liar out of my son, now you want to bring shame to the whole family. Clearly your word isn't to be trusted. Don't come back here unless you want me to call the police.' I remember all their words as if they were said yesterday, how could I forget them?

Without anything left in me, I used all the strength I had to yell back at him. 'Go ahead I'll wait, then we will see whose baby this is and you will find out the truth about your boys.' I had no dignity left but I tried with all my might to walk away with my head held high. I never looked back, until today I had never been back. There, now you know the whole sordid details of my life. I best be getting back to my apartment." Katie's head looks down, she can no longer look at Samson's face. She tries to wiggle out of his legs but he will have nothing of letting her go.

Samson begins to laugh, actually laugh out loud, this infuriates her and her head snaps up. He grabs her hands quickly from across the table. "Your daughter should be about ten years old by now. It would have been really funny if we borrowed my neighbor's kid before we showed up. Would have been priceless. Come on admit it, you'd have laughed too." He smiles at her and she melts, it would have been pretty funny at that.

"I kept her for three months. I tried to be a mommy, but I wasn't ready. I was not mature enough. I know where she is, I gave her to the people I was working for then. I told them she would fit right into their family, she had the same coloring as them and no one would ever know. My boss insisted that we do everything right, he wanted papers drawn up and everything. They were the closest thing I had to parents at the time. His wife helped me through the birth, so she was there when this big head of dark hair came out. Clearly not from my side huh? I became her aunt, she knows me as Aunt Katie to this day. Cora doesn't know this part, she doesn't know I know where she is. But the odd part is, I have no maternal feelings towards her, none at all. Makes me a weirdo for sure. Why are you still here?" she looks at Samson.

"I will never leave you Katie, not now, not ever. Knowing this means you trust me enough to tell me and if we weren't in public, I think I would be crying right now that you hold me in such regard as to tell me this." Before he can say any more.

"Dessert time! Man you guys must have been hungry, not even a morsel is left on your plate. Or my food is that good. Hmmmm, let's go with the food is that good." He laughs out loud.

"It was all very delicious that is for sure." Katie responds.

"You know, I was looking at you from afar and I figured out why I've seen you before. A million years ago, you used to go out with an old friend of mine. He too was in the restaurant business. Guess you like guys who can cook. Have you had Samson's fish tacos yet? Even I can't duplicate them. If you want my opinion, you're much better off with Samson, that other guy, I think, well rumor has it anyway you aren't exactly his type if you catch my drift." He begins to walk away and whips back around.

"Katie, I'm sorry. Oh my god, I'm so sorry. You were the pregnant girl who came to the restaurant one day too. I saw the whole thing happen. I was the one who sent their father out there." He buckles down to his knees on the floor, his head hanging down. He can't believe he brought up the possibly worst part of her life, in public. He is not sure Samson even knows. Oh god, how can he ruin his friend's life like that. He can't get up. He can't face Samson. He stays down on the floor shaking his head.

Samson is the first one down next to his friend. He puts his arms around him. Thankfully, no one in the restaurant is paying attention. "Don't fret. I already know. Weird you remembered, she literally told me about this as we were eating. Jules, really, we're ok."

Jules looks up at his friend then up to Katie. "I'm so sorry. I never knew what happened to you. I went to check and your car was gone. I knew I should have helped but I was bullied by them into submission. That's when I left this town for a while. Didn't come back until I was grown enough not to care. Samson may not have told you I left for a while. Maybe he didn't know why himself. I'm a terrible wimp I suppose. Not backing you up. They still intimidate me when I see them at industry shows. But this has got to end. Katie are you strong enough, because I'm willing to back you up and I'm sure Samson has enough strength for ten of us." He looks to her for an answer.

"I don't see how that will help. My daughter is happy in her life, I don't want to upset her. She has great parents and never needs to know she was adopted. They may tell her at some point in her life, but we've all decided telling her is not necessary. I appreciate your honesty, and the fact that you sent out his father thinking he would help. He was going to kill me, or at least do some serious damage. Besides, with what Samson said to a few customers today, things may change for them anyway." She looks to Samson.

Katie begins to chuckle, "Do you realize what you said? You told people that they don't serve pretty women there. Do you know that that indicates? Can you imagine if their place becomes a gay hangout? Not that I have anything against gay people but they surely do. Oh my, that is the best revenge ever." She begins to laugh.

A laugh Samson hasn't heard in a long time. The three of them begin to laugh even harder. Only takes one stupid incident to have rumors start to spread. "All we have to do is feed the rumor, the rest will take care of itself." She says with confidence.

Jules stands up, and in a voice loud enough for all his patrons to hear he says, "What!!! You've got to be kidding me!!! Kramer's won't let pregnant woman in their establishment?" Katie shakes her head no. She looks around and sees everyone looking at her, she shrugs.

Satisfied, Jules walks back into the kitchen. One woman comes over the table, "Is it true?" she asks Katie.

"Well, I'm not pregnant even and when we went over their tonight, they told me I wasn't welcomed there. So, we came here, the food is much better here anyway." She smiles.

"Game, ...set..." Samson whispers and then pauses.

Another man comes by their table, "Excuse me, were you there tonight you said?"

"Yes sir." Samson answers, "Those were his words, he looked straight at my girl here and said she was not welcome there."

"I work for the Herald, are you willing to be interviewed about this?" he asked Katie.

"No, there is nothing to tell, it was all pretty simple." She answers

"And you're sure about this? This place should be picketed and I know the right group to do just that thing. Thank you for your insight. I will keep your name out of my report. Seems you've suffered enough embarrassment, you don't need publicity too." He says.

"I appreciate that." Katie answers with a smile.

As the man walks away, Samson says, "match". The two of them laugh for a moment.

Katie is once again solemn though. "I never realized people knew. Does that mean others knew? Does that mean people know I gave her away? If it comes out now they may want to go get her, find her....oh my god even take her!" her voice chokes, her tears falling freely now.

Samson grabs her and pulls her close. "Time to leave."

Jules comes running out to see them off. "I'm sorry Katie I started this whole mess. Oh, why can't I keep my mouth shut. Please, please say you forgive me. Please Katie I can't.."

She cuts him off, "I'm worried more about the fact that other people may know too. They knew it was their son's what if they try and get her now?" she shakes her head and leans into Samson.

"That won't happen, remember what Nat always says. Love is key. Oh man, the world is small isn't it. I'm sorry I burst out with the information. I'm usually really good about being discreet. I'm sorry for being such an ass. You were such a blast from the past, a moment in time I wanted to forget. I was young, not as young as you but young and stupid all the same." He continues.

"Me too Jules, me too. I am considered her Aunt Katie, she doesn't know the truth. I used to see her more often, now only holiday times. We decided the time is good now to fade me out at this point before she changes too much and possibly starts to look like my side of the family. This is for the best. She has a happy family. Three siblings now thanks to modern medicine." Katie's voice is soft, reserved. Samson notices that she is not 100% happy with this but knows what is best for the child to never think of herself as a mistake.

"Still Katie I'm sorry. Don't hold my mouth against me. Please come back to my place any time, with or without this big lug. My place is yours. I promise." Jules keeps talking but Katie has zoned out. How many people know? How many others has he been with? Was her boyfriend really gay? Is he? Did they plan this all along? So many questions have come back to her head now.

"Hello, are you listening?" Samson says and this shakes her out of her stupor again.

"No, I'm not. Can we go for a walk?" she asks quietly.

Jules hugs everyone and goes back inside. Samson walks with Katie in silence until they reach the end of the block and begin to walk back. He sees a bench and pulls her to sit down, again. "You do your best thinking on a bench don't you?" he smiles.

Katie lays her head on his shoulder and he puts his arm around her. "Why are you still here? You can leave me you know. I'll go back to my apartment. I'll stop by when no one is around to check on Nat. I can take my work to the next town over, or even further. I am not meant to be grounded anywhere. Time to move on, again." Her tears come without warning, sliding down her face and onto Samson's shirt. He can feel his shirt become wet, he feels her body shake with fear, he pulls her in tighter. "One day I'd like to show you what it means to be loved by a real man." He blurts out.

Katie cries a little longer, she hears him, she feels his heartbeat through his shirt beating faster as she cries harder. She is hurting him, she tries to take deep breaths but it's not working this time, she keeps crying. All her tears she has held in for years are coming out, tears for her lost parents, for her lost baby, for her loss of dignity, for all the losses in her life, and here stays a man promising her love and comfort. Too much at once, her mind, body and soul are not as one right now, she feels torn apart. Piece by broken piece she is falling apart. All from one misjudged night.

Slowly, she is bringing the three parts of herself back to being one. Her breath is slowing, her tears are drying up, her head has stopped spinning. What is left? Samson, he is still here, holding her, comforting her. Is this the love Nat has for his wife? Is she lucky enough to be blessed with such a thing after so much hatred and loss? Can't be, she is not worthy.

"Yes, yes you are my dear, you are worthy of this and more. If you'd only let me in." Samson says in a whisper.

He heard her thoughts, like his father. "Samson, why me?" she asks.

"Hard to say really, from the time we met I knew you were my other half, simple as that." He says.

Katie sits up and faces him now. She sees his eyes are watery, from watching her cry, her pain is his, her joy is his, her inhale is his exhale. Nat knows this for sure, this is why he could not say, he knew. "I don't know if I have it in me to give you all you deserve." She says quietly to him.

Samson pulls her in for their second kiss, this time, as much as the last one, is slow and deliberate. There is no mistaken his feelings right now, Katie realizes there is no mistake in hers either, she simply has to admit them to herself.

When the come apart and she is looking into his eyes again, she smiles, "Some dinner your brother gave us huh?"

"We need to tell them, at least part of the story. They need to know. Your history is part of who you are and that's ok with everyone, we don't care. Do you understand that now?" he asks.

"I'm beginning to. Let's go home." She says.

"Shared home? Or your apartment. I'm fine with either." He wants her to understand she can have her space if she needs it.

"Nat will be waiting, let's go home." She smiles.

~ ~ ~

Another month has gone by, Nat's progress is very slow but at least there is some. He is understanding more but his physical strides are not as great as everyone was hoping for. Even Bart seems to be disappointed. He can feed himself, and stand in the shower but the rest is still too hard. Thankfully, he has not given up hope.

His language has become better, but still slurred. So, at least he can communicate his thoughts better instead of trying to type them out on a computer, typing takes too long and sometimes he was losing his train of thought.

Cora and Kirk are over less and less as they see his progress as hitting an end. Bart has told everyone that sometimes, you only get a small portion back. This could be one of those cases, or it could be, he will take a long, long time and in that case, there is no reason for everyone to disrupt their lives permanently.

Jules has become a bigger part of their lives, sending over meals once a week. Katie and Jules have become friends, ignoring the reason their friendship started and appreciating the oddity of it all. "I have funny news to tell everyone tonight." Jules says as he sets the table for dinner for all of them. He does not use his delivery guy for them because he usually joins in on the dinner.

"Shoot" says Nat slowly.

"I had a customer come over yesterday to tell me he heard that Kramer's has been getting so much slack from protestors that they hardly have any business at all. Some regulars have stopped going because the protestors are still outside every day. They want the place shut down." He looks around the table.

"Wow, I wasn't expecting that. A little bad press yes, but shut down? They've been in business since their grandfather opened the place." Katie recalls.

"Yes, however, in digging deeper, that reporter who was at the restaurant a month ago, found out that they used to be an exclusive club. Only allowed members in, and in order to be a member you had to be recommended by three other members, a legal way of keeping out any ethnic type they didn't want, any religion they didn't want. For example,

Nat here could not have belonged being Jewish. Your neighbors, the Johnsons is their name I believe, couldn't join because of their skin color. Anyway, the bottom line is that even though we may have started the ball rolling, about damn time justice is served." He sits down, now that he placed all the food on the table.

Nat shakes his head, he is not happy about the whole ordeal. Samson and Katie came home and told him, Cora, Kirk and spouses all at the same time. They wanted everyone to hear firsthand. Kirk was very apologetic, almost to the point of tears. Katie had gained strength from sitting next to Samson and assured him that it's only hard because she suppressed the information for so long.

Sure, the adoptive parents of her child know because Katie felt that it was important that they know who the real father is in case of medical emergency down the line. His name is not written down, they keep the name in their heads though.

Nat is banging on the table and everyone watches him. "N,n,no." he said with trouble.

"No what Dad?" Samson asks.

"C,c,cannn't be. N,n,nissssss." Nat's face is frustrated because he can't get the words out.

Samson puts his hand on his father's shoulder. "Dad, calm down. We know they can show to be nice people. That doesn't mean they don't have a dark side. Dad, we don't know what goes on in someone else's mind. They may have been nice in the past, may even have saved a man's life before, who knows, but what we are dealing with right now is a group of people that knowingly allow their own children to break the law and do what they can to let them get away with doing what they do to save face. Dad, try to understand that part. For Katie ok?" Nat looks at his son, he looks over at Katie sitting next to Samson, where his wife told him she should be. A tear rolls down his cheek. His boy has become a man, he has found a woman like his wife.

Katie will be there for all of his life, he knows this in his heart.

"Don't cry Mr. Nat. We won't let anyone get hurt. I promise you that. They've been out there for a month already, the article ran the week after Katie spoke to the reporter. Protests have to die down soon. They will recover. A bump in the road for them, like all their other bumps. Only this one, maybe they won't forget." Jules tells him.

The knock at the door jars everyone from the conversation. Samson looks around at everyone and they all shrug their shoulders. No one is expecting anyone. Samson and Jules go to the door together and stand like bodyguards as the door opens.

"Mr. Kramer?" asks Jules.

Samson quickly establishes his position, "You're not welcome here." He says in his most authoritative voice and his stance gets even firmer.

Mr. Kramer tries to step inside, "Hello, are you listening?" Samson says.

"I need to speak to that tramp of yours, she has ruined my life, my family!! Come out here bitch!!" he calls to Katie. "Face your victim!!" He calls again.

Samson uses all his self control not plow this man into the ground. Nat stands up and pushes his chair out. Katie helps him up and walks him to the door. Jules pushes her behind him. He allows Nat to confront Mr. Kramer.

"N,n,n,no m,mmmmore!" he manages to yell.

Samson holds his father back. Mr. Kramer is fuming. He is trying to push Nat, but Nat is as strong as an ox right now. Katie feels lucky to be protected by these three men. She has a family now, parents, brothers and possibly a partner for life.

Quietly she dials 911 from the land line so that they can find the address without her talking. They operator hears the yelling from Mr. Kramer, the accusations, the threats to everyone's lives. Now all on tape. That' all she needs. The operator whispers – 'someone is on the way, stay on the line.'

Katie's heart is beating so fast she is afraid it will burst through her chest any second now. The sirens are heard quickly because, in this community, everyone knows Nat and if he is in trouble, they come running and running quickly. Not one, not two but three patrol cars pull into the driveway at the same time. Mr. Kramer spins around to see all of this going down. The color immediately drains from his face.

The first officer comes out of the car, "Nat!! you ok?" he calls to Nat.

"Nnnnnnno!" Nat calls back.

With that word, there were six patrol officers on the front porch, three with guns drawn on Mr. Kramer? "I'm unarmed." He says in a quivering voice.

"Put your hands up sir and walk down the stairs. The residents say there is a problem and you look to be the cause. I don't see anyone else. Unless there is someone in the car or someone around back." One officer says.

Mr. Kramer looks behind him and in front of him. This is not something he can talk his way out of, he realizes his mistake. Two of the officers run to the back of the house to make sure there is no one there. To their surprise they see two younger men. One with a club in his hand. "Freeze!" one of them yells.

Upon hearing this, two more of the officers run in the back from the other direction, two more men apprehend Mr. Kramer. Within what feels like seconds, the four officers are bringing Mr. Kramer's two sons to the front in handcuffs.

Katie swallows hard. She cannot believe they were going to try and use force to see them. "Sppppeak!" Nat says.

Mr. Kramer looks over at Nat, "Your little tramp is spreading rumors about us. She will pay!" Forgetting that his hands are cuffed and that they have been caught trying to break into the house in the back, Mr. Kramer continues. "She teases men, then ruins their lives. Watch yourself Nat!!!"

One of the officers starts to push him down to the patrol car, "You have the right to remain silent," he starts to read him his Miranda rights.

Mr. Kramer wiggles and calls over his shoulder, "This is not done!!!! I will ruin you!!!" The boys are quickly put into the other cars and Mr. Kramer and his family are carted off to the place that they have, until now, been able to avoid.

Nat is still shaking as they leave, Samson turns to Katie, "You ok?" he asks.

"I didn't talk on the phone, his rant is all recorded." Katie said quietly.

The four of them walk Nat to the couch. He is crying again. Samson sits next to his father, his arms around him. Katie speaks, "Its ok Nat. Really. You protected me like a father and I'm appreciative. I could not have asked for more from you. You still have a lot of gumption in you. Love is key. I see that now. Really, I do." She lays her hand on top of his on his lap.

Jules chimes in. "Come, let's eat dinner and tell really corny jokes, Nat has a million of them I'm sure. This chapter is done. Over." He smiles at everyone.

The phone rings in Samson's pocket. "What the hell happened? Mr. Johnson told me he saw three patrol cars come to the house." Samson looks at everyone. "Kirk, thankfully the neighbors are watching out for Nat." he turns to Katie and his father, "I'll be right back, start without me." He takes the call in another room.

Katie and Jules help Nat back to the table. The dinner starts in silence, then Nat, who has been working on his speech really hard lately, starts to say an old joke, Jules finishes this one. The three of them laugh. Jules and Katie look at each other, happy to be laughing again, to letting go.

Seeing Nat happy is worth everything.

~ ~ ~

Cora, Kirk and their families have come over. Nat's progress is still slow in his physical development, but his speech is getting less slurred, so the grandkids are able to understand him better now. They like playing on his computer to talk and Nat works hard to answer with his voice.

Today is Jules's birthday and they are surprising him with a special brunch, made by Nat and Samson. Jules has become a great asset to the family. He has taught Cora how to cook things she never thought she could on her own.

He allows Katie to display her artwork at the restaurant and she has received many more orders. Jules and Samson have had many private conversations, Katie doesn't interfere, she knows he needs a confidant, she still uses Nat for that. But when they are together, everything important eventually comes out between Katie and Samson.

The grandkids are running around Nat playing some sort of circle game, the adults are busy finishing this special brunch. The table is set, the balloons are all around and even the presents are set up in a nice way.

The doorbell rings and Katie runs to the door. She pulls it open quickly. "Happy birthday to me!!!" calls Jules as he steps in.

The entire house hears him and regardless of where they are, they are laughing. Katie brings him into the dining room and everyone yells "Surprise!!!"

Jules fights back some real tears. He sees everyone is there and then he sees the balloons and the presents. "Katie, I knew I couldn't go wrong having you as a friend." He smiles softly.

Everyone walks over with either hugs or kisses for Jules. He walks over to Samson and from his back pocket he pulls out a newspaper. "Best birthday present ever!!" he shows everyone the paper then lays it down on the table for everyone to see the front page.

"911 call records released to public. Former Restaurateur charged with aggravated assault and threats of murder."

Everyone around the table lets it all sink in. They had heard that after their arrest they had yet to be released but no one knew why. Kirk reads more out loud, "At the time of this report, as many as a dozen other businesses have come forward with evidence of the bullying tactics of the Kramer family. On top of this, fourteen women have come forward with claims of inappropriate behavior towards them while employed with the Kramer's restaurant."

Kirk looks around the room at each adult. "There could be other children." Katie said. She sits down. All of a sudden feeling the pit in her stomach growing into a tornado.

"Now, none of that. Not on my birthday girlfriend. We will celebrate the fact that justice will be served. Your situation will never come to light because none of us will say anything and we know you won't either. She is safe. Is that pancakes I smell? Let' eat!!" Jules is always good at changing the subject especially if food is involved, he never likes to stay serious for more than a minute or two. Breakfast ensues and everyone is enjoying themselves around the table.

Jules and Samson share a few silent eye conversations that no one notices except for Katie. She always knows what he is doing, even from another room. She has begun to feel his essence inside of her. They have shared a few kisses, since their first one and many hours of hugs. They even fell asleep on each other one night while helping Nat through a bad time.

Everyone cleans up from breakfast and Samson shoos them all out of his kitchen so he can prepare dessert. Katie walks into the kitchen to see if she can help, as she always does. Samson turns around before she is even in the room. "You ok honey?" he asks.

"Yeah, I never knew it was so far reaching but part of me feels like a closed door. I'm done with that part of my life. I had my final visit with my daughter last week. Turns out, her father received a job transfer and so they aren't around to see all of this come forward. Better for them that way. I've closed the door, I promise I have. I'm ok, are you?" she asks.

"Why would you ask that?" he asks.

"Because you and Jules have been secretly talking all morning. What's bothering you? Don't lie to me because I'll know." She smiles.

Samson stares at his beauty. It took her a long time to admit it but she is his and he knows in his heart and his mind. He has been given a gift. His father tells him this all the time. Jules comes running in, "I'll get dessert, you always take too long, bye, you two". He calls as he leaves the room with the tray of desserts.

"Come with me?" Samson extends his hand to Katie, she takes it and they walk outside to the backyard and sit down on the bench holding hands.

"Katie you are my rock star, you are my best girl, my one and only. I wish I was more eloquent with my words but I'm not. I have loved you since my father first brought you home the first time. You complete me, pardon the cliché, but you do." Samson pulls something out of his pocket, it's an old fashion looking box and Katie's heart jumps one more time around this man.

"Samson?" she asks slowly.

"This is my mother's ring. Dad says I'm supposed to give this to you. He said Mom told him to give it away to the right girl. At first, he thought it was for him but then when he met you, he realized how wrong he had been. The ring is yours if you'd like to wear it but there is a catch." He says.

"A catch you say?" she asks with a quiver in her voice.

"You'll have to wear it the rest of our lives together." He says with a smile. He is so nervous right now it's the first time Katie has ever heard his lisp.

Katie's hand is shaking as she puts it out to take the box. Samson takes her hand to steady her and he glides the ring onto her hand. "Is this a yes?" he smiles at her with a tear in his eye.

"Jules knew about this didn't he?" she asks.

"Jules has become a great friend, hard not to tell him. Best present I could give him he says. He made me promise to do this today. Shall we go inside?" he asks.

"No need." Katie says as she points to the smiling crowd who is running towards them.

Photo Shoot

Through tragedy a friendship emerges. Fear and self-worth prevent anything from developing though. Can Tanya and René see what is right in front of them? Will past scars continue to shine or can this friendship help them fade?

Tanya owes her life to René, literally, so when he calls and asks her to be a part of his photo shoot about strength in women, she could not deny him her time. Tanya does not think of herself as strong, she thinks of herself as lucky. Lucky René was there when he was so that she is alive today. Lucky the driver tried to swerve the car away instead of letting himself go head on. Lucky, she has an amazing boss who kept her on payroll despite all the time off she needed to recuperate. She does not have time to be sad or down on herself, she was given a second chance and she intends to live her life, her way. She does not take any day or anything that occurs to her anymore as happenstance.

  Her amazing boss granted her wish by letting her continue to work from home while she had been recovering from her accident. He brought the work to her apartment personally because he did not trust anyone else in keeping their mouths shut about who their clients are and why they need a lawyer. They have some very influential clients who would not want their dirty laundry leaked to any media or anyone for that matter. As far as anyone else is concerned she was on medical leave and only on leave not laid off as the rumors were beginning to indicate. Because her boss values her ethics and her work that he did what he did. René tells her all the time that this is one of her biggest strengths, people trust her.

  Her boss is a lawyer who values confidentiality on the top of his top list. When Tanya asked for work while at home to help keep her busy, he did not hesitate to work something out with her. He dropped by each day around 1:00pm and picked up the completed work on his way home from the office. Now that she is back in the office, all she hears are rumors floating around, she doesn't remember there being so many before. They all seem so trivial, one of them being that people think Tanya and her boss are having a hot and heavy affair, her boss is single so, she is not sure how it can be an affair. She makes a mental note to speak to her boss about the situation, make sure he is aware of what his office staff is talking about. "I guess this is why he can't seem to trust them to do sensitive work at home and for some of them even here in the office." She says out loud to no one in particular. How can you have staff members, you don't trust, deal with sensitive information about your clients? She wonders to herself.

Tanya shakes her head out of her stupor and continues to walk to René's studio. His studio is only about ten blocks from her office, she loves to take this walk on a nice day like today. The sun is not too hot, there is a slight breeze in the air every so often, enough to lift her hair but not enough to make her look messy.

Her phone rings in her pocket. Tanya stops walking and digs out her phone. "Hello." She says calmly as she recognizes the number being her boss's personal number.

"Hi yourself. I come back in the office and there are several folders on my desk that I handed you at the end of the day yesterday. Is there a problem with the files?" he asks with irritation in his voice.

"A problem? What makes you think there is a problem? You had asked me to verify some of the facts in each file. I did that. You had asked me to find the pictures that were missing from file B, I did that and inside the folder you will see where I found them because I took a picture of the places I found them in. I believe the final item you asked about was for me to compare file T with a previously won case from last year. All of the work is done. I took copies of everything that I made and I have put those copies back on your desk. The originals were put in a private and secure place. Have you found that I missed something? I was in the office past 10:00 pm last night getting through the last part of that." Tanya is never cross with her boss, but something in his tone upset her, almost accusatory. She hopes her tone doesn't sound too defensive.

"What are you saying? That you finished all that I had asked you to? I gave those to you at 3:00 yesterday afternoon." His voice a little softer this time.

"Well, I did tell you that I was there past 10:00pm last night. You said this information was urgent, and by the looks of the files and the dates in them, I realized you really needed answers right away. Each file I gave you back is sealed with clear tape, the kind I used while working from home so you could see the finished work and nothing was lost in transit. Seems like a good idea to continue using that system, so I did. If you are able to open them quickly, then there is a bigger problem for sure." She says with annoyance. That would mean someone opened the files and he is finding something missing.

"Hold on." He says.

Tanya hears some rustling about, she hears him moving, he drops the phone then she hears something slam, possibly his door to his office or maybe it was a book being thrown to a wall, "Damn it!!!!! Damn it !!!!!! Tanya where the hell are you?" his voice more frustrated than anything else.

"I'm on my way to René, you know I have this afternoon off to help him out. We spoke about this a week ago and then again yesterday, that's another one of the reasons I finished your work last night. What's wrong sir?" Tanya asks pensively.

Her boss lets out a deep breath, then he does the same thing again. As if he is taking a couple cleansing breaths before he speaks again. "Tanya, there is no tape on any of the folders. I picked each one up and examined them. There isn't even any rip marks where the tape would have been. Someone saw you put these on my desk, they opened them and replaced the folders. I knew there was a problem here, I knew it! Look, this is not your problem, I'm sorry I took my angst out on you. I have a staff that I can no longer trust. What am I to do?" he asks sounding defeated.

Tanya smiles, "Sir, you remember I said that the files I put on your desk were copies, do you not?" she asks.

"When did you...oh, you did say that. I'm sorry again. My mind is so full of anger right now I can't think straight. What does that have to do with anything?" he asks with another deep exhaled breath.

"I'm half way to René's studio right now, I'm sitting down on the bench near the old fashion shoppe, the one with the penny candies. Why don't you come here and I'll explain my madness. But leave angry so people know something is up. Oh, and before you walk out mumble loudly about needing to check all the drawers in the office. You'll understand when you get here." She finishes off in a very calming voice because she knows he is anything but calm.

"You are a puzzle to me Ms. Tanya but somehow I believe you and I'll do what you say. I'll be there in ten minutes." He disconnects quickly.

Tanya calls René and says she will be a few minutes late. He doesn't mind, he tells her he is running late himself, she hangs up relieved. As she waits for her boss, she is smiling, knowing that the trap has been set and they took the bait makes her feel good and actually kind of bad at the same time. Knowing that there are people in the office who are trying to sabotage her boss, makes her angry. Tanya is lost in thought when her boss sits down next to her with two bags of penny candies in his hands.

"Vanilla or Chocolate, I'll eat either." He says smiling. As he began walking, he realized that Tanya must have done something that could not be discussed in the office, and that could only mean, she is on his side and has done something to help him fish out the culprits, he is hoping anyway.

Tanya shakes out of her stupor yet again today, "Chocolate taffy is my favorite, if you don't mind." She responds.

"Good, I happen to enjoy vanilla more, now say what you know my friend, I know we aren't here on a social visit." He says.

"Ok, two things. One, I did finish your work last night, that much is true. I put the originals in the vault in your office. The one you have hidden behind the books. You showed me the vault shortly before the accident remember?" she asks for clarification.

"Ah, yes I did, didn't I. Silly of me, now that I know I can trust no one it's amazing that I even gave you that access. You know I haven't used the thing yet myself." He smiles.

"Yes, I do know because the plastic was still on the inside when I opened the door." She smiles at him.

Tanya continues, "Your original files are safe. So, here is what I found. The missing picture was found in Beatrice's top desk drawer. She didn't hide the evidence well, and I found the picture there completely by accident. I was looking for a permanent marker to mark the pictures I already had, I didn't think she would mind if I borrowed a pen from her desk. I know she uses them, so I opened the top drawer and there the pictures were. I took a picture of the drawer, you will find that in the vault too.

Then, being that I found something you have been looking for in her desk, I decided to check everyone's desk. Not very professional of me and I'm a little ashamed by that. However, I did find other missing items and more. Some of what I found are confidential names and phone numbers of your most prestigious clients. Those were found in one of the intern's desks. Mr. Lawry's paralegal even has his personal phone number and addressed taped to the inside of her desk drawer along with a picture of his kids. That's totally creepy to me. There for all to see on the side of her drawer, I didn't have to move a thing to these items.

The items you asked for were easy to find. I suppose that some of the people you have working for you have taken some liberties with the information they have been privy to. They also like to spread rumors by the way. There has been a lot of talk in the coffee room about the two of us having an affair, which is funny because you could almost be my father, no offense."

"None taken. Any other insights I should know about?" her boss asks cautiously.

"There have been rumors about Mr. Lawry's son being bribed in order to get information on his dad. There is a lot of gossip that I did not like hearing, especially since some of their nonsense involved me. We don't have to get into that, I'll deal with those myself. All of what I found is in your vault. I only removed the items that could be of danger if leaked. Otherwise, I merely took pictures for you and Mr. Lawry to see. Thank you for the taffy by the way." She says lifting the bag in a toast.

Her boss sits back with his hand molding his taffy into something else, he needs to punch something right now but squeezing the taffy is a close second. He tries to grasp all that she has told him. Sounds as if the majority of his staff and his partner's staff have been engaging in some very unethical behaviors and he has to deal with this the right way. "If you don't mind. I'm going to call Mr. Lawry now. Sit tight." Tanya crosses her legs, she was about to stand and leave when he said to sit. He takes out his phone and dials. He tells his partner what is going on.

Tanya waits with him, quietly eating her taffy. The first one she has had in a long time, and it tastes like heaven. What she did not tell her boss was that she also found pictures of herself in more than one desk drawer, both belonging to men. They were from when she was in college and on the cheerleading squad, she is not sure how they found them or why they were keeping them, but she is sure they won't have any more. She replaced them with pictures of an angry German Shepard with a talk bubble above his head saying, "I pity anybody who messes with my owner." She hopes she got her point across.

Tanya notices that her boss is shaking his head yes. "Does she have an explanation as to why it's there?" he asks.

Tanya doesn't hear the answer, however, her boss is shaking his head again. His eyes are closed, he is contemplating something. She recognizes that expression on his face. She looks down at her watch, already fifteen minutes later than she is supposed to be, Tanya starts to stand up again to indicate that she is ready to go, she points to her watch. Her boss grabs her hand, she stops.

"Tanya, Mr. Lawry wants to know why you are doing this? He says he thinks you want something." He says again in an accusatory way.

"Yes sir, he is right. I want a job. I like what I do as a fact checker for you and him. I enjoy solving the mysteries that it entails. What I don't enjoy is the badmouthing that everyone seems to be doing lately, and when the rumors became personal, I had to investigate for myself to make sure my name wasn't going to be smeared. I started off as a purely personal investigation and ended up being far more. If I overstepped my boundaries as a fact checker, I apologize for that, but not for finding out what I did. I hope, in time, you and he will think I did something good. Right now, I need to go to René." Those last words making her choke back tears.

She starts walking away, how could he think I had a different motive? She has always felt that Mr. Lawry never trusted her, now her boss has confirmed those feelings. She starts walking faster. She needs to get to the studio. There is a hand around her arm and she nearly jumps out of her skin. She turns around and sees her boss, a tear forming in his eyes and she doesn't think it's from the pollen in the air.

"Tanya, don't go like this. I had to ask you while he was still on the phone. He was burned very badly by his ex-wife. One of the things she had done was perpetuate lies and rumors in his previous office, this all happened before I signed on with him. He is old school, he would never have believed that his own staff is against him, some in creepier ways than others, I agree. He is holding his paralegal in his office he said until I get back.

    I have to go back now. Go, enjoy being with René, you deserve the time off. I'll go settle things in the office. What you did for us is far beyond the call of duty. I suppose we have both been so busy lately, that we lost track of what was in front of us." Her boss is visibly upset and he is not stating why.

    "Are you ok sir?" she asks.

    "Were you hurt? I mean by anything you found. Did you find anything that upset you because if you did, I'm not sure I can look at anyone in the face without beating them to the ground. You and I are like brother and sister, I take your protection personally. Sorry if that sounds creepy or out of bounds." He says.

    "No, not creepy. Flattering though. As I take my job very seriously. Yes, I found a couple of photos of myself. Some flattering, some not so flattering, with marker drawings on top of them. I'm ok. I got rid of them in the shredder." She says holding her bag a little bit tighter.

    His eyes following her grip, "No, you didn't, they are in your bag. But I won't pry. After all you've been through lately, you are the strongest person I know. No wonder René wants you in a photo shoot about strong women. Many men I know would have crumbled with the thought of having an artificial limb, but not you Tanya. You've made your prosthetic a statement piece. René saved you, and now you have saved me, at least professionally. I am indebted to you." He smiles and finally takes his hand from around her arm.

    Tanya watches as her boss takes a step back from her. "Maybe you and Mr. Lawry should look at the files in the vault before you speak to any more people in the office.

You'll have a better idea as to who is behind what. I'll see you tomorrow." She says as she starts to walk away.

"Ok if I call you later to tell you how things went?" her boss asks.

Tanya turns to smile at him, "That would be fine, thank you." She says.

~ ~ ~

Tanya walks into René's studio about half an hour after her appointed time. "Hello!" she calls in loudly as she walks towards the middle of the studio, already set up for the shoot. She hears a crash behind her and turns around quickly. From the look of things, René was carrying four or five cardboard boxes of equipment that are now all over the floor. "Let me help you clean this up. Why are you so jumpy?" she asks.

"Ah mon Cheri, it is you who makes me nervous. Your beauty overwhelms me." He says with a smile and a silly accent.

Tanya punches him in the shoulder playfully and bends over to help him clean up the mess. The two work together in harmony and finish in only a couple of minutes. Tanya tells René all about what happened in her office and how she feels partly responsible for some of these people who may be losing their jobs today.

"Ah, no. No fault but their own my dear. You did nothing but bring out the truth, which obviously they didn't hide so well. What crazy nonsense. Don't they know this will not look well on a resume? I know the men you work for and they are not too forgiving. Especially that Mr. Lawry, poor guy. His ex, well she knocked him clear out of his shoes with the stunts she pulled. Rumor is that the judge felt so bad for him during the trial that he made his decision to decide in Lawry's favor even if part of it wasn't warranted. In the end, the ex-wife barely got anything. The money for his kids is set up in a trust to make sure they actually get the money themselves and there is an account that he pays his alimony too that is monitored as well. The whole situation is messed up. His children all sided with him too. Last I heard, he is still fighting for full custody of his youngest one, who is the only one left at home." All this said in a manner so calm, she would have thought René was talking about some random person he heard about on the news.

"How do you know all of this my dear René?" she asks.

"I can't reveal my sources, but suffice it to say, I have a few in high places." He grins at her.

"René, the truth is, you are an encyclopedia of gossip in this town. Everyone knows you know everything there is to know. However, they don't know you like I do. They don't know that you really rarely share anything you hear, unless there is something to report to the police. So, let's get down to business, what kind of shoot does a woman have to do to be considered strong?" she asks.

René takes a deep breath. He has been wanting to photograph Tanya since the day he met her. She has been back to work already three months and many months before that since her accident happened. Might even be almost a year at this point or even more. But René, he is a patient person. For the right photos to come out and scream at you in a way that art does, the timing has to be right, otherwise the pictures come out looking crass.

He walks around to where he has the lighting out. He has placed cameras, some hidden, some not. All around a small area of his studio. He does not want to miss a single angle. The right angle can be missed, a perfect shot missed by simply standing in the wrong place. He is not sure he can get her do to this twice, so he is taking all he can today. His brother had shown him how to rig up four or more cameras to take a picture at the same time with the push of only one button. He tried this already five times this morning to see if he can make this idea work. It does, and he can't wait to start.

"René?" Tanya asks slowly this time.

René wiggles out of his thinking, "Ah, yes. Well, here is the thing. I bought for you a monochrome full body suit to put on. All white, actually off white, and I plan on taking the pictures against this black boxed background you see here. The body suit only covers you until your knee." He looks at her hoping she does not blow a gasket. He knows that even though her artificial limb is beautiful, it is still not the one she was born with, she may hate him for this.

Tanya contemplates the idea of being in a full bodysuit in any color. Against her red hair, this may turn out to be some crazy pictures. "René, do you have a rose I can hold in my mouth too?" she says only half joking.

René turns around in his studio and heads for a back room. When he comes back, he is holding on to the rose, dripping with water. "I received this bouquet only yesterday as a matter of fact."

"Ok, let's put the rose on the floor over there and I'll go get dressed. Where is the body suit? You did remember to get one large enough for my top half, right?" she grins.

"Tanya, my muse, there are three different kinds in the changing room. Pick the one that best suits you. I can't thank you enough. You don't know what this means to me." He puts his hands on his heart.

Tanya walks over and kisses René's cheek. "I will forever be indebted to you. This pales in comparison." Before he can rebuttal. She puts her finger on his lips and shakes her head no. Tanya walks slowly to the dressing room. More apprehensive about what she will look like in all white from head to toe than she is about having her prosthetic leg showing. Strange, she thinks.

The first body suit she puts on has three-quarter sleeves ending right past her elbow, a scoop neck and snaps that go between her legs. She puts on the white short pants that are there to complete the outfit, they are the length of nice walking shorts. So far, she has resisted looking in the mirror but she must, at least once, see what she looks like. The camera could make her appearance worse.

Slowly, she turns to see herself in the mirror. Not as bad as she thought she would be. Tanya's figure is average. She may be well endowed on the top but her behind is not proportionately sticking out so she always thinks she looks lopsided. "This is for René. You don't look awful; he could have picked much worse." She says to her own reflection.

Tanya doesn't even try on the other outfits, this one works well enough, so she goes with the first one. "All ready." She calls over to him as she enters the center of the photo shoot area. She sees multiple cameras all around her, the set is inside a black box like he said, so that any angle being taken will have a black background. Interesting, she thinks to herself. Tanya walks over and picks up the rose. She twirls it in her fingers while she tries to smell the beautiful fragrance at the same time.

René watches her and clicks the camera in his hand. Such simple beauty has to be caught. He walks around the room to make sure each camera took that picture. Satisfied, he calls to her, "So, let's get started.

"I want you to relax. Do what you want. No stiff posing this time. I want fluid movements. Can you be fluid?" he asks.

Tanya is not sure how she can be as smooth as he wants, so she thinks for a moment. "Yoga can look fluid, how about some poses? At least those poses are a place to start and you can tell me to stop any time you want. But I'm warning you, if I get in the zone, I may not hear you at all. Really, not at all." She says pointing to her ears.

"Yoga, requires music. I have that." René walks over to his music player and finds some music that would resemble what is heard during a yoga class. Relaxing. He plays this type of music when he is developing his pictures the old fashion way, helps him remain patient.

Tanya starts with a left-facing warrior pose, looking away from René because she doesn't want to see him looking at her. From there she moves easily into the right triangle pose. Tanya does her yoga breathing to get herself in the zone. Her positions are always better when her mind is free of distractions.

She brings her hand down and lifts one leg into downward dog pose, and smoothly adjusts herself into upward bow pose. This is a reminder of her gymnastic days back when she was ten. Then, the same position, was called a back bend.

~ ~ ~

Tanya remembers her days in gymnastics, she tried so hard; she practiced every night. Her instructor was encouraging and told her she could do whatever she wanted. He had told her that her body was primed for this sport. When the school year was over, she spent all summer practicing every movement she could find on gymnastics, she couldn't wait to get back to class in the fall.

The coach was as happy to see her as she was to see him. He challenged her constantly, he gave her harder and harder routines and she made each one look effortless. Each time she proved herself stronger and stronger. By the end of fifth grade, the instructor told her parents that she should start to consider competitions. He gave her a regime to follow for the summer months and told her to come back in the fall ready to compete.

Her parents were encouraging as well, they allowed her to miss family barbeques over the summer so she could practice more; her mom even began to do stretches with her every morning. Her father would spot her for the more difficult floor exercises. They covered a small area in her basement with non-slipping mats so she wouldn't get hurt.

Her summer went great. Her body was in tip top shape by the time the new school year was starting.

At the beginning of sixth grade, she had a whole routine ready for him that she had been working on herself. Her father had helped her perfect this routine. She needed to prove herself. Needed to show the coach she had what it took not only to compete but to go all the way in a competition.

~ ~ ~ ~

Tanya zones in on that old routine. She starts right where she is now, with a back bend. She walks her feet closer to her hands and lifts up one leg, very slowly, then she picks up the other leg. Her body is holding a ninety degree bend now with her legs hanging behind her, her toes pointing upward, supporting herself only on her hands and her will. She brings her legs up ever so slowly, always remaining in perfect control over where her body is, to a full headstand. Her legs fall away from each other in a full upside down split, one leg in front of her one behind her, they are completely straight, she holds her pose to the count of ten, that was how she used to train, Tanya brings her legs up again, trusting herself that she can hold her body in perfect form.

Now, she slowly bends them into another ninety degrees, only this time, her feet are pointing down, she holds this for a moment remembering her instructor's words about holding a pose meaning more than running through the motions. Holding on shows inner strength, he used to tell her. With complete control, she moves her legs down inch by inch, letting her core muscles take the burden of holding her up not her hands.

First, her toes reach the floor, she holds this for a moment, they are barely touching the floor; then she allows her feet to come down to the floor in a two-step process; first the balls of her feet, now her heels. She is completely folded in half now otherwise known as a forward bend yoga pose. Her hair is touching the floor, Tanya brings her chin in to touch her legs and hugs her ankles.

She drops her hands down slowly, vertebrate by vertebrate she raises her body up, half way up she extends her hands and the top half of her body out in one direction, her right leg in the opposite direction. Holding herself out again to the count of ten. To finish off, she lowers her leg and lifts her body continuing to keep her body in a straight line until she stands fully erect.

To complete the circuit, she slides easily into warrior pose but in the opposite direction as before. She opens her eyes as she feels the tears roll down her cheek.

Tanya collapses like a crumpled flower and the tears keep coming. She has not done this routine since then. How can a memory affect her so much?

~ ~ ~

How? She chastises herself. What do you mean how? Ugh, Tanya you're such an idiot!! She screams to herself in her mind. The memories of her routine may have helped her reach her zone but the memories of what happened the fall of sixth grade also came forward and the pain and hurt come crashing through all at once. So long ago!!! What is wrong with you?! She yells to herself.

Puberty hit early in the fall of sixth grade. Her body betrayed her, she developed a chest and a behind faster than you can even say the word puberty. Then the worse night of her entire existence happened, her instructor came to her house one night to discuss this new development, as he called it, with her parents.

Tanya had been hiding at the top of the stairs to see why he had made a private visit. She had been hoping this visit was about the upcoming competition. Instead, he told her parents that they need to stop this or she could no longer compete, he gave them names of doctors who would do this for them. That is when her world turned upside down. She looked down at herself and wondered what was wrong with her. She thought everyone was supposed to "sprout" as her mother said, when they got their period.

    Her father almost physically threw out her instructor for even thinking of such a barbaric act. He told him that he had better look for a different school to work in because he was going to file a suit against him if he didn't leave on his their house on his own at that moment. Her father said anyone willing to alter a young girl for competition should be sued for child abuse.

    In the end, she is who moved schools. Her father could no longer even look at the school knowing they allowed that man to work there for so many years. How many girls did he make alter their natural state? How many even went on to compete? That's when they moved to New York. Her father was lucky enough to be in demand in his field at the time and finding a new job did not take long, thankfully.

    She never went back to gymnastics, she never looked at her body the same either.

    ~ ~ ~

    René watches as Tanya starts, she is doing a pose he actually knows about. The next one too, however, he notices her face soon after these first couple of poses. She is slipping into the place where all yoga instructors want you to be. Her mind elsewhere, he sees her poses changing as well. The full control she has over her body that she is displaying is astounding, he can't click the camera fast enough.

    René knew about her gymnastics background only because she accidently let the information slip once, but he had never seen how beautiful she is doing this. Never seen anyone for that matter have this much total control over their body as she does right now. This is definitely going to show through in the photographs, one of the cameras will capture this strength from every angle.

After a while, René stands and approaches Tanya to get a few close ups, at this time, she is standing on one leg. He is sure that she does not realize that she has her full weight on her prosthetic leg. He continues to snap pictures.

He is more sure now, than ever before, that this will be the pinnacle of his collection. What better way is there of showing you have fully overcome your disability than by showing you have control of it and the disability does not have control of you. Through the lens, he only sees her strength. Through his heart he sees her beauty, today is hard to separate the two.

A piece of him swells with pride knowing she is here for him. As she stands up, René catches something different, though he is not sure he sees, so after he snaps the picture he looks again at the camera at the last picture, yes, that is a tear running down her face.

When he looks back at her over the lens, she is crumpled on the floor. René drops the camera and rushes to her side. He doesn't ask questions; he only holds her and rocks her in his arms until the tears stop and her breathing returns to a normal pattern. This takes some time, but he is not looking at his watch. He sheds a few tears of his own thinking that she must be in pain, that maybe he pushed her too soon. He berates himself in his thoughts for being so selfish.

Tanya is once again saved by the arms of René, she feels she owes him an explanation, but she is not always good with words of her own. For work, yes, but not on her own. "I need to explain." She says softly.

"No, you don't." he answers quietly.

"René, something from my past, not about you or this photo shoot. I promise." She brings herself to a sitting position and looks at him. Damn he is handsome, why doesn't he know this?

"Does it have to do with your zone? I noticed you were definitely somewhere else." he comments. She shakes her head. "Why don't you get changed, I'm sure you've had nothing else to eat besides that chocolate taffy you told me about earlier. I'm going to make some pizza upstairs. You know the way." He says to her, trying to give her time to think about if she really wants to say anything to him or not.

"Yes, I do. I'll be there in a few." Tanya gets up and walks over to the changing room. As she sits down to take off the pants, she rubs her prosthetic leg. She is not sure why it's so sore, but right now she could use some heat. She will get some upstairs. Good thing René lives above his studio, she does not think she could walk too far right now.

Since her accident, Tanya has spent a lot of time with René. They have impromptu lunches and sometimes even late night snacks when she is working late or he has a project he is working on. She has spent the night in his apartment because they talked till all hours of the night and she is too tired to go home.

He has spent a lot of time in her apartment as well, sometimes he takes her home late at night but then they talk even more and he is too tired to leave as well. Tanya spends a lot of time wondering if she cares for him because he saved her or because he is so damn good looking, both inside and out.

There is not a bad bone in his body. How can she allow herself to grow attached? With her mom long gone, she doesn't have anyone to talk to about this. She has a sister, two actually, but one of them hates men and the other is deep in puppy love right now and is hard to talk to about anything else. Her brothers won't understand either.

She has a couple of friends but her closest friend right now is upstairs waiting for her. She had better hurry. Tanya quickly gets changed, places her clothes in the hamper René leaves in the changing room and meanders upstairs. Even though she knows the door is open, she knocks on his door anyway.

René pulls it open with zest, "Ah what a beautiful guest I have. Shall I invite her in?" he smiles.

"Yes," Tanya says pushing past him. "MMM, how do you make pizza so fast from scratch?" she asks.

"Old family recipe, and I always keep at least four pizza doughs in the freezer and two in the fridge at all times. What? You never know who will show up?" he says as he walks towards the kitchen.

Tanya follows him and sits down at the table. She begins talking before he asks and while his back is to her so she doesn't have to face the humiliation again.

René keeps finding things to do at the counter because he knows she does not want to face him. What is confusing him the most is that right now he feels his fists ball up as if he wants to go punch the old instructor and teach him about treating people nicely. He spent his whole childhood not being treated well because of who his parents were, he vowed to never be like all those people he encountered. But right now, he really could punch that man. Why is this confusing? Because, he should not be feeling all these emotions when it comes to Tanya, they are plutonic friends. Aren't they?

Then he begins to smile, and even laugh out loud as he turns to face Tanya. She is looking quite sad at his laughter so he tries to speak through his guffaws. "Can you picture your instructor's face should he see these pictures in a gallery? I mean really, you not only proved him wrong, you did those poses with such finesse he will fall over. You exude strength and power in your poses. You do not need to compete in anything to show the world how wonderful you are. Just be you." His laughter subsides by the time he finishes. His voice soft and endearing to her.

"René, I'm not sure that man is capable of seeing any strength beyond his own bellybutton. But seeing him be in shock over this would be a nice revenge tis true, although I don't hold my breath. I'm sorry I lost control. I'm not sure why though, I suppose because I haven't done that routine since that day." She adds. She rubs her leg unconsciously.

"That routine? You mean to tell me what I saw was *the* routine you had worked on so many years ago? You gave that to me? Me? But why?" René's voice chokes on that thought. He sits down slowly in the chair across from Tanya.

He looks at her in a way he never has before, or maybe he has and he is only recognizing now how he should look at her. The woman in front of him is very special to him but how can he know for sure? How does he know these feelings are not because of all the care he has given her since the accident?

Tanya reaches across the table and holds René's hand. Softly, she rubs her thumb across his knuckles a couple of times. "Because you gave me a piece of you when I had the accident, I wanted to give you a piece of me back." She says still holding his hand.

René takes a deep breath and exhales slowly. He looks at Tanya, beautiful Tanya, in the eyes. He cannot bring her into his world of shame. She must stay in the world of beauty where she belongs. No, this feeling must be because he saved her and knew her at her most vulnerable. This is caring for a friend, nothing more. He tells himself.

The oven buzzer rings and René is thankful for a reason to get up. "By the way, I gave you nothing. I merely tried to pull you out of the way of a car is all." He tries to say matter-of-factly.

Tanya stands up quickly and gets to René before he opens the oven. She pulls on his shoulder and twists him around quickly to face her. "You could have been killed if you pulled me in the other direction, both of us would have been. You somehow had the foresight to know where to go and DON'T you tell me you didn't think about it. I heard you speak to the EMT that day. I know better. You gave me something I can't pay back! Ever!! Don't deny what you did, don't make less than it was!" her voice getting louder. Tanya's breathing is getting faster and her head is spinning. How could he belittle what he did for me?

René is shaking inside right now. She heard me talk to the EMT? Then she knows.... "You heard all of my conversation?" he says hesitantly. This makes René very uncomfortable, if she knows that conversation, then she knows something not only personal but humiliating about him as well.

Tanya puts her hand down from René's shoulder, her own shoulders sagging now, suddenly, they feel very heavy. She takes a step back, René is staring but not at her, he is deep in thought. To distract him she says, "I'm hungry, take out that pizza before you burn my vegetables." She tries to stay firm but she is smiling at the thought of his pizza. Artesian style crust, fresh toppings.

René shakes his head and turns back to the oven. He is no longer hungry, but he serves his guest and enjoys watching her eat and enjoy his cooking. There is so much more to her than her inner beauty. He can get lost in her but he can't allow something to happen between them, he can't. He must talk to his brother.

~ ~ ~

After their pizza, René seems disjointed, as if his mind really isn't with him. This is why she makes an excuse to leave shortly after she finishes eating. On the way home though, she realizes that he knows so much about her because she is always having to explain something about her behavior and usually has to do with her past. True, the decision to disclose is hers, still she seems to do this with him too often.

Walking further, Tanya's leg starts to hurt again, she completely forgot to ask René for ice or a heating pad. She is halfway home already though, she decides the best thing is to keep going on. Tanya goes over the whole conversation she had with René today. Part of her feels very guilty about yelling at him. Today is the first time she ever verbalized what he had done for her. Also, the first time he tried to play down what he had done. So many times he refers to that day as life altering, now he says he did nothing. Tanya's heart hurts, her leg hurts more and her head is in so many places she can't begin to focus.

What does she know about René? She asks herself. Not much. She knows he is not an only child but how many siblings he has is an unknown factor. She knows he compares his parents to the old nursery rhyme of the old lady who lived in a shoe. So many children and not knowing what to do with them and something about sending them to bed without any dinner. Weird comparison. He doesn't speak about his father, ever.

Somehow, they all made it through childhood and have found great professions to be in. He has two brothers that both became accountants because they always had amazing math skills. His baby sister is finishing college now, coming out with a teaching certification and a degree in English. He has made some references to another brother and possibly another sister or step-sister, she can't be sure.

She has seen one family photo in his upstairs apartment but she is convinced not everyone is in there, and the one of the siblings in his studio he always tells her is a partial family picture. He has made his hobby into a very successful career. But that's all she knows about René. She is not even sure his age, although he swears they are only five years apart, she has never seen proof.

The honking of a car horn nearly knocks Tanya off her feet. She is usually so good about paying attention and not getting distracted while walking on the sidewalks since her accident. She scans the area quickly and realizes that the driver at the red light is honking at the car in front of him.

Nearly a year ago, one car was driving at speeds uncharacteristic of city driving when he lost control and drove on to the sidewalk. René's quick thinking in pulling her out of the way and the direction he pulled her, resulted in her losing only the bottom half of one leg as opposed to her whole life, which is what they said would have happened had she continued to walk in the path she was headed. The EMT also told René that had he been coming from the other side and pulled her instead of pushed her, they both would have lost their lives. So many small factors attributed to him being there and doing the right thing, all those pieces were in the right place.

Tanya remembers a lot more than people think she does from that day. She doesn't talk about her memories because no one needs to know what's in her nightmares. She doesn't tell anyone that she looked up from where she was pinned, which was in René's arms, and she saw the driver saying "damn it, damn it, damn it" as he hit the steering wheel; that she saw four other people taking pictures of the accident, none of them reporters, and that the fire fighter that released her from her pinned position was actually cursing under his breath as he saw the carnage that used to be her leg. She never told anyone that she knows that René needed to speak to the EMT about needing to change his pants before going to the hospital. She heard the EMT tell him, "Listen man, if you didn't I would think there is something wrong with you. You saved this woman's life for sure and put your own in danger at the same time. But I've got your back don't worry, there are extra scrubs in the bus."

She remembers the conversations of the two women who were closest to the accident, one of them said she is happy that she walks slowly or she would have been with the redhead pinned by the car. Her friend responded that she would not have been because she would have easily pulled her away from the car. Then they looked at Tanya in the face and cringed. In fact, most of the faces she saw that day had the same look on them. Including the driver.

Tanya's worst memories are of her looking down at herself and seeing the blood but not feeling any pain. As if what she was seeing was all part of someone else, not her. The sirens were loud, the whistles of the police getting people to move were loud as well. The old man from the penny candy shoppe came running out to her, he had tears in his eyes and he promised her she would be ok. He promised her she will always be welcomed in his store. For some reason, right now she also remembers that he leaned down to kiss her forehead and stayed there until the firemen had her on the gurney.

Tanya sits down on the steps to the bank and contemplates her memories. René came into the ambulance with her and kept talking to her about fun things to remember. Flying kites, going on a canoe with a good friend, curling up with a friend on the couch and watching a funny movie. All things the two of them have done since the accident. She remembers the EMT telling her that she is probably in shock which is why the pain hasn't kicked in yet. He told her he gave her pain meds in the IV because he was sure she needed them. He checked her vitals all the time and kept reporting about her leg's condition on the phone. The ride was both long and short at the same time.

René stayed with her at the hospital until her father showed up and one of her brothers. Then he left the room. She found out later, though, that he never really left. He was in the waiting room the whole time she was in the operating room.

His was the first face, not the face of family that she saw when she first awoke. He was there for the all the news from the doctor too. Her father began to think he was her boyfriend and spoke to the doctors freely in front of him. René knew all of what was going on before she did. He is the one who gave the news to her straight, her father could not tell her about her leg without breaking down.

René helped her father and brother deal with the news, he was the one to call her sisters to ask them to come down to the hospital. He called where Tanya worked and let them know what had happened as well. He used her own phone and contacted everyone in it to say she had been in an accident and would not be in touch for a while.

René has done all that he could to help her afterwards too. He comes with her to physical therapy still. In fact, he is the one who found the guy who designs prosthetics limbs into pieces of artwork to help a person cope with their new reality. Her leg no longer looks like a stump with an attachment that reaches the floor, she has a beautifully created prosthetic made of the sturdiest of metals available in a beautiful, one of a kind, filigree design from top to bottom. She has noticed it makes people less uncomfortable when they see her in a skirt.

Tears run down her face for the second time today. She owes René so much more than what she gave him today. A silly old gymnastics routine, she should not have reacted the way she did. René must think she is a complete basket case, how can he see those pictures as strength? There is nothing she can do that will accomplish the same thing for him. Her feelings for him are all over the place, is this love? Is her heart full of admiration? A simple feeling of gratitude extraordinaire confused with the fact that he is the most handsome man she knows or has ever known?

Her phone rings and she picks up mindlessly, "Hello" she says with a catch in her throat.

"Tanya? Where are you right now?" her boss asks calmly.

"I'm sitting on the steps by the old bank contemplating how lucky I am to ever have met René. Why?" she says in a sigh, too tired to deal with office drama now.

"Don't move." He says.

She has no intention. She hangs up and waits for him to show up. Rubbing her leg from the strain she unknowingly put herself through, her tears keep rolling.

Tanya's boss runs up to her as soon as he sees her. He puts out his hand, "Come on, it's time to get you home." She stands without even knowing she is standing. A full on stupor has taken her over. She moves through a cloud into a car with her boss and he directs the driver where to go. He brings her up to her apartment in the same fog she came into the car with. Never letting go of her for fear she may fall over.

Her boss opens the door to her apartment and leads her in. She stops in her tracks as he closes the door. He leads her further and brings her over to the couch in the living room. She lays her head on the arm of the chair and curls up into fetal position there, her eyes close quickly. He looks around to find a blanket and covers her up.

He will wait this out. He can't leave her in this state.

~ ~ ~

The smell of something cooking wakes Tanya. She blinks her eyes a few times and tries to orient herself as to where she is. The last thing she remembers is sitting outside by the bank. She sits up quickly and takes in her surroundings as if she is a frightened animal.

"Good evening." Her boss says to her. Her head turns towards him and he smiles, "You've been sleeping for a little over three hours, I haven't eaten since that candy we shared so I decided to cook some dinner. Would you like to share?" he asks cautiously, noticing her fear.

"What?" she asks.

Her boss tells her how he picked her up earlier in what he refers to as a catatonic state and he is happy to say it was him who found her, another person would have or could have taken advantage of her with the way she was. He is happy to report she came home and slept but he is concerned as to why she keeps rubbing on her leg and wincing, even in her sleep.

"I'm not sure, I don't remember doing much today except working with René." She says quietly, her brain still a bit foggy.

"I hope you don't mind, but I called René from your phone and asked him what you did today. He mentioned something that didn't make sense to me but might to you, something about being on one leg during a pose for close to thirty seconds or more he wasn't sure of the timing." He says in a questioning way.

"Oh, that makes sense now," her mind clearer now, "I was doing some yoga poses, I was in my do not disturb zone and I must have carelessly been on the wrong leg. I'm surprised this held me up. Happy, but surprised. I should put some heat or ice on myself. Maybe I'll take a pain reliever first." Tanya finishes talking and attempts to get up from the couch.

"Whoa there, you stay seated, I'll bring you what you need. Do you want food too?" he asks.

"I had pizza with René. I'm not hungry." She answers.

"I'm sure that was hours ago my dear. Which means you were sitting outside for a lot longer than I had assumed." He says as he walks to her bathroom to find some pain reliever for her to take.

Tanya contemplates what he has said, she sees her phone on the coffee table and reaches for it. She sends René a text and asks what time she left his studio. He quickly texts back to her that she left a little after 4:00. Then he asks if everything is ok.

She writes back, *I apparently lost track of half the afternoon. My boss picked me up, he is here with me now. I'm ok. We should talk. Lunch tomorrow?*

René writes back *I have a lot of appointments this week, can we postpone meeting a day or so?* He is not sure he can see her tomorrow. She brought back a memory that he did not want to revisit. She now knows what a wimp he is, she heard everything she told him. Everything is far too much. Her beauty needs to stay in her world, he says for the second time to himself. She does not need to be privy to his mess. René feels he may have to pull away a bit to sort this out, the best thing in the end, for her anyway.

Tanya's boss walks back to her with a glass of milk and her pills. She looks at him and says, "Apparently, René says I left a little after 4:00, so it wasn't so bad after all." She says as she takes the glass from him and the pills.

Her boss brings over a plate for her to eat and one for himself. He sits across from her on the loveseat and says, "Want to talk about what put you there? Bad memories? The accident?" he asks lovingly.

Tanya starts to explain for the second time today what had happened to her when she was younger, but then she said more, she spoke to him about what and why she feels for René. She asks for his advice and if he thinks it's false or true feelings.

"I suppose even a portion of that could put someone in the catatonic state that you were in and all of that? For certain, however, what has me worried is that you can even get into that state and not know where you are. You had no idea I brought you home. That worries me a lot more that your feelings for René." He states in a concerned voice.

"My biggest fault. My gymnastics instructor used to yell at me all the time about zoning out, when actually I was zoning in. Inwards that is. I would concentrate so hard I would not hear him until I was done. I've been doing this my whole life. I suppose it's a miracle I wasn't hit by a car earlier in life." Tanya looks down at her plate and realizes she must have been hungry after all, because the plate is empty. "Thank you for cooking. I happen to love garlic noodles."

"Bachelorhood teaches you how to cook, or you don't eat and I hate most restaurant food. I wanted to tell you what happened at the office today. You up to hearing some of my drama? Take your mind away from where it's been all day," he smiles. Tanya nods to him.

"First of all, when I got back to the office, Lawry did not have security anywhere, he did, however, have the girl in his office. Sitting silently there, by the time I walked in she was so nervous she sweat through both her shirt and her sweater.

We asked her to empty her purse in front of us to make sure she was not hiding anything else there. Lawry took her phone to make sure no texts or pictures were there that shouldn't be; there were ten pictures of clients taken from their visits in the office. Not hidden or anything. He told her he was going to keep the phone, and she should consider it a gift because he wasn't going to bring charges against her. He then told her to stand up and walk out of the office, not to return, and he watched her go from his doorway. She barely kept herself together as she passed the others.

Then, we went into my office and looked at the files you put in the safe, like you suggested. Tape was still on those by the way. We spent time looking at all the pictures you took of the information you found. Lawry was ready to call the police, but I told him not to, even though technically he probably could. Instead he put on what some people call his court face but I know to be his drill sergeant face and walks out of the office and calls out, 'Atennnntion!' Everyone stopped in their tracks, the worst offenders scrambled to their feet. Tanya guesses the names and the two of them laugh for a minute.

"Then, continuing with that voice Lawry says, 'This is a search and rescue mission, all phones on the desk, all bodies on the east wall.' Everyone looked around the room, Patrick went straight to the east wall." He smiles

Tanya thinks of Patrick as a younger cousin, he is a great kid with tremendous potential. He came in to the office one day asking to meet with the two head lawyers, he told them he has not gone to college yet, not because he can't but because he doesn't want to. He promised them one hundred percent of himself if they gave him a job. They decided to take him on and have been pleasantly surprised ever since. The boy knows how to fact check, he knows how to get people on the phone and he happens to be particularly good at putting clients at ease. She once heard the two lawyers talking about his potential and how they are going to try and convince him to take night or on-line classes for fun and eventually get him a degree.

"I noticed the intern looked as if he was quivering so I walked up behind him and asked, what am I to find if I go in your desk?" his voice rough from remembering how angry he was when he said those words. He stands and paces the room a minute, Tanya watches him for a minute and then says, "He was worried you'd find his porn?" she asks with a laugh in her throat.

"Worse, I knew he had that, we all did. Made us laugh. But this was no laughing matter, his porn is there as a ruse. To keep us from looking underneath. No, so much more than porn. He had files pertaining to Lawry's divorce in the bottom of his drawer, he is spying for his wife. Even though things are final." He says with his head down. He has been beating himself up all day about this, he is the one who pushed to accept this guy over the other intern.

Tanya walks over to him. "Lawry find out?" she asks.

"No, I told the kid he could get disbarred for that even before his certification was broken in. Conflict of interest and all that, besides the completely unethical part. I took the file and ran the whole thing through the shredder, I didn't even want to know what was there. I told him, if he has anything at home about Lawry, he had better cough it up or I will bring him to the board of ethics. He practically pissed on himself running out of the room.

When the dust settled, there was Lawry, myself and Patrick left in the office. Lawry looked defeated. We decided then and there that the four of us will be all there is for a long while."

Tanya watches her boss and for the first time in a really long time, she addresses him by his first name, "Parker, I'm sorry. I can't imagine having to clean house like that all at once. Who will take Junior's clients? There was that woman who applied, she would have been my pick." She says calmly.

"Lawry said the same thing, I think he may have already called her. Give me your dish." He says and brings the dishes to the kitchen and begins to clean up the mess he made.

Tanya follows him into the kitchen and sits down on one of the bar stools. "Seriously, been an emotional day for all of us but can you answer me one thing? Did I do the wrong thing?" she asks.

Parker turns around, "As your boss, and as your friend I would say you did all the right things today, including working with René. I know you're a bit sore physically but you'll be ok. As for the other question you asked? I'm not sure I can quantify your feelings the way you're asking me to.

People feel they love the person who saved them, but you two became fast friends along the way. In the beginning René appeared to be more of a caretaker but now, you guys appear to be the closest of friends. If you're not sure, maybe take a break. Blame the office, with the loss of people you may be very busy in the next couple of weeks anyway. If it feels ok to be without him, then you know you have a strong friendship and nothing more. I'm only guessing. As you can see, I've been a bachelor most of my life. Hard for me to give advice." He says honestly.

"You chose to be a bachelor because you don't want to feel pain again. Pretty dumb reason if you ask me. You're a very nice looking man and you have a lot to offer someone. I have been told that it is definitely possible to find love more than once. Don't sell yourself short." Tanya speaks in a soft voice because she knows how hard and raw his emotions are since his wife died. They did not have a chance to have children, so it left him completely alone.

"Tanya, you are wise beyond your years and here you are asking me for advice?" he smiles.

"I looked at René today when we were on the floor, feeling him hold me again didn't bring back the accident at all this time, it felt good all by itself. He smiles at me with ghosts behind his eyes though. Do you know anything about him? His past? Even how old he is?" she asks.

"I know some, but I'm not sure he would want me talking about him. Although his age is no secret, he is about five years older than you, even though he may appear to be a lot more. Life does that to a person." He says.

"Oh, then I need to speak to him directly. Really speak to him for a change. Thank you for today by the way. I'm sure I would have recovered on my own, I generally do. Thinking about my old instructor and the words he said to my parents was the catalyst of everything. I could not believe it was said then and the words still puts me in a tailspin, obviously." Tanya looks down at her hands, she finds she can't face Parker now.

He finishes with the dishes and sits down across from her, "Tanya, my dear friend, we have a funny relationship, don't we? I'm your boss but I feel I'm your personal protector and your friend first. If I could go back in time, I would knock that man for a loop and ask questions afterwards. He would not have been able to physically stand up during the trial, the judge would have understood." He smiles.

Tanya laughs, "I think that is what René was thinking when I told him the story too. I saw his fists ball up only he doesn't know I saw him because I did not say anything to him. I don't want to lose him Parker, I can't." Tanya allows one tear to roll down her cheek.

Parker watches and takes a deep breath before he responds, "Your feelings are real, the question really is what to do about them. How about we wait a week, let's let everyone figure things out this week and make plans to get together over the weekend, today is only Tuesday, and it may take you that long to dig out of the mess at work anyway. By then you will need a distraction." He watches the pain in her face.

"Your leg?" he asks

Tanya looks up at him, "Throbs once in a while anyway. I think I'm going to shower and head to bed. We have a lot to do tomorrow, I'll be in early." She says as she gets up.

Parker walks around the counter and grabs his briefcase he had brought with him. "Good idea. I'll see you in the morning then." He puts his hand on her shoulder, she pats his hand.

"I'll be ok. I promise." She assures him. He smiles and leaves the apartment.

~ ~ ~

René has been pacing his loft for the past two hours. Why did Parker call him? Why hasn't he called back? Is Tanya ok? She sent a text but it was a weird question. What should he do? His pacing gets faster than slower. First, it is back and forth then the next thing you know he is literally running circles around his studio to burn off this energy.

Finally, he sits down in the middle of the photo shoot set up from earlier in the day. He sits and looks around the whole room. René decides to burry himself in his work. This photo montage is going to be too valuable to mess up. He cannot worry about how Tanya is, she will be fine, he assures himself.

Once the decision has been made, René becomes a man on a mission and hits his own zone. He walks from one camera to the next gathering the films or the digital cards from within the cameras. He takes down the black screen that was the backdrop for the shoot and he plugs in his computer to the white screen left behind.

He sits and watches the digital pictures come to life before him. He flips through each set of pictures with continued awe. He has chosen his subject well, this gallery of pictures needs special attention. René decides he will need the expertise of one of his brothers, with a deep breath he calls JoJo.

"I have the perfect project for you. Us, really." JoJo left the house long before René did even though he is younger than him. He took himself out of the garbage and came out smelling like roses. JoJo has a passion for beauty and is very artistic. He became one of the most sought after set designers this side of the Mississippi. "We will take this to the top, this I assure you. I have everything here; woman, strength, beauty, fluidity, overcoming obstacles, you name it, I've hit this one out of the ballpark I swear to you. I need your expertise though, the display has to be done perfectly or it won't do this montage justice. Can you come by tomorrow?" he asks his brother.

JoJo starts to laugh, "I haven't spoken to you in six months and the first thing you have to say is to ramble on about a photo shoot? What's so special about this one? I'm sure the pictures are cute but really now, René, we've been down this road before." JoJo tried to build the perfect display piece for René before and not only did he fail the pictures, but the critiques had said the display was shabby work. Good thing JoJo never put his name on that one.

René looks down at his computer and forwards the first four pictures from this camera and then four more, and more to complete her routine. Some were taken from her right side, some head on and some the back. "I'm sending you a few, let me know what you think. There are a hundred and fifty-four more to sift through. I am required to produce fifty for this upcoming gallery contest. Winner takes all this time. And when I say all I mean ALL." He says dragging out the last word.

"Hold on, came through on my phone, let me look." JoJo takes the phone from his ear and opens the file his brother sent him. No one in their family made their way through real college, each of them has made a name for themselves but more based on a skill they know well. JoJo has been building with almost any kind of medium since he and René were pre-teens. René always took a photo of the before and after of all the pieces JoJo restored that they found on garage sales and they sold them to other stores or other people.

JoJo finds himself staring at one of the pictures, "Whoa, René is this the girl you saved?" he asks.

"How did you know?" René asks

"I see her prosthetic, amazing work done on that. You told me she had an artist make one for her. You are not kidding that you can see both her inner and outer strength in these pictures. Ok, I'll come by the studio to go through the photos but we should call Audrey too. She has a better eye for compilations than I do." JoJo says.

"JoJo, I haven't talked to her in a very long time. She kicked me out and I've never looked back." Audrey was René's first live-in girlfriend. They were together for three years in their late teens when he needed a sounding board to get him past his family life.

JoJo and René are the only two siblings who actually speak to one another once in a while. The others send texts here and there to say they are still around. He knows everything about René's relationship with Audrey too. She told him. They went out for a while after René left. He has never told his brother this. However, the two of them are still good friends. "She is married now with children René, but she still has a great eye for the details that you and I sometimes miss. You know I'm right." He says.

René answers with, "The day I left when she spit in my face and told me what a loser I was and a disappointment to our mother. A woman she never knew. JoJo, I'm six years older than you and twelve years older than our baby sister. I'm the only one who remembers our mother. I'm also the only one who remembers Audrey's hatred towards a family she didn't know. I can't call her. If you need her as a consultant, you call her." His voice being harsh now. René sits down, he does not want to fight this out now.

JoJo hears his brother loud and clear. "I never knew that man. I dated her afterwards for a short time and never knew. I never told you because it was brief. She met her husband months later and has been living happily ever after since. I still talk to her, we are friends. But if you say no, I can respect a no." JoJo realizes afterwards what he let slip. Quickly he adds, "René, I will respect you on this. I'm sorry I brought her up. That was not fair. I didn't know. I really didn't know." He says softly.

René is the one who bailed JoJo out of jail during his teen years. René again who took the rap and almost went to jail because of their baby sister's bad decisions at a frat party. René carries a lot of burden with him. Their accountant brothers, the only ones who went to some form of traditional college, have always acted like twins even though they are years apart. They regard René with caution because the only mother they knew is the one that kicked him out, their father's second wife.

Theirs is not an unusual family but they each have their share of baggage and JoJo is convinced that this is why

René never lets himself get too close to someone. They may find out his family history. They may find out he has flaws. Who knows? JoJo wants him happy. Maybe this redhead is something he needs to look into, for his brother's sake.

    René tries to control his voice from sounding angry, he needs his brother's expertise here more than he needs a brother, "Ok. I understand why you said her name, but don't bring her up again. I only had one mother, she decided to play god and take her own life, I don't need another woman who thinks she can make life judgements for me too. We'll leave the conversation end at that. Garlic pizza is yours. I'll see you tomorrow then." René hangs up, clenching his teeth down and trying not to scream bloody murder.

    He looks around and on the screen before him is Tanya, big as life itself. Tanya in the beginning of her routine, the one she gave to him. Watching her go through this again and again is the only thing that calms him down right now. He sits on the floor and watches the slide show over and over again.

    René does not know how long he has been sitting on the floor, there is a strange buzzing sound that brings him around to look away from the screen. He gets up and walks to where he left his phone. He missed three phone calls and four texts, all from Tanya.

    Checking in to let you know I'm ok.

    Thought you might have been worried that Parker called you.

    Guess not, ok.

    They let most of the staff go at work, I'll be pretty busy this week, can I reserve some time with you over the weekend, we really need to talk.

    René is happy that she wrote what she did, he finds himself taking a deep breath and exhaling out of relief. He sends a quick message back, although she might be asleep by now, he notices that her last text came in at 10:00pm.

I will be working with JoJo on this project. He is my brother. When the weekend gets closer, I'll let you know. Glad you are well ☺

René drags himself upstairs, time for sleep. He suddenly feels overwhelmed and groggy.

~ ~ ~

JoJo and René have been feverishly working on the picking out the perfect photos for the gallery contest. This is no ordinary contest, you had to be asked to participate number one. And two, you were given a topic of their choosing. The winner will have their photos up in a national gallery for a full year. JoJo keeps commenting on how all of the pictures are near perfect, how René really captured every angle of her strength, they need to put their heads together to come up with the perfect display.

On their third day together JoJo finally screams, "René!!" from down in the studio. René comes running down from the loft. "I sent this photo to our math head brothers; their reaction was amazing. I have received five texts from each of them telling me how perfect the picture is, how perfect her pose is, how the concentration on her face shows the ability to conquer all. Do you know which picture I sent?" he finally comes up for air.

René responds by shrugging his shoulders, he has no real connection with his brothers. "Guess, come on, please." JoJo pleads like a small child.

"Ok, the one where she is holding herself up by her prosthetic leg." He says calmly.

JoJo looks surprised that he guessed the right one. "How did you know?" he asks perplexed.

"Because that one photo answers all the guidelines, strength personified. But I can't let the other pictures go without recognition. This is a whole routine, don't you see that?" he asks a bit irritated.

"Of course I can see that, anyone can. But you also said that we have to pick one out as a feature. Does Tanya have to sign off on these pictures for you to put them on public display?" JoJo asks.

René runs his hands through his hair, he is not sure. He quickly walks to his desk and rummages around for the official letter from the organization running the contest. When he finds the letter, he sits down and reads the whole thing.

Turning to JoJo, he says, "Yes, we do." Softly.

JoJo watches his brother, his heart pulling. "René, you are allowed to feel for this girl, woman, sorry. I've been watching you look through these photos for three days. I look at my wife the way you look at Tanya. You are in awe, and you feel drawn to her. Listen brother, don't let this one go. You may not get another Tanya in your life. Call her. I'm going to call my Zelda and ask her to come down. I don't know why I didn't think of her earlier, she is far better than, well than anyone else I may have mentioned in these past three days. This is a winner man, a definite winner. We're taking this to the top, I can assure you." He walks away to call Zelda.

JoJo explains the pictures to his wife and she says she will bring dinner down to them, she doesn't want to wait until tomorrow to see this. They talk for a few minutes more to throw around ideas, JoJo is kicking himself for ever mentioning Audrey.

René sends Tanya a text, *turns out I need your signature to display these in the contest. Any chance I can bribe you with pizza for dinner to come down and sign off on them?*

~ ~ ~

Tanya's week has not been as bad as expected. At least the work that was done was done correctly and she has been able to clean up and have all her papers prepared on time each day. Patrick has been a tremendous help as well. He loves this work and is grateful for having more to do.

The other intern called on the second day to make sure none of the lawyers were there, he brought over all the papers he had on Mr. Lawry. He apologized and said he was leaving town for a job in another state.

Mr. Lawry even brought her an ice cream shake as a thank you and as an I'm sorry all at the same time. She accepted the drink happily. The decision to have a new intern has been tabled for a while. The four of them have quickly formed a new rhythm of working that has been running very smoothly.

Tanya hears her phone chime, she knows the ring is René because she gave his number a specific ringtone for identification. She reads her text. Her heart beats a bit faster, the idea of seeing him tonight lit a spark inside her that she is not expecting. A smile forms on her face unknowingly.

"Go see him." Parker is standing at her desk smiling. "No one else makes you smile like that. Go see René. You have your answer now." His smiling never leaving his face.

"I have to sign off on being used for the contest is all." She says holding her phone up to him.

"We won't need you past 5:00pm today. Tell him you will come then. Oh, and Tanya, enjoy your evening." Parker walks away still smiling. *Parker says I can leave here at 5:00pm today. Is that too early?*

René writes back quickly, *it's good, I need time to make a fresh batch of dough anyway.*

That's strange, why would he need new dough? He always has some in his freezer and only a couple days ago he had four in there. Tanya wonders who he has been cooking pizza for. None of my business, she says to herself. But the pit in her stomach is not agreeing. Tanya muddles over this the rest of the afternoon. By the time she leaves for the studio, she is full-blown worried. Maybe there is another woman in his life and he really only wants to see her to sign papers. Her walking speeds up without her really noticing, she gets to the studio half out of breath.

She swings the door open and walks in so quickly she almost runs into another man standing in the studio. Quickly, she sidesteps to avoid a full frontal collision. "You must be Tanya, I'll get my brother." JoJo says to her.

"René!! Your muse is here." He calls to him.

"This is my lovely wife Zelda, she is here as a creative consultant. I'm JoJo." He puts out his hand to shake Tanya's.

Tanya is still a bit put off, then she sees René come down from the loft and her world is righted again. He sees her and stops on the steps a minute. She is the most beautiful thing he has ever seen. Even though he has been staring at her picture for the past four days, she is to him, almost intimidatingly beautiful.

René walks over to his desk to grab the papers, he fumbles with them a couple of times. Zelda walks over to him and puts her hand on his back. She whispers, "This is love René, its ok to feel. I promise and love even looks good on you." She smiles. René looks up at her and tries not to grin but is having a hard time.

The four of them spend the next couple of hours eating pizza that René made and the pasta that Zelda picked up on the way over. Tanya has answers to many of her questions about who René is. JoJo even confirmed René is only five years older than her which makes her one year older than JoJo.

René had brought the papers upstairs with him and finally brought them to the table to have Tanya sign. She looks over the papers for a minute or two, occupational hazard. "René, you do know that you have to have these papers in by Monday, which means you have to send this overnight first thing tomorrow morning. And that the rest of the project is due the following Monday. Can you finish building by then?" She asks JoJo.

"That's the problem Tanya, we haven't decided on what that display will be." JoJo answers her

"How about you make one of those old fashion movie circles. I don't remember what they are called, but you used to look through a hole and spin the wheel, on the inside the series of pictures were made to look as if they were moving but you were really seeing sequential pictures taken. Like a flip book. Don't look at me that way, am I the only one who knows what a flip book is?" she asks.

JoJo jumps up and gives her a hug and a kiss on the forehead, "I'm on this. René come with me before the hardware store closes." He grabs his brother and they rush down the stairs from the loft and out the studio in seconds.

Zelda says softly, "René told us about the routine. I hope you don't mind that we know the back story to the shoot."

"No, I suppose my story sounds pretty silly, no?" Tanya is a bit embarrassed knowing that this person knows she broke down after the shoot.

"Not at all, Tanya we all have back stories. René and JoJo probably have a few more than necessary but I love them both for who they are now not then. To tell you the truth one look into those eyes and I probably would have loved JoJo then too, don't tell him though, we don't want him to get a swelled ego." Zelda giggles at herself. Tanya smiles at her. She likes getting to know René's family.

"We had a very basic relationship, I wasn't too close with either of my parents, what about you?" Tanya asks.

"Me? Inseparable with my dad, Mom and I didn't get along too well after I hit fifteen. Two older brothers and two younger ones." Zelda answers

"Is there anything I should know about René that is important?" Tanya asks shyly.

"Everything about René is important to know. Including the fact that he is ticklish behind his ears. JoJo teases him relentlessly about that one. Talk to him Tanya, he will open up when he is ready. He is afraid is all. Let's clean up here before they get back. I have a feeling we will all be using power tools within the hour. Do you have clothes to change into? The work will definitely get messy downstairs." Zelda finishes as she walks into the kitchen with the dishes. Tanya follows with her hands full too.

They clean together in silence and go downstairs to disassemble the studio and get the room ready to be turned into a workshop. "The boys work well together, but they have a tendency to get on each other's nerves as the same time. Our job to distract them during those discussions. A small kiss on the cheek usually foils all their anger, its great fun. Are you game?" Zelda asks her.

Tanya is about to respond when the brothers walk in, carrying all kinds of wood, different colors, different grades and shapes. Plastic, tubing and a variety of other items Tanya doesn't immediately recognize. "Ooooo, this is going to be a long one" Zelda says to her with a smile.

~ ~ ~

Tanya cannot believe that only a few short days ago, she was buried in sawdust helping to create a photo shoot display that is like no other. René's brother is amazingly talented like René, kind, giving, creative, and great in the kitchen. Once the two brothers got started, the energy was contagious. Zelda and Tanya were doomed to catch the rhythm.

They spent the whole night working up ideas and then the whole weekend putting everything all together. Last night they moved the whole thing to the museum for the judging tomorrow. René and JoJo worked meticulously in setting up so everyone who walks in will enjoy the series for what it is, one routine. Zelda decided the simple title of, "Strength".

There is the large spinning view that makes the viewer feel as if they are watching a movie of her routine. There are the group shots of one move from different angles, there are also about a dozen or so different single shots that René played with the coloring on. A couple in sepia, one or two in black and white and even a couple that look like old negatives. Those are Tanya's favorite.

The display in full is quite a site. Took her a while to see past the fact that she was looking at herself. Most of the pictures don't show her face because of the way her body is positioned and the fact that she did not put her hair up. "The title says it all", Zelda told her.

Now, as she gets dressed this morning in a simple blue dress with tiny yellow flowers, sensible shoes yet stylish ones. She puts her hair up and leaves a few tendrils hanging out on the sides. Her stomach is so nervous. She is going as René's girlfriend.

He officially asked her to be his girlfriend one night when they were both exhausted in the studio and JoJo and Zelda had left to sleep at their home. Tanya couldn't believe her ears. He asked her flat out then leaned over and gave her the most tender of kisses she has ever experienced. Since then, there has been many more tender moments shared. Each one a new surge of love inside her and a new connection between them.

Today is the highlight of her life. She notified her family and most of them said they will show up to see her. René actually called all of his siblings and many of them said they would show up to this pinnacle of his career as he has referred to this display. JoJo keeps teasing him that they are actually coming to meet Tanya, the pictures are an excuse.

The brothers have been getting along really well with this project. Given them both a little hope that they can actually become a family again. Tanya and Zelda get along really well and that is helping a lot too.

René is truly happy today; he has his best work out there for the world to see. He has the best girl next to him and his brother JoJo is back in his life. Things could not get any better. The only thing he is nervous about is meeting Tanya's family again. The first time they met was the day of her accident so he is hoping they don't associate the two for the rest of his life, because he is pretty sure this will be a relationship for the rest of his life.

~ ~ ~

The crowd pours into the museum. The advertising for this has been all over social media as well as print media. The curator has already calculated that today is the best turnout since they have started this contest ten years ago. He has been back to René's display already four times and it is only 11:00am. The contest voting is all day.

There are five rooms with photos from photographers from all over the country. One of them used a lot of advanced techniques in lighting and shading but his pictures don't appear to be as strong to Tanya as René's are.

The one woman in the contest decided to photograph only animals. Many of those are stunning but she doesn't see the strength that the requirements called for. Tanya is truly biased, however, there is one other that she feels has tackled the requirements as well as René. Zelda and Tanya have walked around the museum already a few times. Each time they come back to René's display, they see more and more people. They are hoping more people means more votes. Fifty percent of the voting is by viewers, the other is from the judges.

With the day almost over, René grabs Tanya from behind and slides his hands around her stomach, he puts his mouth to her ear and says, "Look to your left my love. Over by your backend pose." He holds on to her as she turns her head to see her parents looking at her pictures.

"They like the display René, they like you too, you know." She says.

"Wrong picture, keep looking a little more to the left." He whispers

Tanya looks at René's eyes and follows them across the room. She finds JoJo standing next to an older looking man, hunched over a bit with very little grey hair left.

Recognition hits her and she freezes. She goes stiff and René feels her, he holds her in tighter, "JoJo contacted him. He personally wanted to be the one to spit in his face. Once JoJo likes someone, he becomes the protector from all things evil. Yes, that is him Tanya, your old instructor, your parents saw him and chose to ignore him. JoJo can't. He is taking full pleasure in rubbing his face in your abilities like a person does to a dog who is house training."

Tanya finally exhales. She does not know how long she held her breath for, but as usual, René is right there holding her. Zelda comes up next to them. "I was with JoJo when he was investigating your instructor online. Turns out he never did produce an Olympian, before or after you. Only got himself to the nationals three times and his girls never placed. Oh, and the piece of info that was best. He was forced to retire when three girls brought him up on charges of abuse. Thought you might want to know. Should you choose to approach him, go with the knowledge you are the winner here."

Tanya turns to her new friend and gives her a tight hug. "Welcome to the family" Zelda whispers. The thought of that made Tanya's stomach flip and flop. The idea is a crazy one, yet exciting at the same time. Why would she say this to her; Tanya thinks to herself.

Wiping a tear from her face, she holds firmly onto René's hand and walks over to her old instructor. "Good afternoon sir, I hope you are enjoying the exhibit." She says with a strong, confident voice.

The old man turns to face her, takes him a moment to register who she is, but it is certainly hard to forget her eyes and that hair. However, before he can answer the bell rings in the museum. The curator began to speak, "Attention everyone. Thank you all for coming. The votes have been tallied and without further ado, I'd like to announce the winner of this year's contest."

"Marry me Tanya, that is all the award I need." René whispers into Tanya's ear from behind her, his hands clasped around hers sliding a ring onto her finger. She grips his hands tight and holds both of his hands in hers against her stomach. Words escape her as the curator continues.

"With great pleasure that I announce that we have had more voters this year than ever before. Our panel of judges have conferred with an almost unanimous vote of our participants. Join me in congratulating René and Tanya!" He begins to clap.

The whole room bursts into clapping and everyone is looking for them, finally the spot light finds them and the entire museum sees the artist and his muse, he is holding on to her, bending her over backwards and kissing her. The museum goes wild, JoJo and Zelda are both shedding tears of joy that René is happy.

The clapping continues until they finally stand up at which time JoJo pushes them up to accept the award, they did not even hear they won.

The Cottage

Caitlin has built a business for herself with a little help from her father. She has never taken any time to discover herself until she is given an assignment by a mystery client. In the course of one day, Caitlin's world will change dramatically, forever.

Caitlin takes pride in her work. She started off as an interior decorator and has since advanced her knowledge and career into something even bigger. She has become, what she likes to call, a business transformer. Residential decorating never held her interest for very long. Caitlin doesn't only look at the aesthetics of a place of business, she also spends time getting to know the people who work there, how and why the facility is run the way it is. Over the past ten years she has saved more than fifty restaurants alone by investigating their facilities and their inner workings. Her first degree is in interior design, her masters degree, however, is in business management. She has made herself a very successful career by learning to combine these two careers. So far, she has discovered she is part of a very small profession which is better for her, more work.

The first restaurant she worked for was a mom-and-pop shop downtown. A small place that was barely floating financially who desperately needed her help. Once Caitlin pointed out the cash flow problems and offered some solutions, she worked on the restaurant structure and redecorated the main room to become what the proprietors wanted in the first place. Three years later, they called her back to help open their second restaurant. From there, they have referred almost everyone they know who has a business to contact Caitlin for a consultation. After that, she has not needed to spend much on advertising, word-of-mouth is the best advertising there is.

Caitlin's dad is a chief financial officer of a large firm, from him she was already taught a lot of the bookkeeping/business concepts before she took her first masters' course. He gives her some pointers throughout each of her ventures and they have all paid off. When Caitlin consults with her dad professionally, she pays him for his services. Although he hates her doing this, he understands why she is, she writes it off as a business expense. Usually, he turns around and donates the money; it's not as if he needs hers, but for her own business practices he respects her not treating him differently because he is family. Makes him feel good that his daughter has come to him and he can't lie, he likes seeing the fire in her eyes on a new project. But as far as her personal life goes, he doesn't much care for that part of her. He tries to be supportive but at this point in her life she feels the only relationship she has with him is professional.

  Today she is going to visit a little-known resort near the mountains about an hour and half from the city. Caitlin always does her research before she goes to any new location; she found this resort has been around for forty-five years and seems to be doing well, however, the client told her he wants her to check things out because he thinks someone is padding the books somewhere, that it can't be doing so well without an active website or aggressive advertisement campaign. She doesn't have the heart to tell him that she doesn't do much advertising herself and she is very successful. Well, successful enough for her, she only has to care for herself right now. This client said he can no longer trust the manager there. His instructions to her are for Caitlin to go to the business and talk with the people, find out what is really going on, and then he'll get the full story from her afterwards.

  This is the first time she has not met with the client in person. The whole transaction took place over the phone. Even the contract was signed and scanned back to her and then the hard copy was sent via regular mail. She called her dad about this one first and he said it's normal to have an unknown insider do this type of investigation, no one knows you so they won't suspect anything. He told her to keep her eyes and ears open for anything out of the ordinary and write everything down after she speaks with people. If something is going on, she will find that something, he told her. This vote of confidence from her father really helps her get into the spirit of this job. This is the only place where she and her father see eye to eye. Professionally, never personal.

Caitlin likes to drive to places on her own, she doesn't like to rely on public transportation or even a cab. Sometimes she has even made comments to the business owners about what she has seen or not seen in the drive to their establishment. The drive up to this place is easy on the eye and on her car. The roads are all paved and there are fences with vines growing on them at various points on both sides of the road. She was afraid that the roads would be half gravel up here this far from the main city roads, thankfully they are not.

As she finds the address, she pulls in to a very nicely manicured parking lot and is instantly amazed to see such beautiful buildings. There are at least four edifices, but she is only interested in one right now, the restaurant. Her research showed these grounds were once used as an old hospital, now the buildings have been turned into a restaurant/bed and breakfast. That is the only information she could find on this place. Caitlin parks to the side of the restaurant and makes her way inside. She is greeted by May, a beautiful young lady with a flower in her hair. May brings her to a back table, as per her request. "Thank you May, I'll let you know if I need anything."

"What do you mean, if? This is a restaurant, I'm assuming you came to eat. No?"

"Actually, I came to observe the place. I'm doing some research on bed and breakfasts." Caitlin almost forgot that no one knew she was coming. Damn, she really didn't want to blow this one so fast. The owner promised a bonus at the end if he was satisfied with what she reported back.

"Well, there's a nip in the air outside, why don't I bring you one of our signature soups?" May is pretty persistent but in a friendly way. Caitlin likes her.

"What kind of soup do you have?" Caitlin loves soup, always is her go-to food.

"First off there is the traditional chicken soup, then we have the chicken vegetable, the regular vegetable, the cream of broccoli, and there is always the chef's surprise. We serve them in a cup or in a bowl with breadsticks. So, what will it be?" May is standing, ready to take her order and the smile never leaves her face.

"What is the chef's surprise?" Caitlin asks tentatively.

"Actually," May starts "not sure about today's but it's creamy and has a garlic taste to it." Then she bends down and whispers, "To tell you the truth I think the chef uses all the produce that is not as good anymore and makes something magical. There are never two surprises that are the same. The other waiters and I always order one bowl and pay for it with our tips, then we taste it ourselves so we can honestly tell our customers what the surprise is. Smart huh?" May stands back up with a proud smile.

"I'm not much of a garlic fan, so thanks for telling me that part. I'll go with the chicken/vegetable, but only a cup please."

"Coming right up. But I warn you, you'll be asking for more." May saunters away with her head held high. She walks briskly to the counter to turn in Caitlin's order, then she meanders over to check on the other tables. This is the first time Caitlin notices that in the few minutes she has been here, all the tables have filled up. Each table being attended to by the courteous wait staff, all of whom have smiles on their faces, as do the customers they speak with. Caitlin waits another few minutes, and looks around with her discerning eyes and notes again that there is not one unhappy-looking person in the room. What a strange affect this place has on people. Probably all that city living has jaded her about how people can actually be happy for the sake of life itself. She could certainly get used to a place like this, maybe she can convince the proprietor to open one up in the city.

When her soup arrives, May serves the cup with a smile and warns her again about wanting that second cup or even a bowl. She leaves behind a menu for Caitlin to look at, which is a good thing because you can't fully process a place unless you at least see their wares. Caitlin takes some time to study the menu, which it is quite extensive. Next to some of the dishes is a strange footnote, reading, *"please indicate if you want Chef Lorainne or the Chef Bob."* She is certainly going to have to ask what that is all about.

    Caitlin looks back around the room again and sees the place abuzz. The wait staff is quite attentive to each and every table, each customer has left with a smile on their face and the atmosphere here is slightly shy of perfect. At first you realize that each table is set up with enough space around it to make the customers feel as if they are alone and not in a room with a hundred strangers. Second, the customer sees that each table has its own lamp and one does not have to rely on room lighting to see the menu or each other. The air smells clean, not perfumed. The wait staff cleans off the table with wet cloths so as not to spray cleaner everywhere to get in the way of someone's taste buds, that is certainly something you don't see in her city. Caitlin assumes that all the chairs feel the same as the one she is sitting on, and while it is not cushioned, the molding of the seat is very comfortable. What could the proprietor want to change? This is going to be hard to analyze. Caitlin figures the real problems are going to show up when she tries to look at the books, but how is she going to get to that? The only way she can think of is to speak directly with her client.

    May is headed her way and Caitlin is still organizing her thoughts, she is caught off guard when May places the most delicious looking sandwich down in front of her. "No one can work this long on only a cup of soup. Here is one of our most popular sandwiches, a Chef Bob specialty."

    Ah, perfect segue. "May, why do they have two chefs here? I've studied other bed and breakfasts and never heard of that before," Caitlin says.

May laughs, "Oh, honey you must not be from these parts. Everyone here knows who the chefs are. They are the most sought-after couple you can find behind a stove. Each a master chef in his or her own right, but they argue sometimes over how something is made – some people prefer one chef and some the other – they are ordered equally so the battle continues. Some people come back and order the same item but from the other chef and then tell us how they can't decide, so they keep taking turns as to which one they want that day. Lorraine and Bob have been here for about ten years together. They were married here right out on the terrace there." May points to the back courtyard with fondness. As if lost in a memory for a second; she sighs; she shakes her head and turns back to Caitlin. "Sorry, my dear, thinking. If you're really not hungry I'll take the sandwich away, I merely thought...."

"No worries, May, I hadn't realized I was hungry until you showed me this amazing looking sandwich. It can stay. Oh, and May...." She calls after her before she leaves.

"Can I speak to Mr. Bennet now? He is expecting me." May looks at her very unsurely and then eases away from the table as if Caitlin asked for a ghost. She regains her step as she turns around and leaves for the back of the store. Caitlin watches her; May is not going to the kitchen area, but instead walks through a different set of doors, possibly to the bed-and-breakfast part of the building.

Meanwhile, Caitlin takes a bite of her sandwich. As she begins to chew her mouth waters even more. The mixture of cheeses and grilled vegetables is tantalizing in her mouth. What is that sauce in here? Hmmmmm. She has never tasted anything like this sandwich. Wow, what could the other foods taste like? The soup was good, too, but this? This is flavor sensationalism. The only other thing that gave her mouth so much pleasure was her old beau. Nah, not even him, this is far better, thinks Caitlin. Then she laughs at herself. Out loud apparently because she hears a voice and looks up.

"Are you the one looking for Mr. Bennet?" Caitlin keeps looking up, this man must be at least 6'8", and his eyes are the kind of green that reminds her of a fresh meadow. She shakes her head and swallows. She starts to stand up and put her hand out to shake his but he sits instead and motions for her to do the same.

Caitlin takes the napkin to her mouth and wipes herself off before she begins speaking. She swallows one more time and takes a drink. "This sandwich is amazing, and this place is incredible, I have to be honest sir, I'm not sure what you would want me to change."

"Change? I don't know what you're talking about. I don't want anything changed here. What I do want though is to know who you think Mr. Bennet is and why are you looking for him?"

This man, looking at her with all the seriousness of a funeral home director, scares the confidence right out of her. "Sir, I'm Caitlin, the one Mr. Bennet contacted about making some changes here, he told me that he no longer could trust ... excuse me, that he wanted me to look into the whole operation." By the time she finishes, Caitlin's voice is cracking. The man's eyes never move, not even one iota. They are staring right through her, she isn't even sure he is breathing, certainly she isn't. Only she isn't sure if it is from the intimidation she feels or if there is something else in those eyes. She is being pulled in by them more every second. Intimidating has gone out, mesmerizing is more like the effect.

He starts to laugh, not any laugh, but a big, hearty belly laugh. May looks over at him and starts to laugh as well. He waves her on and she leaves with a smile. Caitlin is now more self-conscious than she ever has before. "Did I say something funny?" her shaky voice asks.

"Do you have any paper that *Mr. Bennet* signed?" He puts his fingers in quotation marks as he says Mr. Bennet.

"As a matter of fact, yes, I do." She pulls out the papers from her briefcase as proof and hands the contract to him firmly, and a bit annoyed now.

"I'm afraid you've been sent here under false pretenses Ms. Caitlin. There is no Mr. Bennet, never was." He explains.

Caitlin feels her blood rise to her cheeks; she is popping mad. 'I drove all the way out here on a ruse? Is he kidding me?' she thinks to herself. Her fists close around her briefcase but before she bursts out of the room, the man puts his gentle hand on hers, "Why don't you finish your sandwich, on the house, and I'll explain what I think may have happened here ok?"

His hand is smooth and warm, his eyes suggesting truth. Caitlin takes a deep breath and looks back down at the plate; she really did want to enjoy all of that. She slowly picks up the sandwich and he begins to talk.

"Bennet and Marcy Lowenbrow were married fifty years ago, next month. They bought this place for a song with the help of Bennet's uncle, also named Bennet. They had a dream, and Uncle Bennet had the money. Together they made lemonade, as they used to tell us. This place was run-down and broken; they painted all the rooms themselves, had friends re-do the electrical and the plastering wherever it was necessary. They also built two small cottages for the families to live in. This became a community effort. Those friends who helped them never paid for a meal here, ever. Even after they could all pay for themselves. That was the way it was. They did not come from a very religious home but some traditions they kept... always" He looks up lost in a memory for a moment before he continues.

"For example, giving back ten percent to the community in order to remind yourself that what you have is a gift and was not only from your hard work alone but there was always the hand of god in there somewhere. We give back, three hundred and sixty-five days in a year means thirty-six days are given away each year.

"In the spring we have a ten-day retreat for a battered women's shelter. They bring their children. The place is closed off to the public during that time, and these women get pampered like socialites. We hire extra masseuse and beauticians so that each one of them gets a chance to be pampered. The kids are free to roam around the grounds, we put guards around the whole area so this whole place becomes a safe retreat for everyone. There is a second ten-day retreat for families that have children with special needs of any kind; some of them have terminal illnesses, others birth defects. All come here to enjoy some together-time, away from hospitals and therapists.

That leaves a few weekends here and there that are given to various religious groups and non-profits. All in all, we give back and we get paid in triple afterward. Many of these people tell their friends who don't need the free weekend about what a great time they had and how they were treated, and so we get booked without even having to think. Word of mouth is the best advertisement." (Caitlin looks up, where had she heard that phrase before? Oh my, yesterday she said those very words to Mr. Bennet, alleged Mr. Bennet that is.) He pauses a moment again to think about how much he wants to tell her, but since he knows his brother is involved, he feels the whole truth is best. He continues.

"Marcy and Bennet had five children, raised three to adulthood. The youngest is Chef Lorraine. She always had a penchant for food and it certainly shows here. When the kids come, she makes the most creative food items you could ever see. Pancakes in all shapes and sizes, bread that looks like origami, we all have fun during that week.

There is the middle son, that's the one who probably called you. He is always trying to prove to us that this place has no future. He is not exactly the outdoors type, and even as a kid, tried to get our parents to sell this place and move somewhere 'normal', as he would say. I guess this is his last attempt. He figured if a professional tells us this place has no chance, that we would listen. Either that, or you're a reporter that he wanted me to meet and get some advertisement.

So now you have the story for either answer." He is watching this woman in front of him soak up every word he is saying. She is listening so intently it almost makes him uncomfortable but then she smiles and his heart skips a beat. 'Odd' he thinks to himself.

While Caitlin's sandwich is keeping her happy, her heart rate is beating faster and her hands are beginning to clench down on the bread as if she is trying to crush a can. "Whoa there, trying to kill the sandwich won't help you at all." He jests.

Caitlin looks down at the mess she has made, not of the sandwich but of herself. Her idea of opening one in the city flew out of her mind. Why would anyone want to sell this place? Money, it has to be, it's always about money.

"How much debt has your brother gotten himself in that he needs you to sell this place so desperately?" Caitlin knows her word choice is a cheap shot but she has spent an entire week on this place doing research, and she intends to get answers *and* to get paid. Definitely to get paid.

There is that laughter again. "I'm sorry Ms., debt you say? My brother can buy and sell this place ten times over if he wants to. He is a novelist who has had four best sellers and two movies deals in his lifetime already. No, he is not worried about money, he has bad memories here and every time he wants to see us, well, we both live here in the extended wings and he hates to come here. He would give anything to not have to come back here again-- ever.

Speaking of money though, he must owe you something for the time you've spent doing whatever it is he hired you for. But before I pay you, can I at least give you a tour of the place? Considering you traveled all this way. I promise you'll be happy with what you see. You might even see something that we can improve on, we are always open to helpful suggestions, but selling wouldn't be one of them. Never selling."

He stands up and holds his hand out to Caitlin. With all that anger inside her, one look at him and she can't maintain the same level, he is going to pay her, her lunch is free, and tasted amazing, she might add, plus, she is already here, so why not? "OK, I had allotted the whole day to be here anyway" Caitlin wipes off her hands. She turns to pick up her briefcase when she sees that he has already done that for her. His hand outstretched, she takes it and they begin to walk toward the doors that she had seen May go through earlier.

Walking through the door, Caitlin is amazed to see the quick transformation from the rustic restaurant. Immediately she is grabbed by the hallway's walls, painted with climbing vines and a beautiful sunset so realistic you could almost feel the heat from the sun, all this before she walks into the lobby of the bed and breakfast building. The lobby itself is painted in bright hues of reds, blues, greens and yellows. The décor is as if one walked into an English garden, complete with a few trellises and a natural archway over the receptionist desk. As she looks to the left, she notices architectural details that she had not seen when she first drove up. She had been so focused on getting to the job that she didn't take in the whole place, which is very uncharacteristic of her.

Caitlin finds herself walking toward the front of the building, which has floor to ceiling windows with white grids marking off perfect boxes. The doors look straight from a European manufacturer. She feels her legs carry her out the front door and she looks around; the topiaries are professionally manicured, the gardens leading up to the front door were clearly created with great care and extremely good taste. Each flower variety adds not only a different dimension but a different color scheme. Each color scheme lends itself to the next, the order feels and looks natural. Walking up to the door, anyone would feel welcomed and at home by the simplicity of how this all goes together. How could she have missed all this, why on earth was she so focused on the restaurant? 'Have I started to slip?' she asks herself. Caitlin walks back in and "Mr. tall" is standing there waiting for her at the receptionist's desk, smiling. He has one elbow leaning on the desk and his head is cocked enough that he looks like he is straight out of a magazine for menswear. Too bad she isn't a reporter because this would have been a picture-perfect moment.

"So, do you want to see the rest of the place or continue to analyze my courtyard?" he asks. "Did we pass the test? Any recommendations?" His sarcasm is oozing but his eyes are searching for an honest answer. Or they are searching Caitlin, right now, she can't tell the difference.

"I was so focused on coming straight to the restaurant I didn't even look past the door to the other building." Caitlin says. "I parked over there too. By the way, what's with the sarcasm? You offered a tour so I was taking one, I didn't know I needed permission to follow my eyes." Caitlin takes a breath and turns around to walk away. She has never before been so forward with anyone. That was so out of character for her and unprofessional...again. What's happened to her here? There's no way he wants to continue this tour with her now. She walks a little faster, this time to leave.

Before she gets to the door, his hand is on her shoulder. "No harm done, I'm simply having fun with you.

You can't leave before you see the upstairs and the backyard. Our pride and joy and well, I'm sorry for back there, I was out of line. Truce?" In truth he really doesn't want to admit to her that he was mesmerized watching her take in the place He could tell that she was internalizing what she saw and there are so few who understand the purpose of all that is out there, actually she took his breath away and apparently his good sense too.

 Caitlin slowly turns around to face him. How can she resist that smile? His eyes are as inviting as this place. She shakes her head in agreement and he extends his hand once again. Not one to be rude, she holds his hand as he moves her toward the stairs to the left of the front desk. The wood is stained in a rich mahogany and yet they don't look dark against all the colors of the lobby. The steps blend in as a tree in a rainforest.

 "I see you're enjoying what you see, I can assure you that you'll only enjoy the lobby even more from up here." He takes her up the steps and when they get to the top, he walks her to the right and shows her how the balcony was created from what used to be a nurse's station. From one side the whole lobby can be seen, and out the front window and on the other side, there is also a large picture windows overlooking the back courtyards. The view is breathtaking. From here, Caitlin sees all the way to the lake at the end of the property.

 "This was an old hospital, right? Was all this here too?" she asks

 "To my knowledge, the grounds were all here" he says, "It was my mom's vision that brought the beauty out. My uncle knew this about her; she could always see potential. This is why she sent my little brother to the college of his choice because she knew he was going to want to do something else with the degree of his choice, and not stay here, and that is exactly what he did."

"You make it sound as if you and Lorraine didn't attend college," she ventures. She hopes she doesn't sound condescending with that remark.

"I grew up here in more ways than one," he says. "I learned from the inside what this place is all about and how to deal with the good guys and the bad. My father was the best judge of character there ever was this side of the mountain and probably the other side too. He could tell, by the first meeting, whether or not we would do business with someone or not. He was never wrong. This place is either in your blood or not. There really is no in between. My brother does not see this place the same as Lorraine and I do.

"Let's go down this hall, I want to show you some of the rooms. The ones on the other side are currently occupied. We have sixty five rooms on that side but only twenty-five on this side that are rentable."

Caitlin hears his voice change every time he speaks of his brother's opinion of this place. Something must have happened. Caitlin finds herself deep in thought as they walk. "Caitlin? Are you with me? Did you hear what I said?" he asks.

She shakes her head as if to bring herself out of her own thoughts. She remembers what he said earlier, - *'they had five children and raised three to adulthood'* - "Sorry, I get lost in my own thoughts sometimes." She looks at him with soft, curious eyes because she wants to know more, she wants to know all he has to say. How can one place and one man have such a strong effect on her in such a short amount of time? Not even an amount of time, more like moments.

McCoy looks into her eyes; what about them has his whole attention? What can she be thinking about? What is she looking at, certainly not him. Women don't look at him like that, not anymore anyway. Once upon a time, maybe, but not since. Facial blemishes seem to be a big deterrent. He loves his oasis in the mountains, he has plenty of company here and a lot of friends all the time. So why on earth is he hoping she will stay, or, at the very least, come back really soon.

The two of them stand looking at each other for an untold amount of time when the silence is finally broken by a client from across the walkway calling to him. "McCoy!! Thanks for the breakfast in bed today, I really needed the nourishment, feeling much better now. Tell Lorraine those rolls were scrumptious."

"You're welcome Mrs. Morrison. Always a pleasure to see you here. Will you be joining the dinner crowd then?" He calls back to her.

"If Bob is cooking his stew, then you bet," she calls to them as she hurries down the stairs, "My husband will be back from boating soon, so I'm going down to meet him. Have a nice day."

McCoy takes Caitlin's hand again and heads down the hall toward the unrented rooms. "McCoy is a nice name. Were you named after someone? I only ask because I have a cousin named McCoy and he was named after an uncle that had died. A tradition in our family." Caitlin is not sure why she revealed that to him maybe for an excuse to talk. It's not like he asked her to talk but he is so easy to talk to, and so easy on the eye it makes her almost uncomfortable. She can't explain why and that's the part she is questioning. Maybe the thin mountain air is getting to her brain. Yeah, that must be it, ever since she got here, she has not been herself.

"Actually, my mom picked my name out of a hat. Literally. My dad put in three names and so did my mom, but since my dad had the idea, he let her do the picking. So, McCoy. Silly huh? They named Lorraine after my grandmother and Nikky, well Nicholas, is a name they actually both liked. What about Caitlin? Where did your name come from?" McCoy asks more curious than he should be.

McCoy opens the door to another room and once again her breath is taken away. This room is decorated in early American, from top to bottom. "Who thought of all these themed rooms?" she asks, turning around slowly to take in the room in its entirety.

"My mom had fun decorating the first few, then; she would leave inquiries for the clients who were here and ask them for design critiques and ideas. They were happy to be a part of the decorating decisions. If a client chose the winning décor, mom allowed them one free night in that room. Needless to say, everyone was happy to participate."

"I wish I could meet your mom. She might give me some amazing tips in design." Caitlin says this without any forethought, the words are out before she realizes she had no right to say such a thing. She knows nothing about his mom or his family. She only met McCoy and yet......

McCoy is leaning on the doorway, watching Caitlin take in the room. He is entranced by her love and desire for what she sees. This is the same reaction his mother had with each piece she decorated. That "coming alive" feeling she gave to each room. Caitlin feels the aura, he is sure she does, his gut tells him so and so do his eyes. He is thinking of ways to get her to stay here but then reality hits when she mentions his mom. He has to respond, "Um, Caitlin," he stammers because, of anyone on this earth, his mom is the one he misses the most.

Caitlin looks over at him and sees him struggle, she can see in his eyes, she feels as if she can see his thoughts in his eyes. She wants to stare at them for hours. Oh; my, she is doing it again. Caitlin quickly looks down at the carpet to pull herself together. "Mom's gone Cat, she only lived six months without my dad and she couldn't live any longer. They were truly one soul, I know I sound like a dime-store romance novel, but theirs honestly was." McCoy shifts his feet around like a small boy who is embarrassed, because truly he is. He asks himself, 'Who am I to be calling her

Cat? As far as I know she will hate the name! You're such an idiot McCoy. The first woman who walks in here that you're reacting to and you're saying all the wrong things.' Unconsciously, he hits the wall behind him with his foot.

Caitlin looks up. Now she has goose bumps, no one had called her Cat since high school. That's it! She must know him from somewhere. But he said he grew up here, went to local schools, she assumed, but maybe not. Her curiosity gets the best of her and before her mind can stop her mouth she says, "Did you go to high school locally, too? Have you ever been off this mountain?" She is watching him move toward her now, his slow but purposeful movements have her at a complete halt. What hold he has over her, and yet she is not complaining.

"Actually, I went to WestPoint military academy for part of my high school years. Dad said I needed to get out of the house and be at a place that would bring out the man in me. Those were the best years of my life. However, my pull was, and still is; this mountain, I came straight back upon graduation. My guidance officer was a little upset with me, didn't talk to me for months, but he has been here since, and we talk often. He says he is very proud of what I have accomplished here. That's better than any degree I could have achieved in college. Why do you ask?" He is watching her face, her eyes, ah those eyes will tell him everything he knows they will.

Caitlin feels very small next to McCoy and he is standing only about four feet away. She still can't move. Her eyes are on the ground. Her hands are getting that nervous sweat that she sometimes gets before a big presentation. Her heart is pounding and part of her feels as if she should be moving, or running the hell out of the room, but she is still as a doorframe.

To change the subject and not to feel too stupid, as she already does, she answers, "No reason," she says. "I was named Caitlin because it 'is a respectable name', so they tell me. In other words, no thought was put into who I was or will be, except whether or not the name will fit in with their high-society friends." She slowly lifts her head to see him standing even closer. He reaches out his hand yet again.

"I want to show you the back courtyards in person." McCoy says, "The view down below is much better than through the balcony window." What is it about him holding her hand? She doesn't do this normally, even with friends. Truth is, half of what has happened today has never happened before; she is getting scared of herself. She wipes her hand off on her skirt and hands him her hand again. This time the hold feels a little bit tighter from him as if he is telling her not to go too far. Caitlin's head is spinning at the thought. 'Can that be right? No one likes Caitlin, not even her ex- boyfriend, he only used her to get to her father. This, however, this already feels different.' She thinks to herself.

What has possessed him to constantly hold her hand? He can guide her simply by using words, however, he can't be without her touch. Nikky, you've seen her. You knew what she will do to me. I'm going to get you for this. McCoy says all this in his mind, but he means it. Nikky could be quite sneaky especially when it comes to him being single. Both Nikky and Lorraine are happily married with two kids a piece so they are constantly nagging on him. Well, actually, he may end up thanking him. Only time will tell. Still, how can every emotion in his body come forward with one encounter? Help Mom. He thinks as he looks up to the sky.

~ ~ ~

They walk down the rest of the hall and to a door marked with a sign reading, "*Cottage personnel only. Please use lobby doors to get to the courtyards. Thank you.*"

From English gardens to botanical gardens, this place holds magic. Whatever his mom had done, her visions were exceptional. The fact that she was able to visualize this and bring her thoughts to fruition is awe inspiring. Caitlin pulls at his hand as she walks a little faster toward the back. Here she finds two gazebos one on each side, both filled with beautifully carved benches and trellises filled with climbing morning glories. Slightly passed these she finds the small lake where guests can go boating. She has to walk closer to the water; like a siren, the water calls to her. Once she gets there, she pulls up her pant legs one at a time to takes her shoes off and sits down with her feet in the water and her bottom barely on the land. Her legs are short so she has to be close to the water to feel the ripples on her feet. She has found the most tranquil part of her entire state. How she longs to be here for an extended amount of time. But she has to remind herself that she is only here on business, or was anyway. Her friend Mica warns her all the time about relationships and how they can come out of nowhere. That she had better be prepared because one day it will hit her as hard as a stun gun.

Caitlin props her arms behind her to hold herself up. The middle of the day and she is clearly doing everything except her job. The worst part is (or maybe it's the best) is that she is enjoying every moment of this bliss. "Living here, you've led a charmed life." No sooner are the words out when she wants to retract them. Caitlin is having an 'open-mouth- insert-foot day'. Ugh. Why can't she shut up? All she sees is the outside of things, there is no way she can tell how his life was. Wait, what is that phrase again? 'raised three to adulthood'. That phrase is beginning to haunt her. This is why she is tripping on her words. Caitlin hates unanswered questions but she has no right to inquire further on that, nothing to do with the job at hand. Job! Oh man, she is slaking off so much today. Dad where are you when I need a good swift slap? She looks around and sees McCoy standing ten feet away.

"These grounds won't do those fancy pants of yours any good you know," McCoy says. "Grass stains are hell to get out of silk." This is all he could think to say? He has to talk to Nikky, and sooner than later would be best. Caitlin slowly picks up her shoes, then herself, and heads back toward McCoy. That tower of a man is no less intimidating when he is smiling. She comes upon him and as she gets closer, she could swear his smile got bigger as she approaches. She checks her watch.

"It's getting late; if you don't mind, I need to call your brother and tell him of my findings. This is what I'm being paid for anyway. Besides, it's getting dark soon and I should be heading back to the city. If I was honest with myself, I'd have to say it's going to be really hard tearing myself away from here." She looks around at the ground to indicate the place and not the person, but the person is what is holding her more and the feeling is so sudden she is not sure what to do with it. 'UGH, I need to call Mica' she thinks to herself.

McCoy is hearing all the words but he isn't listening anymore. He sees her mouth move, but all he is thinking about is how sweet those lips look and how badly he wants to taste them. With a startle, he stands up straight as he can. He hears her say "away" she plans to leave. Well, of course she is, she doesn't live here, she didn't even want to be here to begin with. He has to stall her, one more hour. He needs time to contact Nikky and find out the real reason he sent her. Oh, Mommy, you would love her. He says to himself as he looks up again for the second time this afternoon. When his face comes down, he realizes he could have said that out loud, but he sees her back is facing him on the gazebo. She is not looking back at the yards of finely pruned trees, or at the banks of the lake. She is looking through the trees at a sight she isn't supposed to notice, the clearing, about fifty feet away, the space of forbidden access to anyone but the three siblings. She has found their secret spot. But how?

Caitlin is taking in all that she can before she is going to call Mr. Bennet, no Nicholas Lowenbrow. She takes out her pad and paper and jots down key points so that she won't forget to say everything she wants to say. She looks back at the buildings, standing so grand before the gardens, and she watches the birds and butterflies enjoying the gardens along with the guests. She looks back over her shoulder and sees wives meeting husbands at the bank of the lake as they come in with fish. This is a vacation spot to be lost in. Then her eyes take in something she isn't sure she sees at first; a clearing.

Maybe new construction; she stares to make sure she sees clearly. Yes, there is a clearing not fifty feet away, a small clearing where there are no trees, no flowers, and even more remarkable, no grass. Her mind starts to wander to all sorts of places. This place holds so much life and yet right there, in the crook of its neck, there is death. Caitlin perks up quickly and unconsciously puts her hand on her heart and her mouth drops open. Those other two children are here. She made a beautiful resting place for those two children, a place for them to frolic, forever happy. Caitlin is fighting back tears when she feels a hand touch gently down on her shoulders.

"May I ask you a question Cat? I'm sorry, may I even call you Cat?" McCoy says. She nods all the while staring out into the trees. "It may seem weird but now that you've seen my place, can you tell me what your place looks like?" What a lame question. McCoy kicks himself mentally but she is way too smart for his own good. He is not ready to go there, not ready to feel anything for someone. The air is thick with something he doesn't recognize. He needs a diversion and short of screaming and scaring the rest of the guests outside, he chose this stupid question.

Yes, this is a weird question, she thinks, but it may take her mind off of where she is right now. Without turning around, she answers him, "I live in a simple apartment. So small the whole thing can probably fit into one of the suites here. From the front door, you walk in to a two foot square foyer, and to your left is a cute galley kitchen complete with bar stools and a counter to drink my morning hot cocoa on" She pauses, then using her hands she shows him, "Straight ahead you will see my living/dining room area. Here I have a basic square table that can barely fit four. In my living room I have a blue denim sectional couch, a coffee table, and a small tv set. To the right you will find a small bathroom tiled in black and white tiles and before you ask, no, it's not done in a nice pattern, scattered black and white tiles," she pauses and takes a breath before continuing, "The bedroom consists of a day bed, glass dresser, and Queen Anne desk. When all is said and done, sounds pretty skimpy compared to the oasis you live in."

"Why on earth would you want a blue denim couch? Sounds kind of strange. No offense."

Nothing can tear Caitlin's eyes away from that patch. She feels her chest rise and fall because she knows for sure what she is feeling, her heart is still racing and she is in real need of some deep cleansing yoga breaths. "None taken" she says. "My folks are not like yours. I was raised by nannies, displayed by my parents and shunned by society. When I saw this couch, I decided it was my rebellious piece. Now it has since become a piece of art. I spend a lot of time doodling on all parts as I sit there and think." She can picture herself attacking that last corner for today's addition.

She turns only slightly to see where he is, and notes he is not more than an arm's-length away. The sun in his eyes makes them shine even more. Caitlin takes her notebook and starts to fan herself. This is unnatural, no one should be reacting like this to a man that they recently met. But he is clearly not any man. Not to her anyway. There is some kind of circuit running around them and until either of them wants to admit this, nothing will take place. The air feels as if it is hugging the two of them, something is here with them, or someone. Caitlin thinks to herself, giving herself chills.

McCoy hears every word this time. He takes each word in and processes it slowly, all the while watching her face as she speaks. She cannot look at him when speaking of her folks, how unfortunate for her. He wouldn't change his childhood for anything, even with all its ups and downs. The part that hits him the most is the end. "I find it hard to believe you'd be shunned by anyone." It's what he thinks is best to say. His heart is aching watching her, his pulse is slowly rising and he is not sure he even wants them to stop. These feelings that are overcoming him scare him to no end. He has to call Nikky, or maybe make an excuse to go find Lorraine, but he doesn't want to leave her. Part of him is frozen right where he stands.

She stands more erect and faces him. "Look at me, McCoy, I mean really look," she says. "I am shorter by a foot or more than any fancy model type. I can't walk in heels if you paid me because my ankles give way. I have more curves than necessary according to all the fashion magazines and that's what my mom has told me for years. She offered to pay to get me "fixed" for graduation. Fixed!!! Did you hear me?! Dogs get fixed, not people. She needs me to be the perfect body type to fit into her version of what a woman is all about. I went away to school and ran like a vampire in sunrise. I've never looked back. They agreed to pay for my college education but there the connection ended. Your folks may not be in your life but that was an act of god. My folks aren't in my life because they think they are god. Ok, I take part of that back, my dad does give me business advice but not because he is proud but because he thinks he is the only one who knows better, and he is the best so I ask him anyway. Don't get me wrong I'm grateful for his advice, he is business smart." She pauses because her body is betraying her right now and all professionalism has left the building.

Stunned at herself, she quickly turns back around and faces that bare spot that took her breath away moments before. She sees this spot more like a symbol for her own life now. There is a bare spot in her life too. Her secret that she is all alone in the world. Even her brother disowned her because of, as he said, "her own status choices". Sure, her father is in her life professionally, but only out of sympathy and ego; he threatened her about going anywhere else. He keeps asking her, "when are you going to come to your senses and take your mom up on her offer?" It's been ten years since college and Caitlin knows she has a successful business, built all by herself. Still, not enough for him or her mother. Nothing will be enough until she fits into "his world", both physically and emotionally, which will never happen. What a disappointment she has been for them.

Caitlin finds herself staring at this blank patch in the ground amongst all the beauty, and accepts this area as her own. This is a true metaphor of her life. She is a black hole in her family, a spot where no life can exist. Waiting out there on her own, surrounded by beauty but having no way of getting there. No way at all. Tears start flowing uncontrollably down her face. She can no longer see clearly, she no longer wants to. She wants it all to end. Caitlin slowly sits down on the bench right where she is, pulls her legs up, and is sitting there holding her legs. This is a moment long in coming, why here? Why in this place? There has to be a connection. Maybe when she sleeps tonight, she will figure out why this place is so connected to her. But for now, her body is in control of her and her mind seems to be going along.

McCoy watches the transformation. Caitlin has gone from a strong-willed, confident woman to a scared child in what seems less time than it took him to take a breath. Watching this is killing him. But he doesn't know what to do. 'Please Poppa, help me this time,' he thinks. After he thinks this a sudden breeze starts from behind him, pushing him forward. McCoy walks slowly with the breeze toward Cat. He goes up right behind her, puts one leg over the bench and sits behind her. His hands are shaking as he puts them on her shoulders, and in a shaky voice, he says, "You will always be safe here, Cat. I promise."

Caitlin takes a deep breath and lets the air out slowly as she leans back into McCoy's chest. He is a full head taller than she is yet she fits comfortably. The tears keep coming as his hands move slowly down her shoulders to her elbows and pauses there for a moment. Then he continues until he finds her hands and intertwines his fingers with hers. He scoots a little closer and there they stay. Neither one of them knows how long it is before either one can entertain the thought of speaking. There are many deep breaths and lots of tears but neither changes their position.

McCoy starts to speak in a voice barely audible except that he is right by her head. She doesn't hear the words, she feels them come through his chest as well as his mouth. "I am not the oldest child. There was a storm, loads of lightning and thunder. The sky was lighting up like fireworks," he begins. "Like most children, we went running to our parent's room, on the way we stopped at the balcony windows because there was a deafening clap and a huge bright flash. When it was over, Mom had met us there thinking we'd be coming to them, that's then we noticed there were only three of us. Looking up at Mom we saw a look of horror on her face. We followed her eyes outside and saw the gazebo on fire and my dad trying to carry our brother and sister, one on each shoulder. Then we looked behind him, that last clap of thunder came with a bolt of lightning that hit the gazebo. My siblings used to have campouts all the time with and without permission, even in the rain and snow. Doctors said they didn't know what hit them. We wouldn't play outside for months afterward. Then Mom started to plant around the area we left that spot as sacred ground. Nikky won't even look out the window on the upstairs balcony."

Caitlin doesn't know what to say. That must have been the hardest thing for McCoy to share. Somehow her tears seem very shallow right now. She clings to his arms and pulls them around her. The moment they are sharing right now is more personal than sharing a bed.

"Cat, I've never told anyone that, I'm not sure why I did now. I'm sorry." McCoy's voice is raspy from his own emotions.

Finding her voice is hard but she finally does; "No one has called me Cat since I was ten years old," she says "I had a good friend that did for a while, but she moved away. I haven't heard the name since. Everything about this place is pulling me in deeper and deeper. I don't know why, McCoy, but I don't want to leave, and I have to. I have to go home." She takes a deep breath again, slowly.

"You don't have to leave today, it's Friday," McCoy pleads. "No work tomorrow. Stay, Cat, please. I don't know why but I can't say goodbye right now, I can't even leave this position, and something tells me you are supposed to be here now and for a long time to come." Something or someone, he thinks to himself. 'Thanks Dad for the push'.

Caitlin shivers and finds herself pulling herself around to face McCoy. She stares into his eyes as best as she can, he is telling the truth, he does want her to stay. Her heart is beating so fast she doesn't know how to control herself anymore. There is a feeling in her stomach that she has never felt before. She cannot explain what is happening, and the lack of control makes her even more nervous. Her eyes can no longer tear, there is nothing left inside. However, her emotions are on overdrive. She looks into his eyes and sees the same thing in his eyes that she is feeling.

McCoy looks down as Cat turns around to face him. Her eyes tell him that she wants to stay, that she is as confused as he is right now. He cannot decide if this is supposed to happen or not but there is a part of him that simply feels right. His heart is telling him other things and his stomach is telling him something else entirely. All of which he does not understand. "No one knows our secret

Cat. We keep this part of our lives to ourselves, I'm not sure why I told you. You have to forget all you heard. I'm not even sure Lorraine has told Bob and I know for sure Nikky has not told his wife, he was very young when the storm happened and quite scarred. What I do know is that somehow I needed to tell you and that same thing could have been why you told me your secret." McCoy takes his hand and pushes the hair away from Cat's eye and back behind her ear. She is definitely heaven sent, it's the only explanation he has. He feels his mother here with him, her hand on his shoulder. Without a doubt, she is here.

"I never told anyone about the relationship I have with my parents," Caitlin says. "It never seemed important. I have to report back to your brother, he is expecting a call. Maybe we should go inside." However, looking into his eyes, she feels something pulling at her to be closer. Her hand moves before her head registers her own actions. She touches his face and softly rubs her thumb against his jawline. He shivers and grabs her wrist as if to take it off his face and throw it somewhere. His eyes are scared.

"I'm sorry. I should go." Caitlin tries to stand up but his hand is still on her wrist. She stands before him and looks into his face. Fear, that is what she sees, yet softness, but she can't tell which one makes her heart stir more. McCoy can't believe what he is feeling, this woman touches his face, his pre-maturely wrinkled, and scarred up face and it feels as if he is kissed by a butterfly. So soft, so sincere, so passionate, yes there is passion in her eyes. He can't let her go. So here she stands for a few minutes until McCoy finds his words again, "I don't scare you?" he whispers.

"To be honest, McCoy, there are a lot of things you do to me but I can assure you scare is not one of them," Caitlin says. "Why would I be scared anyway? You are a kindhearted soul, I want to connect to you. I see that I have upset you, though. Please, McCoy, let go, I need to leave." Being that Caitlin is already standing she turns to face the cottage and tries to walk away only to be pulled back to McCoy who catches her in his arms and turns her around to face him.

"Women tell me my scars are gross, I've been offered free plastic surgery by the doctors that we've had here and you mean to tell me you don't see them?" McCoy's voice comes out a bit gruff but his face is telling her that he is confused and maybe almost hurt.

"We all have scars McCoy some are more obvious than others, that's all." Caitlin pulls back and shakes her hand as he lets her go. She picks up the bottom of her shirt slightly and pauses, she is not going to be able to do this on her own. She looks into his eyes for support, and there it is. Slowly, she pulls her shirt up to uncover what McCoy realizes must have been self-induced scars. A dark moment in her life but she has already exposed so much of herself she might as well go all the way.

McCoy tears his eyes away from hers long enough to see what she is showing him. The only thought he can muster is one of sympathy. What she must have been going through to cause that to herself is something he will never understand. His siblings always had the love and support of their parents and their family. Uncle Bennet even lived with them for a while and taught the boys the things their father didn't have time for. They were always well loved.

"Cat, come here." Carefully she lets her shirt drop and walks back to him. "Mom always said these woods were magical. She used to tell me how she saw my brother and sister playing here all the time that she even heard them sing. It's not a spooky thing that we kept that circle, it's because of the love she felt was still here. But I see that their magic not just there, it's all over. This whole place was created through love and kindness. The aura right here is at its strongest, that's why we have experienced what we have today. Mom and Dad are telling us it's OK. That we," he points to himself and to her a couple times, "we are supposed to be here." McCoy closes his eyes. To himself he sounds like the same ten-year-old boy who used to listen to his mom telling him how beautiful his sister sounded and how she knew that his brother was protecting her. He must sound like a fool.

Caitlin reaches up to touch his face again, and that is all the encouragement he needs. He is so filled with want for her that he practically grabs her face in his hands and pulls her toward him. Only in fairy tales has she heard of true love's first kiss, if this is what they were describing then heaven is definitely achievable on earth. Neither McCoy nor Caitlin want to let go of this collective feeling that is being shared right now, however, they are interrupted by someone clearing his throat behind them. Slowly McCoy withdraws and looks up over Caitlin to see the last person on earth he expected.

He takes a deep breath and slowly turns Cat around, "Cat, I'd like you to meet my brother Nikky." Caitlin stands dumbfounded and speechless, she has no idea what to say or do at that moment. No one moves. Nikky takes one giant step forward and grabs Caitlin out of McCoy's arms, picks her up and swings her around as if she is no heavier than a five-year-old. He puts her down, he kisses the top of her head and goes toward McCoy with outstretched arms. The two brothers hug in a way they have not done in many years. Nikky whispers in McCoy's ear, "Mom told me to, I swear. It was a dream but she showed me her online. I miss them Mic, oh god I miss them so, but now we move on, yes?" he slowly pulls away.

~ ~ ~

As the brothers pull away from each other, there is another cry coming from behind them. Lorraine is running to them. Before Caitlin takes in the full scope of what is going on, she is pulled into a four-way hug. They break apart and together walk to the clearing. This is the first time the siblings have been there since their mother had surrounded the place with plants and created a sacred place. Nikky speaks first, "OK Ms. decorator, what do we do with this spot?"

All eyes are on Caitlin. "First of all, call me Cat," she says. She looks toward McCoy and he reaches up so he can put his hand around her shoulders. He is not letting go, not here, not ever. "Second, my professional brain as well as my gut is telling me that this is the perfect place to put a playground for all the kids who come. The aura is playful and it will always be filled with laughter. Whether of the children that are here physically or in spirit." Caitlin looks into all the eyes that are watching her. They look around the space and look at each other.

It is Lorraine's turn to talk, "I remember they both liked swings. Is that correct McCoy?"

"Yes, Lorraine, they would push each other for hours on the old tire swing," McCoy says. "That tire is still in the garage." He looks to Cat, "how about we turn it into a flower bed? I'm sure it isn't strong enough to hold anyone now." Caitlin smiles and shakes her head. This is the place she belongs, never has she felt as if she actually belongs somewhere, but everything about this place feels right. She finally belongs. Who would have thought?

The four of them start walking toward the cottage and each one is talking quickly, not to be outdone with their imaginations, they are firing ideas at Caitlin as fast as they are coming into their heads. By the time they get back to the cottage, there is a sense of togetherness that has not been felt in a long time.

"Nikky and I are headed in to get ready for the dinner crowd. Are you two coming?" Lorraine says and smiles at McCoy and Cat. She does not remember the last time she saw him smile, well, not that big anyway. 'Thank you Mom.' She says to herself.

"Cat, I'm sorry for the ruse, but would you have come if I asked you to come meet my brother because my dead mother told me to?" Nikky laughs at the whole thing, but mostly because Mom was right as usual.

"Truth?" Caitlin asks. "I might have been intrigued, but this was a much better way. I fell in love with the place long before I even met your brother. I suppose I owe you a great deal of gratitude but I'm not sure thank you covers what needs to be said." Caitlin is still floating from that kiss and her gut is telling her there is more to come.

With that, Lorraine and Nikky walk back into the cottage through the door that Caitlin remembers being marked for official personnel only. McCoy pulls her, however, in a different direction. They pass a couple of rooms marked storage and then they come to a door with a lock. McCoy takes out his keys and turns to her and says, "Close your eyes for a second." She does.

Once the door is open, McCoy reaches for her hand and gently pulls her through the door, which he then closes behind them. In her ear McCoy whispers, "This is where I live, you can open your eyes now."

Caitlin opens her eyes and takes a step back, bumping into McCoy. She cannot believe what she sees. She is standing in a beautiful foyer with colorful tiles. She looks to her left and sees a kitchen that she could probably put her living/dining room in. She walks toward the kitchen and notices something familiar. It isn't only familiar, it is her kitchen, the tiles, the cabinets, and the table is exactly the same as her table, although, her table only fits in her dining room. She turns on her phone and lifts it to him. McCoy sees the picture of her kitchen. He looks around and then back down at the picture. "Mom knows best," he says with a smile.

She walks out of the kitchen and into the dining room. A nice size and it too is open to the living room. Caitlin stops suddenly; she looks back at McCoy and fumbles with her phone again, another picture. McCoy looks and sees what he already knew to be true, that the two of them have identical couches, only hers is beautifully drawn on oh that must be what she means by a work of art. "Why the drawings?" he asks.

Sheepishly she answers, "You know how many kids draw on their jeans to make a statement? Well, one night I was angry and a lot of times I draw when I'm angry. I was curled up on the couch and drawing. It hadn't dawned on me what I was drawing on or with. Turned out to be a black permanent marker. Afterward, I realized that this fit very well with me. I continue whenever the mood hits. Yours looks like a blank canvas to me right now."

"I have a black marker; want to initiate it?" McCoy walks over to the counter and hands her a black, permanent marker. Caitlin jumps up and gives him a peck on the cheek and immediately goes to work. She knows exactly what she wants to draw. Once inspired, it only takes moments to draw what she wants. This is a gift she inherited from her grandmother, the only one who loved her for who she was. Grandma was a talented, accomplished artist but she did it under a pseudonym so no one in the family knew about her success until she died. She was a master with ink and paper. Caitlin spent hours learning from her in her private hideaway studio.

Moments later, she turns around to see that McCoy has not moved. She scoots over so he can see what she has done. She has drawn two flowers sharing the same stem. "Perfect." McCoy walks over to the couch and gives her his hand. She gives him the marker and he laughs. He puts that on the table and reaches out to her again, this time she gives him her hand and he gently pulls her up and into his arms. "Like you." McCoy leans down to kiss her again and Caitlin lets her body feel.

Caitlin lets out a groan from deep inside her because this feels so right. McCoy grabs her even closer, if that were possible. They stand embraced for some time, exchanging physically what there are no words for. Slowly, McCoy leads her to his bedroom. Caitlin's stomach has already done a hundred flip-flops, she is not sure she is ready for this, but she is also not sure she can stop the momentum of the day or this moment, nor does she really want to.

Once inside his room, Caitlin smiles. "Don't tell me, you have this same bedroom set too." McCoy says with a sigh.

"No," Caitlin says. "Just the sheets." She smiles.

"Good," he says. "Then you already know how comfortable they are." He grins as he closes the gap between them.

Caitlin reaches up to touch his face with both hands. It is so smooth, so soft, so waiting to be kissed, she pulls his head down toward her. Only he does much more, he scoops her up and carries her to his bed. What happens next is hard to explain.

From the outside it looks as if two bodies are engaged in physical contact. However, from the inside Caitlin is feeling as though her body is being awakened for the first time. McCoy has never felt this type of pleasure in his life. There they are discovering each other in ways that actually help them discover themselves. It would stand to reason that there are two people breathing, however, for those involved one cannot tell who is breathing in and who is breathing out because there is no longer a him and I, or she and me, this is what becoming an us was meant to be. This is not simply a physical act, it is a merging of souls, it is a conjoining so beautiful it defies explanation.

Sure, there is a lot to talk about, but for right now, conversation remains understood. The cottage, and dinner, can wait.

The Gift

A family is in turmoil, sadness surrounds the house but everyone is pushing through and going on with their daily lives as best as they can. Jo arises one day to find out she has been given a very special gift. Watch how the rest of the family is impacted.

Jo opens her eyes, the room is dark, she turns her head to see the time, its 2:00am and the world around her is silent except for the rhythmic breathing of her first and only love. The love she has had for 38 years now. This man, this warrior who championed all the bad and evil in their lives has lost only one battle. The battle of the cancer inside of her, he could not defeat it, even all the love and devotion in the world could not. He would move heaven and earth if he could have her forever, but forever is not in the cards for them. She knows that, she has known that for a long time, but he has never given up, never wavered from telling her how beautiful she is every morning. Telling her how great she looks in the old tattered concert t-shirt she likes to sleep in now.

     Jo gave it her all, she fought this disease with all her might, her children all came to her aide, except for Angel, but that is no fault of her own; she is in a bad situation of her own. Jo knows that Angel is aware of her illness, she ran into her one day and told her the cold hard truth before he showed up and dragged her away. Her heart knows, Jo can feel her. Angel is hurting badly and she needs to be saved if it's the last thing she does on this earth.

     As Jo looks around the room again, she begins to notice a something. She is pain free. Her arms no longer feel like heavy weights hanging from her shoulders. Her stomach does not feel tied in knots with the burn of all the acid that sits there, her breathing is easy and comfortable. Jo stands up and walks around the room. She walks into her closet and finds a dress she has always loved, she puts it on. The material hangs on her a bit so she finds a belt and adjusts herself to fit better. She walks in front of the mirror and brushes her hair, her hair that is back to being full and curly, she brushes slowly languishing over how good it feels to do such a simple task without pain. How good it feels to have more than strands on her head.

She looks at herself in the mirror and does a twirl to watch the rise and fall of the skirt of the dress. Nothing makes you feel better than a twirl of a skirt. She takes a deep breath and lets the air out slowly. Jo feels so good right now, the only thing she can think to do, however, is to go fix up the house. Ben has let the house go because he has been taking care of her most of the day. She is going to put things right. As her job as wife and mother she will set the house right again, then all will be well and she can move on.

Jo walks into her baby's room and sees she is sleeping soundly. She begins to pick up all the clothes on the floor and hang up what is clean and put the rest in the hamper to be washed at a later date. She picks up her school bag and sees a few papers fall out. They are crumpled, "this must be the reason she is moping around the house confused lately" she says to herself.

Jo opens the first note, 'Hey Kar, thanks for taking me home last night. I was a bit trashed and you came around – no hard feelings." #86

Jo thinks carefully and reminds herself that Karen had mentioned she came home late last week one night because some guy at the party, who lives across town, made her take him home. Karen did this because she owed it to herself to part of his crowd. "Yeah that's what she told me, that she owed it to her reputation as a dweeb to take him home, that it was an honor." Since then she has been spending more time with him and less time on her studies. She has been talking to Jo but in disjointed conversations, like she wants to say more but can't.

Jo knows it's not nice, but right now she begins to read all the correspondences from #86, it is the last one that gets her mom-blood boiling. "Why that piece of trash, he doesn't want to date her, he wants to dethrone her. Oh, my poor baby does not understand this. I'll have to write her a note."

  Jo sits down, after she cleans up Karen's room, she takes a highlighter pen and begins to highlight all the hints he has given her that she is sure Karen has missed. The innuendos to his real purpose. The exacting nature of what he plans on doing at the graduation party. Jo looks over at her daughter and sees she is wearing a t-shirt of his and on the shirt there are tally marks on the back of it as well as the front of it. She counts them up, there are 99. Now she knows what he meant in his note when he said 'wear this t-shirt, all my best girls do'. #86 wants her Karen to be his number 100 conquests in high school. Or so he would like the world to believe. Jo is sure that he may have had ten but definitely not 100.

  Karen goes back to the desk to write a letter to Karen. She is careful with her words, she wants to be firm and yet still a loving mother.

My Dearest Kar Bear,

  I have been listening to you speak of this new boy in your life and your voice always gives away what is in your heart. He is not for you my dear, he is no way near good enough for you.
  I found your notes from him and I have highlighted his code words. I will be blunt. He wants to have sex with you. Not because of you but because you will be number 100. Count the tally marks on his shirt you're wearing. There are 99.
  Count the notches in his belt, I'll bet he has 3 rows of 33 on them and he wants to make one more.
You are no girlfriend to him, you are a conquest. He is convincing you that you don't deserve him and should be happy to be with him, but you deserve so much more.

No, that's not how it works. You ARE far better than the likes of him. You graduate in two weeks, you will have your summer job and your college career ahead of you. I'm so proud of you that you got into your first choice of schools, many don't. Don't let a jerk like him take something so personal away from you. He will not think of you one moment after graduation except that you are the 100th virgin he has had, or as I said before, he would like everyone to believe he has had.

 You are so much more than a night's conquest, you have a brain, you have a future. You have so much inner strength that you can explode mountains if you wanted to. But you can't find that strength when there is a guy in your face pulling on your necklaces to have you kiss him. I've seen the broken chains and the marks on the back of your neck. No, don't allow him access to you anymore. You are soooooo much more and don't let him make you believe you are not.

 Jo gets up from writing, she needs to find something in her room. She pulls open her jewelry box and finds just the right piece. She brings it back to Karen's room and continues to write:

 I am giving you this bracelet and necklace as a symbol of your strength.

 Your father gave me this when we were first married, he said I was the strongest person he had ever met. Wear them both. Let the necklace be a symbol to others that you are strong and wear the bracelet so you can look down every day and see your strengths. Your heart, your mind, your soul are strong. Don't let one stupid high school fling make you question that. He will not be there when you need someone, he will not even be there the morning after.

 Greg will, he always has been there for you, he still will be many years from now. I promise you that.

 Wear this strength on your heart and your hand and know that I am always with you helping you to stand strong.

He, this #86, will be a blip in your life, as insignificant as the ant you stepped on while walking in the park one day.

A time will come when you will meet the man who will be your first, and when that time does come, and he is the right man, you will know. I count myself as being lucky to find my first and only.

I hope you can be so lucky.

Greg, Brian, Wendy, Tricia and your siblings will be there through good and bad.

I love you Kar Bear.

Jo smooths the piece of paper she has written on, she looks at it twice to make sure all the words are really there, that she hasn't missed anything. When she is satisfied, she rests the pen next to the note and walks over to kiss her baby girl.

~ ~ ~

"She can't do that! What is she doing?" he asks confused.

"Ah, but she can, and she is. This is all ok. We are here to only watch." Number two says

"But." He rebuttals

"Shhhhh"

~ ~ ~

Jo leaves Karen's room feeling she has done the right thing. No regrets for reading the notes or cleaning up after her daughter. When she wakes up, her daughter will know everything was done from love. She will know, Greg will be happy too. Jo smiles to herself, she has known that Greg likes Karen since the beginning of high school. But he is Charlie's friend's older brother and she hasn't been able to see the truth yet. She will, Jo smiles.

She picks up the towels in the bathroom and changes them for clean ones from the closet and then walks into Charlie's room. She takes a deep breath. "Oh Charlie" she says to no one. She watches as her for son sleep a few minutes.

Jo begins to pick up his clothes. Each pair of pants holding a small package in one of the pockets. Each shirt holding something small in the folded cuff of the sleeve. She finds a few more packets in his shoes and some other paraphernalia under his bed. Each piece she finds she shakes her head. Jo knows her son has been hanging with the wrong boys this semester, she knows he has not quite been himself, his friends have told her they are worried. She is not as worried as they are, but she appreciates their concern. Each one has come over to talk to her lately. Everyone has. She counts herself as being very lucky to have so many people care.

As a matter of fact, many of her children's friends have come over to say what they feel they needed to say. Gave her promises of keeping up grades and doing the right thing. Told her some secrets they haven't told their own parents yet, and shed a few tears with her.

But for now, she has to concentrate on Charlie. She has finished gathering all of what she believes he has. She puts them all together in a pile on his laptop which is on the floor as usual. But he likes to sit in the corner of his room, on his beanbag chair when he works, so she will leave everything here knowing he will find it easily. She sits down on his bean bag chair. "Hmmm, it is quite comfortable Charlie." She says.

Jo pulls out a notebook from Charlie's bag and begins to write him a note:

Oh Charlie,
Look what I found all over your room. It doesn't make me angry, it makes me sad. Sad to think you really feel

this new group of people are your friends. Maybe one of them will be a real friend, but the rest will drop you like a hot potato as soon as things go sour in your life.

I know you have all of this not because you are dealing but because they keep giving them to you and you tell them you'll have it later. I hope you haven't spent too much money on all of this. What a waste. I suspect you will be flushing this all away when you see this in a pile as I've given you. Charlie, kids will experiment, I'm not stupid.

But this isn't you. Your friends miss you Charlie, they've all come by and each one has told me so. Peter seems to think he can trounce you now in chess, I can't tell you his knew trick but watch his pawns on the left side. I believe his left.

And Big Al? Well, he tells me that with you out of the tournament he is going to easily take the title from you and you'll never get it back. He thinks he can outthink you in math. HA!! He doesn't know my Charlie does he? I know you've been doing your work.

You aren't handing it in because you want to fit in with a group you don't fit in with. Not sure what you see in this group. Is there a girl you like? Then teach her to value herself and make something of herself. Even if she hasn't done so before, doesn't mean she can't do it now, and if she can't? Teach her, don't drop to her level; elevate her to yours. ☺

Take her on walks in the park and show her how the world can be wonderful if she is an active participant not a bystander. Show her how you showed me to appreciate the small things. Remember how we moved the garbage cans closer to the benches so people would actually throw their trash away and not leave papers all over the benches?

Whomever it is that pulled you in, work your Charlie magic and pull them out. You CAN do that. You're my Charlie, my secret hero remember?

Remember how much fun you had last summer working in that special camp? Go back there this summer, find your purpose again. Remember the boy you taught to tie his shoes, took you all summer but he learned and it was a big thing for someone with his condition. You work magic Charlie, it's who you are.

I love you Charlie and expect great things from you, no matter how small, they are all great ♥ do it with a full heart.

Always,

Charlie's proud momma

Jo rises from the beanbag chair and walks over to her son. She sits on the bed and rubs his back for a moment. Charlie curls up with his mother's touch. He pulls his blanket in towards him and hugs it while she rubs his back a few more times. Jo leans downs down and holds him a moment before kissing his cheek. A tear falls off of her and on to him. She leaves it there and walks out of the room.

~ ~ ~

"This is not right I tell you, not right at all!!! Why are you standing for this?! We have to stop her, she will ruin everything!" he says.

"There is nothing to stop, she has been given a gift, we can't take a gift away; we can enjoy it and watch it unfold. Ah, the gift, not given to many but watching never gets old. I am in awe of her, she is doing it all right. All right." Number two says.

The first one walks out of the room infuriated.

~ ~ ~ ~

Jo walks downstairs and picks things up along the way. She brings all the clothes to the laundry room on her way down to the basement to visit Albert, her oldest boy. He recently moved back home as a money saver. He was engaged to be married but she broke off the engagement because she was more interested in marrying into the right family than marrying the right guy.

Albert is saving money now so that he can save up enough to buy his own house. He told Jo he is not going to wait for the right woman to come along, he is going on with his life. He wants his own house, he can afford the payments but not the down-payment right now. So, now he saves, each month he puts away what he was paying for in rent and within a year he feels he may have enough to look for a nice starter house.

If life hands him a good woman to live there with, than that will be a bonus. But for now, he came home to help with Jo and all her needs. Albert has always helped. He is very close with Angel and this horrid relationship she is in now has hurt him terribly. He wants to help her but she won't leave. She has been crushed by this man who has made her feel insignificant. She is a shadow of who she used to be and Albert is ready to accidently find him in an alley. Jo has to stop this from happening. Albert would not do well in prison. Jo opens the door to Albert's bedroom. Thankfully, he is still asleep. Sometimes he goes for a run at 4:00am but today he sleeps, and she is thankful.

Jo picks up his clothes and hangs them back up. Very unusual for him to have left his clothes out. Albert is neater than she is, he must have been distracted last night. She looks around the room and sees a driven man. His academic trophies and accolades are plastered all over his room as if they were each a Nobel Prize.

It would not surprise her if he actually accomplished that too. As soon as Albert moved home again. Sylvana came around again. She is there at least once a week. Jo will have to open his eyes as to why she is around. He gets so focused he probably doesn't even know that Sylvana is the one for him. She always has had her eyes on him, ever since they were in college together. Although Jo still thinks it was a coincidence that they ended up in the same school. She smiles to herself.

She talks to Albert out loud, "Albert, don't be stupid anymore ok? Look at Sylvana and the reason she is here. See her for the beautiful young lady she is."

Albert rolls over in his sleep. He and his mom always had conversations while he was half asleep. "ok Momma" he mumbles.

"Albert listen to me, I'm going to bring Angel home tonight. But she is going to need your understanding and not your criticism. None of it. You hear me?" she asks in a motherly directive.

"yessss Momma, Angel, no criticism." he mumbles back to her.

"Don't yes Momma me, do the right thing. Angel will need a lot of love. She needs unconditional love from you especially. Sylvana will be around to help her too, you'll see. Albert, I hate to pull rank but you are going to have to show your siblings the right way to handle this. Angel is pregnant, I know she is; I feel her pain. I have to get her away from him and tonight I will. I promise you that." She sighs.

"promise Momma, Angel, love, Sylvana lovely." He repeats in his sleep voice.

Jo gets up and kisses her son. She knows he will remember all she said but she takes a sticky note and leaves it on his mirror, *remember your promise. Love you Albert S.W.A.K*

Jo kisses him one more time and walks out of the room, she goes back upstairs and looks around the house. She spends a few minutes in each room putting things back the way they belong. Everyone will know the room has been touched by her, they will know where everything goes now, and hopefully it won't become in such disarray again. They will have a guide now.

~ ~ ~

"She can't possibly drive a car. That is plain nuts!!! A car!! This whole thing doesn't make any sense!" he exclaims.

"For you, no. but it doesn't have to. It has to make sense for her. For them, too many requests to deny this one. The gift is a wonderful thing, you need to understand that. This is not a cold process, maybe that is what you had, but it's not the norm really. This, this here, in front of us is the ultimate gift. Stop looking at regulations or what you think is right. We will get her where she needs to be, only not now, she isn't finished." The second responds

"ok, let's go." Jo says to no one.

~ ~ ~

Within a blink Jo arrives where Angel has been living. It's not a dump, she is thankful for that. She walks around the house a moment and she sees Angel has not been in an unsafe environment, physically anyway. She takes a moment to look into each closet, not knowing exactly what she is looking for until she sees them.

Angel's suitcases, the one she left the house with to move in with this guy eight months ago. She opens one and realizes that she hasn't been wearing her own clothes at all. She puts the suitcase by the front door ready to grab and go. Something pulls her into the kitchen, she looks around each cabinet and she finds what she is looking for, a packet of birth control. He has been forcing her to take pills. Angel can't swallow pills, she gags on them. Now she understands the magnitude of the situation.

He thinks she is on the pill, Angel is not taking them, he does not know. Or maybe he does and all her calling to Jo means that she is afraid. Jo hears her daughter calling to her in her sleep. She hears her pleads with her to come help.

"Ok, baby, I'm here" Jo says holding the packet of pills, Jo puts them in the garbage and looks around again in the kitchen. She finds morning after pills as well. "So you want all the fun without any of the consequences? You are a sick bastard." She says out loud.

Jo is now fearful for her daughter; she runs upstairs and finds her sleeping in her bed. "Wake up!!!" Jo screams at her. "We haven't much time, he went out running and you have to get the hell out of here now!!!!! Angel, wake up!!!"

Angel sees her mom and begins to cry. Jo had brought up Angel's clothes. "Here honey, your big sweatshirt, the one you say you feel loved in because it feels like someone is hugging you when you wear such softness, put this on. Here is a bra, and your own underpants and I brought you soft jeans to wear too. Come, move honey. For once, wake up quickly and do as I say Angel." Jo's voice is quivering, she is not sure this can work.

She looks around the room, she looks down at her wristwatch and shakes her head no. "Angel honey, he is on his way back from his run, it won't be long. Please come with me. It's Momma." Jo pleads

"Momma, I'm pregnant." She cries.

"I know honey, I heard you in my dreams." Jo answers

"It's not the first time." Angel continues as she begins to waken and get dressed in her own clothes. She missed them but didn't know where he put them. "Last time he beat it out of me. It hurt so much, he didn't stop until I bled." She says holding her stomach. "I never thought I would be able to do this again." She cries to her mother.

"Oh Angel, Albert would have come, Daddy would have come, any of them. All you had to do was call. But that doesn't matter now. Now we go home." She says. Jo has tears of her own running down her face at the thought of her child being beaten into an abortion.

"Angel, does he give you vitamins each morning?" Jo asks.

"Yes." She whimpers

"And does he give you a different one after being with you in bed?" Jo asks.

Angel can only nod.

Jo holds her daughter in her arms and pulls her in close. She speaks softly but quickly into her daughter's ear. "Angel, he has been giving you birth control without your consent and the morning after pill after he sleeps with you. He does not want children. But you don't swallow pills what did you do?" she asks.

"I held them under my tongue and swallowed twice whatever he gave me. Then he would leave the room satisfied I took I would flush it in the toilet later. He is going to kill me Momma." Angel leans into her mother she needs to hear her heartbeat.

"I want to go home, are we going home?" she asks through tears.

"Yes baby, we're going home. Albert is waiting up to help you." Jo says. The second one looks around for a clock and sees its 5:00am already, she knows this man's run is about over. Jo knows he will be back much sooner than later. The second one is getting nervous, so is Jo.

She grabs her daughter's hand and together they run out the door and around the back to where he has been hiding Angel's motorcycle. Angel puts on her helmet. Jo sits behind her holding onto the suitcases for dear life. Angel starts it up slowly and walks the bike through the back neighbor's yard to the street in front of that house. She knows her man comes in the front and she doesn't want to be seen.

Once in the street, she heads home. Jo breathes a sigh of relief she sees her car following them and understanding sets in. Jo finds a smile in her heart.

~ ~ ~

Back home, Jo prepares a breakfast fit for a king. She makes homemade biscuits, her special strawberry jam is boiling on the stovetop and she puts up the coffee on the timer. She puts the volume up high so her husband can hear it upstairs when it is ready.

She sets the table for the five of them and she sits down for a moment to think. She writes on a napkin;

Dear Ben, unconditional always
Jo.

"It says it all. Each one a private sentiment between us. Tacky?" she asks.

"No, beautiful" says the second.

"When will Angel be home?" she asks.

"Within ten minutes. About the time the coffee timer will go off. We have to go though." Says the second.

"I know but can you wait till after breakfast?" she asks.

"I will, have you enjoyed your gift?" he asks.

"Oh, more than you know. More than I could ever express. Did I do right? I mean did I blow this gift?" she asks.

"No, you did well and so will they." He answers.

~ ~ ~

Karen sits in class worried about her mother. How can she even contemplate having a relationship with this guy when her mother is up in her house dying? How can she go away to college without her around? She needs her advice, she needs her here for a long time. Even graduation won't mean as much without her.

Tears begin to fall without her wanting them too. 'great, right in the middle of math.' Karen thinks to herself. Tricia leans over and hands her a tissue.

Karen looks at her and sees tears in her eyes as well. Tricia and she have been close friends forever. Going to separate colleges is going to be the hardest thing they have ever done. Tricia practically lives at Karen's house. Thankfully, Greg is going to school with her, at least she will have one familiar face and his is a good face to look at too.

So, why is she with this loser from the basketball team? Is she even with him? He chooses moments to acknowledge her and moments to ignore her, no rhyme or reason to either. Greg is not too fond of him and neither is Tricia but Karen feels stuck dealing with him. Ugh, if only she could have one more conversation with her mom. A real one, the kind where she is blunt with her and doesn't sugar coat life like many other parents do.

One conversation!!!! Is that so much to ask for? Karen wishes she knew how to put in a request where it would be granted. Which voodoo doctor to call, or even a higher spirit, someone. She needs one more day. That's all. After graduation, she can go to college and start anew with new friends and a new world order for her. But for now? She still wants her momma.

She lays her head down on her desk to will herself into a different situation. Tricia is right there for her, as always.

~ ~ ~

Charlie stands among his new friends, if you can call them that, and watches them get high. They are so interested in what they are doing they never noticed that he has yet to join them. He thought a new group of people would give him a new perspective on life. New friends, new ideas, new ways of thinking. But none of them think, do they?

And then they do too much and he is there to pick up the pieces. He comes up with cleaver ways for them to cover for each other while they aren't exactly doing the right thing. None of it is illegal, it's not right either though.

Skipping class to get high, seems pointless to him. But here he is watching it all over again. Making out because no one is there to stop you is not a reason to do that either but they do. They don't care who watches either.

Charlie came to this group by accident. He happened to be around them during a particularly weird moment of two of them getting caught by one of the janitors. He came up with a quick reason why they were there and since then they have pulled him into their group, thinking he is of like mind.

But he is not, and he doesn't want to simply walk away, but in reality, he walked in so why can't he? There are one or two who seem like decent kids but they only want one thing out of life so conversations become limited.

Charlie misses talking to his mother about things. They always talk about everything. He once told Brandy that he talks to his mother about everything and she called him a pansy and a momma's boy. So since then he hasn't told her anything else about himself.

What she doesn't understand is that his mother is his rock. She is the reason he is who he is. She has always believed in him and that he can do anything. His father has always backed him up as well. He has great parents, weird but loving siblings too.

As the baby of the family he gets teased the most, even though they always call Karen the baby in the family, it's only since he grew taller than her. Karen and he are best friends really, he will miss her next year. It's going to change a lot at home in the not so distant future.

It will most likely be only the guys at home. Unless by some miracle Angel comes home. He misses his sister too. She left to live with some jerk who won't let her visit and who changed her phone number.

He knows Albert won't let this last, Albert is ready to knock some sense into the guy, literally. He almost feels sorry for the guy. Albert packs a mean punch, especially when it comes to protection of the family.

Charlie shakes his head out of his thoughts, this can't go on anymore; it can't. This place, these people, they are not him. He is not enjoying this at all. He walks away from the group and they don't even notice. If it was his other friends they would have called to him or something.

"Why can't I talk to my mom?" he says out loud. "One more time, a real conversation. I want to hear from her that I'm going to be ok. She will know. She will be honest with me." He says.

"Who you talking to bud?" someone asks.

Charlie looks up to see is good friends waiting for him outside of the gym. Big Al grins and Peter pushes on Charlie's shoulder. "Come on, Coach Michael is on the prowl, let's get out of here before he finds us skipping gym again." The three friends walk around the building until they find themselves in the parking lot.

Charlie remains quiet. "We've got your back Charlie my friend. That's a promise." Big Al says.

The three friends part and make their way back to the building to sneak in before the next bell. Charlie still pondering where he can put a request in to speak to his mother again.

~ ~ ~

Albert doesn't like living at home. He actually despises being here. He doesn't do sadness well and clearly he doesn't do sickness well either. How will he ever handle his wife or children being sick? He looks on as his father's undying love for his mother drives him to do everything in his power to make her comfortable. He watches as he reads to her their favorite books. He pushes her around the living room on a rolling chair to music as if they were dancing.

No one has that kind of love anymore. He is not sure he is capable of giving love to anyone either. Besides, who would want affection from him? He was turned down already once, and for what? For not having the perfect family.

His family has no connections, no social climbers, no one who is a "somebody" in society. How was she supposed to cope being in a family where social activities revolve around the family and not society? She also hated that he and Angel are so close

She commented on the fact that he speaks to his sister too often. She should not have such a strong hold on a brother, that connection didn't look good. None of this came out until after they were engaged and she took a good hard look at his family.

He thought the whole idea of society and social climbing was only in books and movies. He never really realized that real people do that sort of thing. Better he found out now because he was not about to forsake anyone in his family for an outside person, no matter how beautiful.

Angel, he thinks, has not been in a good place for a long time. But he can't get to her, the jerk she is living with won't let him speak to her, he has tried of several occasions.

He needs his mom is what he needs. He hates to admit, even at his age, but his mom will know what to do. She will know how he should proceed because the only thing he can think of doing right now is pounding some respect into the guy.

Karen is graduating high school soon and she is involved in a jerk as well but she asked him not to get involved. She said she can handle this one. He only hopes she handles the rejection well. He knows the type all too well.

Albert is the lightest sleeper in the family next to his mom. She used to sit in the room with him and have full conversations with him. He never remembered them as well as she did. But if she ever asked him to do something, that part he always remembered in the morning.

As an adult he should not miss those conversations but he does. One more would be nice. One more request. "Just one Mom. What would it be?" he asks out loud.

~ ~ ~

Ben met Jo 35 years ago, they met while he was still in medical school. She was one of the trainers at the nearby farm. She gave horseback riding lessons and tours around campus. He followed her on a tour one day and that was the end of him.

Ever since then he has loved her. She didn't put up much of a fight either. Ben smiles at the memory. He watches her now as she sleeps in her medical induced coma to alleviate the pain they say she is most likely in if she was awake.

It's the hardest thing he ever had to do. He looks around the house and realizes he doesn't even know what is going on with his kids right now, he has been so tunnel focused on her. His whole life he has been focused on her. Her care, her happiness, her everything.

His children came second to her, he knows that but he loves them too. He would go to the moon and back for them, barefoot on nails if he had to. Jo always told him he needs to tell them that. He has tried in his own way.

He is so proud of them, this much he has said numerous times. Especially Angel, how smart she is. He knows Jo will find a way to bring her home. He knows it will happen, he doesn't know how but he knows it will be because of Jo and no one else, that Angel will leave the guy she is with and find her way back to a place where she is loved.

Often Ben finds Karen on the phone with some mystery guy that Charlie says is a jerk. Charlie has been a bit aloof lately but Ben as attributed everything to Jo and her condition. What he wouldn't do to have one question and answer session with her. Only one, he doesn't need much. He will settle on her showing him how to care for the kids, like she did.

So, not even a whole conversation, one answer. His heart pleads for one answer.

~ ~ ~

People don't understand that even through all the pain, you can hear what they are saying about you. Jo knew the moment the meds were being given to her to make her sleep. She didn't mind getting rid of the pain, but getting rid of everyone else was hard.

The kids have been confiding in her telling her things she may have had to pry out of them in the past, but now they probably think she isn't listening. She is, she did, and she heard every word.

Oh, if she could get one day, one, is all she needs to put everyone back on track. Once there, they will be ok, she needs one day is all. Maybe even a few hours, she will take a few hours.

~ ~ ~

"This is not how it's supposed to happen. No conversations, no notes read or written, no assisted help in finding a daughter, none of this. It's ALL wrong." He says.

"No, it's ALL right. You still don't get it do you? There were multiple requests for the same thing. Look at the transcript again, I showed you the whole thing, it's all written down. Each and every one of them asked for one thing, one more day. A gift was granted. It may not be the way they were thinking it would be, but they received what they asked for. A gift. Understand that and we can move forward." The second answers

"What do you mean we can move forward? You mean we can't until I understand? We hang out here until I get what is going on? Why is this all on me? I didn't ask for this." He says annoyance in his voice.

"No, but you need to learn about life's gifts all the same. You need to see wonder again or your position will be changed. You will have a different job if you can't grasp or understand the gift when it is given." He instructs.

~ ~ ~

Angel knows she has missed her period again. He has been avoiding her lately though. As if he is disinterested now. Almost as if he doesn't see her, doesn't want her around anymore. When Angel goes to sleep she thinks of her mother, she wonders if the illness is as bad as her heart tells her.

She dreams of her mother several nights in a row. Each time she is calling to her to come get her. Each time she wakes to see she is still locked in her bedroom and can't leave until morning when he needs breakfast.

He will want sex tomorrow night, he will notice her breast getting fuller like they did last time right away. She cries herself to sleep screaming in her head to her mother. She needs her so badly right now. No one else will understand how she is trapped here.

No one at work understands why her boyfriend takes her to and from work. They think it's romantic that he packs her lunch when romance is the last thing his bringing her is about. He tells her what she is allowed to eat and weighs her every other week to make sure she is not eating anything else other than what he says.

He decides her clothes in the morning as well as after work. This is not what she signed up for, she thought he was a giving man, but his giving was all a lure.

Angel has a good job, she works with an accountant as his second in command. She can do anything he asks of her professionally. He likes her, a lot too. She can tell. Some days he actually can get her to smile, but then she is reminded that she lives with a man who would not want her smiling at another man's jokes.

Mr. Beagly, Manuel, is probably the only person she could call a friend outside of college. He is passionate about what he does and believes his job can really help people.

Angel feels the wind in her face again and is enjoying every second. She is headed home in the wee hours of the morning. She knows she will be home before the coffee timer goes off. That is her goal.

Her boyfriend will not follow her, he doesn't work that way. At least she doesn't think he does. He may want to possess her but with his recent disinterest she is hoping he will find another, maybe someone who likes being told what to do all day.

Being back on her bike, Angel is feeling free again. She can't wait to be home. The drive home, the wind in her face, it's all giving her the revitalization she needs right now.

~ ~ ~

The coffee timer is going on. Tweeting loudly. Ben wakes to hear the noise. He looks to his wife and is wondering how she is sleeping through the piercing sound. He makes his way downstairs quickly to turn it off. Albert beats him by a second and turns off the alarm.

Albert looks to his dad with a sticky note in his hand, tears are in his eyes. "Angel is coming home, Mom told me last night." Albert manages to say.

Ben looks around the room, he sees biscuits on the table and the jam on the stove. "When did you wake up?" he asks.

Albert looks to his dad, 'When the coffee was ready why?"

"You didn't do this?" he asks as he looks around again. He sees the napkin on the table and sits down to look at the writing. It says it all, the answer he was waiting for. Love them, as long as there is a sun, moon and stars in the sky.

Ben begins to cry, "When? How?" he is baffled.

Albert sits next to him and puts his hand on his father's which is still holding the napkin. "Last night. I told you, Mom and I talked. She said Angel"

The front door slowly creaks open, the men both jump to run to the door. They freeze when they see Angel. "I came home." She says as she drops her suitcases on the floor.

Albert runs over to hug his sister and picks her up and swings her around. He puts her down and hold her head in his hands. It's really her, not a ghost. "Did you speak to Mom too?" he asks simply

Angel's eyes fill with tears. Ben is in front of her in seconds. He holds his daughter like he has never held her before. This time he will never let go.

~ ~ ~

Karen wakes to the sound of the coffee timer. "Damn, I don't want to get up this early. Why can't Dad set a normal timer? Or at least turn this one down." She says as she starts to sit up in bed.

Something is amiss. She looks around her room. Everything is in its place. Everything has been touched, all of her belongings, she looks to her closet, closed, she runs over and sees everything hanging up. Her book bag is sitting neatly next to her gym bag, her shoes are all put back on the shoe rack, her dresser has been arranged the way it used to be and her desk has a bunch of papers on top.

As Karen stands over the papers she begins to tremble. She sits down and pours over everything that is written before her. The highlighted words, the clues that she missed. She takes off the shirt she is wearing and realizes Mom is right, this is not a design but actual tally marks, she counts them, than she lets out a scream at the realization of it all.

Seconds later her father opens her door, "Honey are you ok?" he asks with concern in his voice. Albert is right behind him, then Angel.

Upon seeing Angel, Karen begins to cry, "I didn't imagine her? She kissed me last night?" she asks.

Ben looks at his daughter, "I believe somehow she did, yes." He looks at how she is holding onto the t-shirt. "Should we burn that? Or bleach to take out all the marks?" he asks. He has seen such stupidity before he knows what the shirt is intended to show.

"Hmmm, bleach sounds good, then I can say I washed it before returning it." She smiles.

Albert holds up his sticky note, "You too?" he asks.

Before she can answer Charlie says from behind Albert, "Can I join the party?" They all look at him, he is holding up his note as well.

"Breakfast is on the table, let's go eat and discuss our next moves together, yes?" Ben asks his children.

Everyone follows downstairs and begins to sit down at the kitchen table. After plates are passed and filled and the eating starts, Charlie speaks, "I don't know what happened last night, I don't care for an explanation but I do care that Angel is home. We missed you." He smiles at her

Angel looks around the room, ahhh, love. This is what she needs. "Long story short, I'm pregnant, he will kill me, literally, if he finds out, Mom came to get me last night. Here I am, with all my baggage." She rubs her belly.

"Ok, so first on the agenda is get you to a doctor to make sure all is well. You don't do this without a doctor young lady, too risky. Next?" Ben asks.

"I don't want to go to graduation parties with people who think it's about losing virginity and not a stepping stone to our future." Karen says.

"Ok, bleaching the shirt will be a loud statement to him. Then we get to plan a family celebration which you rejected before. Can I invite grandparents? Aunts and uncles?" Ben asks.

"The whole nine yards please. Albert, can you bake me a pineapple upside down cake?" Karen pleads

"If that's all you want, you got it." He smiles.

Another knock at the door.

"Who the hell can that be so early in the morning?" Ben asks. His children all look to him confused.

"What the hell? Ooo, Sorry Sylvana, I couldn't imagine who was here this early. Come in, we're having breakfast." He says

Albert stands up to greet her only to sit down quickly after he realizes he is still in his batman pajama pants. "Morning Syl, what brings you out of bed?"

"A motorcycle's engine." She smiles at Angel and gives her a kiss hello. "Welcome home." Sylvana looks around, she knows immediately what has happened.

"She was given a gift. This is the most beautiful thing I've ever witnessed. I mean I've heard of such things but never seen it before." Sylvana looks around the room, clearly everyone else is confused. She explains what she believes has happened, with each person she said that Jo either spoke to them or gave them the answer they were looking for. Each one held up their note, except Albert, he is too awestruck by her understanding to know what to do.

"Oh, I'm sorry to go on so, my grandmother told me about getting a gift many years ago. She said it is as much for the living as it is for the departed." Sylvana slapped her hand over her mouth.

"It's ok Syl" Ben says. "We've been expecting this for days now. But after this, it will be easier to accept." He looks around the room, his children all agree.

~ ~ ~

"So this gift allows her to follow us now peacefully. No fighting, no kicking and screaming they want one more of something?" he asks.

"Now you're understanding. Come, let's go get Jo. She is ready." The second one replies.

"Jo?" he asks.

"Yes, I've been waiting for you to come back. Did Angel make it back in time?" she asks.

"I can only answer one question, is that the one you want answered?" the second one asks.

Jo thinks a moment, the rest will be ok, she knows they will. "Yes." She says.

"She is in the arms of a loving family now." The second one answers, giving a little more than necessary.

"Ok, let's go then." Jo responds

"Just like that? You're ready?" he asks.

"Yes, unless there is something else for me to do?" she asks.

"No, he is a rookie, come, let's go." Says the second one.

~ ~ ~

After the funeral Karen is wandering around her house thinking of all the things her mother had a hand in designing. Greg finds her in her father's office. "You ok?" he asks.

Wendy and Tricia had finally left and Karen was still feeling the need to be held and cry with someone but they were spent. They loved Karen's mom and were having a hard time staying in the house. They will come back tomorrow, she knows for sure.

"Maybe" she says.

Greg walks over to her with open arms. She falls into his arms and begins to cry all over again. He stays with her that night on the couch and lets her fall asleep on his lap.

Sylvana and Albert cleaned the kitchen up after everyone left. "Syl, why did you really come over yesterday morning?" he asks.

"Your driveway is right near my bedroom remember? Motorcycle's aren't exactly quiet at 5:00am. I came because I felt there had to be a reason she is home out of the blue. My instincts were right. Angry?" she asks worried.

"Scared, actually." He says thinking how his mother had mentioned her in his sleep conversation with him.

"OK." Sylvana could not say more, she has more in her head but now is not the time to tell him. In time, she hopes he will understand they are meant to be together.

"Syl?" he looks at her

"Yes?" she looks to Albert who looks like a little boy right now about to burst.

She opens her arms and he falls into them holding onto her like he never did before, and loving how she feels.

~ ~ ~

"Damn, how can you still beat me?" Peter asks.

"I told you that you won't be able to beat me at chess." Charlie says.

"If I didn't know better, I'd think someone told you about my secret weapon, but that can't be possible." He tells Charlie

"You should always believe in possibilities, life can surprise you." Charlie answers with a smile, thinking of his mom.

"Hey Charlie, heard about your mom. Been there, done that. If you need a pal, give a call." Brandy says.

Charlie looks over to her wondering how she got to his house. Peter speaks up first, "Brandy, you need a ride home? It's a two bus trip ride over here." He says.

"You took two buses?" Charlie asks.

"Yeah, well, for a momma's boy you're ok." Brandy says.

"Play chess?" Charlie asks.

"I'd love to learn." She says sitting down next to Charlie to watch him and Peter play again.

'Bringing her up, one step at a time' he thinks to himself.

~ ~ ~

Ben has been numb for most of the morning but then he watches his children and held them and mourned with them instead of by himself. They are all in this together, and together they will stay.

Angel is seeing a doctor tomorrow, he is driving her himself and they filed for a restraining order on her boyfriend, in case it matters. The police officer said he has been reported on before but having solid evidence is even better, they were going to try and get a search warrant to find the pills she was forced to take. Even if she never actually took them

Ben walks around the house and sees Charlie with a girl leaning on him. "Hmmm, nice to see," he thinks to himself.

He finds Greg and Karen in his office sitting on the couch not talking which is saying more than words to each other.

Then he goes to find Albert and to his shock and surprise, but in a good way, he is in Sylvana's arms.

Ben walks over to the living room picture of his wedding. He stares at Jo, to him the sun, the moon and stars revolved around her, he is surprised the sun came up today. "Daddy, we're going to be ok." Angel says. "Together"

"Yes, Angel, yes we will." Ben says.

~ ~ ~

A year to the day Jo was given her gift, Albert and Sylvana decide it is a good day to get married. They have a simple ceremony with only family and a few friends at the park.

Angel stands next to Albert with her son as his best man. Who says a boy can't have a close sister? Albert was there when the baby was born. The family decided to name him Joe. He certainly has the strength and determination as his namesake did.

Charlie and Brandy have been an item ever since, his friend Big Al has been coming around the house with a girl as well, one of Brandy's friends. They are quite the foursome, now instead of planning which class to skip they plan on which colleges to apply to, career goals and how to stick together through all life will throw at them.

Karen and Greg enjoyed a great first year in college, Ben couldn't be prouder. The two of them have made promises to each other that they are trying to keep. Mainly, to stay in each other's lives.

After the wedding, Ben drives off to the cemetery. He sits on the bench from his backyard that he and Jo used to make their plans on. He paid to have it transferred to the cemetery. "Ok Jo, we did it. You did really. Everyone is settled here, as you can see. No, I haven't started dating anyone and for right now I'm content with that so don't pester me.

Albert and Sylvana want to stay at the house for six more months because they said they will have their money then for a down-payment on a house with a bit left over to fix whatever needs fixing." He fidgets with his hands a moment.

"Little Joe is a wonder to us all. His curiosity for the world around him makes us all marvel at the simple things in life. We miss you Jo, and there is one thing I forgot to tell you a year ago today. You look beautiful." Ben smiles down at the stone in front of him that bears Jo's name. He said the same thing from the first day together to her last. Every day.

Ben stands to leave when he sees something in front of him falling, he reaches out his hand to find a feather landing on his palm. It's brown, he thinks a moment, upon realization he smiles, the name of Jo's horse when they first met, Brownfeather. He looks up and lets a tear fall, then walks to his car smiling.

The Night of a Full Moon

Petunia has been getting ready for the next stage in her life, motherhood. She lives on her own and has created a wonderful life for herself. It may be different from the rest of her community but she likes what she is doing. However, tonight is about to change all that she has thought to be true.

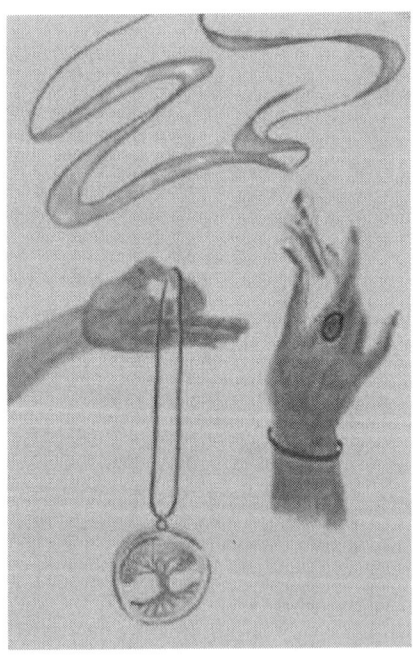

The night has a full harvest moon, with only a few cloud wisps gliding across the sky in slow motion, the air is warm and the mist within it has enveloped all who venture out. It is on this night that Petunia's stomach starts rumbling in ways that she has not known before. The life inside of her has chosen this night, this night of a full moon to come and join her in the world.

Petunia walks into the kitchen slowly so as not to speed up this life changing event that is coming, she opens the window slightly. She reaches into the cabinet and takes down her life amulet to put around her neck, she quietly moves over to the stovetop and puts the water on to boil. Carefully taking out the extract and herbs required to make the soothing tea she needs, suddenly, she feels a harder rumble inside. Petunia lays her left hand on her belly, "Slow down new life, I'm getting ready. We will do this the way it's supposed to be done. The way all new life comes in." She pats her belly again for comfort.

She makes her tea and takes her crystals from her pocket, Petunia rubs them together in a very specific rhythm over the cup of tea and they begin to glow a soft blue, she rubs them a few more times then, circles one over the other. The blue hue rises from the crystals and swirls around her hands, holding them together like a handshake. She opens her hands and lets the blue roam, first around her heart, then it breaks into two and finds itself traveling around the house, until each stream finds the open window and leaves with a sudden whoosh. Each to their own direction.

The years of learning the craft of her community had seemed difficult to swallow at an earlier time in her life. All the rules and regulations, the right time for this the wrong time for that. Every time something changed in her life there was another reason to pull out the life amulet. All of these specifics had worn her down, to the point where she had told her parents she needs a break. She put her foot down when it came time to further her education, she wanted more. She insisted on going to a school of the non-spirited, as they were known to her. She wanted to learn about all people, not only her own.

    Surprisingly, her parents supported her wholeheartedly. They told her that they would even pay for the education and that, in time, she may see the value of what she has learned living in their community and how to apply her lessons to her new life. Her mom gave her a blessing before she left and her father gave her a bracelet for her protection. The bracelet is so beautiful, she is still wearing it today, she rubs it now as her body is twisting in ways she didn't learn about yet. This new life is going to come whether she is ready or not. Whether she can find the father or not. Whether she is alone or with family.

    Right now, the answers to so many of those things are open ended. Before she finishes getting ready, she sends a message through her mind's meditation to her parents. She sits with her elbows on the table, one hand on her belly and the other hand on her heart. Many years ago, she was told her parents could "hear" her anytime she did this with full concentration. Concentration is hard right now with the life becoming so active, but she needs to try. Calling on the phone would not tell them of the urgency.

    She sits for only a minute when suddenly the window closes on its own, she gets up and closes the lock, now she knows it's time to leave. But before she does, she tries one more time to "reach" her parents. This time her thoughts work, she knows for certain because the bracelet becomes heated and she begins to feel as if her father is holding her hand. She never expected her thoughts to work, she never expects any of what she does to work and yet, they always do for her. Her grandmother used to tell her that she has a special gift and that one day she will appreciate receiving this special gift. Not many receive.

During her early school years, she tried hard not to use any of her "talents". She wanted to be like a non-spirit and yet she found them all lacking in something. She could never quite put her finger on what was missing, but something was always missing. She loves her friends very much but when they get close enough to her and realized she is a spirited one they treat her differently. Asked completely uneducated questions. For example, they always asked, "Can you look and see what is on the next exam?" or her other favorite was, "Is it true spirited ones have green blood?" where did they come up with this stuff? None of it made any sense to her. Still, she loves them for who they are, simple, nice people who only understand the world from what they have read or seen. They do not feel the world around them at all, they cannot connect to the elements the way she does. This is why during a rain storm they run inside while Petunia sits on the park bench soaking up life's water energy.

Petunia gathers her bag and waits for her ride to show up. There is no telling whom will be driving her. For this, she relies on the blue hue. Petunia hears her ride before she sees it. Slowly the white car comes into her driveway and pulls right in front of her. Smoothly, she opens the back door and slides in, again being careful not to jostle the life inside of her. "Got the blue and came as soon as I could, not the white horse you were expecting eh Tunie, but it's all I could find on short notice." He smiles.

"It's ok, my old friend, there are few people I'd like to share this with, I'm glad you're here. Besides, it's white and can move fast through this kind of night with ample protection for the life within me, which, by the way, is telling me it's in a hurry, so we best be moving on." She leans back into her seat and starts to feel her stomach becoming harder and harder. Her breath becomes uneasy with this one. The driver senses things are moving faster than they should so he mumbles a few words of magic of his own; *help me help her oh wise one, bring the pain to two and not one – I will help her through this time, in the end, she will see she is mine.*

Eli is not completely ready for the power of energy that hits him the minute his words are finished. He grips onto the steering wheel as this pain comes and goes. "How are you doing my friend?" he calls back to Petunia. Glancing in his review mirror he can see that Petunia is lost in mediation. To himself he says, 'good Tunie, find a comfortable place, let me help you through this'.

Petunia is using an old family recipe to get through stressful times - meditation. All her life the elders in the community have spoken about how meditation and mind over body therapy will help you through everything physically challenging and this sure is challenging. This being the most difficult thing she has experienced, she decides to try to reach a deep meditative state. At the last traffic light she did notice that the pain was not as hard as it was in the house. Petunia is cautious about changes, so instead of letting her mind run amok and go to worst case scenario, she has decided to bring herself back to the what lead up to this moment. Giving herself a point in which to focus her meditation.

~ ~ ~

The day she left for school her parents packed up her car, on loan until school is over, and wished her well. Her father was so proud that she was able to get in to this school and that she received some academic scholarship made him overjoyed with pride. The night before she left, he sat down with her and gave her some life guidelines to help her sift through the mumble she will see in school. He talked with her about the difference between and college boy and a man. Her mom spent time with her as well. She made sure she was prepared for anything. It was her mom that had taught her self-defense moves as soon as she turned sixteen.

She went over all of them again that night, and then, for added protection, she snuck a few amulets in her belongings.

She always considered herself lucky compared to the classmates Petunia had met and what they said about their parents. However, she did have someone tell her that she should not always believe all that they say. This was the first life lesson she had with the non-spirited. Her closest friend at school was a boy named Eliezar. He explained life in school for her, taught her the ins and outs about campus life and showed her how to believe in her own decisions. Something that was taught in her community as well but the lessons never sank in when you are trying to break away from all that has been taught to you. Trying to be your own person and not only a follower, being unique was always her goal.

She never wanted to forget her community, she simply felt that she did not belong and that there was more to life than being inside their insular community. Being in a college setting she was meeting a whole slew of people from different backgrounds, different walks of life completely. Her brain was on permanent overload with what she had to take in around her. Some days the cultural differences would take her hours to understand.

Each night she went back to her apartment and spent some time meditating to gain perspective on what she had learned that was not from the professors. Eliezar, as it turned out, lived in the same apartment building. The only request from her parents was that she lived off of the campus and did not become involved in the dormitory life. This, she felt, was a small concession considering they were paying for all of her education and housing. These new friends did not understand why she felt living alone was better than the perpetual party of their dorm life.

Petunia quickly learned how to get from her apartment to her classes on time, she even found herself a job on campus to fill up her days each semester. One of the many things she did not understand is how much time was wasted at school. Once her classes were over, which usually was by 1:00 or 2:00 in the afternoon because she loved morning classes, she became restless and board. Her anatomy professor showed her the job board where she quickly found herself various positions on campus.

During her third semester in school her job was in the chemistry lab. They actually paid students to clean up and prepare the lab for the next group of people to come in. Petunia always prided herself on her efficiency and she completed the job in half the time the professor allotted for her. Even on her first day, she went to find him to tell him she was done. The man looked infuriated and stormed out of his office towards the lab, picturing a half done job and ready to yell at this new student intern. When he stood in the doorway of the lab he looked around, not only had she cleaned the tables, counters, sinks and chairs but the lab was set up for the next class, materials out and easily found. He turned to her, now calm, "How did you do this so fast? Did you have help? Because I can't afford to pay more than one of you."

Petunia had taken offense to this accusation; did he know she was spirited? If so, he must have assumed she used some sort of trick, little did he know you can't use tricks to clean, you can only give the illusion of clean while the real mess was still there. She spoke rather abruptly, "Not on your life. Efficiency gets everything done in a timely fashion. Is there anything else I can do for you? I am on schedule to be here another hour and a half."

He smiled at her and looked back at the lab again. "You can come clean like this on lab days; that will be great. If you are as good in an office as you are in the lab, I could use some help in my office, getting my papers straightened out there too." He has smiled at her.

The pain came on strong this time and without warning like the other times, Petunia arose from her meditation and grabbed her belly as well as the seat in front of her. Eli was gripping onto the steering wheel and trying to stay in control of the car. 'wow that was a whopper' he says to himself.

"What did you say Eli?" she asked him.

Forgetting for a moment that she does not know that he is feeling her pain and listening into her thoughts he calls back to her, "I said that must have been a whopper, the way you grabbed my seat dear."

"Oh, I'm sorry, it came on so fast and furious I didn't know what to do. Are you ok, you look like you're sweating. I'm a little hot in here too, so you can turn down the heat. How much longer before we get to the hospital?" she asks in a much calmer voice.

"We are still about twenty minutes away, however, there seems to be a bit of traffic here. We'll be ok Tunie, I promise. This baby will be delivered in the proper fashion. Don't you worry; I got this covered." Eli is trying to talk in a calm voice, however his insides are completely jumbled around and he is not sure how much more he can take. If he is feeling half, he has now gained a whole new respect for his mother having done this eight times.

"I'm going to try and get back to my meditation I hope I'm not making too much noise. Sometimes I moan." She says shyly.

"Go ahead dear, all is good." Eli doesn't want to think anything of his own so as not to disturb her; he had no idea the connection would be to her thoughts as well as feelings. He knows that she is coming to a point in her life on campus that was not good but he wants her to think the whole day through. Been a long time and he is not sure she ever really addressed this. It has to be done. She has never been able to tell him the whole truth and now he will know. Although he is not sure if this will be a good thing or a bad thing.

Slowly, Petunia gets herself back into her dream-like state. She is following the professor back to his office. He pointed towards the file cabinet and said, "If you can make sense of that for the next hour and a half than go ahead." Petunia opened the first drawer on the bottom. Her mother had always told her the foundation was first, so she figured these were the least looked at files and probably the ones where she should start.

Each week had become the same thing, she went to classes, went to lab, then went to the office. From there she would go home, sometimes meeting up with friends and sometimes meeting only Eliezar on the green to study and talk about what's been going on in each other's classes as well as work.

Eliezar was very helpful in giving her ideas as to how to make sense of the jumbled mess the professor called an office. She had been so disgusted by someone living in such a mess, she almost didn't want to finish the job, but she knew better than that. If she didn't do this, no one she knew would and he would forever be in this mess. However, with midterms coming up she needed the time to study so she told the professor that she will continue to do the lab but is postponing her office duties until after midterms. He seemed to be ok with this.

During this heavy study time, Eliezar spent a lot of time in her apartment. He was in his last semester of graduate study and would be getting full time work soon. Having already been given an offer by a place where he had done his internship, Eliezar was enjoying his last months of freedom. She remembers him saying, "Once classes are over, its full time work. I'll only be able to see you after work. Most likely only in the apartment too because I have already been told there will be some late nights."

Petunia remembered feeling a bit sad by this news but did not fully knowing why. She enjoyed her time with Eliezar, he made life easy, made her comfortable. He made coming to college the right decision. There was so much about him that she enjoyed, it was hard to tell when her feelings changed but she definitely noticed that they did. "You're not leaving the area are you?" she remembered asking with a quivering voice.

"Of course not, but I won't see you on campus is all." He smiled at her. He walked over to her and gave her a hug. They stayed that way for a long time and then they both went back to studying. Neither of them ready to admit anything was going on between them.

With midterms behind her, Petunia headed back to the professor's office to finish the job she had started. Nothing had been moved since she was there last. It disappointed her, but she was not surprised. She continued her work, tirelessly and efficiently.

Week after week she whittled away at the years of discourse in the office until she was satisfied it was in a respectable condition. The way she finished would allow any newcomer to understand where everything is and how to put the papers back to keep the office running efficiently. She only hopes the professor knows how, it is his mess after all. The day she had finished the professor was not in his office. She left him a note and told him she was finished and explained how everything was put and in the order it was in so he could keep it going.

Upon going back to the lab for the final time before winter break, Petunia found the professor in the lab with her. He sat there and watched her work, she moved with ease from one station to the next and did everything that had to be done. It was unnerving being watched but she figured he was board before break and was avoiding grading exams.

When she finished, he applauded and asked her to come back to the office so that they can discuss whether or not she will be continuing next semester. Petunia followed him in, "Close the door Petunia please." Petunia's inner alarm went off, but she did not know why, so she closed the door anyway. The professor approached her and asked, "What else do you do with such efficiency?" This time he was smiling at her in a way a professor should not. He walked towards her again but instead of backing up to the door where she could leave, she found him pushing her towards the couch in the office, the now uncovered couch.

She tripped backwards and fell onto the couch. He eased onto the couch next to her and started to touch her face, Petunia's bracelet became hot, she knew to get out. Her father's protection was on high alert and she needed to listen. "I need to leave sir. I have people waiting for me."

"Listen oh spirited one – we both know you are lying, we both know you are here to taunt me all these weeks with your claim of efficiency. I can smell a spirited one a mile away. We have a few on campus now, more and more each year. Now I have one of my own. I've heard that if you capture one, they are yours for life. Isn't that true?" he said in a slimy voice that made her skin crawl.

Petunia had never wanted to be found out as a spirited one. She wanted to live a normal life on campus. Her head was screaming for Eliezar, he was the only one she wanted to see right at that moment. Her heart beat quickly and her arm was beginning to burn from the bracelet. In a millisecond he was all over her, his hand traveling to places that should not be discovered by someone who is not your husband or lover. His head was on her chest and with his mouth he was ripping off each of her buttons, like an animal. He had her hands held down on her side, then she turned one hand enough for the burn to hit him. He jumped from being touched by her bracelet, this had started getting him angry in a way that she never saw coming either.

He was clearly going to hurt her and fight her in the process. Her only defense was the bracelet which continued to send out heat. As his hand came down on her face, he fell to the ground. Petunia looked up and saw Eliezar. He had pulled the professor off of her and had his hands behind his back and he was putting something on his wrists.

"How did you know to come?" she asked quietly and ashamedly

"I heard you Petunia. Simple as that." With those words he stood up and other men had come into the room. Eliezar gave them his phone and after pushing a few buttons, they gave it back to him. He put out a hand to her and she got up, but when she did her shirt fell off, from all the rips, he turned around and took off his shirt and handed it to her, he was wearing and undershirt anyway. She quietly accepted the shirt and the two of them walked out.

They walked hand in hand back to her apartment. He waited for her to take a shower and come out in clean clothes. "Will you be ok tonight or would you like me to sleep on the couch here?" he had asked her.

"How did you hear me Eliezar?" was all she could say.

"How do you think I could?" he answered

Petunia thought for sure that she was going to be able to avoid all spirited people, now she was glad she had fallen for the one man who could have helped her. "I don't understand why? I did everything right, didn't I? Did I wear the wrong cloth...."

"Stop!" he yelled at her. "Do not ever think this was your fault – the man has a reputation and I'm glad it was you in a way, because other girls have claimed he tried the same thing on them too but no one had proof and he has been getting away with this for far too long. Because it was you, I came running in with my camera on and took a picture first before I called the campus police and pulled him off of you. Now it will end. So, in a strange way, your being spirited has saved countless women from the same fate." He finished with his head down, he was ashamed that he yelled at her right now. "I should go if you're ok" he stood to leave.

Petunia caught his arm. "What if I don't want you to leave?" she took a step closer to him. "What if, I would like you to hold me on the couch until we both fall asleep?"
With no words the two of them did just that.

"Whoo hoo! This.......is......a......doozy" Petunia says very breathy.

"I see that." Eli replies trying to keep his own breath smooth.

"How much longer?"

"We passed the accident that was causing the traffic a few minutes ago, so I'd say less than fifteen more minutes assuming all is well with the road. I'm not sure meditating is good for you right now Tunie – you seemed to be fighting in your chair there. Maybe think of happier times." Eli's heart is pounding with guilt knowing that he should have gone with the first call from her. She would have endured less.

"I'm ok, but you're right. There are a lot of better places to take myself than where I did. I'm going to close my eyes again, I'm sure this little life will wake me soon enough though." She smiles and leans her head back onto the seat of the car.

Petunia's heart is racing, she should have gone back to a better time than that, Eli is right. He always is. Petunia thinks back to when she and Eli met. She must have been only fourteen and Eli was twenty. There was a community wide celebration about harvest time and Petunia had been bored out of her mind sitting in the park watching all the goings on.

Eli had approached her and immediately they were talking. It was always so easy with him. They talked with each other as if they'd known each other all their lives. It was an instantaneous friendship, but it was more than that. Wasn't it?

Eli had left for school shortly after that, he continued to talk her via emails and their cellular phone connections. They talked about school, parents, life, bubble gum ice cream and pretty much anything under the sun. There was never a shortage of conversation between them.

Until she went to college, she had never experienced anything like that with any other male person she knew. Her first semester she met Eliezar and they hit it off very quickly as well. She remembers thinking that she will have to tell Eli about him, and often times she did.

Eli was a friendship she never wanted to lose. She had older siblings, it's not like she needed him for advice, no their relationship was different. Although she could not put a finger on this either, it could only be explained as different.

For a long time after the incident with the professor, Petunia found it hard to work in quiet places, she opted for working at the cafeteria. The cafeteria became a great place to work. She saw all of her friends from previous semesters show up there and everyone greeted her well. Until the rumors started. It got around before midterms of the next semester that she was the one that finally got the chemistry professor fired. Girls from every year in college were coming up to her and thanking her for her heroics.

The boys, on the other hand, began to tease her that she was probably leading him on in the first place, some of them were even hostile towards her. They yelled things to her about how when a girl says no, they really mean not now but when a guy is ready, she has no choice.

The campus became divided on the issue of date rape and her face was being used as an example. She couldn't go anywhere without people knowing about what happened, even though it didn't fully happen. No one would believe her.

This cruel world became something she wanted no part of, but how could she tell her parents? How could she come crawling back to them under these circumstances? She wrote to Eli, she cried to Eliezar. She was a mess. Then, she came home from class one day to see a familiar car in front of her apartment. Her parents had come to surprise her.

She ran up to her apartment and saw that Eliezar had let them in, the three of them were sitting on the couch talking easily. She could not have been happier. She ran to her mother and held on for dear life. The two of them went to her bedroom.

"We heard what you did on campus, then Eliezar confirmed it all." Her mother stated.

"I'm sorry Momma, I brought shame to the family. I do not know what to do but it's become so much bigger than I can handle. I want to leave but you've invested so much in me, I sound like a failure. I am a failure, aren't I? I will never make my way in the non-spirited world. You knew that, didn't you?" She cried her words out to her mother.

"No, you are not a failure. They are. All of them for believing that a woman brings this upon herself. Those are the boys your father told you about. Real men, listen when the word is no. Real men listen when there is silence too, they will understand uncertainty as much as they will understand certainty. Unfortunately, there will always be those who treat others as objects or possessions. You are neither, you are your own person.

Oh, and one more thing. Eli is the one who told us what is going on. Don't be angry at him, he is very sweet on you and said it out of caring and love. You know that, right?" her mother was holding her hands in her own and looking Petunia right in the eye.

Her mom never lied to her and there was no reason to think she was now. She bowed her head, "Yes, Momma, I know he always means well when it comes to me. He is a great person, as is Eliezar." She said to her.

"Really Tunie, did you just say that?" her mother looked at her puzzled.

"Ahhhhhhhhhhhhh, hooo, hoooo, hoooo" Petunia blows out her breath slowly, trying to catch it before this new life jumps right through her skin.

Eli, having a hard time himself at this point, checks their location and calls back to her, "Three more blocks my love. Hang in there."

"Three? .....hooo....hoooo more?" Petunia is no longer going to be able to relax. It is now, the time has come that she has to give full attention to what is going on inside of her. She tries to think about what the birthing coach taught her before she left that class of uneducated individuals.

What a dumb bunch they were, many of them did not even know the anatomy of their own bodies and how the baby is going to have to travel out. They asked the most inane questions she thought that she could stay no more. She relied on the teachings she received in college and the rest she relied on the teaching of her mother, who seemed to know everything there is to know about a woman's body and how things work. She is glad she called on them now.

The last pain caused her to pass out a bit from exhaustion, her mind went to the time when Eliezar and she were hanging out again. He changed his work schedule so that he had the freedom to come and go as he pleased and he came to walk her to class and come back two hours later to walk her to the next. The whole semester stayed that way.

The petitions died down after a couple of weeks. Her mom stayed with her during that time. Her father walked in to the cafeteria and made a speech in front of everyone about the meaning of what it means to be a real man. Many of the "men" in the room applauded him. Those too immature to understand, walked out believing whatever he said didn't pertain to them.

Her father remained on campus and spoke to various groups and even in a variety of classes about the same topic. No one knew who he was to Petunia and she was grateful he kept his identity that way. With strength given back to the women, with the knowledge that date rape is as much of a crime as any rape, the campus seemed to calm down a bit. Less outbursts meant that Petunia could go back to the life that she had established here on campus.

 Her parents continued to support her in all that she did. Eliezar found her a job in his office for the summer and her parents allowed her to stay. They loved him already, and that made her very happy. She couldn't believe how lucky she was to have it all. How did she get so lucky to have her parents like the man she found herself falling in love with? How did she get so lucky as to find a spirited one who understood her need to be part of the un-spirited world as well as her own?

 "Now!!!!!! Are........we...........there.......now?" she says in between heavy breaths

 Eli takes a deep breath himself, "Pulling in right now." He parks the car next to the emergency room doors, there are only five parking spots that are allowed to be used, he will probably have to move his car later.

 Eli runs in first to tell the nurse at the desk that he has someone in labor and the baby is coming fast. Two attendants come out with a wheel chair and help her sit down. Eli is trying to keep is cool while his insides are being twisted in knots unimaginable, but he can't let her know that he took this away from her. With the amount of pain and discomfort she is in, he can't imagine her going through this fully on her own. How does any non spirited woman do this?

 They are rushed to the maternity ward where a handful of nurses immediately grab her wheelchair and bring her to a room. Eli stays at the desk and gives them all the information that they need. He too is puffing a bit and they asked him if he is ok. He nods to them and smiles, "The stress of getting here, we hit a lot of traffic." He tries to calmly walk towards the room they put Petunia in.

 Her parents come running into the maternity ward and see Eli about to go into the room. He stops and nods, her father gives him a knowing smile. Her mom rushes past both of them to find her daughter. Petunia's father puts a hand on Eli's shoulder, "Let this go, she has to feel the full effect to give birth. Besides, I have to tell you, if you don't, you're likely to have a heart attack yourself. Many spirited men have done so, and then they were worthless afterwards and needed more care than the new mother."

Given permission to revert the pain back to Petunia, he leans his head down to touch the forehead of her father. "I can't remember the words right now" he says breathlessly.

"I got this." Her father says and puts an arm on Eli's shoulder. To onlookers it looks as if the father is giving his son in law support. No one hears the words being said in the chant like manner.

When the words are out, it is none too soon, for they hear Petunia yell as never before. "Good timing I'd say." Her father grins. "No guilt son, we aren't equipped to do what they do." He pats his shoulder again and the two of them walk into the room and see that Petunia is all prepped and everyone is waiting for the doctor to come and check how far along she is.

"My guess is nine pounds four ounces, boy." Her father smiles his knowing smile.

Her mom smiles, "I hate to tell you this, but in all my years of childbirth, he has never been wrong. He can't see inside you, nor can he predict anything else, but this, well, this is a special talent of your father." She laughs a girlish laugh at her husband.

Eli pulls up a chair next to the bed. "How are you feeling?" he can't seem to ask anything more.

"Eli, my dear Eliiiiiiiiiiiiiiiiiiiiiiiiiiii!" she screams as her stomach begins to tighten and her legs are actually shaking.

The doctor walks in as this is happening. "Nurse, we will need to close the door now." He remarks. After the door is shut, he walks over to the bed and says, "Don't worry, he will come out fine. I do have two things to say after I examine you."

The examination does not take long and the doctor shakes his head yes to the nurse, who speedily starts preparing the bassinet soon to be occupied by the life inside of her. "First things first," he hits the side of Eli's head hard, "do NOT try that again. Always new dads who try and help. It does not help that after you get tired you get to stop and she then has to take the full brunt in double time."

"Duly noted." Eli muttered under his breath.

Petunia looks over at him and a flash of love comes to her heart. "You did that for me?" she asks

He only nods in defeat, his thoughts are all over the place now. His son is about to be born. The woman he has loved for years is in so much pain and he can't help, his hopefully future mother in law is wondering what kind of spell he put on her daughter, his hopefully future father in law knows what was done out of wedlock and with whom and to top it off, Petunia still thinks someone else is the father.

"Second question my dear goes to you." The doctor continues in his professional voice. "Do you know what happens to the blue smoke you sent out tonight?" he watches her reaction. No one ever realizes, it always makes him laugh. She can only muster to shake her head no as her stomach is contracting again and this time it does not want to let up. Her father comes around to the back of her and puts a wet wash cloth on her forehead.

"I will explain it to you as I always have to, not sure why they don't teach this part when they teach the women to make the smoke. Here goes, when you take out your crystals, it does two things. It finds your heart first and foremost. It listens to it and then it splits in two. One of the streams comes to me to tell me you're on your way and the other one, well, the other one always goes to the father of the child. Simple as that. That's why infidelity rates are really low in our community because both parties will always be found out." He smirks as he says this, remembering how many DNA tests he has had to do over the years to tell the husbands that the blue hue is always true.

Petunia is not processing this right now. How can it go to the father of the child when the father doesn't even know because he cut off ties with her? Their night together was his night to say goodbye. He was transferred to another state and he didn't want her to wait but he wanted to give her something she deserved.

She looks over at Eli, whose head is bowed down out of embarrassment. He knew this was the case but forgot when he got the blue hue – he forgot the ramifications. Now she will know, now she will hate him. He pulls his head up to look at her, he needs to regain some amount of dignity. She is smiling, then she screams in pain.

"Show time people!" the doctor calls. He walks over to the intercom and calls in two other nurses, they come in with another bassinet. Everyone is confused. With her mom on one side, Eli on the other and her father at her head, Petunia begins to push out this life inside of her that will soon reveal itself as a boy or a girl. Up until now she has always referred to it as the life inside of her.

She follows the instructions of the doctor and holds on to her mom and Eli as she pushes out this new life. It is really hard, harder than anything she has ever done. Now that she knows the size, what is going on scares her even more. The baby comes out and the doctor is very busy, he hands the baby to the nurse and he remains down there waiting for something else.

'oh' she thinks to herself, 'the afterbirth' Then, another contraction comes out of nowhere. "Hey, I'm done, aren't I?!" she screams at the doctor.

"Almost my dear, there is another one right behind this one. One big push and we got him." He says rather matter-of-factly.

The second baby comes out. Both are nice looking boys. One is really little though. There is a team of nurses and doctors looking at the two babies and all Petunia can do is lay her head back and rest. She can't comprehend all that has taken place in the last couple hours. The pain, the revelations, the love, the pain.

Eliezar came to her about nine months ago and said he had to leave. He told her that it would be for the best. He told her that it may be temporary but he has to go where the job tells him to go. The job pays well and he doesn't want to lose the opportunity. They talked all night long about life and about what each of them want out of it. They were so in sync with each other she couldn't understand why he didn't want her to transfer schools.

They talked throughout the next day as well. She experienced one of the longest weekends of her life. Then in the midst of all that talking they started to kiss. A kiss that transformed her life. By lunchtime they were in bed and giving to each other the most they could give another person. Themselves.

The moment was magical, in every sense of the word. That connection gave her the strength to go on. She knew then that she could carry on. She didn't know how but she knew she had the strength. Shortly after he left, she still lay in bed and the only person she could think to talk to about what had happened was Eli.

He sounded so tired when she spoke to him.....................sooooo tired. He was so tired!! But Eli has stereotypical hair coloring of a spirited one and Eliezar only had red hair with a tiny hint of brown. She reaches down to take hold of Eli's hand and she brings his hand to her lips and she kisses his hand. He watches her as she does this. Realization has hit and she doesn't hate him. Eli takes a deep breath and lets the air out but before he can speak the doctor starts to talk.

"Well, you two are the proud parents of two wonderfully looking healthy baby boys, one is five pounds, two ounces and the other is four pounds two ounces. We will keep them for observation as they are on the small side, but you do have the choice of having them room in here with you instead. However, keep in mind there will be nurses in here every couple of hours or more to check their status. Your call." He announces more than talks with them.

Her mother speaks first, "nine pounds four ounces – you're still right damn you." She hits her husband then she turns to the doctor and says definitively, "they will stay here." Everyone shakes their heads in agreement. All eyes are on Petunia.

"Momma, I'm tired. Can you take first watch?" is all she can muster out. Then she turns on her side, still holding on to Eli's hand and closes her eyes. She deserves some rest she decides. Her mom smiles from ear to ear. She whispers to Eli, "I suppose a wedding should be in order, soon no? All this time she would not tell us who she was with. Her father thought for sure it was a non-spirited one who talked her into being with him." She lowers her eyes as that chapter of her daughter's life was a tough one to go through for all of them.

Her father decides it's time for him to say a few words next, "How did you pull off this dual life? And for so long?"

"It seemed to take a life of its own. I saw Tunie on campus almost the first day she was there. She did not know who I was. I had to change my hair there, I am too obvious a spirited one and I wanted to be treated like everyone else there – so did she. She saw a different man there but for some reason she only saw my outside and not my eyes, she didn't see in me. Maybe if she did, she would not have taken to writing to me emails about the man she met in school and she would not have spoken to me about her best friend back home. Sometimes I didn't know who I was. That last night together in her campus apartment, turned into a thirty-six hour conversation and we were both tired of talking so our bodies took over. To say what words could not say. I'm sorry, you must hate me now. Not exactly the gentleman you thought I was. I will leave if that's what you want sir." He resolves to obey whatever Tunie's father wants.

"Hate is a strong word Eli and not one I'm accustomed to using. Petunia has one more year left at school. Her apartment is big enough for all four of you and you're going to have to make it work. It's a good thing she moved down to the garden apartment last year, because carrying a double tram up two flights would have been a pain in the, well a pain." Her mother says.

Petunia starts to stir. She pulls Eli's hand even closer in and holds on for dear life. "Let's give these two a few minutes to get used to their boys Grandma." Petunia's dad smirks. The idea of being a grandmother never occurred to her, she knew her daughter was pregnant but it didn't register what that meant to her. "Ok old man, let's go." She retorts smiling.

Petunia stays quiet for a few minutes after her parents leave. She sits up and looks Eli in the eyes, really deep into his eyes. "If only I had looked, you're right." She pulls him in for a kiss and he was not one to argue, oh, how he missed these lips.

Petunia takes a deep inhale, "Eli, Eliezar or whatever you want to be called, we are parents now. Do you want to bring them over so we can be a family?"

Eli gets up to get the babies. He picks them both up and brings them over to their mother, placing them in each of her arms. Tears fall freely from her eyes as they do his. "How could I have been so dumb as to not see? How could I have missed all the clues? No wonder college has been so hard, I'm really not smart enough." The tears keep falling and thankfully, Eli knows it's the hormones talking so he does not respond at all to what she has said. Instead he interjects with, "Do you even have two boy's names?"

She looks to him and laughs, they both laugh a few minutes until one of the babies start to cry and she puts him on her breast and is amazed to see how naturally he suckles on her, then she takes the other one as well before he gets too fussy. "How do they know how to do that?" she turns to Eli.

"Beats me." He smiles at her.

When she is done feeding them, Eli holds them one at a time to burp them. Love is instantly bestowed upon him by the nuzzling of their heads into his neck. Her parents come back in time to see this bonding going on.

"Give me a few months Mom. Can we wait a little for a wedding? I want to have the strength to dance at my own wedding." All eyes are now on Eli. Shocked to his core what she blurted out, he responds with, "I'll check my calendar." And a smile from ear to ear.

"We have to check the stars anyway. Each couple has a designated time they are supposed to get married. I know its old fashion and not your way but allow me this please." Petunia's mom says in a quiet voice.

"You were right Mom, I have come to appreciate the ways of our community, but that does not mean I won't still live among with the non-spirited. I have to finish school. Dad?" Petunia watches her father closely.

"What color is your bracelet?" he asks.

Petunia looks down, for the first time ever the bracelet is green, she looks to Eli, same as his eyes. She looks to her father, "Green" she says slowly.

"Then we know for sure you are with the right man. We will consult the elders about what the stars say. It could be months as you wish but it could be sooner. Tell me now if you will listen, if not there is no point in going to them." He states firmly.

"I understand," Petunia says, she looks to Eli, "as you wish." She waits for an answer.

"It is an honor and a privilege that I do not take lightly. I will stand and protect those who have been given to me today and all those that will come hereafter." He raises his arm and everyone sees that the mark of twins is on his wrist already, along with the full moon, the marks are the color of Petunia's eyes, lavender.

"This makes me happy children. I accept your way of life but it makes me happy to know you will not abandon where you came from. I will go make the call now." Her father says.

~ ~ ~

Three months to the day that Petunia went into labor, she is being prepared to walk down the aisle of roses as is their tradition. The carpet of rose petals is set before her, her feet have been properly adorned to walk on the soft path to her beloved.

Her mother and father are wearing their traditional garb as are her brothers and sisters to escort her down the way. Her youngest brother will be pushing the stroller down behind her.

Eli and his family are waiting for them under the tree of life, the place that gives birth to all the life amulets, their children will be receiving their first ones as they enter under the canopy. This will shield them from any harm that may come their way. They have been dubbed, Nathanial and Jacob, each with their own individual eye color, as all spirited ones have.

Eli takes Petunia from her parents and they all stand around the tree with the elders performing the ceremony under the same full moon that started this family. The hues dancing around the tree make for a magnificent sight.

Timmy and Kim's Longest Year

Timmy and Kim live together with their mom. They go to school, have friends, love basketball and enjoy picnics and ice cream. Only life isn't always happy, Kim is also a frequent visitor to the free medical clinic. Her friendship with Robert is put through the hardest test ever one night. Protection and safety doesn't always come easy for Kim. Will reaching out to her father cause more harm than good?

Most of my evenings were spent in front of the mirror drying tears or wiping blood off from my nightly encounters with Mom. Timmy, my little brother, would be crying himself to sleep with his teddy, JoJo, close by. JoJo is Timmy's best friend and also the only thing our father ever gave him besides his blonde hair, freckles and green eyes. After each 'encounter' with Mom, she would usually try and convince herself that I deserved what I received, then she would come upstairs, wrestle me to the ground, and proceed to jam a fork into my back, in order to," drive the point into me" she would say. After a while her actions seemed like s.o.p. (standard operating procedure), I even would fit it into my evening's schedule. My back had so many little dots on it that I didn't give them a second thought. I stopped fighting her also. There were times I went upstairs and took off my shirt, lying in bed waiting for her. These nights I would get even more of her wrath because she thought I was mocking her. I think she wanted me to fight her, but most nights I didn't have the strength or the desire any more.

Timmy began to count the dots on my back. Sometimes he would even take a marker and play connect-the-dots. Occasionally, he even made a picture. This would get us both to laugh, then cry ourselves to sleep. On these nights, Timmy slept with me, on the lower bed of my high-riser. I would leave the bottom bed pulled out almost all the time, no reason to push back since he became a frequent visitor at night.

The doctors at the clinic told me that in about ten to fifteen years I won't notice about ninety percent of my scars. But then again, ten percent is still too much for me. They tried to tell me that as I grew my body may hide the scars on its own and that I was lucky in that so many were in places that are covered by the type of clothes I wore. Were they so stupid as to think I wore these clothes by choice? Didn't it ever occur to them that I wore what I did to cover up the part of my life that I never wanted to be public? Their actions began to give me reason to question the doctors I was dealing with as to whether they were on my side or hers. Around that time, it seemed to be hers. I began to read up about first aide and started treating myself for as much as possible. My life began to feel as if I was in an atmosphere of me against them and I was losing. So, I had to take responsibility for myself and Timmy, always Timmy.

Our father was not to be heard from. Not his fault really. He is in the military and is sought after for his expertise. At a point when he was gone more than he was here, my mother decided that she could do adulthood alone and handed him divorce papers one day while he was on leave. The day didn't matter to her, but it was my birthday. He left before I got home from school. She decided this way was better. Turns out the only person it was better for was her. It became apparent to me that this whole divorce was an excuse to get one man to pay for her room and board while getting another to satisfy her more primal needs. 'Military men were so unpredictable', she would tell me. 'Find a man who has a local job' another one of her favorite phrases. To me there was no need for that, she seemed to be finding them all by herself and for herself. There was none of this 'looking for a good father', thing because no one ever panned out to more than two or three dates.

~ ~

There were many nights when Timmy came to see me before going to bed and cried himself to sleep in my arms. He knew what was about to happen, his being ten years old didn't deter his understanding of the situation. He loved to smile too, at me anyway. Tall, curly hair and his sea-green eyes that sparkled somehow, made things a little more bearable. Things became so routine that we even began to make jokes about what went on in our home. I know maybe people think our jokes were in bad taste but we decided better to laugh every day than cry. We were each other's sounding boards and still are.

It was, however, a little embarrassing to admit that my baby brother was the only one I could turn to that would hear me. I tried writing to my father and explain the situation since he had left. I gave explicit details about everything and all I received from him was one phone call. To tell me he was shipping out and would not be available for a while. He was unable to tell me where he was going or for how long. Only that he would be gone. I asked him if he received my letter and he said it was a bit confusing, that it had so many crossed out lines in it. He blamed these scratch outs on the military censorship – but I knew better, I knew the scratches came from Mom. If only I had found a stamp myself instead of asking her to mail the letter for me.

When I hung up from his call, I knew precisely what had happen. Mom must have found my letter in the mailbox and either edited it or only sent the first page where I was talking about school and Timmy's potential learning difficulties. I knew the letter was risky, but I was so fuming that my insides were burning. At that moment that I understood what the phrase 'blood boiling' meant. I checked the house to make sure Mom was not home. I called her at work and asked when she might be home, to confirm she wasn't coming home anytime soon, and then I checked the house again.

I went into her room and looked through every drawer, every box in the closet. Only to find some drugs and a couple of old pictures of some previous one-night stands. (the only thing she was good at anymore). Right before I was about to leave her room, I saw something sticking out from between the mattress and the box spring. I recognized the color of the paper from across the room. I pulled out my letter and saw that she had written 'ungrateful witch' with her lipstick across each page. If ever there was a last straw for her, I suppose this was it. This was the turning point of my life. For fear of my life, I slipped the letter back to where she had stuffed the paper, making careful notation as to how far it was in before I even took out one page so that I could be precise in putting it back.

I needed to sit down at that moment. However, my body had other things on its mind and I proceeded to dash down the hall, barely making it to the bathroom in time to puke my guts up. I did not realize how long I was in the bathroom until I heard Timmy at the door. Timmy had been at a baseball game at the park about a block away, and I forgot to get him so he told me he walked home by himself. Then he saw that I was upset and he said he would not tell Mom I got sick as long as I did not tell her he walked home by himself. We were so uncertain at that moment as to what would set her off and what would not. There was this aura above us and around us that made us both realize we were the only people we had. Feeling alone in the world was pretty heavy. Neither one of us knew quite what to do with this feeling.

While in the bathroom, interestingly enough, there was a part of me that felt some amount of pity towards my mother at that moment. Imagining, being her to find something her child had written. Something so graphically detailed about herself, so profoundly jarring. A letter that was screaming for help, when this moment of pity left, I felt quite guilty for writing those words in the first place. My every nerve began to shake internally. My guilt quickly turned to fear about how long and how often I would be punished for trying to reach out to the only other adult in my life. I also began to realize that maybe my father had tried to keep in touch, but to no avail. I blocked that out quickly too because if he really wanted to see or speak to us, we were not the ones moving around – we were easy enough to find.

Strange as it may seem, we decided to go about our normal routine that night. Timmy set the table, I made dinner and he started his homework. We said nothing to each other for the next hour and a half I remember that clearly, until Mom walked in. She usually would walk in, wait for us to give her dinner, mumble something about how her day was and then leave again to her nightly watering hole. There were a few within a couple mile's radius of the house and this is where she would be the rest of the night. Then she would come home four out of five nights a week with another lonely soul as she would call them, never to remember their names in the morning. This was our life, our routine; we realized nothing was going to change. Not anymore.

Timmy and my thoughts always fell under the category of 'things could not get any worse.' But when you think like that, something always changes. That was the day that I brought home the progress report from my eleventh grade teacher, life started to mushroom from occasionally horrible to always horrible occurrences.

~ ~

That day? Of course I remember but do we have to get into the details of everything? Yes sir, I will answer the question.

~ ~

Well, it is still pretty much branded into my mind. Same as every day since then. Each day started out the same as any other day in a suburban neighborhood. Each person finds themselves jumping out of bed, grabbing clothes, throwing backpacks and briefcases together and running into the kitchen for breakfast and finishing last minute homework. Oh, yeah, we had to make something for lunch as well. Mornings started out as if they were straight from a 1950's television show. Morning greetings were always projected through a smile, as if this day were the best day. Memories of the night before were never discussed, and any indiscretion that might have been seen, has been forgotten. This was understood, no one ever had to say a word, the house was silent.

That particular day started out like any other, and yet something told me to be apprehensive about going to school, Timmy was also. Somehow, we began to be able to sense when a bad day was about to happen. Like a person with arthritis sensing a weather change. The rain came during third period for me, in the form of a howling thunderstorm or possibly a level four hurricane. I was fully understood why I was feeling the way I was that morning, because there it was, smacked right on top of my books right before she walked out of the class. That's how the teacher gave these to you; she felt that if she didn't the students would not take her seriously. Well, good or bad didn't matter much to me, a note from a teacher meant they were watching you too much, or at least giving me too much attention. Of course, we all know that giving a child attention is a cardinal sin. In the world of my mom, any attention that was not given to her was not good attention.

      I began to understand the word terror as I walked home from the bus that day. I always got off about two stops before mine, I had to, to give myself time to unwind and to prepare for the unknown. I even bummed a couple of cigarettes off a friend knowing full well that my mother wouldn't notice the smell being that she also smoked, even at home, my cigarettes wouldn't be a foreign smell. You see, my father had a rule that if she had to do that nasty thing, she had to go outside the house and away from the kids. With each step I took, however, my legs became increasingly heavier. By the time I reached the driveway I could hardly stand. My insides began to crumble, I felt some of my body parts go numb. Maybe my body sensed something my brain didn't and was preparing for the pain it was about to receive. Maybe, my mind had willed itself into a self- induced state of disbelief. If one could not image something happening then maybe it won't.

      Lucky for me, my mother was working late that night so I had plenty of time to "prepare" myself. The only thing I could compare my feelings to was that of how a turkey must feel on the eve of Thanksgiving in this country. Knowing full well what the farmers ax is out for.

    Timmy would stay next door after school every day until I would call to tell him I was home. That day it was particularly difficult because part of my preparation, was to inform Timmy of the report. I always told him ahead of time that something was going to happen. Doing this would usually create a rainfall of tears in thirty seconds or less. Not that I could blame him, he was only ten (even younger when all this started). I have always seen my little brother as a small man trapped inside a child's body. I knew full well that he was one hundred percent aware of what went on behind the "closed doors" of my room every night. That night he ran up to his room, crying and yelling inaudibly, I couldn't understand him through the tears. I was convinced of one thing though; his tears were about what was to come. I made a couple of frozen dinners for the two of us and didn't go after him until they were ready.

    I was not and am not a particularly religious person, however, on this night I felt compelled to pray for a miracle but, in reality, I needed something even more. On those occasions when Mom said she was working late, she usually meant that she was going out after work and therefore, would not be home the regular time. It was expected of me to hold down the fort on these nights. The house was expected to be particularly clean and quiet by the time she would come home. One had to always be prepared for the potential guest.

    While cleaning up from dinner it had dawned on me that when Mom was sober punishments took on a more routine nature as if sometimes she had to convince herself that this was the right thing to do and the only way to handle her child. Then there were the times when she was drunk, her emotions intensified to an immeasurable amount. As I put away each dish the pit in my stomach had grown into an erupting volcano and I, once again, made a bee-line for the bathroom to throw up. The last thing I needed was to get sick in the kitchen.

    I tried as hard as I could to read to Timmy that night, but in the end, he wanted to be held, as if to say he was there for me and that things would be all right somehow. We held onto each other until he fell asleep. Slowly, I made my way downstairs, finally hearing the car door close. Then I heard a second door. As quick as a superhero, I darted down the rest of the stairs and gathered up any remnants of inhabitants in the living room and dining room and ran back upstairs as the keys were jingling in the door. After splashing myself with water, I made my way back downstairs to open the door that was apparently 'stuck'. I had become so used to hearing the keys that I knew precisely the moment before Mom would bang on the door to get in and claim the keys were not working. I took pride in knowing exactly when to open the door. It became an inside joke that I could play on my mother. This particular night, however, I was not laughing inside but shaking when I opened the door.

    Lenny, her new friend, introduced himself to me. I thought this kind of peculiar, being that I didn't remember the last time there was even a hint of a gentleman in the house let alone the fact that he was good looking. Somehow, I couldn't figure out how he got stuck with *my* mother. Something had to be wrong with him, and I'm sure I'd find out sooner or later.

    You know I seemed to have forgotten a thing or two, let me back up here for a moment. Two years prior to this night, my folks got divorced. This was no sweat off our backs, my dad was a Major in the army and hardly at home anyway. We, Timmy and I, figured that not much would change with the exception that the two of them would no longer be yelling and she won't be throwing things around.

    We were used to seeing Mom around, and many times it was good. Then there were times when we saw her a little too much. If Dad was out of town, her anger was always vented on me. However, we figured without him around at all to provoke all this anger life would change and everything would be calm and everybody would be safe.

At first, I thought that he was aware of what Mom did to me while he was away, until the day he said," Kim, you act too much like a tomboy, besides you're getting to old too have these black eyes. Don't you ever want to date?" With that I got my answer and needless to say we didn't miss him so much after that. Things became quite apparent to us that he didn't care. The phrase says, 'actions speak louder than words,' but in this case no-action screamed volumes to us.

Meanwhile, back on the couch Mom and Lenny were laughing and singing up a storm. I went to fix them a drink. Yeah, that was my job for her "guests". I called them to the table and went to get them something to snack on. They were a sight, Lenny holding on to Mom and she to the furniture, they finally walked to the table and she sat down right in front of the report.

Boy what a dope, I suppose you're wondering why I didn't hide the note. I guess I could have but she would have found out anyway because the school always makes follow up calls to these things, to see if there is anything the teachers can do to assist the child. If you can believe me, a phone call would have been far worse.

Still in her laughing phase of the evening she hadn't noticed the paper yet. Then all of a sudden sobriety hit like a fire ball on dried straw, as she read the note out loud:

Your child has really been having a rough time in English this semester.
Please take care of this matter accordingly, I'd hate to see her take this course over.

Does the word rage mean anything to you? Well at that moment it meant Mom. I could literally see the smoke coming from her ears as well as the fire in her eyes. She was staring down at me so hard that I almost fell over. I had wanted to run but there was no place or no one to run to. She had her hand clenched onto the report as if she were my holding my neck. My throat felt her grip and was dry as could be. I could hardly hold onto the napkins that were in my hand, let alone my breath. After nearly dropping them on the floor I ran to the kitchen and threw up. Yeah, again. The fear she had instilled in me in the next room was so intense that I felt a prisoner to her.

Trying to help, Lenny took the report out of her hand and said, "Don't worry, she has plenty of time to learn English, she is only in high school. Why let a silly note bother you?" Kind words from a man about to pass out, and then he did.

We walked his six foot body over to the couch and somehow got him to lay down. He felt as heavy as a car. I'll give him this much, he was no doubt the largest person she ever dated.

From the look in her eyes I knew the time was near. Running upstairs, mainly to prolong the upcoming disaster, I went to get a blanket and pillow. When I passed Timmy's room, I noticed he was clinging to JoJo and staring up at the stars, as if praying. I remember calling to him and that as he turned around, I could already see the red and very wet cheeks, his eyes were swollen and the look of fear was upon him.

He ran to me, still holding JoJo. JoJo was the only stable thing he had in his life then. That doll never went away, was always there for him and it never hurt anyone or anything. Holding back my own tears, that I knew would be shed later, I pried him off of me and put him back in bed. I told him, "You take care of JoJo and I'll take care of you. OK?" That usually helped, except for that night.

Then I realized that I had taken too long, she was bellowing already for me to come down. As I got down the stairs, she was standing with a fireplace tool in her hand. My heart was in my throat along with my stomach and anything else that would fit. I walked with my head held as high as I could over to the couch, threw the blanket and pillow onto Lenny. As I leaned over to tuck the pillow under his head I happened to glance up and see the pick coming down towards me.

Thank goodness for great reflexes, I fell onto the floor as fast as I could and only got hit in the ribs as opposed to my head. You could tell she was upset she missed her target. I had fallen into the coffee table and broken one of the glasses they had been drinking from. Like a vulture on its prey, she was on top of me and my hand was being rubbed into the glass and alcohol on the table.

"Now you have a reason not to write well!!! No one, I repeat NO one has ever or WILL ever not pass English!! Is that understood?!" Yep, I remember that day very well, do you Mom?

After the second hand was punished, by the same treatment, I was finally able to pull myself away. I couldn't feel much more pain even if she wanted me to. The pain goes deeper than a cut nerve here or there. My body was hurt and mangled at times but what about my heart? I hurt more inside at times like these than anywhere else. Sometimes I couldn't tell what part of me did not hurt.

She got me down again in a wrestling hold and as I looked up, I remember seeing Timmy peering down through the banister. His mouth was moving but I heard nothing over my own screaming at that point.

Moments like that when I would hate her even more. She had no idea that he knew what was going on. She always figured that he was asleep and his door was soundproof. Had she known though? I don't think she would have been any different.

I wanted to hold him and tell him I was going to be fine, but who was I kidding. Timmy was no dummy and I couldn't fool him anymore with excuses like being a tomboy. Tomboys don't put their hands in broken glass on purpose. He also had witnessed her actions many times already and had begun to fear my mom as though he was next.

There was a time when he even said to me that he wished she would go away, or that our dad would come back so that he could fight with her and not me. Pretty smart ten-year-old, don't you think?

In a flash, I was pulled into the kitchen for a lesson in my writing skills. First came the ruler over the knuckles a couple of times then, the note-board in the kitchen. You know the kind you leave messages on to one another? She made me write, neatly I might add, that I was sorry ten times. Obviously, I had to clean up the mess that was made in the other room afterwards too. I always did.

The only thing I was thankful for was that she only took as much time as it would take for her "friend" to wake up. And then, as if right on schedule, the doorbell rang, and Lenny started getting up. I probably fell to the floor. She had few words for me, "you know what to do."

Shoving a handful of mints in her mouth, a comb through her hair, and the blanket over the coffee table as she proceeded to answer the door. All in one breath.

Through her grand command of the English language and her new found sobriety, she convinced the police that all was calm in her home and that it was probably the music or T.V. "You know how violent the shows can be nowadays." she would say.

I, on the other hand, would wait until she closed the door before walking out the back door for my two mile hike to the free clinic. She was also good at cleaning up before her "guests" would see.

The neighbors, as well as the police, knew Mom was lying but they had no "solid" proof because no one ever saw me, except for Mom.

The cops passed me by numerous times on my way to the clinic, but when I would wave or start jogging, they went by.

I had slowly become a regular patient those past couple of months. Things were different when Dad was around at least she could take half her anger out on him and only give me what was left over. Now, I received her full undivided attention. Lucky me.

Although I have to admit it wasn't all bad. Every Saturday, winter or summer, we went to the park and/or the zoo. We would get so wrapped up in the days' events we would all forget the night before. We even went to the movies once in a while too.

The best was when the three of us would even go on our occasional picnics. These moments were cherished but never seemed to last long enough, even when they were more frequent.

Anyway, I liked the clinic, no one ever asked questions. Until that evening of course. When I had gotten there, Dr. Bons, or Randy, started to ask about my family and my "home life". All he had to do was look into my eyes and know he was right so why bother me with the questions?

They patched me up and gave me a note, for my teachers, requesting that I be given oral tests and homework for the next couple of weeks. Took them a couple of hours to fix my hands, they had to be careful to make sure they picked out all the glass.

I remember wanting to take a nice long and very slow, walk home but Randy insisted that he drive me. "Besides," he said "it is already 3:00 a.m." Soon after we sat into the car he said, "Let's talk." Playing innocent, and being very scared I asked about what. "Cut the garbage, Kim, this is getting worse isn't it? Each time I've seen you in the past couple of months I've taken almost an hour and a half to get you fixed up. And tonight! I had to dig out glass, not wood splinters. Don't you know that I want to be your friend, your confidant if needed? Please don't look out the window. I want to help." He had pleaded with me.

He had stopped the car to get a reaction, so I turned around. His eyes were sincere and so were his words but she is my mother and deep down I felt life had to get worse before it got better. To me this was the worse, I mean how much further can she go? I looked up again and he caught me with his eyes, then I realized he really was a friend and I finally broke down. His arms were the first thing to show me a sign that there really is such a thing called love and caring. You might think I'm crazy but the one thing my father taught me that was worthwhile was that, "A man's eyes never lie."

    I didn't want to give this up. I wanted to share the news with Timmy. I was finally able to let go and I remember seeing tears in his eyes as well.

    Randy, by the way, was only twenty-eight then and doing his internship at Berger Hospital nearby. He volunteered some of his evening hours to the clinic. He said his family lived near one and he used to volunteer there in high school. To him the clinic was a great idea, to have medical care readily available to anyone at all hours of the day and night.

    Then to bring me back to reality he said, "Remember I do care, and when you are ready to talk, come find me." The rest of the ride was quiet and long, yet short. He dropped me off a couple of houses down from mine so that she wouldn't hear the car door and think I was getting any help from a neighbor, or worse, a cop. As the car door opened, the warmth I had felt disappeared, and reality set in. First, the cozy warmth of being cared for, then the hell of not being cared about at all. If only I could have taken a piece of the warmth home, I would have been able to sleep more than two hours that night.

    As I walked back in Mom and Lenny, how shall I say this politely, were enjoying each other's' company, funny how she could go from a violent bull to a tender pussy cat in a matter of minutes. But that's what always happened. That's what would happen any hard night after that too.

    Trying not to be noticed I would walk upstairs slowly and quietly. That evening I found Timmy in the same place as I left him, his hands still on the banister, and JoJo in his lap. I picked him up the best I could and brought him to his room.

As I laid him down, I saw the dried tears on his cheeks and eyes. For a ten-year-old he had seen and experienced more than most kids my age or even older. He may not have understood completely what he saw but he knew enough to know that what was happening was wrong.

~ ~ ~

When I went back to school the next day, I received a hundred questions, but gave only one answer, "clumsy I guess." Everyone knew what must have really happened though. I had been popular with a lot more kids before that night. Now many of the kids were scared of me, actually they were scared of Mom in that she might hurt me if they said or did the wrong thing while they were in front of her. If they had only seen her at the zoo or at the park with us, they would not have been afraid. She always made sure we were dressed well too. Oh, and one more thing – Mom's a great baker – she always made sure we had fresh bread in the house – 'no store bought crap' she would say and we always had home made cookies available. She was happiest when she baked something good in the kitchen.

I was also the "manager" of the boys' basketball team. That meant I collected the balls for the games and drills, which they let me play in too. The guys liked me, considered me a pal and "one of the team". I think I was the only girl in school invited to their victory parties. They didn't even invite their girlfriends, because most of the time was spent patting each other on the back for a job well done, and talking about the game.

The first practice after the Lenny incident, some of the guys were really fired up and some mortified. They started saying things like, "give me five minutes with her, just five." or "my mom would have been more than happy to sign that note for you." They had a point, but knowing her, she would have found out anyway. She always did, and a lie was....let's say, was not worth giving my life for.

After seeing that I wasn't responding the gang apologized and offered to help in getting my homework done. I also remember numerous shoulders being offered, even the coach. He is a strange sort, never got close to the kids on the team, but he had taken a liking to me and to that year's team specifically. No one knows why. The absolutely most grueling part of the day was after practice, when my English teacher came down and apologized for not offering to give assistance before the letter was to be sent out. She looked like a lost puppy. The whole town knew what was going on in my home, yet, without proof, no one could do anything about the situation for me.

"Please don't hate me," she groveled it was weird to watch an adult act like this. "... it's standard for anyone with your grades. I was not aware of your....... situation." She had barely finished her sentence when she had put her head down, shaking and running off in the other direction. To this day, I'm not sure if she felt guilty or simply didn't know what to do with me.

You need to understand that I'm not dumb or anything, I was in the honors class and you had to pull a B+ average or you were required to take the class over or be subjected to being put in a lower class where I would need to get an A+ to be moved back up. Those were the school rules. Big deal, I had a C, and it was mostly due to my lack of time to give the class.

Shortly after that time with Lenny I decided to stay with friends for a couple of days. I don't know why but that one really seemed to sting me and I needed the rest.

I had never really gone away before, this was the first, and it was the first night without Timmy. I wasn't really happy about that thought, I was scared for him. I stayed with Randy. Many of my school friends actually had their parents scared of some kind of legal ramifications if they took me in. Except for the guys on the team, they thought it might start some bad rumors that they could not afford to have. It was fine with me, I think, in the long run, Randy's home worked out better.

Many kids also didn't know how to talk to me anymore or whether or not I would watch anything but a comedy on T.V. Their limited understanding was because no one took the time to try. Not even my closest friend on the team, Robert.

Randy has a two bedroom apartment so it wasn't too inconvenient for him. I was pretty silent, not knowing how I felt about him or the situation. My biggest concern or fear was for Timmy. I had usually taken him with me when I went away, but for some reason, I felt I owed myself a day or two reprieve from her.

My fears were justified the second day I was away. Randy came home from the clinic with the news. My mother had brought Timmy in with a broken arm, four stitches and a black eye. The pain, the hatred, and the confusion that I had felt at that moment rendered me motionless. I can't even begin to tell you what I was feeling at that moment. Then all at once I lost my self-control. I fell to the floor kicking and screaming as a toddler would having a tantrum, but no sound came out. I really didn't know what to do first, or where to go. Randy was quickly by my side trying to hold me down and prevent me from getting hysterical, or doing something stupid. As much as I wanted him to be there with me, I wanted my Timmy more. I *really* wanted her though. He forced me down into his arms, so I would calm down first. I don't think I have ever stopped crying since.

When I was finally calm though, he sat me down holding me in his lap. This was fine to me because his were the only arms, besides Timmy's, that I ever liked. There was no place I wanted to be more, however, I could not stop thinking of what had happened which made the warmth turn cold. Everything went cold, I started to shiver at the thought that maybe it hasn't gotten worse yet, and maybe something else was going to have to happen before our lives got better.

But then I had a new thought, it was at that moment that I realized that maybe my mom was sick and really didn't want to hurt us, she had to. She needed some sort of help. I remember not being able to get Timmy out of my mind the way he must feel, the physical as well as emotional pain he must have been feeling. Especially since I wasn't even there to protect him like I promised I always would.

Then I started crying again because here I was enjoying Randy's arms and Timmy was home probably wondering where I am and why I haven't come home yet. I jumped out of Randy's arms and made a jump for the door. He ran after me, grabbed my arm and said, "Why don't you at least pack first, and I'll drive you, you're in no condition to be making the walk. You may need all your strength for when you get there, don't waste it on a walk. OK?"

I had listened, there was no reason not to. Randy dropped me off, at what had become our "usual spot", and I walked the rest the last four blocks home, praying he was wrong and that I would not need any strength when I got there.

As I was walking those last two blocks that day, I remember wondering what was going to happen when I opened the door. My arms and legs were numb before I even went two blocks. In fact, I had to throw up before I finished the third block. When I was younger, I never threw up so much, but I learned that fear seemed to bring up all that I had. Randy, watching from his car which he strategically parked, got out of the car. But I signaled that I was going to be fine, and he went back in. When I finally did open the door, I wanted to run to Timmy and hold him. And yet I didn't have to, he was sitting in front of the T.V. eating the largest chocolate sundae that I had ever seen, holding JoJo and watching a funny movie with my mom. I walked in very slowly, when I caught Timmy's eye, I asked if I could sign his cast.

Mom laughed. "You noticed already! Wow, you're good, for that you get the sundae of your choice, which will it be?" I told her hot fudge and then went to sit next to Timmy to find out what was going on. He told me how she "accidently" bumped into the swing as she was pushing him, and how she didn't mean to push him off, oh, and how she thought she saw a spider by his eye that needed to be "wiped" off. As for the stitches, I guess she couldn't come up with a good enough story for that one. My assumption was that this is what she told the people down at the clinic. The weird part was they bought her story with no additional questions - I mean seriously, what ten year old still needs to be pushed on the swing? And who ever needs to smack that hard at a spider?

When Mom came back, she asked me where I was staying and I told her at a new friend's house. His name was Randy. Then I got the third degree. Who, how old, how did I know him? Where is he from? You get the general idea. Eventually, due to my wonderful mood, I told her flat out that he was the intern down at the clinic that has been patching me up for the past couple of months, and what did she think of that. Yes, I was trying to get her dander up. Why? So that I can express how I was truly feeling about what happened earlier that day with Timmy.

Her response was simple, "Oh, and did he fix you up in bed too? Because if he did, I guess we'll have to charge him with statutory rape. If not, too bad you could have had a nice time." Then she, very frankly, put down my sundae on top of my head, and walked away. I calmly went into the kitchen to get cleaned up, the best I could with my hands still bandaged up. I was quite surprised that nothing further happened that day, or for some time after that.

For several weeks, my bandages were still there, I think the doctors elongated the healing time. But eventually they have to come off and in that healing time things were looking a lot better. The nightly beatings had become less frequent and less damage was done. I went to the clinic one night to visit and Randy's remark was something like," I guess you were right, it had to get worse before it got better. I only hope this does not put an end to our friendship. I hope this will give us an opportunity to grow even closer." With that he gave me a kiss on my head like you would a younger sister and went to see his next patient.

~ ~ ~

It would really be nice if I could change the subject and tell you about a wonderful love story, but things don't work out like that. My friendship with Randy did grow, we became very close. I learned that it was ok to open up to someone that they really would listen without making judgments. He became much more to me than a doctor/friend. But neither one of us knew what to do with the way we felt, so we went on and hoped an answer would show up.

The road to the recovery of my hands was the only reason things had cooled down for a while. Mom even told that to me, on the night of the big game. Another quote I won't soon forget, "...and when you come home, don't expect a warm welcome, and don't come alone, you may need some help." I couldn't believe that the final game of the season, our championship could be ruined. I figured she was only jesting, being that the worst that had happened since Timmy's incident was that I had a couple of minor cuts and only a sprained ankle. I didn't give her words a second thought, I felt it was only her mood because things were busy at work.

Timmy was excited too, the big game was going to be fun. All the guys loved him they even taught him how to play. What was going to make the game even more fun was that this game was on his eleventh birthday and his favorite player had the number eleven. I also had a birthday during that five week reprieve from Mom. I was seventeen now and driving. So, the two of us got in the car and off we went to the game.

The game was tremendous, no fouls, no fights, no nothing; pure fun and a great game to watch. We won, was there any doubt? There is no need to go on about what happened during the game with the exception of the part when number eleven got his eleventh basket he yelled, "Just for you sport!" to Timmy. I had never seen Timmy as happy as that moment or since. Sometimes to cheer him up I repeat, "Just for you sport." But somehow that moment is gone.

    The drive home was good, I dropped Timmy off at his friends for his first sleep over party. He and his friend Craig had celebrated every birthday together since they were two, but this was different. This time they were really together. Usually they would exchange gifts at the mall and my mom would leave. Tonight, was very special to Timmy, nothing could damper his night, and I was going to make sure nothing would. That's why I wanted to drive him there myself. All the other kids were at the game too because most of them had brothers on the wining team. But none were as happy as Timmy, he got the wining number eleven jersey. Did I tell you number eleven was also my closest buddy and truest friend? No matter what had happen in my life, he always treated me the same. His name is Robert. I guess I have good luck with R's. Maybe I mentioned him before, I don't remember.

    As I pulled into the driveway, I noticed something hanging from the doorknob. But I could not figure out what it was until I started going up the walkway. There was a set of boxing gloves with a note on them saying, and I quote, "Now that you can fight back, we can begin to have quality time together again. I'd advise you putting them on before you come in." Still on a high from the game, and looking forward to the victory dance tomorrow night, I still could not believe that she was even remotely serious, things had been too good to go back to being that bad. I opened the door with them in my hand, and **BAMO!!** A right cross to the chin knocked me right onto the floor.

    Mom closed the door behind me and asked me why I didn't listen to her and put the gloves on, "now the fight won't be fair, but it will still be fun, ...at least for me." I scrambled to my feet in time to miss the next right but not the left. I was so stunned I couldn't even cry. What had happened, had the past few weeks been a dream was it really only a day after the bandages were gone? I looked down to see that it was not, that my bandages were really off and I was really wearing my uniform.

The conversation that followed this opening act is still pretty vivid in my mind:

"What is going on here, what happened Mom, I thought we were becoming friends again. I thought we were finished fighting, I thought you loved me." I said rather softly

"Fighting! So now you think I fight you!? I only discipline you the best way I know how. You think it's easy raising a punk like you and your whining brat brother? I work hard to support you and what does your father do? He sits around and plays soldier. He sends you a used car for your birthday, why didn't you tell me you wanted a car? Maybe I could have gotten one for you. Besides, don't go thinking he spent any money on you, that piece of junk is army surplus and he had nothing else to do with something so old."

"It's the thought that counts. Besides, I don't take as much pride in it as I do in the necklace that you gave me. See I have it on all the time now. I think your necklace brought me a lot of luck. Like my grades being brought up, the game tonight that we won. And most of all, the friendship I thought we were developing." I told her

"You do like the necklace don't you," she said calmly and proudly. Then she proceeded to knock off my dad. "You think your father put any thought into that gift? He doesn't think about you anymore. He thinks of you even less now that you're seventeen. You see, no more money from him will be coming to you. Not that he ever sent that much to begin with. So now my pretty, you will be supporting yourself somehow because I'll be damned if I'm working any harder for you. Now come closer so I can beat this message into you." She started running towards me.

I had freaked out a bit and ducked to the floor then she pounded down on me with a force I'd never seen or felt before. My face was bleeding and my ribs were as sore as I'd ever felt them. Then when she got too hot, she took the gloves off. During this small reprieve, I crept up to my feet and tried to get away. She gave a kick to my ribs with the force of ten. I don't know where she found this energy source that she seemed to have that night but if all this had to do with money than I was determined to find a job. Which is what I told her, which she responded with, "A job! You had better find more than one because of your sarcasm and the fact that you don't have the guts to fight back, you better be earning enough for two."

"*Fight back? I can't hit you, you're my mother, and if I did, you'd beat me senseless, as if you're not already.*" I screamed

"*At least you know your place young lady. But if you mention the fact that you think I abuse or beat you one more time, than maybe I should start, we don't want to make you out to be a liar.*" She had said that with a menacing voice that I had never heard before. What I mean to say is that she said it so that I should feel that my life was being threatened.

She then dragged me into her office to show me the letter that my father had sent her about not paying for me anymore. She was not lying on that part, he was not going to send any more child support. She also began to show me the costs she claimed I ran up, and how much I was going to have to earn to be able to still live under "her" roof.

The figures were astronomical. These were figures of someone who was working full time and paying rent and all that went with a place of their own. She had even broken down the mortgage and told me how much was mine. When she finished her speech, she made me sign a paper that was worded like a real lease, in that I promised her I would come up with $1000 a month for two years to pay for everything she feels I owe her. These were expenses that were not covered by my dad's money. Money, she felt was for frivolous things.

For fear of my life, I signed, turned around and asked permission to go get fixed up. She told me she wasn't finished with me yet. She kicked me over to the back door and handed me a new key, "If you're going to be a boarder than you need to know the rules. First - no bringing guests; Second - put your groceries on the left side of the fridge only; Third - only use this back door, you're not worthy of more; Fourth - when someone comes to visit they have to sign in and out; Fifth and final rule - Don't ever call me mom, I'm now your landlord!! Now you may go on with your life, but if you neglect to tell me anything I should know, I can't be responsible for my actions. Oh, and there's an additional charge to use the driveway."

With that, she let me go, out the back door of course. If there was a way to put more burden on someone's shoulders, than I don't know what that way would be. I was in no condition to drive, but then again, I had to, I was afraid of her additional charges. The money situation was to start right away. I had only one more month of school, I was going to have to cancel my college plans and look for a job. Where was I going to find a part time job where I could still attend school and work plus was going to take home $1000 a month?

I didn't know what problem to solve first. I didn't know where to run, could I hide. Then it dawned on me -- Timmy!! How was I going to tell him that he no longer had a room? Oh, sorry sir, did I neglect to tell you? Mom had taken everything that Timmy and I owned and put our belongings in the den. A room that had been a porch, so it has its own back door and another door into the kitchen. The kitchen was the only room in the regular house we were allowed to use, and the bathroom was right off the kitchen. No shower or tub, a sink and a toilet.

In my dazed mental state, I drove right past the clinic and almost into another car. I pulled over at the next available street and planned on walking back to the clinic. Of course, my luck was not with me that day, because the car I had almost hit also stopped. As I got out of my car, I fell to the street and there he was, with his usual helping hand, Robert. He had not been home yet after the game and was going there now. He lives about three blocks from the clinic.

One look into his eyes and I started to cry. He said nothing, and helped me into the clinic. The nurses ran to get Randy, who was about to leave. They all knew me. I guess I should rephrase what I said before, Robert carried me into the clinic. They immediately put me in the X-ray room. The good news was that the broken ribs didn't puncture anything, however, there were two that were broken through. My shoulder was dislocated, and there was more black and blue skin than white in many places. Robert held me the whole time. I had never known how much he cared about me until then. When I looked up, he simply turned to me, with a tear in his eyes and said, "I'm sorry I can't kiss this and make your troubles go away. But I want to."

Two minutes later, Randy walked in and about fainted. This was about the worst I had ever looked. I think it probably still is. She never touched my face again, after that one. She said visual blemishes made people too suspicious. Robert helped Randy and the nurses the entire time I was there. He would not leave me alone for a minute.

When they finally finished, and I was in the recovery room, Robert asked what had happened. He then asked me why I hadn't believed her warning, why had I not told him, he would have loved to put the gloves on for me. I told him, as I said before, I didn't believe her because things had been so darned good.

Robert came onto the clinic's bed with me and held me. Then he began to say things that were obviously bottled up inside him for a long time. Another conversation I remember verbatim, "Why, don't you tell me things anymore? I want to know what's going on with you. I need to know, you're my best friend. Well, you're really more than a friend to me. I was going to surprise you at the victory dance tomorrow night with a full dance card - all in my name. Then I had plans to ask you to the prom, as well as the graduation dance. I want to spend all my time with you. I never knew I did before until I saw you at the game tonight. You came in in such a good mood, you cheered not with your mouth but with your heart as well, and I felt you. Timmy and I have always been close friends too. He is the brother I never had.

Now I want to do even more than take you to a couple of dances. I want you two to move in with us. There is no reason that you should say no. If you want to pay rent, you can work something out with my father, but we have an entire suite of the house that was originally made for a live-in maid which we never use. It's like a two bedroom apartment. Has a separate entrance and everything. Please don't go back to her. I can't see you like this ever again. It hurts too much, and as soon as my mom sees you, she will insist that you come, Timmy as well. Don't say no now, you have to go somewhere, at least until you heal or until school is over which may be the same time anyway." Then he leaned over and gave me a quick tender kiss. He picked up his head, caught my eyes, and repeated that kiss.

I guess I knew then why nothing ever progressed with Randy. Well, besides our age difference. The feelings were there, but not as deep as they were for Robert. He was, and still is, always there for me.

I then proceeded to tell him about the financial bind I was in now, and how my mom was expecting all the back pay within two years or less. I needed, in total, about $24,000 after taxes, plus I needed to make enough to support Timmy and myself.

If I didn't live under her roof, I felt that life would be worse for Timmy, because he is a minor and she would pull all sorts of legal garbage to keep him home. And I already explained what happened the last time I left him alone with her. If I wasn't there, he may not ever get to his elementary graduation.

"You know Robert, you're right," I said softly "I should stay somewhere, at least for recovery, but don't you think it would be better for us to stay somewhere where people won't see me? Not that I mind being seen at your house, but, well... oh, I can't think straight now. Tell me one thing though, how come you never told me how you felt before?"

"You never gave me enough time. Every time our conversation led to a point where you might reveal a part of yourself you cracked a joke or excused yourself and left. I've always cared very deeply for you. When you first told me about Randy, I nearly died until I figured out that he doesn't know about me which makes me special, special enough to you that you would share your feelings for him with only me. We've been friends for as long as I can remember. Who was with you the day your father said goodbye? Well left..... Me, and who was with you after the very first punch was thrown, me. I've never left you behind, in fact neither has the team. We always worry about you. If you don't show up to a game, at least one of us calls the clinic, and/or hospital after the game. If only you'd let us in, you would have known that the guys have always had your back. As far as my personal feelings are concerned, I guess I never realized them until I picked you up off the street about three hours ago. How about you?"

That whole time, he was holding me, brushing my hair and rubbing my legs with medication to help the redness go away. And yet all the while he was somehow looking into my eyes.

Randy walked in before I could answer. He had been rather hesitant to touch me the whole evening. Then he finally said why, he had met someone recently whom he thought was the right one. He had mentioned her to me before, but it was during the time my mom was my friend so I didn't really hear him. I was so happy that my home life was resembling normal at the time, I really didn't hear any bad news. It wasn't actually bad, though. "I'm sorry," he said "I can't let you stay with me this time. I really am sorry, do you have a place to go? If not,

I'll put you and Timmy up somewhere at my own expense." He was very solemn

"Don't worry about us, you go pursue what is best for you. We will be fine, and I know you're still there if I really need a friend, right?" I said this rather questionably because I didn't know if this girl would let him be so close to me anymore.

"She knows all about you, she won't stand in the way if you need more than medical attention from me, and please do call if you ever need more. As your doctor, though, I must say that you cannot drive for at least three weeks, and schedule a recheck with the nurses. I do care, don't ever forget that." He walked out with his head a bit lower than normal. I knew he felt he had betrayed me but I also knew that was not the truth.

Besides, he had meant what he said about putting us up, he has always been there, and has remained my doctor since then. Randy is now a partner at a private practice, but they still treat me as a clinic patient because of my history with Randy.

Robert called his mom to come meet us where the cars were. She drove his car and he drove mine. We went to their house. From there I immediately called Craig's house to tell his mom not to let Timmy go home with my mom, but to wait for Robert to pick him up early in the morning. Then I called my mom to tell her where I was. I got the usual reaction, "So, what should I do? Throw a party?"

I then asked if the house was back to the way it was or if she really wants to treat us like boarders. "No honey, you know you have your own room here, and so does Timmy. You have no doors though, because you deserve no privacy since I have not gotten any ever since you were born. I put everything I felt you needed back, the rest I am selling to start you off. Any questions?" She was quite smug on the phone but she never lied, so I knew the house was at least back to normal. Well, as normal as it could be under the circumstances. I actually did have a question but was afraid to ask it, however, what did I have to lose?

"Do you mind if Timmy and I stay here with Robert while I recover?"

"Actually, I prefer that you do. That will probably give me at least three weeks of peace, right?" She was still very smug, but calm. Believe it or not, calm was a good sign to me.

"No Mom, Randy said I won't be able to drive for five weeks." I was holding my breath, I thought for sure she was going to call my bluff on this one.

"Five? Really, how nice. Well, since he did me a favor by saying five weeks, the least I could do, is do you a favor back, by saying you don't have to make your first payment until you get back. See you in five weeks. Oh, and I hope you have enough clothes with you. Bye." And she hung up.

I had brought some clothes this time, two weeks' worth though because I knew how I felt, I knew this was bad. Five weeks however was more than I had ever had away from her. At least we would be able to finish school in peace. During the summer we didn't see many people anyway, most of our friends went to sleep away camp or vacation homes. Oh, well, you see sir, ever since the first time I left to stay away, I had kept a suitcase packed hidden in the back yard, for me and Timmy. I was able to get to this without going in the house. I took it when I left that night.

~ ~ ~

I turned around and Robert was still there. He led me into the living room, sat me down on the biggest sectional couch you'd ever seen, he put my feet up, and gave me a pillow for my back and side. Then he introduced me to his parents, and proceeded to tell them all about me. Before I could get a word in to object, he put his hand over my mouth.

His parents sat there in amazement. Nobody moved, and what made their reaction worse was that everybody was silent, until I piped in and said, "You really don't have to put us up, we can find ..."

"Not another word," his mom interrupted "you will most definitely stay with us. And we're about the same size so you can borrow my clothes if you need extra. As for Timmy, I have a nephew that is about the same size, we'll get plenty of clothes for him too. Sit, Robert's dad is a lawyer, and he will talk to you about what you should do next. That is, if you're up to doing anything. We want to help but only if you want the help." Then she left to go get the rooms ready.

His father had stayed back for a bit, "It's true, I am a lawyer, but I'm not sure what I or you can do at this point, I'm a tax lawyer. I know enough people though, but I will not pursue any options with anyone unless you want me to." His father's voice was very gentile. Like Robert

"Of course, she wants to do something, the woman almost killed her this time..."blurted Robert

"No son, she may not, this decision is up to her. As her friend, you must stand behind her decision whether you agree or not." His father walked out after that, with a very perplexed look on his face, almost as if he was hurt too.

"Why wouldn't you do anything? Please tell me you would, you're not going to sit there and let this go on and on,...are you? Are you?" Robert was very concerned you see.

At this point neither of us knew what to say. Then, he came over to me, sat down and put his arm around my shoulder, as if to say he was sorry. It's a difficult enough for someone who is in the situation, but to be someone who only sees the bad half of a relationship is even harder.

We spent that whole night talking about all the things we never said to each other. About all the things we have done for each other out of a sense of love and not friendship. It totally amazed both of us to realize how much love we really had for each other, and how natural we felt to give of ourselves to each other.

In the morning we got a phone call from my mom. No one knows why she really called, but the conversation went something like this, "So, honey, how are you feeling this morning? I do have your room put back together waiting for you. I even bought Timmy a new bedspread, on account I ripped up his old one. Have you picked him up yet?"

"No, remember I can't drive, Robert is going to pick him up in about five minutes." With that said Robert grabbed his keys and was out the door before she got a chance to get there first.

"How are you?" I continued.

"OK, a little tired, but ok. I wanted to let you know that I heard from your father last night. He wanted to ask how the car was for you and who won the big game. I hope I was right in saying that you guys did, and that the car is giving you no trouble. He also asked about Timmy, can you believe he did that? Never asked before. Did you call him last night or something?" She was searching for something she wasn't going to get; I didn't even know where my father was stationed those days.

"No, I have no reason to call a man who walked out on me when I was so young, without even so much as a goodbye. Besides, I gave you a thank you note to send him with your other papers he needed, you know the ones to discontinue the child support." I was praying that I said the right words, but you never know. Turned out that I was playing with all aces that morning. She loves when I bad mouth him. Truth be known though, I wasn't really searching for words. Hard on a child to realize that your father not only divorced your mother but you as well.

We only heard from him through mom. That is, if he had any legal reason to write her, he would stick in a two or three line letter for the two of us.

Then with recent events, you'd think I'd want to tell him what was going on. But as far as I knew, he would have been the same way. After all, the two of them fought all the time, who's to say they both wouldn't have loved to punch my lights out once or twice.

"So my dear," Mom had continued "I see you're not all that thrilled with the present situation either. I'll tell you what, take up to six weeks to give the first payment because your father said he would give one last payment. Tell Timmy I'll send him some clothes tomorrow, and I suppose I could find some clothes for you as well.

Tell me my dear, is this Robert a good boy? Is he treating you good? Do they have enough space for you to have your own room? I'd hate for you to be mistreated by some misguided young man." She was starting to get smug so I tried to end the conversation.

"Things are good here, they have a different room for me and for Timmy. They even have a separate entrance for us, kind of like our own apartment, not that we need one though because we plan on being home real soon, if that's ok with you. I hope to recover before the five weeks are up. You know me, I always bounce back quickly. Thanks for the clothes, but you don't have to bring them, I'll send Robert to pick up whatever you want to give us if you prefer. This way you don't have to make a special trip. Whatever is easier on you, let me know." With that I began to say goodbye, then I heard a voice in the background, sounded a lot like Lenny, one of her old friends.

I think I already told you about him. Right? Yeah, thought so. He must have been there last night. Not that I'm surprised, she always had someone with her after a bad beating. I guess men made her feel less guilty. She then said, "Pick it up? Sure, I'll put a bag outside tonight." She hung up with a giggle in her voice.

Timmy walked in as I hung up the phone and I told him that it was Mom, who sends her love and Dad's too.

I thought Robert was going to kill me. He mouthed to me the word, "Love? Love?" I introduced Timmy to Robert's parents and then brought him to his new temporary home. I never had to explain things to him. He would take one look at me and cry. This time was different, Robert had told him in the car and by the time he saw me he was already cried out. The two of us sat on the bed together and he laid his head on my lap. Considering all the bandages and stuff I had, my lap was the only place that he could touch without hurting me.

    I told him we would be going home after I recovered and was able to drive, he then jumped up and started yelling at me, "I will not go back to that house again. She is an evil person and should be taken away from us. Daddy will come and take care of us, you'll see. I'll call him myself. I'll tell him what is going on here. She will not hurt you anymore. I need you. I love you." With that he lost himself once again, lucky for him Robert had come in and heard the whole thing because he collapsed on the floor. If it were not for Robert, he would have hit his head on the bedpost. I never felt so bad in my life, this time I could not physically pick him up at all. I wasn't even allowed to. I couldn't tell him things would be good now, because last time I did I ended up like this. I couldn't even hold him. As I looked over at Robert stroking Timmy's hair and telling him that he loved him, that he would help now and protect him, I started to cry. He had no idea what he was saying, I had been telling Timmy I would protect him too, and then she turned on him as well.

~ ~ ~

    Those weeks with Robert went fast and peaceful. Not one interruption from Mom. Then again, not even a phone call for the first two weeks. We did get a pizza delivery every Wednesday from her, like we do at home. Wednesday is Mom's late night, so we always got treated. The delivery guy knew us already. He was a bit puzzled at the change of address but he didn't question getting his tip. Mom was still paying for the pizza, and she tipped him well too.

    Oh, and we also got a delivery of our favorite ice cream on the day I got all my bandages off. That day was fun all around. I was able to drive myself to the clinic, Randy took off all my bandages himself and told me he was engaged. I was so happy for him I jumped off the table. Then I sat back down really quickly. To top off the morning, Robert and Timmy came by the clinic with roses printed on a T-shirt, so that I could keep them longer. We all went down the school yard to watch the baseball game, and then off to Robert's house for what would be our last night. When we got there, Mom was there with the bucket of ice cream and new keys to the house. This was about as big of an invitation as I could have asked for from her.

    I really thought she was sorry for that one, I kept telling everyone that it was probably the last time she'll ever raise a hand to me. Robert still had a lot of hatred for my mom and never even cracked a smile when she came by or we ran into her. Even that day, he cringed and clung onto Timmy as if to hold him away from her.

    "See ya tonight." she said with a smile and even kissed my forehead as she left. She couldn't get to Timmy, Robert wouldn't let her.

    The one thing that did come up during the weeks at Robert's was a "way out" as they kept saying. His father told me that if I wanted to bring her up on charges of child abuse, I could now that I was seventeen. However, that did not ensure that I would be the one to take care of Timmy since legally I had to be eighteen for that in our area. He would probably have to go to some foster home or something like that. Also, without any witnesses to the actual fights the case would be slim. As I saw my options, I had no choice but to stay home and look for the job I so desperately needed now. There were too many ifs in their "way out". There were also too many people I would have to involve. Besides I wasn't even sure seventeen was old enough I'd really have to do some research.

    Robert and I made plans to go to the prom together as well as graduation. After that we could not make any plans because he was going off to college and I had to stick around and take care of Timmy. He wanted us to always be together, so did I, but it wasn't in the cards. Not at that time anyway.

Robert helped out a lot though. He came home with me every day and stayed until my mom kicked him out every night. Things were going as I thought they would. Good. There were only the normal verbal fights that all teens have with their parents. Robert and I were inseparable, and neither of us minded. We never felt we needed our own space. Things felt natural, and right.

Prom was approaching and my mom finally got a glimpse of my dress that I had bought. With my own money, I might add. I had gotten a job at a local bar, being a waitress for food, not drinks. My mom frequented the place, so the boss knew her and hired me right away. He assumed I was good because my mom was always so nice to everyone there.

Anyway, my dress was very sophisticated looking, at least I thought so. I had gone shopping with Robert's mom and Timmy, both of whom loved how the dress looked on me. But my mom did not. She walked by and then came back to my room with a scissors and began to cut the dress into shreds. I remember sitting there dumbfounded.

"The dress is not even yours, I bought this one with my own money, the money you told me to go out and get...for myself.!" I was so angry that I yelled, figuring that that was the only thing we had done in a few weeks.

"You bought this with your own money, but you did not buy this with your *own* mom. Did you think I wanted nothing to do with your biggest day? Well, you didn't even ask me, you couldn't be bothered to find out, could you? After all these days you and I have not fought, this is how you repay me? I think not young lady!! You want to go to the prom? You best find something that will cover up this....."

~ ~

Do I have to go on? Yes sir, I understand, my oath. The whole truth.

~ ~ ~ ~

You probably already guessed what happened, the scissor went right into my arm. But then something strange happened. She fell to the floor with me and said she was sorry. She even gave me a hug, and rushed me to the clinic herself. Timmy was out with Robert grocery shopping. They got home before us. When Timmy didn't hear me answer he sent Robert upstairs.

When he saw the torn dress, and the blood, Robert told me he knelt down and started cleaning up. Timmy waited on the couch for me and Mom. But only I came home. Mom went on to the bar laughing. I knew then, all she had shown us recently was all an act. She never really cared, not that day anyhow. If I was honest with myself, I would say not any day.

Do you mind if we take a break now? I'm a bit tired of talking. Thank you sir.

~ ~ ~

As I go outside the room, I see Timmy and Robert playing some silly game with cards, they both looked up as I came to them. Timmy jumps onto my lap and gives me a huge hug around my neck. Plus a million kisses, "These are to say how proud I am of you!! You're the best girl ever Kimmy! I want to be as strong as you when I get bigger. Robert says he is going to make sure of it too."

Robert smiles and reaches out to hold Kim's hand. They do not need words to speak to each other anymore and today Kim has already spoken enough words – with many more to come.

We sit together and have ice cream – some people need chocolate to heal them but Timmy and I always prefer mint ice cream to drown our sorrows and joys in.

There have been a cast of characters here all day but now that I'm getting my turn – everyone has been so quiet. It's weird thinking that so many people want to hear what I have to say.

An officer comes by to find me, Oh well, "Time to go back, Timmy, stay here with Robert ok?" Timmy looks a bit shaken already but he stands strong like a soldier and gives me a salute that would have make any general proud.

"Yes sir, I understand I need to continue from where I left off. Thank you for the break I really needed that.

~ ~ ~

Back into position, Kim begins to speak again, "Where was I? Oh, yeah prom. As I walked in the door I saw something amazing. Not only was Robert there dressed and ready for the prom but so was Timmy. I asked them what was going on because prom didn't start for another two hours.

Well, Robert and a bunch of the guys from the team decided to ditch the real prom and create our own. One where no one cared what you wore or who you were with. He said he was going to do this party with or without my mom's permission and that if she had given him a hard time he would have called the cops this time.

That aside, he told me to go upstairs and put on my dress. I went slowly upstairs while the two of them were busy setting up the dining and living rooms with chairs and decorations. When I got upstairs, I saw a different dress, one that looked to have come from a bridal store. I put it on because it was all I had to put on and I didn't want to disappoint my men waiting for me. This took a while because my arm was quite sore and I had to try and wash myself with one arm. I received forty-five stitches this time. Good thing we only had one week left of school. At this point though, wasn't even real school, mostly graduation practices – yearbook signings and those types of things.

By the time I got downstairs there was already eight other people in the house all wearing their best clothing and putting out Chinese food containers. Robert's mom decided it was the quickest way to get everyone fed. She was apparently instrumental in getting the dress and the paper goods as well. One of the other guys had brought along their dad because he was a photographer and he was taking pictures of all the couples – like a real prom.

We all danced a million slow dances and a few faster ones – sat around and ate and laughed until about 11:30. At that time, everyone pitched in and cleaned up my house. Not from the prom but everywhere. They made sure the kitchen was spotless, the floors were vacuumed, the bathrooms were wiped down, and every other chore I was expected to do and then some. One person was even doing laundry the whole time they were there – they didn't tell me until the end of the night. We voted Timmy the king of the prom and Robert gave him a crown before he went to bed.

By the time my mom got home that night Robert and I were sitting on the couch in regular clothes and playing a board game. She came in alone for some reason. She actually asked me how my arm was. Wanted to make sure I was still able to go and enjoy prom that evening. I had to put pressure on Robert's thigh so he wouldn't say anything. "I had fun Mom, thank you for asking. Did you have a good night as well? You look rather pretty tonight." She responded with an unusual comment, "Honey, I always have a good time, prom night is every night for me." Then her eyes bore into Robert for a split second when she continued, "Only I hope you did not enjoy your prom the way I enjoyed my evening. If you did there will be some serious consequences to pay for both of you."

With that Robert stood up and said very calmly, "I hope you aren't referring to having sex because I respect Kim too much for that. I intend to wait until I'm married before doing anything like that. I thought you knew that about me maám." As he saw the look in her eye calm down, he continued with "Besides, only a fool would make a woman do what she does not want to do."

"Exactly, I'm glad to see you understand me. You are a good influence on my daughter. She needs someone with good morals to help keep her doing good things and not running around with hooligans." She smirked at him but in a weird way, thinking about it still makes me uneasy.

Then she went straight to bed. Neither one of us knew what to do with that exchange. Robert had been ready to fight and my mom had surrendered. To me any calm was always good sign, one that meant she really was changing. It may take a while but she was ready to change, I really thought she was. I had my hopes up, however, Robert has his guard up. Robert left shortly after that.

I went up to my room expecting to sleep and found my mom in my room sitting on my bed waiting for me. Then life got even weirder, "What's wrong with you? Why wouldn't he want to sleep with you are you some sort of tease? Did I raise you to be a slut and a tease? Women in our family are refined. We are able to find a man on our looks alone but clearly you are not." Her voice was getting louder with each sentence. I did not understand what she had wanted from me. Had I slept with Robert I probably would have been beaten but now that I hadn't? I was going to get a beating anyway because she felt I was dishonoring her family. Before she took the first swing she screamed, "You must get this from your father's side!"

Out from behind her came a fry pan to the side of my head, had I not picked up a pillow I would have been dead for sure. I woke up on the floor of my room at about 4:00am. I looked down at myself and saw my clothes were ripped and my legs were bruised up. She must have knocked me out because thankfully I don't remember any of the rest of what happened.

~ ~ ~

"How could you not remember it was your prom night!! You got what was coming to you. You're so stupid, you've always been stupid! I'll never forget my prom night because you came nine months later but YOU!! But you don't even remember what happened – what an idiot!! You call dancing in the liv…" she put her hand over her mouth then and looked around the room, sits down and with the next breath was sitting there like nothing happened.

~ ~

"I'd like to point out sir that this sort of outburst didn't usually happen at home. She always tells me to do better in school and teaches me what I do wrong. I do not believe for a minute that she thinks I'm stupid because she always has told me that I get my brains from her. She graduated from college with honors. Didn't you Mom? See, see how proud she is. We are both smart aren't we Mom? Mom?
"Can't you see my baby needs another break? Must we do this all in one day?" Kim's father interjects.
"With all due respect Major, I prefer to have this done today and the sooner the better. We all need to put this behind us. Continue please."
"But why won't she answer me? Why?"
"I can't tell you Ms., continue please." He answers

~ ~ ~ ~

"OK, the rest of the school year went uneventful. Actually, half of the summer did as well. Robert and I were making plans as to how we can continue our relationship and Robert's mom was helping me work out ways to learn at the local college and still work and watch over Timmy at home. I was beginning to see value in all we planned.
July 4th weekend was coming up and we always went to the lake to watch the fireworks together, never missed one

– Mom makes her famous picnic and we have a great time together. However, that year was to be different. Lenny was back or still in the picture and he had invited my mom to go with him somewhere for the whole three-day weekend.

When I opened my mouth to protest she put her hand up and told me I was old enough to hold down a job and pay rent then I was surely old enough to watch my little brother for a couple of days. It was quite crushing to me, July 4th was a time we always enjoyed together. Right Mom? Didn't we always enjoy that night watching all the colors fall into the lake and eat your amazing biscuits?

She's still not answering me. Mom, are you ok? Why is she staring out into space? I think something is wrong with her – is she having some sort of catatonic episode?"

"We will watch her, I promise she is fine." Kim watches everyone for a moment.

Kim shrugs and continues the best she can, "Mom left without so much as a goodbye and that had gotten me very scared. What if she was gone for good? What if she was really leaving us – I remember running to her room to make sure she didn't pack all her clothes. She hadn't but she also hadn't been too careful about putting things away that day either so I decided to clean up a bit while I was in her room.

I was putting away all the clothes she left on her bed when suddenly a box I had never seen before had fallen from somewhere on the upper shelves of her closet. Yes, I knew it was wrong then and I still know now but some of the items that fell out had my name on them, so I started to look at them.

Every card, every birthday, holiday, congratulatory on making a team card was there. Every letter my dad had ever sent me was in this box. He had not abandoned me after all. Inside each card he always wrote 'ps here is a little cash for you to buy something a little fun and not always practical, enjoy your birthday' or whatever the occasion he was sending the card for.

I sat there too long because Timmy came looking for me calling my name in a panic. I had to reassure him I was not hurt a dozen times and that I had not fallen and she did not leave any booby traps for me but the tears were because my dad still loved me and there was no reason for me to hate him anymore. But, I told him the most important part was that now we have his current address and we can write him a letter and send them out before Mom gets home. We can tell him to respond to Robert's house so Mom won't get rid of his response this time and we can actually read what he wants to say to us directly.

    Timmy went straight to his paper and began to write. So did I. I decided to not hold back and let him know what was going on. All of what was on my mind – no censoring. I was taking a huge risk in doing this again and I know that now for sure, however, I decided the time was now or never. The last one he had sent was only a few months before that day and he mentioned being sent away for another ten months overseas. We both spent the entire afternoon on our letters. I did not read his nor did he read mine. We decided to allow each other to have a private conversation with our own dad.

    We drove over the Robert's house because we were going to be celebrating with their family. But things were not quite the same, no biscuits, no silly jokes or tickling on a picnic blanket but we had a great time. I spoke with his mom about getting mail sent to their house and she was delighted and hoped my dad would respond.

    I also spoke in depth to Timmy explaining that because we found an address doesn't mean he wants to hear from us. That we may never know, he could have sent all those cards when he was in a good mood like Mom does. Timmy got angry at this he actually yelled at me for the first time, I think he said something like, "just because one of our parents hates us doesn't mean all parents are like that – look at Robert's family, look at my friends and yours not everyone is afraid of their own shadow in their own house."

"Yes sir, not a dumb kid for his age, is he? Anyway, we went through the motions of the 4th of July with Robert's family but, in reality, neither one of us felt like the day was right. Before they left for the fireworks, we had decided to head home. The night really wasn't the same without our mom. We really did have a good time with her on this day, every year, without fail. Despite what she may think of me now - Timmy and I do have some fond memories of being with her.

When we got home though, something seemed weird. We could always tell there was something amiss in our house, I can't explain any better than saying that we felt something different. We always did, even Robert was able to tell a few times. That house feels things and the occupants know.

Back to the 4th, Timmy and I pulled up to the house and parked on the street like usual because I didn't want to pay for parking in the driveway. We walked in through our back door and the feeling was really heavy. Without knowing what to do we called to our mom to see if she was home. The first thoughts that went through my mind was to make sure we put everything back the way it was before we found the letters and Timmy must have had the same thought because he looked at me and said that we counted everything and didn't miss a thing. What was going on?

We kept calling my mom and no one answered. We looked outside again to see if her car was there and it wasn't, we weren't sure if that was a good sign or a bad one. Then at the top of the stairs we saw her. She had a black eye and her clothes were ripped. Immediately I asked her if there was anything we should do for her, if I should drive her to the clinic? Get her bandages? Timmy had already run into the kitchen for a bag of frozen peas to put on her eye. She came down the steps so slowly I thought she was going to fall. As she got to the bottom, I took her hand and brought her to the couch. Then Timmy offered to make her a tea and she burst into tears. Real tears, I'm not kidding.

We both sat near her and held her hands. Finally, she stopped and looked up at us. "You came home! You didn't like 4th of July without me, did you?"

Timmy told her there were no biscuits and no picnic and definitely no tickling. Then he said we came home before the fireworks because no one enjoys them like our mom and it wouldn't be right without her.

She had hugged us both – a real hug not a fake one, we could tell. Then I looked at the time and said we could still make them if she wanted to go. She turned to me and said running out would not be necessary, this year we will watch them on TV with ice cream. That's exactly what we did.

It wasn't until Timmy was washed up and in bed that she told me what had happened. She and Lenny had a fight at his place and in the process of leaving, he smacked her in the face and actually tried to rape her – that's her version of the story anyway. To this day I still don't know what happened and to tell you the truth I don't really care. You see, after that we all got along. We had a great July and most of August.

Well, I guess that part is obvious.

The whole month of July we did not hear from our dad – not through him or any military messenger so we both assumed he didn't get our letters, or he didn't care, either way we were ok with the results. Besides things were really looking good for us.

We were going on picnics every Sunday that I wasn't working and Mom had lessened the amount of money she needed from me. She said she was proud of me how I was bringing in what I was required and that I was even using my own tips to help buy groceries.

We went shopping together a few times and she treated us to some new clothes – then she realized that we both wear about the same size so she was excited because now every outfit she bought became a two for one sale to her.

Even Robert was seeing a change in her and he had to admit that she could be a lot of fun. Robert even joined us a few times on our picnics. Sometimes we had ice cream for no reason – because Mom wanted some.

We were a family – for the first time in forever, we had become a family. I really could not complain about anything.

Things started to change by mid-August. One day a woman came by asking us weird questions at the door, like my name, age and questions about my mom. I closed the door on her afraid someone was reporting something and immediately called my mom at work. She screamed on the phone at me and it took me some time to calm her down and for me to convince her that I did not give any information to this woman, that it scared me that someone knew who I was and was asking me questions.

She came home fifteen minutes later and asked for complete details, even though I had given her them on the phone. Robert was there and he confirmed all that had happened. She was furious. Screaming things about Lenny and that she would get back at him for this – which he had no right to meddle in our business.

I asked for clarification and got a stare. One that I hadn't seen in a long time, and boy did it have me scared. Thankfully I didn't think she would do anything in front of Robert. She glared at us and said if anyone else comes by here, or at work or anywhere else and they ask questions that I am to get their name and department and immediately call her lawyer and she gave me his name and number. Then she ran into her office and was rummaging through everything. She came out with a crazed look on her face and said, "Everything is where it belongs- don't let anyone in my office - or in my room. NO ONE is allowed to touch or see anything that is mine without a warrant and without me present!!!! Is that understood?!"

We both gave a resounding yes to that. Timmy woke up from the commotion and asked if everything was ok. She asked him if anyone came up to him in the park and asked him questions about her or about where we live and he said no - not any real stranger but a policeman did but Timmy said he told him, don't worry I'm not lost I know where I live and my sister is picking me up and then you did remember?

My mom's head was about to pop off her shoulders from swinging back and forth so fast. "A policeman?! You saw him with a policeman and didn't tell me?"

I tried to convince her that there are always police at the park and they talk to all the kids I've seen them there many times so no I didn't think anything of him talking to Timmy.

Then I offered to make her a drink to calm her down. She seemed upset and so I wanted to make her more comfortable. To this she screamed, "Do you think I'm some kind of alcoholic that needs a drink to calm down!!!!! I'll calm down when I'm good and ready to calm down.!!!

Doorbell - she shook herself off, went to the mirror and took a couple cleansing breaths and calmly walked over to the door and answered it sweet as pie, "Yes, can I help you?"

It was Robert's dad, he introduced himself and asked if he could speak to my mom for a moment. Robert had no idea he was coming and shook his head at his dad vehemently. Yet, somehow, he didn't get the message and he looked up at Timmy and said, "Hey little man, you left your truck at our house so I wanted to bring it by on my way home from work - I was seeing a client in your neighborhood."

To which Mom said, "I thought you said you were coming to talk to me? Robert why would your father say he needed to talk to me and then talk to Timmy instead?"

Well, there was no good way out of this one – neither one of us knew what was happening right at that minute nor were we sure we wanted to. So he did the only thing he could and that was to tell the truth, "I have no idea maám, perhaps he wants to talk about the same things I talked to you about the other day – about how your daughter and I would like to find a way to continue dating when I go back to school. You had some very good ideas that I think we may look into them more because they seem to be the best ones so far. Very perceptive."

She grinned but gave us her evil grin – I knew that one well, to me I heard, 'wait till they leave then we will have some fun'. In the background I could have sworn I heard a car door – maybe more than one in fact but I had to keep my attention on what was in front of me.

Robert's dad called him over to him and kind of pushed him towards the door and mumbling something about it being time he go home for the day. Neither of us knew what was going on so he waved at me and Timmy – who, by the way, was all the way down the stairs and waiting near my mom for this truck that was promised to him. As Robert walked out the door, Mom addressed his dad. "So was you son right? Do you want to talk about the future of our children or was there something more pressing you wanted to talk about?"

At that moment, I knew something was going down – something bad, I saw figures in the back yard moving around and I signaled to Timmy to come near me. As he was about to walk over to me, Robert's dad was reminded about the truck and took the item out quickly to give to him. My mom intercepted the toy and threw it over to me. Thankfully, I caught this one before it landed on the glass in front of us. Then she pushed Timmy towards me with more force than necessary. Oh, this was going to be bad. The air in the house was so thick you could cut it. The walls were moaning – I swear to you they were.

"Delivery made, and as far as our children are concerned sir, there is nothing to worry about. You heard your son, we already talked about what he is going to do, all of what *I* said. They both are. Now, if you'll excuse me, we are about to have a family meeting before you so rudely interrupted. Aren't we my dears?"

Timmy was only half way to me as she slammed the door. She was on him so fast I couldn't react. She picked him up and threw him down on the floor, his hand smashed into the glass coffee table and spilled the drink I had made for her. The only thing I could think of doing was telling Timmy to stay down on the floor.

I remember asking, "What has you so angry?!" Then as a protective mother hen, I found myself hovering over Timmy. I was not going to let her get to him again. What happened then was such a blur – but I will tell you the best I can.

First off, I began to hear people outside the house yelling, banging on the doors and windows. I heard my mom ranting above all the noise saying something about how I was an ungrateful brat and this little one that was supposed to bring her marriage back only pushed her husband to sign up for another tour of duty and another. It was the first time I had ever heard her blame Timmy for the break-up of her marriage.

She was walking around the room – actually more like hovering around the room looking at us as her trapped prey. Her eyes were the color of rage and I could swear that her pupils took over her eyes. 'You were a mistake – one that I was excited to keep because I was getting the man I loved – well never really loved but I sure lusted after him enough. But life with a military man didn't allow much lusting to go on and so I had to satisfy my desires elsewhere

– then one day he came home and said he would be here for a while and he was, long enough for us to have Timmy and for his first birthday. Then I found him boring.'

Whatever she was passing that was movable was being thrown at both of us. Each time I either batted the object away or caught it, anything I could to keep them from hitting Timmy. I would not let him get off the ground – would not let him see her face this way. It was as if all the anger she had pent up over these past good weeks was coming out at once. But why, I couldn't tell you.

I had to ask, I figured I had nothing to lose. Her response was that I brought it upon myself. That I chose to write my dad, and so did Timmy.

I guess the look of surprised was obvious because she said, 'Oh, you didn't think I would find out, because you sent a letter from somewhere else? I have been getting suspicious calls lately like the ones at home – asking about the welfare of my kids my home. So now I know the truth – I can see guilt on your face – you wrote your dad a letter and told him I was mistreating you, didn't you? What else did you tell him? Did you tell him about Lenny? Doesn't matter – I'm going to make sure that neither one of you speaks about me again if it's the last thing I do.'

Four bottles thrown at us later and so much noise outside banging and ringing or sirens – I wasn't sure what else was going on. I thought I heard my dad's voice but what would I know about how sounded anymore huh? Then I thought I heard Robert's voice crying out to me to stop, to grab him and run. All this yelling – all the screaming on the inside and the crashing of bottles, chairs and books. Then through all the craziness she came running at Timmy with a chair and I blocked her but the impact knocked me down and I landed on him, but cat like – I was over him but my body was not on him. Through the haze of my own tears I looked up and saw my mom holding a long metal object – then all at once I heard the door bust open – glass breaking from one side people yelling stop as the loudest crack I had ever heard came down on me.

There I lay on top of Timmy - unable to move - my back was certainly broken. Mom was still screaming at me about how horrible a child I was and that I shouldn't have even been born - I heard police grabbing my mom - then I heard and felt Robert's tears on my face as he lay next to me saying how sorry he was that his dad was supposed to be a diversion so that my own dad and the police could get inside - no one was expecting her to preempt this and double lock all the doors to the house and the windows.

The EMTs were afraid to move me - they slid Timmy out very slowly and cautiously. Robert took a ring out of his pocket and gave it to me to remind me of his love. As they finally lifted me onto the gurney, I saw my dad. He had as many tears running down his face as did Timmy in his arms.

The next day I woke up in a fog. My dad, Timmy and Robert were all in my room with me. Robert was the first to notice my eyes open. I'll never forget what he said to me, "So, you won't walk again doesn't mean we can't still go skiing like I promised you."

I tried to laugh but all I could do was cry - and then he joined me on the bed and we cried together silently. We both fell asleep for an unknown amount of time and when I woke up again, I saw my dad and Timmy still attached.

"I got your letters, I couldn't believe what you were saying so before I could do anything about the information - I had some people check into the story - sorry this took so long. I contacted your doctor Randy and found out how often he saw you. I contacted your boss and found out when you were hired and that your mom had slept with him a few times and made some promises if he hired you. Promises she could not keep and eventually he knew she wouldn't but he loved your work ethic and vowed to keep you working so you could pay her the rent she wanted.

We tried to set something up that was supposed to catch her in the act - but we had no idea what act we would catch - it was enough that she threw Timmy that would have been sufficient - I.... I don't know what to say."

Well, after that introduction from my dad, we all sat around and talked for hours. Randy came by and visited with his fiancé, so did many others from the clinic.

As you can see sir, things kind of suck right now as for my recovery - well, I've been told I may not walk ever, not fully anyway - possibly I'll be able to stand but never really walk.

But you don't have to feel sorry for me, I still have a family - a brother, a dad and a great boyfriend who may end up being my fiancé one day. I guess there is nothing left to say, may I get down now?"

"Will there be any cross examinations?" the judge asks.

"No sir, my client does not want any more questioning." Mom's lawyer replied.

"Alright, then we will take a recess until tomorrow morning 9:00am. At that time, I will give my verdict. Court is dismissed."

Timmy runs up to Kim and jumps onto her lap again as soon as he sees her close enough. He holds on to her around her neck and cries. For someone so young he didn't have the words to say. That is ok with Kim because she has the same nothing to say to him. She has already spent hours in front of the judge telling everything she remembered about her life these past couple years. She is done talking.

Robert comes up behind her, "Ice cream first then Italian food for a change, I think." As he wheels her over to the elevator, Dad and Timmy follow. They ride in silence, they walk in silence too all the way to the ice cream store two blocks away.

"Ok Dad, I get you don't know what to say, you feel guilty or whatever it is you feel but don't. I'm ok, really, I am. I'm so ok that I'm ordering a hot fudge sundae and I'm not going to share one drop with any of you. Just talk to me, please don't let her win over you too. No more silence from you.

You heard me in the judge's chambers - we had some great times too. Mom snapped when you left - and I understand leaving was a mutual decision but she apparently never got over being alone. We're going to be ok as soon as we sell the house and get something that is all on one floor. An apartment would be fine - huh Timmy?"

"Can we get a doorman too - Billy has a doorman at their apartment he is really nice - his name is Salvador isn't that cool?"

To that they all laugh and the rest of the afternoon goes smoothly as well. They begin to talk about everything that their dad missed; all the games, milestones, and even the mishaps. Robert is happy to be part of this family - he loves them all.

No one blames their dad - except for their dad. Robert's parents have prepared a grand dinner for them after their long day. Everyone is staying at his house for now because no one wants to go back to the other house. Kim's dad is having the whole place professionally cleaned out and only personal belongings of Timmy and Kim are being kept - everything else is being donated or thrown out.

~ ~ ~

At 9:00 am sharp everyone is in the judge's chambers again. Judge Rutherford is known to be one of the toughest judges on abuse cases. Kim and Timmy's dad made sure that this would not go to a public trial and that everything could be handled in the privacy of a judge's chamber. He did not want his kids on display for the press to get to.

His lawyers had plenty of ammunition and her lawyer was obligated to be there pro-bono because otherwise she would have told his wife why she knows where his birthmark is. As he sat listening to Kim yesterday his body language was showing, that he wanted nothing to do with his client. There was no way he was even going to try and plead insanity, the evidence was clear he wanted her to be put away for her crimes as much as anyone.

The judge enters the room and all who could – stand up for him.

"Are there any last arguments?" he asks. Timmy speaks up then, it is the first time he has been allowed into the room, "Are you going to put my mom in jail?"

Without even a hint of a smile, the judge simply replies, "For a very long time my friend, a very long time. Now with nothing further from counsel, I will state my verdict. Mrs. Carlyle, you sat here in my chambers for hours yesterday listening to you daughter describe her life with you and never once did you show remorse, half the time you actually looked bored. I wonder if my sentencing might knock that smirk off your face for a long time. The way I see the events, the previous two years you have spent abusing your children and for that you would get only ten to fifteen years in prison, however, with this last attack you vowed to end their ability to breathe and to me that sounds like pre-mediated murder. The only way I can see true justice being served here is hereby sentencing you to multiple counts of child abuse coupled with two charges of attempted murder which wins you life in prison, without parole, in my book."

The room is silent – no one was expecting that, not the lawyers and certainly not Kim. She finds herself crying uncontrollably. "Your Honor – maybe I said things too harshly, maybe you misunderstood me – she is my mother, I want her to get help. You don't have put her away forever. Mom, I'm sorry this was not supposed to happen – someone do something – someone say something ---oh my god, I put my mom away for mur....." The crying is too much she can't get the word out at all.

Until her mom decides to speak, "You are so stupid – the judge is right – I was not planning on you or your brother making it into the next morning. Why do you think it took them so long to get into the house? I bolted the doors and windows – I didn't want you running out – you were going to be gone and then the house was going to conveniently have an electrical fire. No harm no foul and nothing to clean up except my insurance claim and my freedom from you two." She says with no emotion in her voice at all.

Even the judge can't believe what he is hearing. The air in the room is so thick that everyone starts for the door at once – the place has become a toxic atmosphere that they all want to get away from. Once outside the door everyone is taking slow deep breaths. One by one they disperse to their own lives and Robert and Kim head for the elevator where he vows to never leave her even if it means doing college at home – he waits until Kim agrees that he takes her straight down to her car where her dad and Timmy are waiting already because her dad had grabbed Timmy and bolted down the stairs.

To the right of them, there is a strange man who is in full military regalia coming forward and calling out "Major." In his hands he has an ominous looking envelope that he hands her dad. She puts her hand up for Robert to stop moving and all is still. Her world has stopped.

"Nothing to worry about my dear," he calls to Kim "my discharge papers – I'm all yours now." Dad says. Timmy cheers. Robert smiles and Kim, well, Kim exhales the breath she has been holding in since she heard the verdict. One last tear rolls down her right cheek.

With that they get into the car and go 'home'.

Made in the USA
Columbia, SC
21 April 2021